Secrets of Ghosts

Secrets of Ghosts

MARDI ORLANDO

Order this book online at www.trafford.com
or email orders@trafford.com

Most Trafford titles are also available at major online book retailers.

Printed in the United States of America.

ISBN: 978-1-4669-3921-9 (sc)
ISBN: 978-1-4669-3920-2 (hc)
ISBN: 978-1-4669-3922-6 (e)

Library of Congress Control Number: 2012909903

Trafford rev. 06/12/2012

 www.trafford.com

North America & international
toll-free: 1 888 232 4444 (USA & Canada)
phone: 250 383 6864 ♦ fax: 812 355 4082

Other Titles by
MARDI ORLANDO

THE LIGHT VOYAGER

THE AMAZING LIFE OF GEORGE FRED FIDDLINGTON

ADVENTURES OF THE WISHALL

THE LIFE EXPECTANCY OF WIND

THE WISHALL

For News and Updates on these and other works, please visit
www.mardiorlando.com

~Present day~

~A Fast Bus to Nowhere~
~Santu of Visions~
~Daffodil of Diamonds~

There was something very wrong with this whole venture.

Santu was woken from his insipid sleep by the howling echo of a wounded animal, only to find himself back in the stormy night on the same lurching bus, going nowhere, fast. The vehicle was rattling violently in the torrential downpour, hurtling at an alarming speed. Every now and then, its wheels would slide on the the slick road making Santu's stomach twist. Musty, dank air filled his nostrils and the freezing cold air was making it difficult to think—but it didn't stop the visions.

Outside, past the clammy windows, the highway was dark and empty save for the black silhouettes of leafless trees ebbing from a low eerie mist. Thunder ached in the deadened gloom like a far-off warning, and lightning flashed in bursts across the sodden, starless sky. Rain hammered on the roof of the pitching bus and frosty clouds drifted through the aisles as if seeking refuge. Why hadn't they told him he was going somewhere this damn cold?

Santu's gaze slid up to the full moon—he could swear it had a face. Its distant light shone on his dark Spanish skin and shoulder length black curls. Shivering, he huddled into his leather jacket to keep in whatever warmth he could and tried to concentrate on the visions. They had been growing stronger and more controlling since he had agreed to this 'research mission' but in his heart, he knew the truth had already been seized and locked away.

Santu skimmed a look at those on board. Six other duped kids that had somehow managed to abandon their lives to attend a Secret Society Program: All of them masters of their own secrets; all of them masters of a skill unusual enough to be accepted by the underground group.

None of them seemed to be interested in making eye contact or conversation. If his visions were anything to go by, they'd have to talk eventually. He wondered if any of them could match his skills.

Santu was an anomaly, a glitch in the human strain, a genetic aberration that had already seen his mother die. The reminder made him angry and he tried to bend his thoughts back to the unacceptable cold.

As he rose to complain to the uninterested and apparently unaffected bus driver, the vehicle abruptly lurched to a halt. The unexpected shift threw Santu forward, smashing his face into the back of the seat in front of him. As his face struck the metal railing he heard a horrible crack: His nose had broken. As blood trickled from his nostrils the horrible stench of mould and death filled his mind before a shrill voice erupted from the front of the bus.

"I am Madame Glizsnort," screeched the woman who had just alighted. Dressed in a long, gray, woolen skirt, short high-heeled boots and a gray jacket which displayed two looping 'G's' on its lapel, she exuded cold indifference. "For your stay on this trip you will be under *my* guidance." The woman's piercing gaze regarded everyone from the front of the bus.

With her pale eyes, gray complexion and high silver bun, Santu thought she could have been an ice-sculpture hung with clothes and a wig. Motioning to complain, he felt himself being forced back into the seat.

"Sit down!" Madame Glizsnort shrieked. "I will not have insolence in my presence!"

And probably for the first time in his life, Santu felt hesitant. Apparently he was not alone. Furtive glances darted from one to the other across the bus—eye-contact finally, mused Santu to himself. But the worry was creeping around him, icy fingers curling across his skin. He was not getting any visions from this strange woman and that scared him more than he cared to admit.

"Now," Madame Glizsnort began again trying to sound just a little less harsh. "I am to be your guardian and tutor for this undertaking." Her tone was practiced, almost calculated. "I know you have all come from far away, some further than others." Her icy stare focused on the girl with the messy blond hair and patchwork clothes. There was something about her.

Daffodil thought her heart may freeze instantly with the intensity of Madame Glizsnort's gaze. In fact, Daffodil *was* from a very long way away and had a history of secrets that would make the discovery of the Holy Grail seem mundane. As far as Daffodil knew, absolutely no one had a clue about her past—except her parents, and they couldn't tell anyone, obviously. But right now it felt like this strange woman with the cold silver eyes was staring into her brain, reading her very thoughts, seeing into her memories and exhuming her life; bit by bit.

"Your name girl?! What's your name?!"

"D . . . Daffodil, Madame," she replied, her Australian twang sounding broken in the silence.

"Try to remember it then!" The ice-sculpture shook her head.

Daffodil nodded, her big, brown eyes, wide and unblinking. If Madame Glizsnort hadn't finally moved her stare to the back of the bus Daffodil would have vomited. Not a good start to her first Secret Society mission. Had her escape from The Institution been a foolish decision? Was the whole research thing real? Had her grueling admission been a sham? Blinking a few times, she let salty tears wash over her burning eyes.

Madame Glizsnort seemed disgusted with them all. "There will be an introduction ceremony once we reach our destination," she continued determinedly, "and then we have a very demanding schedule of advanced research. After this, you will put your abilities into action." She paused for a moment as she eyed each of them. "And remember, I am not interested in cry babies! The quicker you follow the imperative and perform, the quicker you will be *finished*!"

Santu didn't like the way she emphasized the word 'finished'. If his nose hadn't been throbbing so badly, he may have tried to focus on his visions, but the pain was making it impossible for him to judge just how serious this situation was.

And then a flood of arctic water rushed through Santu's brain. It felt like time had stopped, as if all the knowledge he had ever accumulated was suddenly dissolving into nothingness. Just before everything began to fade, a few thoughts pushed themselves to the frosty surface of his mind: In the freezing-cold midnight hours of this strange rain-soaked night, how had this gaunt, shrew woman managed to stop a speeding bus and alight without a single droplet marking her clothes?

As this thought formed, another whole, and completely overwhelming notion, swelled in his mind. And that's when Santu noticed Madame Glizsnort was staring straight at him.

And a small trickle of blood oozed from his damaged nose.

Blackwater Herald Moon Tribune Tuesday, September 5ᵗʰ, 1939— One penny

WORLD NEWS HEADLINES
FIRST DAYS OF WAR
WAR DECLARED BY BRITAIN AND FRANCE

*A*t 11 O'clock, September 4ᵗʰ, Great Britain declares war on Germany. Six hours later France follows. Britain and France state their determination to fulfill to the uttermost, their obligations to Poland in this full scale attack.

Australia declares war on Germany September 3ʳᵈ. New Zealand has cabled her full support to Britain. Rush of recruits in Canada. Over 2000 men lined up outside the Recruiting Office yesterday.

LOCAL NEWS HEADLINES
MYSTERIOUS SIGHTINGS CONFOUND LOCALS

After the First Great War and terrible period of Depression we hoped there would be a long time of peace, but the fervent attacks do not augur well for any of us. Just days after the terrifying announcement that Germany has invaded Poland, Blackwater has made a discovery so unsettling that it brings the ghosts of suffering home to us again.

Our Herald Moon Tribune journalist, Mr. Henry Frienly, has discovered a rather strange mystery. With help from Miss Grace Durand of Marchenby Street, Mr. Frienly has uncovered a strange tale indeed.

According to the information, it is believed a group of approximately nine children has been seen lingering around the town. They are very hard to keep *track of, even disappearing whilst being followed! They tend to move as a group, which makes it even more remarkable that they have not been caught, and they do not appear to have any guardians present. This strange group seems to be unaware of the attention they are receiving. When Miss Durand calls out to them they are oblivious to her utterances and their immediate escape seems uncanny.*

The children were noticed on September 1ˢᵗ, by a visitor to the area, Mrs. Agnes McReady of Bluberry Falls. Mrs. McReady immediately reported it to the police whereby Constable Macalister Glizsnort took all the details.

In a rather curious turn, Constable Glizsnort states to the Herald Moon Tribune, that after considerable research, he has discovered that similar sightings were reported in the area about 20 years prior. This just adds to the peculiarity of the situation. Constable Glizsnort also speculates that it is no coincidence that the sightings have begun again just as the Second Great War has been declared.

Even though the Constable is unsure whether these children are of an unearthly nature or not, he affirms that he will not give up trying to locate the children despite the obvious difficulties. He also suggests there may be many a reason why these children have no homes. In such circumstances, he says, those being of the war and all, there are a variety of events that would allow these children to find themselves in very difficult circumstances. It is quite possible that these children are vagabonds or worse: They may be homeless and without parents; they each may have experienced something tragic and may be very frightened; or they could be serious trouble makers.

At this stage he is not prepared to commit either way. Constable Glizsnort insists that once the children are located they will be treated with kindness and compassion before being judged. "It is the Godly thing to do," he said.

However, journalist, Henry Frienly, concedes that others in the community do not see it so simply. Many have expressed concerns regarding their own safety and it is believed that the kind of lenience the Constable affords will give the children open opportunity to commit crime.

Enid Highly of Plain Place Road suggests: "They may try coercion or even thievery; or they may attempt to inflict physical harm on the people of the town—the population should be afraid!"

Even more negative correspondence includes alarming implications that these children may be creating some kind of gang and that they plan to steal the offspring of the neighborhood to expand their group.

"It all reeks of sinister undertones!" Miss Maimsbun of Hawkesmeade Avenue cried when interviewed.

But Mrs. Lightbottom of January Court, believes, "We should take them in and care for them as a community. Obviously no one else is concerned about their whereabouts."

Miss Maimsbun replied with a curt retort about Mrs. Lightbottom being unable to have children of her own and added, "Mrs. Lightbottom's opinion should be ignored as she has obviously displeased the Lord for she has been rendered barren."

Mrs. Lightbottom refused to reply to these allegations.

However, as Constable Glizsnort reminds us, until we actually catch these children, it is all speculation. Miss Durand would like any person aware of their whereabouts to pass the information on to her at 132 Marchenby Street (call exchange B243).

And a very interesting story it is.

Blackout time tonight is 6.57pm.

EVENING EDITION CHANGE

Due to the declaration of war, our standard edition will now be an evening publication only. Therefore, the paper has changed its name from the Herald Tribune to the Herald Moon Tribune.

WAR NEWS
POLAND INVADED BY GERMANY

Warsaw and many other Polish towns bombed by German warplanes on September 1st. As troops march into Poland, Hitler, in an address to the Reichstag, says: 'From now on bomb after bomb is falling.' He continued with: 'The German Army today is better than that of 1914!' Hitler finished his speech with 'Sieg Heil' (Hail Victory).

The Poles latest estimate of casualties in the German air raids on local towns and villages on Friday and Saturday is 1,500 people—a considerable proportion were woman and children. (Continued Page 3.)

FIRST AIR RAID WARNING

London remains calm as it hears its first air raid warning. (Page 4.)

Brought to you by Cadbury's Bournville chocolate—Every man's secret vice!

~Present day~

~The Trees are Alive~
~Blaze of Fire~

The tumbling rain had turned to snow. Blaze peered at the icicles forming on the bus windows—they were growing in front of her eyes. She had never been this cold in her life and she had lived through plenty of Irish winters.

The empty highway had begun to narrow and the black skeletons of dead trees clustered closer to the road, their gnarled branches screaming as they scraped the paintwork. It was so dark out there. The ivory moon didn't seem to shed any light on anything. Even the sporadic flashes of lightning did little to help her make out what was beyond the bus windows.

It was only annoyance that had overpowered her anxiety. Really, who was this shrieking old woman? And why was everyone so scared of her? And that complexion. Was the woman adverse to a little bit of sun? Maybe, Blaze thought, when you're that old you just don't care anymore.

Either way, Blaze knew she had gotten herself into this mess and now she had to suffer the consequences. So much for the 'exciting experience of world travel' and the huge benefits she could make 'all in the name of research'. This felt like the dungeons of Siberia. All she'd wanted to do was get away from her life and her past: A past that dragged behind her like an enormous shadow. She tried to shake away the memories, but as always, they curled around and around like slithering snakes full of poison just waiting to strike.

And then Blaze was struck with an odd thought. How had this woman boarded the bus in a heavy rainstorm, without a raindrop on her? No umbrella, no overcoat, and not a hair out of place.

"You, the redhead!" Madame Glizsnort looked furious. "Address me immediately!"

Against her will, Blaze snapped to attention. Her whole body stiffened into a perfectly erect posture. Slightly puzzled, she blinked and stared at the sickly looking woman.

"Um, hello . . . Madame Glizsnort?" said Blaze in her lilting Irish accent. Was that an 'address' Blaze wondered? "Um, I am Blaze Montgomery?"

Madame Glizsnort had thrown her coolest stare at the freckled girl with the wild mane of red hair and golden-flecked, green eyes. Except for a slight stiffening of the body, the girl had barely reacted. That wouldn't do.

"Well," Madame Glizsnort's voice was breathtakingly cold, "if you want to survive this experience I suggest you start learning some manners."

A shiver ran up Blaze's spine and into her brain. Okay, now she got the fear in everyone else's eyes. This woman was crazy. "Er, sorry Madame Glizsnort," Blaze stammered as she felt the eyes of the other children on her. "I will try harder." Her voice trembled on the last word making Blaze annoyed with herself. Showing fear to strangers could get you in a lot of trouble. And there was a lot of trouble waiting for her if the truth got out. She would just do what she was told and then make a run for it. Although, god-only-knew where she was going to run to.

Finding a way to control whatever this woman was doing to her would be difficult but Blaze wasn't shy of a challenge. Fear on the other hand could be her undoing. The threat of Madame Glizsnort unearthing her secrets was tantamount to suicide.

Madame Glizsnort had tried her stare on the girl again, and yes, she could feel the fear thrilling through her. Good. Without feeling danger, none of their true instincts would kick in. Their resistance surprised her. It was troubling to some extent, but nothing she couldn't work on. These children were supposed to be the best, the ones who could master the situation quickly—before the Callers could find out. Still she wasn't sure. This was much too important a task for her to risk any of them crumbling. And time was running out.

Turning to the front of the bus Madame Glizsnort tried to recoup her energy. She could feel the mist growing stronger. There was not far to go now. It was a good decision to join them in the last stage of the journey.

"Everyone!" Madame Glizsnort screeched. "Be quiet until we arrive!" Taking a seat near the driver, she resisted the wave of exhaustion that threatened her attendance and reminded herself why they were all here.

Blackwater Herald Moon Tribune Saturday, October 21st, 1939— One penny

WORLD NEWS HEADLINES
GERMAN BOMBS FALL ON BRITAIN

German bombs have fallen on Britain for the first time since the war has begun. Miss Hilda Marchant of Queensferry describes the terror. "I was sitting at home with my sister when we heard the terrible thunder of several planes coming toward us. Two big black aircrafts were visible outside my window and we saw bombs hurtling from them." Follow this amazing story—Page 3.

LOCAL NEWS HEADLINES
HORROR STRIKES AS CHURCH BURNS

In the midst of the war, a disaster of another kind has horrified the small local community of Blackwater. It was during the fierce storms early yesterday morning that the citizens stood in horror as their small beloved church, The Church of Mortimus, burned to the ground. It was apparently struck by a lightning bolt early Monday morning, only hours after the last service, and the extent of the damage is devastating. All efforts to stop the fire were useless.

Certain community members have indicated a belief that the act was one of God Himself and that the church was burnt down to show the populace that they have not done enough to worship the Lord and are therefore, being punished.

11

John Melmbry of Citizen Square says, "Perhaps we did not worship hard enough on Sunday, or perhaps there was an unbeliever amongst us!"

Yet, still other community members feel this attitude is dangerous. Already, factions are beginning to form and fights are breaking out all over town. The local Constable in charge of the issue has been very busy containing these arguments and has expressed publicly that God would not want people to take their anger out on each other.

Unfortunately, this does not seem to have stopped the fights.

Others still, agree that the church was burned by the hand of God to rebuke the community because of the lax attitude toward the strange children that have been sighted around town. Many suggest they may have brought with them, the fury of the Lord. Further action will be required to control the problem.

The more pressing issue is that the people will not have a church to worship in next Sunday. Suggestions that the town hall be used as a temporary place of devotion have been faced with outrage.

Ted Newgan of Plabuly Lane says: "I cannot see what the problem is. It is not like God cannot hear us if we are not in a church. The town hall has even more room than that old wooden church and there is a lovely piano in there too."

But Noel Cordenly disagrees. "The church is the only place our worship and hymns will be accepted by the Lord. If we begin to accord reverence in any old building we shall suffer greater punishment."

The matter continues.

Blackout time tonight zero hour until 7:45 am.

OTHER WAR NEWS
POLAND'S LOSSES

The last Polish ground troops surrendered on October 6th. Polish national losses stand at: 700,000 men captured by the Germans; 200,000 men captured by the Russians; and many more from loss of life. Germany has lost 10,000 men and Russia several hundred.

Mass at the Polish Church in North London was attended by Cardinal Hinsley. Together they prayed for their homeland as they faced news that Poland has surrendered.

RUSSIAN INVOLVEMENT

Russia will gain about two-thirds of Poland and approximately half the population under the agreement reached by Berlin and Moscow. It has been revealed that Hitler and Stalin have signed a non-aggression pact which includes clauses for the division of Poland even though Russia is still claiming neutral status. (Page 5.)

HITLER'S SPEECH

The Fuehrer states that: Neither armed force nor time will conquer Germany. November 1918 will not occur again! I do not doubt for one moment that Germany will win. Hitler concludes that the business of annihilation is grim and says that one day the frontier dividing Germany and France will be a border of graveyards. He thanks God to have shown justice in his cause and prays that God will guide him further in his ventures.

JAPAN'S ASSURANCES

Japan *assures Britain of her neutrality in the present war. (Page 5.)*

UPDATES

Cinema "Shuttlecock" has begun. *Two groups of cinemas will take alternate weekly spells. This week the Plaza, the Odeon, Warner Theatre, Ritz and the Rialto will take the first turn.*
Gardening, Radio, Crossword, Comics, Page 6.

~Brought to you by ~

Bear Brand Stockings—*A sheer necessity!*
And, Grow More Food at Home with Mr. Middleton's Garden Book 3'6.

~Present day~

~Jake of The Inaudible~
~Annabelle of Accolades~

Jake watched the interaction between the redheaded girl and the old squawking lady. It was all just horrible noise to him. Jake didn't like being here, he didn't like any of these other kids and he definitely did not like the ugly lady and her screeching voice. It reminded him of fingernails on a blackboard. That's what stupid kids did to upset him. They would trap him in the unused classroom at the back of the school, lock the door and then watch him writhe on the ground in pain as they each took turns to scratch their nails down the old fashioned slate boards. He didn't like *them* either.

The air smelled putrid: A mix of wet earth, rotting carcasses, and anxiety. And the eerie blackness outside was making him feel claustrophobic. His worn pullover and tattered jeans weren't of much use in this bitter cold.

All Jake could think about was being back at the foster home and he hated that place. But, at least there, he could be in his room with all the things that made him feel safe. The Secret Society for Gifted Teens hadn't said anything about taking away his stuff. He needed *everything* he had packed. Why had they insisted on taking all of his devices?

Jake wondered if the people at the foster home would even notice he was gone. He doubted it. They were overloaded with kids. The day he had arrived, his new foster parents had discussed the welfare reimbursements right outside his bedroom door. There was a whole list of things the two of them wanted to buy. They may have been whispering but Jake had heard it all. Of course he had heard it. They knew what his hearing was like.

Outside, the lonely darkness murmured and whistled at him like a warrior who had lost his battle. There was something out there. He could feel it. Jake squinted past the falling snow into the distance. Rows of gleaming stones flickered under a flash of lightning before dissolving into the blackness again. Jake shivered, and covering his ears, he tried to remember how he got here.

Why couldn't he recall the flight from South Africa? The vague image of being picked up at the terminal on his arrival was shrouded in mist. But he didn't forget what had shocked him into panic: The bus driver had confiscated all his electronic devices. 'To be returned in due course,' the young man had said to Jake with a shimmer of a smile. There was no way Jake could sleep without his static. Without it, every single insignificant high-frequency sound would ping inside his head until it felt like his brain was screaming. He tried to explain it to the driver but his words were strangled with anxiety, and so, he was shuffled onto the rickety, old-fashioned bus to endure this nightmare of a trip.

Something had been wrong about all this from the start. Jake had sensed it as soon as those 'academics' came to his school—The Port-Elisabeth Instructional School of South Africa. They claimed they were representatives of a research program for gifted pupils, but it was obvious to Jake they were lying. He knew they were from the Secret Society by the mottos they used—the very same Secret Society that he had applied to 6 months prior under the banner: 'Risk is the requirement, Sacrifice is the spirit'. He had come across the website by accident and only filled in the application to keep himself distracted while all the other foster kids in the house were running amok. There were very strict guidelines and he never expected to get in, especially when he had spent most of his time answering the question about 'unusual talents'. It was really just to get it all off his chest.

The representatives had searched each class with their strangely penetrating stares and finally picked him. The principle practically bowed as they left the school only to then announce over the sound system, that he, Jake, had been chosen as the most gifted child in the school and would be rewarded with the overseas 'trip of a lifetime'. Only a select few other students from around the world would join him. All expenses paid. Most of the kids just sniggered and pointed at him: Always the odd one out.

To be honest, Jake hadn't really been listening: Too much noise. No one could understand the discomfort some voices caused him. Instead he had closed his eyes and concentrated on his favorite topic: Antiques. Facts about the past had always made him feel safer. That day he had focused on Chinese Abacus Cases, finally stopping when he came to the one that had really tested his knowledge in the European contest in Munich, Germany. It was the red one, made using the traditional techniques of 1500 years before—the Tang Dynasty Era—and which was owned by Emperor Tang Taizong. The lid was decorated with a dragon and a phoenix and was of the finest craftsmanship Jake had ever seen. His distraction had only slightly dulled the pain but at least he could cope.

The note received from the Principal was deftly forged by Jake and returned. Although surprised that he was capable of such deceit, Jake quickly packed and fought the hoard of 'brothers and sisters' to escape. A last glimpse revealed his foster parents studying their beer labels and smoking next to already full ashtrays. No one even noticed the disheveled boy with the short brown hair and sad, dark-blue eyes traipsing toward the front door gripping a small bag with nearly everything he owned in it; his headphones blocking out any of those awful sounds.

And now he was stuck here with all these other strangers. Strangers that could never understand the terrible things that had happened to him; strangers that would end up teasing him and torturing him like all the others. Even the counselor had been too upset to listen to his stories so he had lied to make her stop crying.

Jake just hoped they would all stay away from him.

Annabelle could have sworn the icicles on the bus window were pointing, like fingers, toward danger. The icy glass reflected her perfect features: Her pale blue eyes stared back at her without warmth, her silky, long blond hair curled around her pale creamy skin and her cherry lips hinted at an unattainable smile. Eyes weren't supposed to change color as you grew older but Annabelle's had. When she was young they were a deep blue, almost purple, and had been the focus of a great deal of admiration. But as she grew into her tall lithe frame, they had faded to an almost arctic blue.

Annabelle wondered if your eyes were the first part of your body to die.

The cold was unrelenting, sinking into her skin like acid. Her tight black Prada jeans and fur-trimmed Gucci jacket were of no help whatsoever. It was making her so tired. And the shrill tones of Madame Glizsnort made her head ache. She leant back against the worn leather headrest, the smell of the damp hide making her queasy.

Before the woman had started screeching at them, Annabelle had been day dreaming about jazzing up Tchaikovsky's Concerto Number One. Having played it in concerts around the world, it was the one piece of music that had given her spirit the freedom to breathe. Now she was forced to impress the audiences with Rachmaninov, Stravinsky and Sorabji. And she did so unfailingly—it was just that she did so without heart.

When the invitation from the Secret Society for Gifted Teens arrived, Annabelle took it as the perfect opportunity to escape. The couple, who had taken her in, cared only for her exceptional musical ability, taking her thousands of miles away from her own country of England to live in America because that was where the money was. Their lives revolved around her lessons and her endurance. They were grueling task masters 'for her own good' and she hated them. Her reward was a large home with every gadget she could ever want but Annabelle had never been interested in things: She had only one wish, but it was, she knew, pure folly.

She didn't deny that music had given her a focus to help her forget but it had also torn away whatever was left of her tattered childhood. This particular escape had her lying to them, claiming she was attending a very prestigious musical trip and that she needed to attend alone. Despite their protestations, Annabelle's manipulative mind found an exit strategy. Right now, they were none the wiser and hopefully it would stay that way. This was her chance to pull away from them, and maybe her chance to run—run as far away as possible. It felt like Annabelle had been dreaming of escaping since she was eight. Maybe she could find her real mother? These pseudo parents wouldn't let her look: 'It will damage your ability', they had said. But they didn't have a clue about what she was really capable of. If they knew about her real gift she would have been dragged around the world and displayed in circuses and freak shows for eternity. No one could find out. Ever.

At least the horrible old woman at the front of the bus hadn't singled her out with one of her death-stares. In fact she didn't seem to be interested in Annabelle at all. Maybe the stupid woman didn't think Annabelle should be here? Yet Annabelle knew her IQ was at genius level—plus she had received straight A's in all four of her instrumental exams, each several grades higher than was required at her age. And that didn't include her feats with the piano. Was she being tested? Someone was always pressuring her. Annabelle pushed the memories deep down. Why did people treat her like this? Closing her eyes, she concentrated. '*Yes, that's it,*' she whispered to herself, '*harden yourself; make yourself impenetrable.*'

Santu screwed up his nose to see how bad the damage to his cartilage was. The blood had stopped trickling, probably because he was so damn cold, but it still throbbed relentlessly. He had started to shiver now and his whole body vibrated like he had some kind of nerve disorder. His teeth were chattering and his head ached. Had he momentarily fallen asleep? He seemed to have difficulty remembering the last few minutes: The chill he felt deep inside his brain when Madame Glizsnort had stared at him with those piercing eyes was mind numbing. He remembered having some kind of revelatory thoughts, but they were gone—like ice-shards on a tongue. Santu squeezed his eyes shut. When would this hateful journey end?

"Right!" came the demanding screech of Madame Glizsnort. "We are nearly there. I want everyone to be ready to alight shortly and everyone is to exit the bus in orderly fashion!"

'*Exit?*' thought Annabelle. This wasn't anywhere. And how else did this woman think they were going to exit? There were only 7 teenagers on board—all of which were virtually incapacitated by the cold. A chill of uneasiness swelled inside her. 'No matter,' she thought, 'there isn't much time for me anyway.'

The speeding bus suddenly came to a complete stop in a matter of seconds. But Santu was prepared this time and held on tightly to the railing. It didn't stop him hitting his head on the seat rail in front of him but the cold and the already existing headache took care of any further pain.

Unfortunately he was the only one who had done this and there were some angry faces directed at the oblivious Madame Glizsnort.

If anyone had been looking at *her* instead of smashing themselves into the seats in front, they would have seen that Madame Glizsnort had not moved an inch: She had not swayed; she had not moved her feet to align her balance; she had simply stood perfectly and flawlessly still.

Static Recording No. 126—On Loop

BITSY. 1908–1916. GHOSTED AGED 8.

H ello, my name is Bitsy. They call me that because I like to collect all sorts of bits and pieces. Also, I am very good at putting things together and making them work.

I don't remember my real name. No one does here. I don't know how long I have been here. I don't like it very much but I think it's safer than the other place. I think I have been here a long time but I don't know how long.

I am tired. There is no sleep here. There is no eating. There is no time. I miss the things I used to be able to do but I don't remember what they were.

I want to tell you about my life before I ghosted. I was only 8 you know. And I was very sad and scared. If Oscar hadn't found me I could have been even more lost. I remember before I came here there was a war and lots of people in the whole world were fighting. Mommy said there had never been a war like it. I couldn't understand why the whole world wanted to fight. Why should everyone be so angry with each other? I got a bit angry once when mommy wouldn't let me play out in the rain but I didn't want to start a war.

I don't like snow and I don't like being alone. I was alone when I lost my mommy and daddy. I remember mommy said there was a mass-evacumation or something—I didn't know what it was but everyone was running away. I made sure my dolly, Poppy, came with us because it sounded scary and I knew she wouldn't want to be left by herself. Tell them Poppy, tell them about it.

Oh . . . Poppy is shy today but don't worry, she'll tell you all about it next time. I can tell it today. We were in a huge crowd and all the people were running. I held on tight to mommy's hand and to dolly. Daddy looked scared which was bad. I don't know what happened but suddenly mommy and daddy weren't beside me anymore. There were so many people. The crowd was pulling me away from them. When I looked back I saw mommy screaming. I think she was screaming at me to come back. I tried. But I just kept being pushed along by the people. It was like that time we went swimming and the ocean pulled me away from mommy. That time she brought me back but this time it was different.

It's very strange but I don't remember much after that. There was a bright explosion like a 'sunburst'. My mommy used to love that word. She would say it in the mornings a lot. But after that my mommy and daddy couldn't see me anymore.

Then I was somewhere else, I think. Then I met Oscar. It was much better than being alone. And then that scary Shadow came and we hid in this old building. It felt much safer.

Sometimes we play games. My favorite game is Whispers.

I like songbirds. They remind me of my mommy's voice. I like looking out the window too.

Sometimes I scream like mommy did when I lost her. I think, maybe she might hear me and run against the crowd to come and get me.

At least my dolly, Poppy is with me.

I don't like being alone. And sometimes it seems really dark here. I keep saying it's too cold but Oscar says that's silly. He says if you're a ghost you don't feel the cold. I don't know how he knows so much about being a ghost. I know I'm cold. I don't like being cold. Neither does my dolly.

I wish there would be a sunburst. My mommy would love that.

~Present day~

~SUB ZERO TEMPERATURES~
~DUEL OF HONOR~
~DUETTE OF MIND~

After exiting the bus in as 'orderly' a fashion as possible, they found themselves standing in the dark night in a large snow-laden clearing. The clearing was dotted with several dead trees erupting from the icy ground, and was encircled by enormous forest pines lit only by the obscured moon hanging somewhere in the distance. Beyond the ring of trees, a thick opaque mist ebbed back and forth as if it were breathing. One large wooden cabin glowed with dim orange light on the right, which each and every student hoped was the result of a log fire, and another larger structure stood further ahead of them: The expanse in between was covered with compacted ice, the result of enduring snowfall. Far over to their left stood an old pitched roofed building, completely unlit, and looking like it could collapse at any moment. And that was all there was. This was where The Secret Society for Gifted Teens had been sent for their mission: The middle of nowhere.

"Your introductions shall take place in the mess hall straight ahead of you," yelled Madame Glizsnort as if they were all 20 miles away. "You will have supper and establish relations for 45 minutes before being assigned a bed number and then you will be required to go immediately to your quarters."

Blaze thought this sounded like some kind of military mission. She looked around the group to catch the responses of the others and that's when she noticed the blood on Santu's face.

"Your nose is bleeding! Oh my god your nose is smashed! This boy has a broken nose!" Blaze was shaking her brilliant red hair and pointing a purposeful finger at Santu.

"Enough!" returned Madame Glizsnort. "You will not blaspheme in my presence! His nose is not broken and impudence will not be tolerated. One more example of this behavior and there will be consequences." How did these modern day children get away with such rude conduct? If the redheaded girl only knew her part in all this, she would be concentrating on herself rather than concerning herself with others. Indeed, the truth would be a mighty blow for her and she would, no doubt, need to prepare for it.

Blaze held in her fury, but if anyone had looked into her eyes, they would have seen gold fiery flecks spark across her deep green eyes. Blaze had already decided: She would figure out a way to deal with this woman—and then get the hell out of here.

The students all stared at Santu's damaged nose but quick bursts of head-shaking and wide-eyed glares from the victim made them all turn back to face their instructor whose complexion had paled even further.

"Now," Madame Glizsnort continued trying to sound more strident than she felt. She was well aware that dealing with these children would be very different to what she had been used to and this time she must guide them carefully, perhaps use a more placatory tone. Another mistake would ruin everything. "*Please* go forth and make your introductions. Your luggage will be placed beside your beds by Bert," she motioned toward the practically comatose young bus driver. "Hurry now, before supper gets cold."

'*Cold!?*' thought Annabelle, '*unless there was a log fire big enough to heat a circus stadium everything would be frozen.*'

"I said there is to be no insolence!" Madame Glizsnort shot a ferocious look at the designer clad Annabelle with her silky long blond hair and perfect skin. Looks meant nothing here.

The icy pain that hit Annabelle was intolerably severe. It shot through her brain, down her spine and into her abdomen—as if looking for its rightful place. She tried to gasp for air but it was too late: Annabelle had fainted.

Several gaping mouths were rendered speechless.

"Quickly!" Madame Glizsnort had forgotten what kind of power she could wield. This girl was definitely the weakest. "All of you help her inside!"

The group rallied together, half carrying and half dragging, the beautiful Annabelle over the icy ground and into the warmth of the mess hall. As Blaze passed Madame Glizsnort, a distinct odor of dead lizard greeted her nostrils but she had no time to let it concern her.

It wasn't until they had laid Annabelle down by the fire and looked around for someone to help that they realized they were here alone. Madame Glizsnort was nowhere to be seen.

"What the hell?" yelled Blaze, her Irish accent slamming the syllables together like cymbals. "Where has she gone?"

Santu smiled and nodded. He enjoyed a bit of attitude in a girl—and the redhead was very pretty: All dark green eyes and fiery hair tumbling around her creamy skin. If he were back in Guernica . . . he stopped himself. There would be plenty of time for that—*if* he ever got back home.

"It's probably past her bedtime," Daffodil said, her warm brown eyes smiling as she rested Annabelle's head on her patchwork skirt. "Oh, look, she's starting to come around."

Annabelle was shaking her head. In the darkness of unconsciousness, visions had floated in her mind: Icy, cold, white apparitions reaching for her, making her insides squirm. Shivering, she tried to force herself up but someone's hands were holding her down.

"It's okay, you just need to lie still a minute," said Daffodil, her frizzy blond hair framing her face like a halo.

Opening her eyes, Annabelle was faced with the concerned expression of the crazy girl with the terrible accent and horrible dress sense. She was dressed like a 1960's hippie: All multicolored layers and groovy hair attachments—it was quite off-putting.

Annabelle pushed away from the girl's insistent grip and sat up. Dizziness swam like coils behind her but she managed to scan the rest of the group. Carefully lifting herself up, she tried to look casual but everything had changed. Finally, her destiny had found her. It had crept inside her and made its mark. It was as if that awful woman knew and wanted Annabelle to know that it would be coming for her now. Annabelle tried to act as if nothing out of the ordinary had happened but the icy feeling inside her had at last taken control. With her strength of mind summoned, Annabelle tried to stop shivering. There was no need for these people to know anything. But then her eyes rested on a very good looking boy with deeply suntanned skin and dark, shiny hair that curled in perfect swirls to his leather jacket clad shoulders. Quickly, she lit up with the most perfect smile. She definitely would not be ignoring him.

"Hi," Santu said as she stared at him. "I am Santu." He was grateful that the girl with the icy blue eyes had come around so quickly. If the old woman didn't care that he had a broken nose then what *would* she care about?

"Hi," said Annabelle staring at Santu and wondering what country had created his melodious tone. "I'm Annabelle." She was shivering inside and out. "And I'm so cold I could reverse global warming."

"Quick," said Daffodil, "come over near the fire."

Swiftly, Santu dragged one of the old school chairs from the long tables and offered it to Annabelle.

"Well," said Blaze, sidling up to the fire and smiling sweetly at everyone, "I'm Blaze and I hate this place."

Daffodil laughed. "What?!" she cried in mock horror. "But it's so cold and creepy!"

"What a shame I have to leave," replied Blaze, her green eyes glimmering with firelight, "I think I'd like you."

"Not staying?" asked Daffodil feigning surprise.

Blaze's words had sent flashing visions into Santu's reluctant mind: Fire and frightened green eyes. The images always came with people's words. It didn't matter exactly what people were saying; it was their souls filling the sounds that gave him the visions. Their words were his curse. Unable to understand, he pushed them away. How was she going to feel when she realized none of them were going anywhere anytime soon? No need to tell her yet. Instead Santu nodded to the boy and girl standing next to each other. Neither of them had said a single word.

"Who are you two?" Santu asked staring at the well dressed duo with their smart haircuts and intense hazel eyes.

"We," said the boy with very short, light-brown hair, "are Duette and Duel. I am Duel." The boy's unusual accent drew their attention. "It's French. The accent. It's French. This is my sister. We are twins." He shrugged his shoulders at the inevitability he would never escape. "She hardly speaks any English."

"Welcome French twins," said Daffodil. "Nice clothes," she added. The French boy looked like he'd stepped off the set of a James Bond movie and the girl looked like a well dressed secret agent with her perfectly groomed bob and asymmetrical fringe and her very fashionable military style raincoat. Daffodil looked down at her own outfit with layers of different materials and patchwork pieces: All made by her own hand with whatever scraps she could find. She liked to call it hippie-chick but next to Duette and Annabelle she felt less than fashionable.

"Thank you," replied Duel. Duette barely acknowledged anyone.

As usual, no one had noticed that there was another boy still standing near the entrance, his fingers clenched and his shoulders scrunched inside an over-sized pullover. In his discomfort, Jake was blinking his eyes quickly as if he were sending Morse code signals to an invisible watcher. In fact, all he was doing was flicking through images of all the different methods of bottle closure for antique bottles. His favorites: South African ginger beer bottles with rare patented methods for securing corks with a steel spike: Reids Bloemfontein (patent number 4172) and W.H. & J Morgan from Port Elisabeth; both from Price Bristol Potteries.

"Who's that?" Blaze asked as she eyed the boy with dark-brown 'bed hair' and tattered jeans who seemed to be having some kind of seizure.

"I do not know," replied Santu, "but I am thinking we need to be finding out." As he slowly approached the boy he knew straight away that this kid had something else going on. "Hi, I'm Santu."

Jake immediately opened his eyes in shock. Dark blue irises stared back at everyone. How long would it take for them to start punching him?

Everyone had followed behind Santu and stood smiling as they introduced themselves to the sad looking boy. Jake wasn't sure what was happening: No one was laughing at him.

"And-I'm-Jake-and-I'm-so-cold-I-could-create-a-black-hole," he said, his sentence running on without stops.

Santu burst out laughing. Jake flinched and waited for the strike. Daffodil threw Santu a fierce look.

"What?" said Santu raising a characteristically emotive expression. "Black holes, global warming." He shrugged. "It is funny."

The lilt of Santu's accent softened each word and Daffodil wondered how many people he had coerced with those smooth inflections. Ignoring Santu, she addressed the anxious boy.

"It *is* funny Jake. Are you into the universe and stuff?"

Jake nodded quickly and then shook his head. Wasn't anyone going to hit him? "Yes-but-my-field-is-antiques. I-am-an-encyclopedia-when-it-comes-to-antiques. I-am-an-assessor-for-many-highly-esteemed-companies. I-was-named-top-prize-in-the-Youth-Worldwide-Judging-Competition. I-won-because-I-named-a-very-fine-and-very-rare-Patek-Philippe-perpetual-calendar-moonphase-minute-repeater-chronograph-antique-pocket-watch-circa 1889. It-was-worth-about-$180,000-American-Dollars." Jake's South African accent clipped the vowels, digging small holes in each of his words.

Even if Santu had wanted to, he couldn't have made a joke. From Jake's words, came the visions. Santu tried not to reveal what he was seeing but it was difficult given the dreadful reflections that rolled past his eyes: Words; images; secrets. And now he knew why the boy was so fearful.

Jake being unusual was not the surprise for Santu—none of them were here because they were ordinary—but the fact that this stammering kid was *so* extraordinary was quite astonishing. And yet, neither Santu's ego nor his competitiveness was anywhere to be found. Santu smiled to himself and guessed that there was a first time for everything.

"Well," said Daffodil looking up into Jake's sad eyes, "that's really good to know."

As a general rule, Jake didn't like people standing too close to him but this girl was different. She may have messy blond hair and crazy clothes but she felt . . . was 'safe' the word he was looking for? Jake had never used that word before. He checked her again. Daffodil's brown eyes were warm and gentle, he knew that for sure. How long had it been that he'd been certain of something? He smiled at her. Nice eyes. Crazy hair.

For just a moment, Jake felt a very brief and very rare moment of confidence: Short-lived, but distinct nonetheless. It was a strange sensation, like a rush of air to his lungs. What would it be like to know the feeling again? As everyone ushered Jake over to the fire he finally felt like he might actually be able to make a friend.

Blackwater Herald Moon Tribune Thursday, November 30ᵗʰ, 1939— One penny

CURRENT WAR UPDATE
ASSASINATION ATTEMPT KILLS 6

*J*ust 27 minutes after Hitler ended a speech in which he cried that he was ready for a five-year war with Britain and that Germany would never capitulate, the Buerngerbrau Beer Cellar in Munich was shaken by an explosion which killed six members of the Nazi party and injured sixty other people. Hitler had already left and was unhurt but the ceiling collapsed and Hitler's platform was buried under 10ft of debris. The perpetrator is believed to be a carpenter named George Elser. (Page 3.)

LOCAL NEWS HEADLINES
CASE OF THE LOST CHILDREN CONTINUES

The case of the missing children has taken another turn. News has spread far and wide and is causing more problems for the once quiet town of Blackwater.

Now dubbed the 'Lost Children' these runaways, as they are thought to be, are being spotted all over the region by citizens as far away as Snowfall Mountains. However, as yet, neither the police nor the Herald Moon Tribune has been able to substantiate any sightings.

Currently, some of the townsfolk believe that the presence of these children and the fate of their Church, The Church of Mortimus, are related. The church was burned to a cinder over one month ago due to a lightning bolt striking its newly thatched roof.

Now there is a movement pushing toward building a new church on the same site but the majority of these folk will only rebuild when they can source a sufficient amount of bluestone to reduce the likelihood of the building burning down again.

Mr. Jeffery Pennyfarther, a farmer and well-known builder states: "The building will go ahead! I will build it alone if I have to."

However, as is the continuing problem with this issue, there are many folk who do not want the church rebuilt over the same site. To them, it seems blasphemous. This is because they believe that the church was intentionally destroyed by the Almighty, and to build over the same area would be offensive to the Lord.

However, these same protestors object to the current alternative of praising God in the town hall. Instead, they have been traveling over 150 miles to attend church in Balisbury Plains at the 'Church of All Saints' where they say they have been welcomed.

Mr. Barnaby Georgeson of Trentstoke Street says: "My wife and I are deeply devoted to God and we believe He is telling us that the site of our old church is now cursed beyond redemption. We must all gather together in these desperate times of war and challenge and find a way to appease our Creator. And if we find these children we must do what we must do."

But Madame Corsila, originally of Burgundy, France, and now living on the Harrow Hill says: "Too many people are trying to find a reason for the church's demise. It was just a wooden structure and wood burns. The children have nothing to do with it."

Whether the mysterious sightings and the demise of the church are related is yet to be discovered.

Miss Grace Durand is still anxious for any clues that will lead to the whereabouts of the Lost Children. If anyone knows anything at all please pass this information on to her at 132 Marchenby Street.

Blackout tonight from zero hour until 7:40am.

OTHER NEWS HEADLINES
IN HITLER'S WORDS

German radio *has announced that Hitler has demanded that no flowers be thrown at him during his visits to the front. The Fuehrer has also told German wives to forgo their gold wedding rings to finance the 'Hitler Fund'.*

MR. CHURCHILL ADDRESSES THE NATION

Mr. Churchill declares that: Our struggle at sea will be long and unrelenting but in the end we shall break their hearts. (Page 3.)

RUSSIAN TROOPS INVADE FINLAND

Now the Second Great War has come to Finland. Moltov, Russian's Premier, says to expect a Soviet invasion at any hour. But the people are remaining calm and orchestras were still playing dance music in the cafés until midnight. But the people were saying to each other: 'Now it has come.' (Page 4.)

N.Z. PILOTS FLY ONE-WINGED PLANE

An R.A.F. plane operated by two young New Zealand pilots—one a schoolmaster and one a wool buyer—was struck by a blinding yellow light and big bang when they were flying at about 2,000 feet over north-west Germany on Monday. The plane began to circle uncontrollably and they realized they had been stripped of the starboard wing—Full story back page.

~ Brought to you by ~

White Point Wines—*A new start to the day for hard working housewives! The wine to drink for your mid morning rest!*

His Master's Voice—*This Radiogramophone is the key to the cheerfulness we must have on the home front! Money well spent!*

~Present day~

~Truth or Dare~

B ert, the bus driver, had broken the chatter, issuing everyone with a bed number before shuffling them out of the mess hall. None of them had a chance to find out anything much about each other, let alone attempt to eat any of the unappealing food.

Madame Glizsnort had assumed they would eat what they were given. They could have no appreciation of how difficult it had been to organize edibles in these conditions. Bert had fulfilled his duties so far— even the children's electronic devices had been dealt with swiftly. Too many suspicions would have arisen if their strange modern phones and mechanical gadgets had not worked here. The idea was to distract them from the peripherals, get them to focus on the task at hand.

It was all a calculated risk; but a risk that had to be taken. Madame Glizsnort had waited and watched for so very long. This was about unfinished business and she would do whatever it took to bring it all to finality no matter what the cost. And there would definitely be a price to pay for them all.

Right now, all Madame Glizsnort could concentrate on was resisting the Calling. It was trying to pull her away, and for good reason. That was understood. But she had defied it for so long. It had been grueling, but she couldn't let it happen. Not yet; not before all this was taken care of. The Calling would have to wait.

The cabin itself was quite large inside and had two bedrooms with several windows and a washroom. The first bedroom was larger with a log fire and it occupied the girls: Annabelle, Blaze, Daffodil and Duette. The second bedroom was for the boys: Santu, Jake and Duel. The bunk beds looked hard and that's because they were. There was only minimal lighting (an old fashioned lamp lit by kerosene oil) and the washroom was a small rudimentary room to be shared by everyone.

There was also a huge pile of wood to keep them going for a long time which worried Santu. They were only supposed to be here for a few days and there was enough wood to keep them going for weeks. At least the fire would make up for the single scratchy green blanket covering each of the beds.

"We're going to have to make sure that fire doesn't go out," said Blaze as she hesitated beside it. The issue of having fire burning so close to her while she slept was a big concern. She tugged at her long sleeves making sure they covered her arms down to her knuckles. To Blaze, fire was conversely fascinating and terrible. How could it not be after what she had been through? If she could keep watch, then perhaps she could protect them.

"Well, they didn't take *my* watch," replied Daffodil holding up her wrist. "It looks like a wind up one but I've jigged it with an alarm," she smiled mischievously, "and a few other little additions I've invented."

"Well done!" said Blaze, her red hair glowing in the firelight. She had immediately liked this hippie chick, dressed in all the colors of the rainbow.

"Thanks, I've always loved gadgets," nodded Daffodil as she lugged a huge suitcase full of crystals and stones onto her bunk to check the safety of its contents.

"You have a funny accent," added Blaze, "where are you from?"

"Australia," Daffodil winked. "From the south. I live on the coast. It's so beautiful there. I kind of miss it already. And please don't pronounce the 'A' in Australia, just pronounce it like 'Us-tralia'."

"Ustralia," Blaze repeated, green eyes glinting. "I'm from Ireland."

"Yep," replied Daffodil, "I kinda picked that up." Daffodil was fiddling with one of the compartments in her case. "Where in Ireland?"

"Cork. Have you heard of the Blarney Castle?" Blaze scanned the vacant expressions that greeted her. "You lean backwards over the top of the tower and kiss the Blarney Stone. It's to help with the gift of the gab."

"Oh," said Daffodil, "to help you talk more?"

Blaze was too tired. "Sort of."

Duette climbed into bed. She had no need to enter the conversation. Anyway, she generally only spoke when it was absolutely necessary. There was also the fact that she didn't have a very good grasp of English. Duel had learnt to speak the language very well but Duette had never bothered. After all, every language is decipherable in the mind. Being a mind-reader had a lot of benefits. Her and her brother had read each other's minds since they were babies. Duette didn't care about being left out anyway; she wasn't here to make friends.

"So," said Daffodil as she tore her interest away from her crystals, "we've got a couple of Frenchies, an Irish lassie, an Ozzie," Daffodil pointed to herself, "and . . ." Daffodil looked over to Santu who was standing with his back to the fire, still in jeans but with his leather jacket removed to reveal a tight white tee shirt and a strong, tanned torso. She also noticed that Annabelle seemed suddenly very interested in what he was about to say.

"I am from Basque Country."

"That's Spain right?" asked Daffodil trying to tie back her frizzy blond hair.

"Basque country is actually bordering Northeastern Spain and Southwestern France but I am from the Spanish part." Santu shrugged. "So yes."

Everyone could see now that it made sense: The soft rounded words; the slight lisp; his darkly tanned skin and shiny black shoulder-length curls.

"You speak English very well," said Blaze trying to get some attention from the good looking boy.

"Yes, I have learned from Americans. I have all the cold terms you know."

"Um, I think you mean 'cool' terms," replied Blaze trying to hide a smile.

"Yes and those too." Santu ignored his mistake and nodded. "So," he continued as he eyed the tall blond with the cool, pale-blue eyes—frosted seascapes of impossibility. "Where are you coming from?"

"Live in America but born in England." Annabelle's reply was intentionally brusque and she threw in a deliberate American twang. Personal questions were to be avoided at all costs. Everyone waited for more information but Annabelle ignored them, pretending to check the contents of her luggage.

It sounded to Daffodil like Annabelle was forcing that stupid American accent. The soft English tones still resided there on her palette but it seemed like Annabelle just wanted to chew them and eat them instead.

There was only one left. Daffodil smiled at the boy called Jake. "You're accent sounds a bit like mine."

"South-Africa," Jake said feeling excited to be part of a conversation. "Port-Elisabeth. It's-in-the-The-Transkei-Wild-Coast-on-the-Indian-Ocean-coastline. It's-one-of-the-last-remaining-untouched-regions. Very-beautiful. It-was-formerly-a-Bantustan-or-black-homeland-during-the-days-of-the-apartheid-regime-but-it's-largely-been-forgotten-by-the-powers-to-be. Some-really-good-schools-there." Jake realized he was reciting practiced information again. He could have gone on for an hour. He forced himself to stop.

"Well," said Santu laughing, "It is very good that you are liking where you live."

Jake didn't understand it when people laughed at him. It reminded him that he didn't belong. He covered his ears with his palms. Daffodil felt bad for him. She threw a glare in Santu's direction. Santu shook his head. Why was this crazy-haired girl always angry with him? The boy was funny, that was all.

"Oh, no, Jake," said Santu, "don't be blowing up a fuse about it. I am not laughing *at* you. Your answer is very . . . full, yes?" Santu smiled and nodded at Jake reassuringly. He waited until Jake took his hands away from his ears. "You would like Biscay, especially Guernica. This is where I am coming from. There are lots of churches and museums. You know Guernica is where the famous 'Tree of Guernica' grows—it is where the King of Castile swore an oath to uphold the laws of Biscay—right underneath this tree." Santu was stretching his arms wide and high. "It is like a dinosaur, you know?"

"Mammoth," said Blaze wondering if she was going to be Santu's 'slang translator'.

"Yes, mammoth! Then you have got the coast of the Cantabrian Sea. There are many beautiful coves where you can escape the world and hide . . . and then of course, there are the girls." He winked and raised an eyebrow, his flecked brown eyes roaming the room for understanding. They settled on Daffodil. She didn't understand. He turned back to Jake with a shrug.

Jake smiled at Santu. He liked the sound of Santu's voice. It was full of rolling tones and confidence but it wasn't condescending or cruel. He was very expressive too—his hands and eyes moving with emotion. It was just that Santu was kind of loud. Tiredness and confusion had taken their toll and loud noise was the last thing he needed. Hoping the heat of the fire would follow him to the boys' room, he moved toward the second room to go to bed.

"Well, that's all very fascinating," said Blaze, her tone tinged with feigned excitement, "but shouldn't we be trying to get some sleep?" She set another log on the fire watching the curling flames as if they were alive: simultaneously powerful and terrifying. "I think this log will last us until about 4am. Can you put your alarm on for then, Daffodil?"

"Done," Daffodil said feeling suddenly exhausted. It had been such a strange day.

"Then tomorrow I'm getting out of here." Blaze threw the poker down beside the fire.

Santu tossed up whether to make the call or not. He decided to let it go. There was no use getting the redhead agitated when they all needed sleep. She would find out soon enough that they weren't going anywhere, anytime soon.

"I do not want to be around that Glizsnotty woman for one more second than I have to," added Blaze.

"She's a bit . . . well, strange," admitted Daffodil.

"She's not strange," said Annabelle trying to forget the horrible vision that had ended in her fainting. "She's clearly insane. And dangerous." She flicked her blond hair demonstratively.

Santu usually liked foreign girls but Annabelle's American twang distracted from her beauty. That sort of thing had never bothered him before and he wondered if it wasn't so much her accent but the deceit behind it that bothered him. What he did know about her was that she had some very dark secrets that took a lot of work to imprison. He had been having trouble with his visions here—he wasn't sure if it was the throbbing nose or something else, but his senses were definitely dulled—but he knew enough to know she had deep dark pain that had been buried for much too long. And there was one vision her words had forced upon him that was truly frightening.

"Maybe it will be better tomorrow?" added Daffodil hopefully.

"It will be better because I'll be gone," said Blaze.

"That *would* make it better," said Daffodil stifling a yawn. But she was skeptical. Where exactly did Blaze think she was going to go?

"I have got to sleep," said Blaze and without another word she sank her head into the surprisingly soft pillows and drifted quickly into dreams.

"Also me, I must go to sleep. You ladies sleep well." Santu threw them a generous wave before disappearing into the next room.

Annabelle looked anxiously out into the black night. Her bed was seated right beside the window and there was an eerie glow that shrouded the room. Outside, the opal moon was hovering behind the pines like a mystery. Although the falling snow was suffocatingly silent, the trees made strange whispering sounds that ebbed around her. Annabelle begged the moon not to leave—she knew it was ridiculous but still, she wished. The only thing that frightened her more than anything was the dark. The couple who had taken her in had never understood her terror. And that was the only thing *she* really needed from *them*: Understanding her greatest fear.

Static recording No. 375—On Loop

BUTT⊕NS & BRUISES. 19⊕6-1916.
GH⊕STED AGED I⊕.

Hello. We have forgotten our real names. We have made-up names here. Oscar helped us choose. He asked us what our favorite things were.

I wasn't sure. There's lots of nice things: More nice things than bad things. But I decided on Buttons because I've always liked them. When I was little, my granny used to take us to the fastener shop on Fridays. There were so many jars of colored buttons. Once I even saw some shaped like faces. My sister doesn't like buttons at all. She likes Bruises. She has lots on her legs. She likes to sit and trace them with her fingers.

We like opposite things which is weird seeing as we're twins. I like birds and sunshine and she likes dark corners and storms; I like butterflies and bright colors and she likes bugs and spiders. I definitely don't like spiders. I think it's important that you know that.

When we ghosted we were 10. It was only a few months after our house got hit by a big bomb. Both mommy and daddy were at home which was odd because they spent so much time making steel things for the war. I wish they had been at the factory then because they both got blown up when that bomb hit our house. My sister and I were badly hurt but someone dug under the rubble and got us out. They took us to a hospital to fix us. I don't know where my brother was. I didn't see him after that.

Bruises didn't last long in the hospital. Her legs were crushed very badly. But when she ghosted she stayed by my bedside. I didn't like the hospital. It smelt of awful things; things I can't explain. Bruises and I would talk late into the night and the nurses thought I was just imagining my sister; they didn't believe that she was really there.

Someone came to get me from the hospital. He seemed nice. I can't remember his name. If that man hadn't died his mean old wife wouldn't have made me leave. After that I had to scrounge from bins. Not that there was much in the bins anyway. I just remember always being hungry. That's when Bruises found a ghosted cat. We called him Fidget because he didn't like being cuddled. But he never left our side. He followed us everywhere. With Bruises and Fidget I wasn't lonely.

I remember sometimes people gave me small handouts. It was nice of them but it wasn't enough. One time I got a whole loaf of bread that lasted me nine days. A long time ago we met a boy that had trouble eating the food I had scrounged. He told us that he ate garbage and even raw potatoes and paper to stop himself from feeling hungry. He even acted a bit like rat. He smelled bad too. I think that's why I remember him. It wasn't that he didn't wash, it was because of something else. The smell made us scared and so we ran away.

I was glad that Bruises and Fidget didn't have to be hungry. I don't know what happened but it wasn't very long after that man died that I ghosted too. I always tease Bruises that I'm older than her since I lived a few months longer.

I wish I could see my mommy again. I think it would help Bruises. I'm not sure I remember what Bruises was like Before but I feel like she has changed. She is lost in thought and doesn't talk much now. When we first started our static recordings she would always join in and add something funny. She seems to have lost all her courage. Now she just sits in a dark corner and whispers to herself. Bitsy thinks she is trying to play her favorite game called Whispers but Bruises isn't playing. I've told Bitsy over and over again but she is lonely so I guess she likes to pretend a lot. Sometimes I can get my sister to play with her bugs and spiders. That seems to make her happier.

I wonder if anyone will find us. I wonder if the Shadow will find us. I wonder if our mommy will ever find us. That would be so nice, to see mommy again.

I hope you can hear me.

~Present day~

~Sleep Little Children, Sleep~

S antu climbed into the tight bed sheets. His nose was throbbing and the pain was shooting into his brain. He was really worried now. This was all wrong. They were in trouble and he didn't know how to deal with it. Putting on a show for everyone wasn't going to keep them distracted for long. This wasn't where they were supposed to be and this had nothing to do with a research program. Before his head hit the pillow he wondered exactly what kind of danger they were in and how he was going to save himself.

Jake felt tired but he was worried: He still didn't know how he was going to sleep without listening to his static. Hopefully he was tired enough to fall straight into REM dreams. The bed was hard as concrete and he struggled to get comfortable but once his head sank into the feather pillow he felt his mind drifting away. It was the first time since he was a baby that he had fallen asleep unaided. His father had discovered while tuning the radio that his crying had settled when he struck static, and ever since, that had been how Jake had found the comfort of slumber. Even now, so many years later, Jake still felt the devastation of his father's death. His father had been the one to protect Jake from his mother's unpredictable and malicious fury. When his father had died, Jake's life had become unbearable. The only light in his day was when he disappeared into the dreams of his static.

And now, for the first time in his life, he would discover nightmares. Really awful nightmares.

When the alarm woke Daffodil at 4am she was wrenched from one of the deepest sleeps she could remember. The strange dream that had traversed the sand dunes of her mind had vanished from her memory immediately but had left her with an odd feeling of gravity. It was as if she had been floating high in the sky like a breeze, and waking up had made her feel like lead. Managing to force her eyes open, she peered over at the fire. If it was still burning she could stay where she was, try to find that dream again.

But then she realized how cold it was.

The fire had burned dangerously low. The 4am call should have been for at least an hour earlier. Daffodil shivered in her bed for a moment and looked out the window at the bitter night-air. The fright she felt at what she saw next nearly paralyzed her.

A boy was wandering around outside in the pale moonlight. He was wearing a faded ghost-busters tee shirt and pajama bottoms and he was walking across the frozen ground under the falling snow with bare feet. He was heading for the large pitch-roofed building opposite their cabin: The one that looked virtually derelict.

Daffodil forgot the cold; she forgot the fire and she forgot her own safety. Jumping out of bed, she ran for the door. That's why it was so cold! The door had been left wide open. She slammed it shut behind her as she ran out into the freezing night toward the ambling boy, her own feet burning on the ice. Grabbing him around the middle, she dragged him back to their lodgings. In the fleeting moment that Daffodil took hold of him and turned back toward the cabin, something caught her eye.

It was something she never wanted to see again.

Static Recording No. 3743—On Loop

BABY. 1916–1916. GHOSTED AGED 0.
MELODY. 1907–1916. GHOSTED AGED 9.

Hello. I've been named Melody and this is Baby. Baby has asked me to do the recording for him as he is too young to speak recordable words on this loop. I found Baby in a field. He was all naked and freezing cold until he ghosted. We don't know how old he is. He is so very tiny that he might be a newborn. He doesn't remember anything at all, which is a shame.

He seems to enjoy the crib we made for him. At least he is happy not to be cold anymore. He wants me to say that he likes cuddles and he likes it when we hold his tiny hands. He likes kisses that make lots of noise and he likes shiny things like ghosted bugs. I think the ghosted bugs like him too because they like to fly around his crib in circles. He likes different sounds too, so I play the strange piano here for him. It's an odd piano with pipes but it makes a nice breathy sound when you press the keys. It took me a long time to figure out how to make the keys go down. My ghosted fingers didn't make contact with them at first. But if I think hard enough they work.

I seem to remember more about Before than the others. I don't know why. I know I like the piano. Something I remember about Before, is that my daddy gave me a piano on my 6th birthday. That was before the war started though. He gave it to me because I couldn't play outside the same

40

way as the other children. You see, I got polio and it crippled my legs. I did get to play daddy's piano for a few years before they came to take it away. My mommy cried but I told her it would be alright. I drew a picture of a piano keyboard on some paper and said I could use that until we got another one. I guess I've got one now—and a much bigger one too.

Both my mommy and daddy were teachers but when daddy went to war mommy also started working with other ladies to help the war along. I remember one night there was lots of attacks and mommy took me to the next door neighbor's cellar. We stayed there all night long.

The next day we went back to school just like normal but there were only seven children left in the class. Fourteen children and their families had all been killed. Mommy tried to teach us that day but she kept crying and had to tell the students to go home.

Then mommy got a very big tummy. She said I was going to get a little brother or sister soon. Then she got very sick and had to stay in bed. I thought it was because they had taken the piano away and she couldn't hear me play anymore. So I sat by her bed and hummed all the tunes I had learned. I don't think my singing was as good as my playing because I couldn't make mommy better.

When she started screaming I called the doctor but he didn't come for a really long time. Mommy was in horrible pain and there was blood everywhere. When the doctor came he didn't do much. He said mommy had gone to heaven.

After mommy died I was sent to a big house with lots of kids in it. There were some really mean ones there too. I never saw my mommy or daddy again. I wasn't there very long before I ghosted.

Like the others, I don't remember how I ghosted. I don't remember my name or what year I was born but I do remember my mommy and daddy and I miss them a lot. At least I have Baby to take care of and I'm in a safe place. Oscar says if we keep sending out these recordings, someone will hear us and then we can go home. We have been doing this a long time and no one has come yet.

If you can hear, me and Baby would like to go home now. I will record some playing after I put Baby down.

Maybe my mommy and daddy will hear me play.

~Fire Isn't All They Need~

Daffodil could see the image in her mind. The shocking vision stared at her as if it was burned into her brain. The strange distorted face had stared at her desperately from the window pane of the old peeked-roof building—and it wasn't normal. It was strangely old and young at the same time and it had been surrounded by an unearthly glow. It was gruesome and intriguing and terrifying. Her mother would have encouraged her to go ahead and investigate. And if her mother were here with her she may have done exactly that. But her mother wasn't. Of course she wasn't—she was dead, or 'spirited', as her father would have called it. But he was dead too so what did it matter?

The cold and the noise of Daffodil's breathless cries—both because of the half-dead boy she had dragged in and the horror she had just seen—woke the others.

As usual, Blaze had not slept well and the noise of the slamming door had woken her in an instant. By the time Daffodil had dragged the boy's body toward the rapidly disappearing fire, Blaze was wide awake.

"Jake!" cried Daffodil as she shook the half-dead boy on the floor. "Don't know how long he was out there! Help me drag him to the fire."

These days Blaze was good under pressure. Jumping off her bunk in her clover leaf pajamas, she helped Daffodil drag him to the fire and checked all his signs.

"Why were you two out there?" asked Blaze as she opened Jake's eyelids to check dilation. She looked Daffodil up and down. Her messy blond hair had escaped its elastic and she wore patched tracksuit pants and a long sleeved jersey covered in bright yellow daffodils.

"I went to get him. He was just walking around out there in some kind of trance or something. I think he was headed toward that building." She pointed to the darkened structure beyond them. "It was like he was hypnotized."

Annabelle was staring at the three of them without emotion. "Calm down," she said, "I'm sure he's fine." The hippy girl did have a tendency to carry on. The boy had obviously been sleep-walking.

Blaze and Daffodil swapped knowing glances: *No one should rely on Annabelle for help.*

By this time Santu and Duel had woken and sauntered out to see what the commotion was about. They were faced with something unexpected: Jake was lying on the hard concrete ground of the cabin, with a stone white complexion and a deathly look on his face.

"Quickly," yelled Santu, "be stoking the fire!"

Annabelle rolled her eyes. Another dramatic one.

Blaze stopped herself from laughing at Santu's love heart covered pajamas—a token of some girl's affection perhaps—and jumped up to thrust the poker underneath the dying embers before throwing on some small branches and then a larger log. The flames swelled, and Blaze felt their life inside her. '*No,*' she thought to herself, '*don't.*'

In the daze of wakening, Duette was trying to understand what was going on. Someone was hurt and the others, well all except Annabelle with her cool blue eyes, were panicked. Their thoughts were screaming out in fear. But Annabelle wasn't like the others—or anyone Duette had ever met. Duette had never come across anyone that could resist her infiltration; she had been able to read everyone's mind for as long as she could remember. Not one to be put off by a challenge, Duette decided to push harder—maybe when the girl was asleep she would find out what she was hiding behind that distrustful gaze. Until then she would keep an eye on her. Maybe, thought Duette, Annabelle didn't trust other people because she was not trustworthy herself.

Duette felt her brother's reprimand: '*Leave what you don't understand alone.*' Duette smiled and sent a message back to Duel—which he didn't appreciate at all. But Duel had dealt with his sister for much too long to be offended. Duette had been bossy since she was born, even pushing him aside to get out of the womb first. It was incredible to him how different they both were. He added, *'Perhaps you don't want to know what's beyond Annabelle's icy wall. Perhaps there is a very good reason you should not be reading her thoughts.'* Duette threw the mental version of rolling her eyes at Duel. It was a fairly typical response which deserved to be ignored.

For now though, Duette disregarded the girl's resistance (and her brother's interruption) and pulled her scratchy green blanket off the bed to throw it over Jake.

"Should we call someone?" asked Daffodil.

"I do not think there is anyone else here." Santu peered out into the dark, his self-assurance still evident even though he was swathed in love hearts.

"What!?" cried Annabelle. She had been watching Daffodil gently slap Jake's face. "Where's Madame Snotty then!?"

Blaze didn't like the blond American one bit. "Oh so *now* you care?"

"Well, if he's dead maybe they'll let us go home." Annabelle sneered at Blaze. Redheads were so . . . ugly.

"Annabelle!" cried Daffodil. "That is a disgusting thing to say!"

Annabelle shrugged her shoulders. She was joking: Kind of. Anyway it was fun to mess with the drama students. Huffing out a sigh, she breezed over toward the prostrate boy, her pink, silk nightgown gusting around her as if she were a queen. Kneeling beside Jake, she reached for his wrist. His pulse was weak but definitely still thumping away.

"He's fine. He just needs to warm up."

Daffodil wanted to greet Annabelle's lack of compassion with hatred but she knew better than that. Ignoring her, she grabbed each of Jake's hands and rubbed them together to create some heat.

"Rub his feet Blaze," Daffodil said as she nodded toward Jake's bright red toes. For some reason Daffodil felt attached to this boy even though they had only just met.

"What was he doing out there?" asked Santu, watching the curling flames that Blaze had created.

"I don't know," said Daffodil. The vision of the face at the window returned. "But there's something else out there."

Annabelle stared out into the dark hating her fear and hating the battle it came with. 'I know.' Annabelle's voice was a whisper that no one heard.

It was a shame because her words would have helped them prepare.

But Jake was starting to come around and everyone's attention was drawn to him. He squeezed open his eyes to see the pretty face of the brown-eyed blond hovering over him. His surprise turned immediately to fear. He hated people being very close to him and she was *touching* him. He quickly shut his eyes again before sitting up and pushing himself backward trying to get away from her. He bumped into Duette, who was standing next to Duel. Jake was horrified. He felt like he was in a box with no way out. He jumped up and tried to run but his blistered feet made him cry out. He crumpled to the ground and covered his head with his arms. It was a childish gesture but one he had learnt very early in life. Rule number one: Protection.

"Jake it's okay," Daffodil said to him quietly. "Everyone needs to give Jake some room." She motioned for everyone to move as far away from him as possible. "Jake if you can try and open your eyes—you don't have to look at anyone—it's just so you can see that we're all far away now." Daffodil's voice was quiet, gentle, trustworthy. Slowly Jake opened his eyes.

"Not-usually-this-bad," Jake stammered with his eyes to the ground. "Seems-worse-right-now."

"That's okay Jake," said Daffodil. "Do you remember going outside?"

Jake looked up suddenly and stared straight at Daffodil. Shocked, he shook his head slowly.

Daffodil was at least pleased he could look at her again.

"I-went-outside? In-the-dark?"

Jake's sentences were still running on but he was managing to speak a bit more slowly. Daffodil didn't know why; maybe it was the shock but she thought if she could gain his trust he might relax enough to talk freely.

"That's why you're feet are hurt," said Daffodil gently.

"Why-did-I-go-outside?" Jake asked bewildered.

"We don't know," said Daffodil. "You were headed for that building over there." Daffodil pointed in the direction of the structure with the peaked roof.

Jake suddenly shivered. The color in his face drained and he bent over as if he were going to be sick.

"That-was-my-dream," he said.

Blackwater Herald Moon Tribune
Saturday, January 6th, 1940—
One penny

WORLD NEWS HEADLINES
SPEE BLOWN UP BY OWN CREW

*O*n December 13th, the Battle of the River Plate began the first major naval battle of this Second Great War. The Nazi pocket battleship, the Graff Spee, was caught off guard by British cruisers in the South Atlantic Ocean, but with only superficial damage, it continued to rally against merchant shipping with attacks in the area. The Spee carried on to Montevideo where, after fierce fighting in the open sea, Captain Langsdorff was driven to scuttle the battleship by removing the crew in lifeboats and blowing the vessel up so that it would not fall into enemy hands. December 20th, Captain Langsdorff shoots himself in the head in his hotel room. Page 4.

LOCAL NEWS HEADLINES
BLACKWATER CHURCH TO BE RENAMED

Despite protests regarding the rebuilding of the Church of Mortimus, a new and sturdy structure is well under way on the Cross Roads site.

Many surrounding areas have helped in the sourcing of some first-rate bluestone and Mr. Jeffery Pennyfarther has done a magnificent job organizing the builders on site. In an excellent effort, an extraordinary amount of locals, although without knowledge of the building trade, have come to participate in any way possible.

"The offering of volunteers is astounding!" cried Mr. Albury Figus of Stanthom Creek Court when the Herald Moon Tribune showed up. "It has proved that this building is of Godly aspiration."

But there are still those who fear impending wrath if this building is against the will of The Almighty.

In a rather dramatic speech at the building site, Mrs. Ethel Pettigrew of Waterbury Road, said, "The final brick shall be placed and the doors shall open for the first time and that is when we shall all be struck down."

The new church is to be renamed St. Catherine's Church of Redeemus. It has been so named after Saint Catherine of Sienna who had visions of saints at the age of 6 and is, of course, the patron saint of fire protection.

Due to reopen on Sunday 16th, June, the Herald Moon Tribune ensures the reading public that it will be there to report on the outcome.

It remains to be seen what will come of the new construction but it is quite evident that if the people do not come together on this matter, the protests and disputes will continue to disrupt the previously harmonious town of Blackwater.

The current circumstances of war are not helping to appease the situation. With bombing threats, rationing and the ever-present concern for loved ones away at war, many feel like they are losing control of their lives. Perhaps this fight is the one nobody will give up on easily.

THE LOST CHILDREN UPDATE

More sightings of the Lost Children have been recorded far and wide. Constable Macalister Glizsnort is trying to follow up on each of these reports but admits there are many other matters that are keeping him busy these days. The Constable states that the infighting between those who do believe and those who do not believe that it has been God's will to burn down the church, are creating such friction, that fights are constantly erupting. "The matter definitely strikes at the heart of the town," says the Constable. "In all my years in the force, I have never seen such strongly divided opinions; opinions that will surely be very damaging if each side does not learn to make peace with the other."

Miss Grace Durand has stated to the Herald Moon Tribune that she believes the Second Great War has been the catalyst to cause the renewed sightings. She has also made a bold announcement, claiming that these children are not of the living world.

Grace Durand's declaration: "These children are ghosts and I believe that they have been ghosts for a very long time. If these children had a terrible experience in the First Great War and have been in limbo all this time, it is conceivable to me that this new war could have exacerbated their terror. We must try to help them somehow."

But many disagree. Ernest Harlington says: "If these children are ghosts and reside in limbo then they are evil and do not belong in heaven. We must find a way to rid this town of their devil energies."

It looks to the Herald Moon Tribune, that at this stage, no one is likely to back down.

Blackout: Zero hour tonight until 7:37am.

OTHER NEWS HEADLINES
FRANCE—Clashes on Western Front.

PARIS, FRANCE, Jan. 5—The French war communiqué issued this morning reported: "Local patrol activity on both sides." There were hand-grenade attacks, trench-mortar fire, and artillery shelling over 125 miles of the front yesterday with 1,300 men fighting on each side for hours. But the French penetration of two miles showed that the Germans held only a light front line. The French managed to surprise the Germans causing heavy losses.

2,000,000 MORE BRITONS

LONDON, Eng., Jan. 2.—A proclamation by King George V1 calling 2,000,000 more Britons to the service gives the British a potential army of at least 3,500,000 men. The King's proclamation, which he signed last night after a hurried return from a holiday at Sandringham, requires that all male Britons between 19 and 27 years of age register for service.

AUSTRALIAN'S HEROISM

AUSTRALIA, Jan. 5. A young Western Australian (a wireless operator and gunner) in a reconnaissance plane which was attacked over Germany at a height of three miles at a temperature of 30 degrees below zero, is the latest B.A.F. hero. His hands and feet were severely frost-bitten, but despite intense pain, he continued firing and sending messages.

RATIONING BEGINS JANUARY 8TH

Rationing shall be as follows from January 8th. Bacon is ¼ lb, Butter is ¼ lb, Meat is 2 lbs and Sugar is ¾ lb each week. Don't forget to register at your butcher by January 8th to procure your meat rations. If you are making marmalade, extra sugar can be acquired but you will have to produce documentary evidence that you have purchased oranges. **Value Basis.** *To save sugar Mr. Morrison suggests that more use can be made of potatoes as a substitute in your diet. Recipes Page 9.*

SABOTAGE ROUND UP IN NEW YORK U.S

Evidence of sabotage has resulted in a monster round-up of saboteurs, spies, and exponents of anti-Semitism in the United States. In just 24 hours the Department of Justice had received 500 complaints of sabotage. Deportation is threatened. (Page 5.)

SAINSBURY'S—*All under one roof! How important is that in a blackout! Unbeatable value in the rationed meats section: Butter, bacon, sugar, meat; plus the widest range of unrationed meats: Liver, kidneys, tongues, poultry and game! All this value together at Sainsbury's!*

~Brought to you by~

Oporto Port *tones you up! The real dessert wine from Oporto in Portugal.*
Harlene Camomile Golden Hair Wash—*Wash dullness away and be the envy of all your friends! Make your fair hair sparkle and shine with our golden hair wash today!*

~Present day~

~Sleep-walking isn't for Strangers~

"What was your dream Jake?" Daffodil was still speaking softly but couldn't hide the tremor in her voice. The thought of that little girl's screaming face was still fresh in her mind.

"I-dreamt-I-heard-a high-pitched-scream." Jake shook his head with the memory of it. Ordinarily he wouldn't have confessed, but as afraid as he was, he felt like Daffodil was a person he could trust. Still, he hesitated.

"Jake," said Daffodil, "you can tell us. We will understand. And please Jake talk slowly for us. We're not here to judge you. Okay?"

Daffodil's soft brown eyes were pleading with him to act normal. She couldn't have understood how much he *wanted* to *be* normal. It was time for him to learn how to communicate without fear. It was just that nobody had actually listened to him for so long, Jake wasn't sure he knew how.

"Well," started Jake as if testing his ability to speak in proper syllables. "I am able to hear very high pitched sounds." Jake looked defensive.

"That's fantastic Jake," said Daffodil, her kind eyes still trained on his. It was important he didn't lose his focus. "I mean we can all understand you if you just talk a bit slower. The high pitched thing is good too though." Trying to recover she added, "keep going."

Jake nodded, not sure exactly which part he was nodding to. "Sounds that humans can't normally hear." He looked at her hopefully

"Yes, that's great Jake. So you can hear sounds that are inaudible to normal humans?" Daffodil wondered what had happened to this boy to have shredded his self esteem into dust. "Go on."

There it was again. Jake wasn't normal. "I hate it. It hurts."

Daffodil's blood ran cold. Her suspicions were becoming much too real. Daffodil stopped herself from desperately blurting out the information. There was no reason at this stage to frighten anyone.

Everyone was exchanging curious looks but no one said a word. Jake was actually talking in sentences that weren't like staccato stabbings. How had the hippie girl got him to do that?

Blaze had done a brilliant job of restarting the fire. She had nurtured the flames as if they were creatures to be roused, tending to them like she was solely responsible for their existence. But it was getting really hot where Daffodil sat. There was no way she could move now, not with Jake looking at her and talking to her like she was the only one in the room. Moving might distract him. From being freezing cold, Daffodil was now much too hot and the stress was starting to show.

"Jake, it's okay. You're with us and you can trust that we'll all protect each other. We're safe here together."

Jake was relieved—Daffodil knew just what to say to make him feel less threatened. He knew there were others in the room but right now he could only focus on the girl with the big brown eyes and the funny hair. He tried to remember all the coping strategies he had been taught by the therapist. But really, thinking about his favorite antiques was the only way he could make it all right.

"Blind-children-still-use-the-abacus-today-to-learn-calculation." Jake was frowning at Daffodil. She was looking strange.

"That's really interesting Jake, but tell us more about your dream. Just try to concentrate." Daffodil wondered if a person could catch fire from being too hot.

"Well," said Jake trying to speak slowly, "I normally sleep with static on the radio to dull the high pitched sounds but they took all my stuff. Last night was the first time I've ever gone to sleep without static. And it was the first time I've had a dream like that." Jake's mind was panicking. "It-was-terrifying."

"What was so terrifying Jake?" asked Daffodil trying to shift slightly to the right of the fire. "Slowly."

"Well the scream came from over there," he tilted his head slightly toward the door without taking his eyes of Daffodil. "And-it-came-with-a-vision."

"Go on," she said softly. Daffodil tried to stop herself from squirming: The girl, the scream, the heat. Had Jake seen that girl's face too? "You're doing really well."

"It was a little girl's face. She was screaming from a window. The little girl was so upset. It was like she was trapped and she couldn't get out. It-was-awful." Jake took a deep breath. "I guess I just went to save her."

Daffodil felt like she was melting: The heat; the vision; her own burned skin from the dash outside. It was all too much.

"I saw her!" she cried. "I saw her at the window when I was dragging Jake back! Oh god, she's real! Oh my god!" Daffodil felt hysterical; it was as if all her blood vessels were exploding.

Jake moved away in shock. The safe girl was screaming and the noise was piercing his brain.

Blaze laid a hand on Daffodil's shoulder. "Daffodil, you need to relax, you're upsetting Jake."

Daffodil's petrified face looked straight back at Jake. He had moved backwards; away from the fire and away from her. Trying to calm herself down she moved to the left of the fire, she patted the imaginary flames on her back. Speaking calmly again, she apologized.

"Jake, I'm sorry. But I need you to know that you didn't dream that vision. It was real." Daffodil took a deep breath.

Jake was in shock. Not only was his 'dream' real but he had been called out in his sleep without his consent. And now Daffodil had seen it all too and she was obviously terrified.

Annabelle sat there, silent and stunned. The vision she had seen when Madame Glizsnort had stared at her with those icy cold eyes, returned to her. It was why she had fainted. But it wasn't just a girl crying in a window, oh no, her vision was much worse: There was a deep dark abyss and symbols that blazed all around her and . . . she shook her head to clear her mind of the images. If she told the others she would have to confess and that could never happen. So, risking everyone's future, Annabelle chose to stay silent.

"Alright," said Duel, his lovely French accent bending the letters like they were rubber, "everyone needs to calm down here." The environment was electric. "Let's just be rational for one minute." He was pumping his palms like a minister. "I agree that everything about this voyage has been very strange: The Glizsnort woman and her crazy behavior and then there is the fact that we seem to be out here all alone, and now all this . . ." his voice trailed off for a moment while he thought. "But we are all together and we can work this out. After all, don't we all belong to the Secret Society for Gifted Teens?"

It was the first time that anyone had acknowledged the link between them. Each had assumed, due to the manner of their invitations, that it must be so, but secrecy kept them from coming clean. Now, under the circumstances, that meant nothing. So it was Duel to bring them all toward the understanding that they each were capable of extraordinary things.

"No offense," piped up Annabelle, "but some of us are more capable than others." Annabelle threw a raised eyebrow towards Jake who was still hugging his knees and looking distraught.

"This is not so true," said Santu. His dislike for the girl with the fake accent was growing by the minute. "We should all know we are here because we are having something, something others do not and there is no test to tell what is the more important." Santu stared coldly at Annabelle. "I know that to be accepted by this 'Secret Society' you have to have been doing something academically extraordinary or you have to have received an important award, but this is not all you are needing to join. Yes?" Santu took a moment. "And I am thinking *everyone*," he stared again at Annabelle, "is knowing what I mean." Santu looked over at Jake who was eyeing the floor in front of him. "I mean, how many people are hearing these high pitched noises Jake?"

Jake was jolted from his abstraction. "Two," he answered. "In-the-whole-world-only-2-have-been-proved-to-hear-such-high-frequencies—including-me." Jake was remembering all the horrible tests he had gone through: Over and over and over.

"You see!" said Santu sounding like this was a good thing. "I am thinking we are here for a reason and that this reason is because of our *other* abilities. Like this one of Jake's."

Everyone had secrets they didn't want to reveal; had promised never to reveal but Santu had tapped their egg shells and his penetrating stare gave them reason to believe he would not let them alone until he had broken their boundaries. Defensive tactics were engaged immediately but Santu had had enough of denial.

He was about to break all his own rules. It was a huge judgment call and a potentially dangerous strategy.

Santu was about to tell the truth.

Static Recording No. 2765—On Loop

⊕scar. 1903-1917. Gh⊕sted Aged 14.

Hello. My name is Oscar. I chose my name because it has the word 'car' in it. I really like cars. I think it was my grandfather who used to take me to car shows. I remember I sat in one once. It had a huge steering wheel in the front and 4 wooden artillery wheels. I was saving my pocket money so that one day I would be able to buy one. My favorite is the Model T Ford. It has a 20 horsepower engine and can go 45 miles an hour! So fast. Their headlights are acetylene lamps and the brass horn is super shiny and makes lots of noise. My grandfather always complained about the hand crank at the front which started the engine. He says too many people break their arms trying to get it to go! Maybe they should let young people like me do it for them. The car I want costs $690! It's called a Tin Lizzie. I really like that name.

I have strange memories of Before. I think I was the only one who survived a mortar attack. I have a strange feeling that my whole family died when our house was struck that night. I was very young at the time, maybe 12. I know I was very scared. And I'm not sure what happened straight after that. The things I remember don't really make sense. Perhaps you will understand them.

I remember being around lots of soldiers and begging for food. I was at the frontlines. I don't remember how I got there. They were very nice to me which I wasn't used to. One soldier took care of me for a while which was a swell time. But then there was an attack and he got killed. I got hurt too. I have a deep gash on my side now. They sent me to a soldier's hospital and I got fed three times a day and slept in a bed! But I missed the soldier who got killed and when they let me out of the hospital I went back to the frontlines. This time the whole squadron took me in and they made me an honorary soldier. But soon after that, the war was over and all the soldiers had to leave and I was alone again. I remember being in trouble but I don't know why. I think I got hurt again. But this time there was no hospital.

I was 14 when I ghosted. I am the oldest here and had more time than the others to understand.

At first I could feel the call of newly ghosted children and I would go and find them and bring them here where it's safe. I have tried to band everyone together. I also found a few ghosted animals. They are good for keeping us company. I found a canary which we call Yellow. It has a lovely singing voice and really likes it when Melody plays the piano. I also found a cat which we call Kat. It's very mischievous and has really loud meows. There is also a duck. I know: Out of all the animals I could sense, one of them was a duck! We call her Duck—as in 'duck for cover'. She likes to run at you and peck your shins. Often, she has us all running around in circles trying to get away from her. Buttons and Bruises brought a cat with them too, called Fidget. And there are lots of ghosted bugs and spiders and stuff as well. Sadly, I haven't been able to sense anymore animals since we have been holed up here.

I don't know how much the others have figured out but I am very worried for us. I know our time is running out. I don't think we are supposed to stay here but we can't leave or the Shadow will get us. None of us like the Shadow. I can tell that we are fading. When I look at everyone they are starting to look different and Bruises is almost gone. I know that if we fade before we are found we will never be able to go home. If we fade, we disappear forever as if we never existed. That is very dangerous for everyone, ghosted or not.

This may be my last recording. I will send it out on loop. If no one comes for us in the next two moons I will have to go out and find someone to help us. I know the Shadow is waiting but I will have to risk it. I cannot let all these ghosted ones fade away. It's not right. We need someone to tell us who we, where we come from and when we come from. Then maybe we can find our way home.

Please if you can hear me you must come and help us. I fear it may be too late already.

Blackwater Herald Moon Tribune Monday, June 17th, 1940— One penny

CURRENT WAR UPDATE
WINSTON CHURCHILL'S DECLARATION

*W*inston Churchill's speech to the British House of Commons: "We shall defend our island whatever the cost may be. We shall fight them on the beaches, we shall fight on the landing grounds, in the fields, in the streets and in the hills. We Shall Never Surrender." As Neville Chamberlain resigns from Prime Ministerial Duties, Winston Churchill proves to be an inspiring replacement—Page 3.

LOCAL NEWS HEADLINES
FIRST SERVICE OF BLACKWATER CHURCH

Journalist, Mr. Henry Frienly of the Herald Moon Tribune has reported that the opening of the new church on Sunday 16th, June at the Cross Roads location went without a hitch. Despite previous warnings about being struck down at the moment the doors opened, nothing but a brief breeze rustled through the air.

"The moment was electric!" cried 13 year old Miss Jane Thumly of Orchard Place. "Everyone was holding their breath. Even though I did not believe all that nonsense Thelma Pettigrew was sprouting, it was still rather scary. But as the doors opened, the sun came out from behind a cloud and we all just knew it was the precise place to rebuild."

Unfortunately, those protesting the rebuild had traveled the great distance to The Church of All Saints for their Sunday worship and were not available for comment.

Mr. Jeffery Pennyfarther, the main builder of the church said, "Perhaps the silly fools were praying for us not to be struck down! Either way it just proves that the church was meant to be here."

Bishop John Biggs commented on the day: "The service began with several readings and then a most enjoyable time was spent singing hymns. It was just like the old days—very pleasant. Perhaps next week the congregation might include all those that did not attend today."

After the service, the Bishop took our journalist on a tour of the church which proved to be very interesting. He reports that there is an organ with full floor-to-ceiling pipes and there is a lovely upper level attic area that is quite large. On the ground level, there are small but beautifully crafted stained glass windows with images of the shining sun and children dancing which, although not highly religious, do create an atmosphere of warmth and comfort in the building. At the foyer, one is greeted with a statue of a beautiful angel apparently reaching out to the worshipers as they enter, and the surrounding walls have been specially engraved with peaceful and loving symbols like doves and crosses.

The Bishop suggests that more open attitudes may upset those who were opposed to the building in the first place but he hopes that they will evoke the community spirit he is trying to encourage. "During these harsh times we must all come together as one; be good to one another and try to understand those we are different from," he said.

There will be another collection next Sunday in aid of the local widows who have recently lost their husbands in the war.

OUR CONSTABLE AND DOCTOR SIGN UP

The Herald Moon Tribune would like to wish both Constable Macalister Glizsnort and Doctor Alfred Williams good luck. The two local men of Blackwater, both highly regarded in their professions, have joined the droves of countrymen and signed up to join the war. The town of Blackwater wishes them Godspeed.

Blackout time is 9:41 p.m.-4:15 a.m.

WORLD NEWS HEADLINES
LATEST RUNDOWN (Follow up stories Page 3 & 4.)

February—British destroyer 'Cossack' rescues 299 British seamen from German prison ship Altmark in the Norwegian 'Josing-fjord'. Sweden refuses to intervene on the side of Finland.

March—Adolf Hitler and Benito Mussolini hold conference at Brenner Pass where Italy joins the war with Germany. Finland signs a treaty with Russia giving up a large amount of territory.

April/May—Hitler invades and occupies Denmark and Norway. Germany severely bombs Northern region of Scandinavia.

British, French and Polish units sent to assist the Norwegians but their efforts are uncoordinated and poorly planned. Failing to dislodge the Germans, withdrawal follows.

General Guderian, in an address to his troops who have fought the Blitzkrieg campaign through Belgium and France, says: 'I asked you to go without for 48 hours. You have gone for seventeen days. I compelled you to take risks . . . you never faltered.'

May 10th—Nazi's invade neutral Holland, Belgium, Luxemburg. Airports Bombed. Rotterdam bombed almost to extinction—death toll 30,000. Both Holland and Belgium occupied.

June 4th—British Forces Successfully Complete the Evacuation of more than 300,000 Troops from Dunkirk in France.

June 10th—Italy Declares War on France and the United Kingdom, bringing to the battlefield 1,500,000 men, more than 1,700 aircraft and a naval fleet of 6 capital ships, 19 cruisers, 59 destroyers, 67 torpedo-boats and 116 submarines.

June 14th—Paris falls under German Occupation.

OTHER NEWS HEADLINES
BALISBURY WOMAN'S CLUB DECLARATIONS

BALISBURY: 'More Than Two-thirds of the World's Population is Engaged in War.'

This startling fact was driven home yesterday to members of the BALISBURY Woman's club when Mrs. Mary Mcnulty gave her annual detailing of world events. She also pointed out that war operations covered more than three-fourths of the total area of the world and that the populations remaining at *peace were either actively preparing for war or retaining a strategy of watchful waiting. Performing after the speeches was Ernest Bailey, who presented such musical pieces as "O Sole Mio, and "Ah, Sweet Mystery of Life."*

SURMON OF THE MONTH

Excerpt from: Verses about Jesus from Mark—"And the second commandment, namely this, Thou shalt love thy neighbor as thyself."

~Brought to you by~

Horlicks—gives you Group 1 sleep! *Do you struggle with war worry? Is it hard to get to sleep? Are you tired during the day? You may belong to the sleep groups 2 & 3. Group 1 sleep ensures you are best fortified to stand war strain. The longer the war lasts, the more urgently you need the restful, restorative sleep that Horlicks gives.*

SPIRELLA CORSETS. *Garments for Health, Style and Comfort. Made to Measure. Free Demonstration. Ida E. Jenkins. 72a Main Street. Phone. B1362*

~Present day~

~THE TRUTH HURTS, THEN BLEEDS~

Everyone in the room was staring at Santu as if he were going to reveal the mysteries of the universe. Even though he had left a few top buttons undone on his love-heart-festooned pajama top to reveal his tanned chest, he looked the worse for wear. Dark bruises had formed under his eyes due to his broken nose and the pain had made his tanned face pale. But perhaps, the fact that he *was* injured and had not complained about it even once made him all that much more credible.

In fact, Santu was pushing back the panic. He surmised that there was only one way out of here and he knew no one was going to like it. Santu's sense of foreboding wasn't limited to this new discovery by Jake and Daffodil. It had been building since he got on the bus. The long journey had at least afforded him one thing and that was time to get emotionally prepared.

"Ever since I was really young . . ." Santu took a depth breath. He couldn't believe he was doing this: Not a soul had been privy to the forthcoming information except his mother and she had begged him not to tell another living soul. For she alone had known what it was to have such a gift; she had known the strength it took to face a knowing world; and she had known what it was to be killed for such a gift. "Ever since I can remember I am being able to see things—I mean like . . . spontaneously. I guess it is like having a 3 Dimensional vision of the emotional world. The visions come to me when a person is speaking—the words are bringing the visions." It was impossible to explain. He waited for the disbelievers to voice their dismissal as they had with his mother.

Instead, he was faced with a group of terrified people and their alarm didn't come from the fear that they were in the company of a lunatic. The panic came from the fact that each and every one of them was afraid Santu would find out their secrets.

Everyone except Jake: Jake clapped. Finally, for the first time in his life, he was not the only person in the room who was weird. Jake's buoyancy lifted the intensity of the moment.

Santu was surprised. Not so much about Jake's clapping, that was just funny. He liked Jake. It was the silence that was more interesting. He had expected scorn, especially from Annabelle, but no one had uttered a word.

Perhaps they were all scared of him? Santu gritted his teeth and flicked his forehead to dislodge an annoying curl. It was a trademark move that they would all get used to, but right now, it came across as conceited. "Has anyone, besides Jake of course, got anything to add?"

Daffodil was struggling with whether she should tell them or not. "So you can see stuff?" she asked Santu testing the group's reaction.

"Yes." Santu was going to keep the answers short. Detail could come later.

Daffodil guessed her secret would come out sooner or later but she hoped it would be later. "That's great," she added nonchalantly. "Have you read *my* mind?"

"No, I cannot read minds. Not at all. I am just seeing visions. You know?"

Duette smiled, her hazel eyes glinting beneath her perfectly asymmetrical fringe. Of course *he* couldn't read minds. She would have known that straight away. Duette delved into Santu's mind. It was interesting terrain. His overconfident appearance was a ruse. The boy was really worried, worried for his life. If she hadn't been distracted by Daffodil's very loud defenses at work, Duette would have probed deeper. Needless now really, she had heard most of his troubled thoughts but she would have to find out why he believed his life was in danger.

Annabelle thought about it for just a second. She was only 4 years old when her mother abandoned her; left her to find her own way in the pitch-black dark. What had ended up happening that night would haunt her for the rest of her life. Then came all the foster homes, and finally, the couple that had taken her in under the pretence of caring for her: They didn't. Annabelle knew that. Her music kept them interested, or more realistically, Annabelle's paying audiences kept them interested.

"Got nothing," Annabelle said as she shrugged her shoulders. Annabelle had learned two things early on: Love was not only impractical, it was destructive; and there was always a choice. And her choice was to never tell anybody anything that didn't concern them. Ever.

Santu knew Annabelle was lying. That was fine for now. But if he needed to, he *would* find out. No question. His visions never lied and what he had seen of her life proved she had a lot more to offer than a cold heart.

Santu could see the others fighting with themselves. On one hand they desperately wanted to confess, on the other, they had kept these secrets all their lives, just like him. He knew how hard it was to reveal the truth.

"Daffodil," Santu nodded in her direction, "are you sure you cannot be adding anything?"

Daffodil had plenty to add. And she knew *he* knew. It was that look in his dark brown eyes: All knowing. Was that why he seemed so confident? Oh well, she thought, she'd probably never see these people again anyway and ridicule had been part of her life for so long; what did it matter if it followed her here?

"I dunno." Daffodil chewed her lip, and tugged at her patchwork skirt. "Can anyone else see their dead parents?" She was sure if her parents were still alive she would have told *them* she could see dead people. But then, if they hadn't died she wouldn't have been able to see them and she wouldn't know she could see dead people. Daffodil was looking very agitated. Her mouth was all twisted and she was fumbling with her watch trying to distract herself by conjecturing how she could make it create static for Jake.

"Thank you, Daffodil." Santu was relieved someone else had confessed. "Now is anyone else seeing anything dead?"

The secret keepers were all looking at their feet.

"Blaze," said Santu, "what about you?"

"I have never felt *any* of that stuff." Blaze was pulling at the cuffs of her sleeves. Her flaming green eyes were turned away from Santu, focused on the fire.

"You are sure?" Santu wondered why everyone's first reaction was to lie. It was a sad state of the world that fear came before truth. But he had done the same all his life too. It was easier in the short term, yet such a burden to walk it to your gravestone.

"My you do like to be right don't you?" said Annabelle, heavy on the twang.

"Generally, yes, but not right now." Santu knew Annabelle would try to play with him like a cat toy. Her beauty was such a waste.

Santu directed his gaze toward Blaze.

"What about fire? Does this help?"

Blaze was horrified. How did he know? It was all some horrible joke. She shook her head fervently. And then she shook her head a little less and a little less after that. Perhaps she could just give him part of the story? But which bit? If he had seen something maybe she could tell him something that would make him second-guess his vision? Anxiety was making her eyes blaze.

Glances darted from Blaze to Santu as the observers watched the redhead fall into a confused stupor.

A delicious smile emerged on Annabelle's cherry lips. The good looking boy was accosting the girl with the ugly hair. Hilarious. Hopefully Blaze really would try to run away, then Annabelle could tease Santu as much as she wanted.

"Blaze," said Daffodil, "in this place, being a freak is a good thing. It might help us get out of here. If you've got something to tell, just do it."

Blaze wasn't ready. "Why can't we just get that Bert guy to drive us all back to the airport?"

Santu knew exactly why. "Do you *see* that bus out there? Do you know where Bert is?"

Blaze jolted to the window. The bus had been parked out the front of the cabins. She looked into the empty darkness desperately.

"Where's the bus?" she cried. "Maybe he moved it?" Blaze went to run out into the freezing air to find it.

Daffodil grabbed her. "Blaze, the bus is gone." Daffodil had already been out there and there was no sign of a vehicle or a bus driver.

"Where did he go?!" Blaze yelled. "They can't leave us out here all alone! I have to leave!"

The noise was hurting Jake's brain. He covered his ears with his hands and started reciting everything he could remember on embossed Medicine bottles from Oregon in the late 1800's, and the most popular medicines like Oregon Blood Purifier, and Oregon Unk-Weed cure.

"Madame Glizsnort is around somewhere. She'll come and get us and I'm sure she'll explain whatever is going on. Okay?" Daffodil was guiding Blaze back to the fire. "Now why don't you just try and answer Santu's question?"

Blaze tried to pull herself together.

"Honestly, I don't have anything like that. Sometimes I get a feeling. That's all." Blaze had no intention of admitting to anything just yet. She certainly wasn't going to tell them about that awful medal that they had forced on her. And there was no way she was going to tell them what had happened after the fire. The memory of all the others that did not make it made her want to dry wretch: Those awful ghostly faces begging her to make them alive again. She had run from them, left them all alone and lost. But it didn't matter how far she ran, Blaze could never outrun the truth. Shivering, she yanked on the hems of her sleeves, pulling her hands inside them.

"What is this feeling?" pressed Santu.

Blaze shook her head. "Things happen sometimes. It hurts." The alarm in her eyes told Santu she was desperate for him to leave her alone.

Santu felt sorry for her. Now the vision that had come from Blaze's words made sense. "I know," he said. "The truth hurts."

As the words came out of Santu's mouth he felt a strange and icy pressure coming toward them. This time he had a chance to grab a piece of tissue before his nose discharged a wave of blood.

Static Recording No. 2012—On Loop

Dog. 1906-1918. Ghosted Aged 12.

Hello. I have been named Dog. It's a stupid name. I don't care what my name is anyway. I mean, who cares right? I put up with everyone here but I don't deserve to be here. I mean the world owes me big time. All that stuff I had to go through and what do I get? This place. And you know, I've been watching everyone for all this eternity of nothingness and they're all fading anyway. I know it, Oscar knows it, and I reckon some of the others know too. But no one says anything—like it's a big secret that we're all going to disappear. But I don't care. Nothing worse can happen to me.

I've thought about getting out of here but what's the point really? I'm just waiting until it's all over. Disappearing is not that bad. I mean, I'll be gone so I won't care. I'm not responsible for what's left behind. And my existence is better dissolved into the abyss. And who cares if that deep hole takes a few more innocents with it? We are all going to disappear anyway. It didn't make any difference what kind of person I was like in the Before. What does it matter now?

Yeah, yeah, Oscar, take it easy. Oscar is getting mad at me. He says I'm venting. Whatever the hell that is. Yeah alright. Oscar is insisting I tell you my story. Again. I've done this a million times already but we all have to do what Oscar says. Yes sir, Oscar!

Let's see. I was born in nowheresville and my name was nothing and no one gave a . . . .

Hey, let me down. Very funny Oscar.

Oscar thought it would be amusing to put me on the ceiling. I don't know how he does that but I'm gonna learn—so help me god.

Fine I'll tell it again. Oscar says it will help listeners to identify us. (You mean all the listeners in the last eon?) Well, I remember having a big family when I was really little. I think my baby sister went first. She got Chicken Pox. She was three. Then my brother got German Measles. He was seven. Not long after that my other two sisters and my father were going to the market in our horse and cart and there was a bad snow storm which trapped them in the middle of nowhere. They were six and eleven. I can't remember how old my father was. It was just my mother and me left. I guess *God* needed some more occupants because then my mother caught Typhus. She was twenty-nine. You don't like that story? Oh, so sorry to upset you. I'm not telling anymore except that I was twelve when I ghosted. It was a while after my mother and too much other stuff happened that was all horrible. A lot of it I don't even remember—like how I ghosted.

Anyway, I guess *God's* place was full then 'cos I'm still here. Waiting. I've never seen any of my family in this empty nowhere—so they must've done something right. What is this place anyway?

Oscar is telling me to tell you why I'm called Dog. For some reason this stupid small scruffy dog was right beside me after I ghosted. I don't know why. He follows me around like I'm gonna feed him or something. I keep telling him he's not gonna eat here but he doesn't get it.

Yes, alright! Bitsy wants me to tell you he's called Scruffy. Brilliant. Thank you. Do you wanna do a recording Bitsy or do you want me to finish? No? Not in the mood? Geez.

Anyway, so I have to put up with a dim-witted dog following me around with big goopy eyes. Yeah, I don't love you back dog. You're just annoying me. Oh, that's great, now he's trying to bark into the transistor. Yeah, that's just great idiot.

I'm done anyway.

Our time's done too. This'll all be over soon.

Yeah, ha ha, Oscar thinks it's funny that dog spelt backwards is god.

~Present day~

~IF WE WERE CLOCKS WE WOULD TICK~

In the darkness of the early morning, the unexpected return of Madame Glizsnort was almost amusing. To those who had been brave enough and confronted their truths, an exhilarating rebellion hovered.

Madame Glizsnort did not knock. She just seemed to appear from nowhere. There was no vehicle, there was no sound before the door opened and straight away she was making demands. The freezing cold air that rushed in at them was shocking and made them gasp.

"Everybody is still in their nightclothes!" she cried. "You must be ready for your advanced research classes on time! And by this time I would have already expected you to have gone to the mess hall for breakfast. You have wasted too much food already!"

Daffodil took a sly glimpse of her watch. It was nearly 7:30am. How had the time flown by so quickly?

"Well, Madame Glizsnort, please excuse me," Blaze began, "but we are not clocks. We are used to having alarms wake us up and since you have removed all our electronic devices we are unable to tell the time." The others tried to hide amazed smiles.

This made Madame Glizsnort most confused. She was used to children working, well, like clockwork. "I will issue you with an alarm," she said out of surprise. "Now quickly, get ready and go to the mess hall and meet me at the church at 08:00 hours. We will have our morning sessions there.

The light only comes out here between 11 hundred hours and 15 hundred hours. This will be when we have our break. Then we shall rejoin from 16 hundred hours until 20 hundred hours. This is an intensive program and I expect you all to produce high energy during these times. Now hurry up!" Madame Glizsnort made a hasty retreat and the door conveniently closed behind her.

Curious looks were exchanged.

"The church?" cried Blaze. "It's a *church*?!"

"Apparently," replied Daffodil running over to stoke the fire back to life after Madame Glizsnort's appearance.

"We have to spend every morning with Madame Snotty?!" cried Blaze still aghast.

"Actually," Santu said, "I am thinking this is good." Horrified expressions were directed his way. "This way we are getting to go in and check the layout, so when we go back tonight we will be able to figure out where to go. Yes?"

"*Go back?! Tonight?!*" screamed Annabelle. "*In the dark?!*"

"Shh," said Santu trying to hide his amusement: Finally Annabelle was showing some emotion. "You will wake the dead."

Annabelle went sheet white and shook her head.

"Santu is right," said Daffodil. "We're going to have to go and check it out."

Annabelle didn't want to go anywhere near the church. The arctic feeling in the pit of her stomach was growing colder and harder every time the hideous woman came near her. Trying to dull her anxiety about it wouldn't change how this was going to go down: The ice in her stomach would manifest and the life she now knew would be lost and with that loss would be the chance to find her real mother. She stared at the cocky boy who apparently thought that this was all a bit of an adventure.

"Well, she makes your nose bleed every time she comes near us." Annabelle's voice was hard.

"And how is she making your stomach feel?" Santu could play this game until the end of time.

Annabelle didn't do very well at hiding her shock. So the boy *did* know. Very clever, she thought. Well he better watch out because if he delved too deep he might just get a very unpleasant surprise.

"My stomach is fine, thank you," Annabelle replied in the same cool tone. "But I still have no intention of going into that building."

"You don't have to go," said Santu. Everyone was watching the exchange like a tennis match. "But I hope you do not get lonely sitting out here in the cabin all by yourself—in the *dark*."

Annabelle nearly choked. How much did he know? She was furious with her stupid, mindless fear. What did Madame Glizsnort say? The sun would only be out between 11a.m. and 3 p.m.? Oh god, those dark stretches would be intolerable. Where the hell was this place anyway?

"Fine," Annabelle pulled herself together. If Santu didn't tell anyone else then maybe she could at least keep her secret from the others. "I will go to the *church*." The anger Annabelle directed at Santu shocked and confused the others.

Daffodil watched, wondering why Annabelle had given in so easily. No matter, at least they would all stay together as a group. For some reason that seemed important. For now all they could do was follow their imposed routine. Soon they would place all the pieces in this puzzle and get out of here.

✻　✻　✻

Annabelle was wearing completely inappropriate designer jeans with high heels and the same fur lined Gucci jacket which did a lot to make her look like a model but not much to keep the cold out. Blaze had spent a reasonable amount of time laughing at her until Annabelle had scanned Blaze from head to toe and smirked at her ridiculously ugly outfit of green leggings and matching cardigan, brown wool skirt and brown leather, flat-soled shoes. Daffodil had consoled Blaze, giving her a brief look at the contents of her own suitcase which looked like a pile of throw outs from a second hand fabric store.

Santu had caught the three of them eyeing each other and had decided to steer clear of the lot of them. He pulled his jeans on over his pajama bottoms, layered his tee shirts in the same way as Jake, and zipped his leather jacket up to his neck. Looking cool was one thing, freezing to death was another thing entirely.

Both Duel and Duette wore their beige trench coats with large belts and multitudinous pockets: Spy twins—Him with his light-brown army cut, hands plunged into deep pockets; her with her perfect bob and distrustful expression; both with their wide-set hazel eyes staring intensely into the snow.

Jake hobbled along on his damaged feet grateful for the relieving ointment Daffodil had treated them with. Even though he had pulled on every tee shirt he had packed, his worn pullover—two sizes too big—still flapped at his sides.

After an uninspired breakfast of watery gray oats and powdered orange drink, they all made their way across the frozen ground toward the church. The darkness hadn't lifted at all and the slowly falling snow just made it all the more claustrophobic. In the silence of the frosty morning air, all that could be heard was the ice crunching beneath their feet. No one spoke: Everyone was trying to think of a way out.

Except Jake. As strange as it was to him, it was the first time he had belonged to a group. He was trying to figure out a way to stay. There were too many things he had to work out, and although this seemed a most unlikely place to do that, it also seemed the most appropriate.

As Jake approached the building, he stared up at the clear glass windows on the top story. Was that where the little girl had screamed? At least now Jake could make out some of the building's features. The steeply pitched roof reminded him of Gothic architecture but this building was very simple. The outer walls were of stone with a fine coating of cement which seemed a shame because Jake was sure it was bluestone underneath. There was a bell tower and a spire. The lower floor windows were covered with dirt but even so, Jake could see they were once vibrant stained-glass depictions. Of what, Jake couldn't tell.

When the huge church door creaked open before they had even walked its steps, they stood in the snow waiting for something bizarre to happen. But the world stayed still and so, they each took a deep breath and walked on in, through the old oak doorway.

Inside, the decoration belied the simple exterior. At the entrance, the enormous statue of an ivory angel greeted them. Frozen in a moment of grief and pain, her arms reached out, waiting perhaps for an invisible need; her breath caught; her eyes pleading for something out of reach, something unseen.

Jake apologized to her as he passed.

The inside walls were of stone and cement, plastered and stuccoed. The layout was in the form of the Latin cross and there was incredible scroll work covered in gold leaf. The tiny stones of numerous mosaics, now obscured by too many years of dust, still clung to the upper walls as if trying to stay close to the tarnished gold trim near the ceiling.

Perched at the back of the church and to the left stood a huge organ, its pipes climbing toward the high ceiling like an unfinished alleluia. At the front, behind the altar, Jake could see a narrow staircase that must have led to the upper floor and the bell tower. It looked as if it could crumble with a strong breeze but he could feel the great energy, perseverance, and indomitable will that had gone into making this church. Someone had cared deeply about its beauty. It seemed a terrible shame to keep it in such an awful state. On the door leading to the vestry was the name of its builder: Mr. Jeffery Pennyfarther. 'Nice church,' Jake said to the man who had obviously been dead for years, 'Nice church'.

The heavy air fell upon them like the weight of water. Emotions struck them all at once and each and every one of them slumped a little as it poured across their shoulders pushing down the back of their heads and their spines. It was indescribable: Distant but immediate; taciturn but overwhelming. Each of them understood that this place was full of sadness, regret and sorrow. And, simultaneously, each and every one of them knew that they were in grave danger.

Blackwater Herald Moon Tribune
Tuesday, December 31st, 1940—
One penny

CURRENT WAR UPDATE
HITLER PLANNED LONDON BLAZE

*H*itler's plans to destroy London by generating the Second Great Fire were a prelude to an invasion in the New Year. Soon after 10:00 p.m. on Sunday night, the German Air Command sent out instructions for 1000 air bombers of the Luftwaffe Air Force, to attack. It is estimated that 10,000 bombs were dropped on London within 3 hours starting 1,500 fires. It is only because of the dreadful weather that more of the city wasn't ruined. Many famous buildings, including the Guildhall and Trinity House, have been damaged or destroyed.

The roar of the barrage mingling with the fury of the flames was terrifying for the people of the city. Mr. Churchill visited the site yesterday. PAGE 4.

LOCAL NEWS HEADLINES
NEW PROOF OF SIGHTINGS

Only 6 months after the new church, St. Catherine's Church of Redeemus has been erected; the fascinating story of the Lost Children has taken another turn. There have been no sightings since the church's reconstruction. It seems the children have disappeared completely. This leads many to believe that the two curiosities are linked.

Speculation is rife that the children either accidentally or deliberately, burned it down. This attitude seems to be despite several witnesses reporting they saw it struck by lightning right before bursting into flame. Others believe that the very presence of the children near the church caused the hand of God to force them out.

"They were evil," claims Mr. Frederick Pinchinbury of Strawberry Road. "They must have been so bad that God would not allow them to atone for their sins and cast them to the devil."

But Mrs. Edna Maybunch disagrees. "Children are not evil. And anyway I do not believe they were in the church at the time. I would swear on the bible that I saw them after it was burnt down. They were loitering near the Blackwater graveyard."

Miss Grace Durand, the woman who has taken it upon herself to try to help these children, agrees with Mrs. Maybunch. "They could not have been in the church. We would have found their bodies."

Our journalist, Mr. Henry Frienly can add some researched information to the bizarre case by sighting an article from The Herald Tribune of 1924. According to a report of that time, a group of children was spotted by the esteemed Bishop Paul Augustus O'Connor. He states in the article that the children seemed to be trying, unsuccessfully, to enter the church. "The children came and went before our eyes. They were ghostly in image," he said, "and appeared to be lost. I have not seen anything like it. I was, however, unafraid of them. Instead I felt driven to offer them succor. But as I approached, they vanished—as surely as an apparition from God himself."

The Bishop said he left the church door open for several days, even in the freezing cold. He stated that he believed the church could offer them a gateway to the afterlife.

Miss Durand says this is evidence of the Lost Children's demise and she continues in her determination to search for legitimacy of fact. "As I had initially assumed, they have been appearing here for about twenty years—since the First Great War." Her final words on the matter-at-hand are: "If their souls are to be at peace we must discover their burden of truth." Any information can be passed on to her at 132 Marchenby Street.

Blackout tonight—5:38pm-7:53am. Moon rises 6:32 pm.

WORLD NEWS HEADLINES
GAS MASKS MUST BE CARRIED

The Minister of Security states that the carrying of gas masks by the public—including children—is essential. Gas drills will be a regular feature of *air raid precaution, training and practice. The public must acquaint themselves with shelters and first aid posts.*

SCIENTIFIC PROGRESS IN NEW YORK

*Dean Smith of the Southern California **Telephone Company** has visited the Bell Laboratories in New York and is very pleased to report to the world, that five thousand men are employed there in scientific research. In one-fifth of a second, the voice can travel around the world by Telephone. **Television** is now employed, but its extended use is limited until the required equipment can be installed. **The Largest Microscope** in the world has also been developed (7,000 diameters). And a **Radio Altimeter** can tell the aviator how far he is above the ground!*

The enormous rate of technical advancements augurs well for the future of technology.

***OF OVERSEAS MAIL**—In a reminder that mail for overseas is subject to censorship, the Acting Deputy Director of Posts and Telegraphs, Mr. R. W. Hamilton yesterday suggested methods which would facilitate the work of the censors—see Page 9.*

Every alien will have to stay at home all night after Monday, by order: 10:30 p.m. to 6:00 a.m.

HOYTS PLAZA TODAY: "SUSANNAH of the MOUNTIES"—Starring Shirley Temple. A thrilling romantic drama from 20ᵗʰ Century Fox.

Macleans Toothpaste—Did you MACLEAN your teeth today?

Buzz—Bee Quicker, Bee Smarter—Use Olive Oil Brushless Shave!

Static Recording No. 2012—On Loop

WONDERBOY. 1910~1918.
GHOSTED AGED 8.

Hello. I'm Wonderboy. I love comics. We found some up here in the attic. I wish I had more. I don't remember if I had comics Before. I don't remember hardly anything. Oscar says I told him stuff when he found me. But I don't remember any of that now. We don't know how old I was when I ghosted. Oscar thinks I must have been about seven. We don't know much about me. That makes me feel sad. I can only remember one thing.

I used to like playing tic-tac-toe. I think it is a girl's game but I liked playing with the girls. They were pretty and funny. I guess it was mostly because of that girl I liked. I can't remember her name but she was lovely. She had fiery red hair and a fiery temper to match but gosh she was lovely.

I don't know what happened to her. I have bad feeling though. I remember her best because I saw her here once. Not in the church. I saw her before Oscar came to get me. I pointed her out to Oscar but he said it was too late for her. He seemed upset with himself. He told me we had to hurry and then the next thing I remember was looking up at the front door of the church. We walked in like we were allowed to. I was amazed. I'd never been inside a church in my life. I couldn't believe how big it was. And then I met some of the others and I guess I forgot about the redheaded girl. I remember now though, and that's good, right?

Oscar has been very nice to me. And I like Bitsy, Buttons and Melody. Sometimes we play tic-tac-toe here. I like that. I feel confused though. Sometimes a memory will flash into my head but it doesn't make sense. It could be about night monsters or werewolves but I don't think that I met monsters or werewolves Before. I don't know why I think that.

I wish I could remember where I came from. I would like to remember my parents like some of the others. But it hurts my insides if I try too hard. If I wasn't ghosted I would think I was lucky to have met everyone here but I have a bad feeling. It's like the night monsters know where I am and they are coming to find me. Sometimes I think they know where I am but they are just waiting to make their move. I don't know what I think the monsters will do when they get me.

Oscar is telling me there are no monsters. I hope he is right. But if he is, why was it too late for the redheaded girl? She was lovely Before.

Oh, I just remembered something. It's a face. I don't know who it is but it looks a bit like the redheaded girl but much older. I like her image. Her face is soft and smiling. I think she is looking down at me. I wonder who she is? I would like to meet her.

It's snowing now. Did I tell you that? It's snowing and it's cold. Oscar says I shouldn't feel cold but I do. I don't think I did when I first came here. Sometimes I see Bitsy shivering and I know she feels it too. I'm too scared to ask her. I know I'm called Wonderboy but I'm not really very brave and I might not want to know. Would you?

I am going to finish up early this time. I know I can go on for ages but I don't feel like it. I feel afraid. I feel strange. Recordings take a lot of energy. Afterwards it feels like I felt Before—tired and weak. Those feelings of Before are definitely something I won't forget, although I don't remember why I felt like that.

And it's nearly light now so we will be still. Oscar calls it stasis. The light seems to take our energy and we find it hard to move. Stasis is awful. It's lonely and it feels weird. It didn't used to be like that.

Perhaps the nice lady I've just remembered will hear our messages. Maybe I will see her again. Oh! I just saw an image of a steam engine. I wonder what that's about? Wonderboy on a steam engine with a kind faced redheaded lady. You see, being ghosted doesn't stop wishes and wonders and Wonderboy!

It's really cold now and I am tired.

Please if you can hear me will you help us?

~Present day~

~Some Lessons Can't be taught~

A few kerosene lamps lit the walls, stretching long shadows up toward the ceiling. The rows of student chairs were just old fashioned church pews; hard and oddly permanent in this weird and obscure gloominess.

Daffodil sat as still as possible, her pieced together dress pulled tightly over her legs to keep out the cold. She was glad she was wearing her amulets to ward off grief. She had even chosen zircon which she knew protected travelers against injury—it even stopped the owner from being struck by lightning. She wasn't sure why lightening had been a consideration, still there it was. But even with all this protection it felt like small daggers of sorrow were scoring her soul. Flicking a look around the room confirmed her fears: Everyone here was feeling it.

Madame Glizsnort had appeared from behind the altar and immediately began with her orders. Everyone opened the texts that sat beside them on the long wooden seating.

"What the hell is going on with the heaters in this place," whispered Blaze to Santu as if it was his fault. The room was freezing. In Ireland, her mane of hair had always helped keep her warm; today she felt she may as well have been bald.

The cold was the least of their problems. Santu thought it smelt like his grandmother's house—all musty and stained with memories. He couldn't concentrate. The tension in this place was beyond comprehension. Couldn't the others feel it? The icy centre of the church was fragmented. It was like there was a host of foreign icicles strewn in all different directions. For some reason Santu was feeling particularly angry. His mood had gotten worse since entering the old building. Hatred seemed to be building inside him like lava bubbling in a volcano. It felt terrible and powerful and dangerous. He fidgeted in the overpowering cold trying to listen to Madame Glizsnort. What *was* she talking about? It was like she was speaking a foreign language. And why did he want to swipe at a panting dog? Pressure was building inside him, inside his head. Everything felt like it was vibrating. He clamped his hands over his ears as if to settle his brain.

"Who can name the three elements to Divine Autonomy?" Madame Glizsnort screeched.

Everyone sat silent.

"Alright then we shall start with something a little simpler shall we?" Madame Glizsnort held her patience. "What is the formula to calculate the Enigma of Spirit Forces?"

Jake knew mathematics but this wasn't a calculation he could formulate. His mind felt as if it were going numb: The icy cold, the woman's shrieking voice, and that crowding force that was making his brain feel like it was going to freeze solid. What was going on here? Was this some kind of torture? Jake had endured his fair share and he couldn't, no, he wouldn't, deal with any more.

"I am confused," squawked a frustrated Madame Glizsnort. "I thought I was amongst 'the chosen ones' from the Secret Society! What am I supposed to make of this?"

Confused glances were exchanged but everyone remained silent.

Madame Glizsnort was horrified. Why didn't they understand any of the subject matter? It had been formulated over decades just for this exact scenario. Weren't they sensing it? It had to work this time, there were no more options. Another debacle like the last time would ruin it all. There must be a way to speed this up.

Duette wasn't used to coping with such an influx of unwanted thoughts—she was used to controlling the flow of information: Whatever she needed to know she would invite from people's minds. It wasn't difficult to make people think about whatever she wanted them to—people were generally oblivious and, she had to admit, fairly inept when it came to understanding their own bodies. Then she would read their thoughts. It was that easy. Sometimes Duel would shut her out. She knew she could easily have butted in if she wanted to, but there were some things she just didn't want to know.

They had begun reading each other's minds early, too early really for Duette to remember. Being born to a deaf father and a mother who died in childbirth, may have given her more reason than most to develop such a skill.

They had never known what their father was like before they were born but, to Duette, he always seemed somehow less than he should have been. Even as babies, Duette and Duel had felt the isolation and had learned to sense his thoughts. By the time they were three they could read his mind and they could also make him hear their thoughts. The first time their father realized what was happening he cried.

It gave little reason for Duette to speak. Over the years her and Duel had formed an inimitable relationship and apparently, unique abilities: Abilities that had been tested over and over again by all manner of skeptics, cynics and disbelievers—all of whom were left speechless in the discovery that it was true—these two individuals in fact did have the ability to read each other's minds.

None of those tests however, prepared Duette for this. It felt like a million thoughts pulsing through her brain: throbbing heartbeats; forgotten, desperate heartbeats. And the other factor that was disturbing her more than she wanted to admit to herself was, that it was impossible to read Madame Glizsnort's mind. Now there were two people that had rendered Duette incapable of her most natural faculty: This crazy old woman and Annabelle. And it scared the living daylights out of her.

"I am going to give you some time to read your text books," Madame Glizsnort was sounding exhausted already. "I want you to concentrate, I need you to focus. Do not assume the text is the absolute. Find answers in-between the lines."

It was the most bizarre thing Annabelle had ever heard from a teacher. It was as if she were in some fantastical world—perhaps Alice in Wonderland—except this was no wonderland. Annabelle could feel it, could feel it all. This sickly place was filled with remorse and sadness and loss. It was making her feel desperately ill. The ice in her belly was getting harder as if it would freeze her from the inside out. Why was it still so dark? It felt like the shadows were stealing in under the back of her collar and creeping, like cool breath, down her spine. The darkness felt alive and it felt like it could suck the life out of her if it wanted to. She shivered and tried not to be sick.

The lessons were endless and infuriatingly obscure to Santu. But he sat and listened. What else was there to do? There were Syncronomity classes about the passage of time (that were ridiculous in the face of current theories). There were classes about Epigenesis in the Electric Body, Electromagnetic brain currents, and Wave Evolution in the Division of Symmetry.

To Santu it was all just a distraction. What was the point of all this? These classes were ridiculous. And why couldn't he get any visions from Madame Glizsnort? Having lived with the ability all his life, it felt to Santu like his heart wasn't beating properly. He heaved a sigh and gently patted his nose. Even though it was swollen Santu could still feel that it was misshapen. A fleeting image of the familiar streets of Biscay conjured an image of the very pretty Anna inspecting his damaged nose. He smiled. He would definitely give her a call when he got home. If he ever got home.

Their fatigue was becoming almost tangible, which both scared and amused Madame Glizsnort. But she would not give up. She would never give up until the battlements had fallen and it was all too late. Not until she had exhausted every dimension of every time of every existence would she stop. Just as those fiery thoughts rose up inside her and finally pushed some strength into her archaic body she sensed the coming daylight. The heavy night was descending and the sun was pushing desperately from the icy clouds to find a face in the murky sky. Today's session was over.

Blaze had her hand raised high in the air, her fingers clasped down on the cuff of her shirt. "Excuse me Madame Glizsnort," she tried in her most pleasant manner.

"Yes Blaze? Please be concise." Madame Glizsnort was nervous. The light was almost here.

"I would like to go home now," said Blaze with a big smile.

Madame Glizsnort didn't have time for foolishness. "Don't be ridiculous!" she screeched. "I will not attend to any other discussions of this manner!" Madame Glizsnort's eyes narrowed and her icy stare rested on each of them, one at a time. Immobility struck as the weight of her of potential cruelty fell upon them. It was only a threat this time but the threat was enough: Their pale faces reflected the pain she had forced upon them.

"It is almost light!" Madame Glizsnort screamed. "You must all attend your break now. Immediately!" She was looking completely fraught. "I will expect you back here at 4 o'clock sharp. Now go!" Madame Glizsnort anxiously disappeared into the darkness. One moment she was cruel and unforgiving and the next she was, well, gone.

With Madame Glizsnort's shock removal, came an injection of wakefulness.

"Can we go now!?" Annabelle was desperate to get out of the gloomy freezing building and into the daylight.

Blaze wasn't waiting for anyone's permission and had already headed for the door, quickly followed by the others. Jake hobbled rapidly on his blistered feet. He wasn't going to be left behind. He could have sworn he had heard noises coming from the church's attic.

Outside, even the daylight was murky. Falling snow sashayed silently to the ground; dying butterflies on their cyclical and inevitable journey. At least the tension had slightly decreased. Following orders like they were prisoners, they trudged toward the mess hall. There was nowhere else to go. Obviously Madame Glizsnort had no intention of letting them leave and there seemed little chance they could safely find their way out of here. There was nobody around for perhaps a hundred miles and there was a thick white mist that encircled the entire area which looked dangerously impassable.

The tables were laden with unappealing foods but again there was no one around.

"Who does the cooking and cleaning?" asked Blaze pulling her mane of brilliant red hair into a ponytail. "I haven't seen anyone come or go yet." She was studying a colorless plate of cold sliced roast meat in front of her. "And can anyone tell me how it is possible to make all these foods the same color?"

"I want go home." It was Duette. Only one shining hazel eye was peering up from under her angular fringe and her hands were firmly planted in her French-styled trench coat. In surprise, everyone turned to face the girl who hadn't said a single word since they'd arrived.

"We all *want* to go home," said Daffodil. "But we can't."

"Why? Why I not go home?" Her tone was pitching with emotion. Duel was looking at his sister amazed. He thought she could barely speak English.

Duel tried to drive his thoughts into her head but for the first time in her life she didn't want to talk with her mind. She realized she had been cut out of nearly every single conversation because she had never bothered to speak to anyone.

"Not want to," she pointed to her head. What was the word she was looking for? "Want to speech."

"You *want* to speak?" Duel couldn't contain his astonishment. He was trying to read her mind and she was shutting him out! "Are you alright?"

"No! Not aright! I want go home!" she was sounding urgent now.

"Duette," it was Daffodil, "I think we are stuck here until we can figure out what's going on. Who knows, maybe it's some kind of test? Maybe we figure out the puzzle and then we get to go home?"

"No puzzle. Bad place." Duette had never been so frustrated. This is why she had never wanted to talk to people—they were stupid. "Not speech to me like child!"

"Duette," her brother was trying to suppress his concern, "you have to just relax, alright? There is something going on that we have to deal with here. We cannot go home yet. Even if we wanted to, how do you propose we get out of here? We don't even know where *here* is."

Jake was getting scared. The tension in the room was at maximum and he didn't understand why. He closed his eyes and visualized all the rare swords he had come across at competitions: The Sword of Goujian, a 500 BC Chinese bronze sword belonging to King Goujian; The 16th century swords of Muramasa made with iron, carbon, and human blood; and the exquisite Masamune swords. It was like humming a rhythm only no one could hear him.

Daffodil could see Jake had disappeared into his own world. She spoke softly and calmly.

"Duette, I don't know what any of this is about. But my parents are telling me to stay."

"Huh," retorted Duette, "they dead! They not tell you anything!"

Duel threw a furious glance at his sister. "You have passed every test known to man that proves you can read minds. You did those tests because you wanted people to know that the impossible *is* possible. It was years and years of awful experiments and I did it for you because you needed to prove yourself. And now you're telling someone else exactly what those cynics told you." He shook his head in disgust.

Everyone was silent, unsure what to do.

Duette felt suddenly awful. She had never said so many words out loud and now she feared she had ruined her chance to be understood. Her lip was quivering and her hazel eyes were shining with impending tears. Daffodil knew what was coming.

"It's okay Duette," Daffodil moved over to her, smiled and winked, "I know they're dead." A tiny smile flickered across Duette's distraught face.

"Well," smiled Annabelle, "they better be dead because I don't care what *living* adults are saying."

"Pardon! Etre desole." Duette was on the verge of tears.

"It's going to be okay," Daffodil said gently as she placed her arm around Duette's shoulders. "We just all need to support each other."

"Anyone want some gray peas?" Blaze was holding up a bowl of unrecognizable content.

"Is that what those are?" said Daffodil giving Duette a little squeeze and a smile. "I would *love* some."

"Oh, yes, and me please also," added Santu with his lovely rounded tones, "I have been craving these 'gray peas'." Sauntering over to Blaze's side he pretended to admire the dish she was holding out. He pointed to the dish directly in front of him. "And this is . . ." he shook his shiny dark curls in shock, "this is . . . oh, it's eggs!" Holding the plate in the air as if it were an award, Santu smiled. "Yes, of course, gray rubber. This is eggs." He nodded satisfactorily. "We can really chow up on this. Delicious."

That did it. The darkness had lifted.

"Um, I think you mean 'chow down'," Blaze said throwing Santu a green eyed smile which he didn't notice because he was busy trying to charm the tall blond. Dislike and attraction weren't mutually exclusive to Santu.

Annabelle was used to boys trying to get her attention. She composed a playful smile which was only noticed by Jake. Jake wondered what had happened to Annabelle's face. She looked suddenly strange. Was she making a joke? Jake would have laughed but no one else was.

Daffodil guided Duette over to the table where everyone managed to chat about mundane everyday things as they searched the plates of food for something edible. If an outsider had peered in, they would have assumed it was an ordinary bunch of teenagers gossiping about nothing in particular, with no special interests or abilities that would make them stand out amongst the crowd.

And that is why strangers shouldn't peer in windows and make assumptions about people they know nothing about.

Static Recording No. 650—On Loop

Scraps. 1909–1919. Ghosted Aged 10.

Bonjour. I am called Scraps. I am the only one who remembers how they ghosted. That is how I got named: I ate scraps. Everyone thinks it is funny to call me this. I do not argue. My English is not so good. It is true that I deserve this name: I did eat scraps and it made me very sick. I am only upset because everyone else here is named for things in *this* place and I have been named for what I left behind. I guess it is better that they call me this instead of 'frog'. This is what peoples called me before—because I'm from France.

It is funny that I remember the nickname that I so despised but that I cannot remember the name my parents did give to me. I think it is like some kind of test. A test we have all failed. Perhaps I used to remember it, but not anymore.

It was a green potato. How I ghosted. It was a green potato. I was twelve. I did not know that it was such a bad thing to eat. I have eaten much much worse. I ate a rat once and they are full of plague. But this rat did not make me ghost—that took just a little green potato.

I have a tiny mouse with me. It is called Tooting. I was patting my mouse when I did ghost. It was giving me comfort while the green potato took away my life. I hope I didn't hurt it with the pain I was feeling. I didn't mean to. It does come everywhere with me now and it does know how much I love it.

I still am having some very sharp images in my memory about Before. But they are like a second in the emptiness of my mind. And they are fading too quickly. I must record them before they are all gone. I think we are doomed if we are forgetting everything.

Yes, I was a foreigner but I had a good childhood until the war. I lived in a nice house and had nice food—no rats or green potatoes you see. My papa was a pilot and my mama was a nurse.

I can be seeing the image of my papa leaving, walking down the road and away from us and toward the war. Even though I was being very young, I did know that flying passenger planes and piloting war planes was a very different occupation. But I did not know that it was the difference between the living and the dying. He did not last long flying these war planes. This is how I found out the difference.

Of course, it did not stop them calling me 'frog'—just because my papa was gone. My mama did take on extra work as a nurse. I can be seeing the image in my head of the day she turned away from me. It was not her fault. My papa was very strong and my mama felt lost. Of course, he was not so strong to withstand bullets, but how many men of war are?

My mama was sent to work in the infectious ward. I did not know that there would be a terrible social dishonor attached to all of us who lived among infectious patients, and I felt its cruelty. I was not allowed to be sitting with classmates at school, but was put at the back of the room with other unfortunate students. The teachers did not like to talk to us, and did not spend time explaining the lessons. Now I was a foreigner *and* maybe poisonous.

Then mama caught the Tuberculosis. I am forgetting which kind. One minute both my parents were there; the next minute they were both gone.

There was no one else to take care of me and I do not remember anyone even coming to help me. I do not know how I did end up on the streets but I was not liking it at all. I had to steal food. This part was terrible. I do not like stealing but I was so hungry. I preferred to steal food from the gardens of the people rather than shops. I could do this at night you see.

And now I am here: Slowly, slowly forgetting everything. I know Oscar is worried, I can see it. I am also this worried. It feels strange to fade away. And it feels wrong, as if something very bad will happen because of it. It is impossible to explain to you. Perhaps I can explain it like sand sieving through your fingers as you try to hold on tight. I have not been telling

Oscar my worries about this. He seems worried enough for everybody. It is as if he is feeling responsible for us. I do not know why.

Oscar has just heard me and now tells me to be more positive. He says being positive will bring the good things in the universe to us. So I shall try this.

What do I do all this time in this place? Well, I like to play Jacks. I play it with ghosted spiders. When I am in the middle of a flip, they 'play dead'—if they remember—they are having short memories. Often I will be making a very difficult trick and one of the 'dead' spiders will scurry off for no reason. It is most annoying.

I also like playing Whispers with Bitsy. With my accent all the whispers turn out . . . you know, stupid. But it is hard to play now. Even our whispers are being forgotten. It feels the same as the ghosted spiders—scurrying off in my mind before my thoughts can form. I was not like this when I first did come here. Something is trying to disappear me. And I do not like it. It feels like I am being slowly undone.

It is much worse than ghosting.

Can you help me? Can you help Oscar? I think if you can help Oscar he may be able to stop us from disappearing. This is about my 650th recording. I can still count you know!

Can you?

~Present day~

~QUESTIONS BEFORE ANSWERS~

After returning to the cabin and warming themselves by the fire the seven teenagers discussed their situation. Santu had tried to find something in the texts they had been given that could help him understand why they were here. But after reading forty or so pages, he was just as confused as before. Daffodil had fiddled with her crystals which entertained Blaze for a while, and Annabelle sat on her bed silently reading some of her favorite musical scores, surprised at how much she missed playing.

By the time 4 o'clock came around, dead ends and boredom were beginning to tear at their new found sociability. The sky had filled itself up with inky blackness and the group had traipsed through the falling snow to return to the church and Madame Glizsnort. The only plan they had come up with was to join together and fight the old woman's stares. They would demand to know what was going on or refuse to help.

But as they waited in the eerie quietude, only one thing became clear: Madame Glizsnort wasn't coming. Blaze's suggestion of going back to the cabin didn't take much convincing. To be free of the stifling chill of the church was exhilarating.

And in that exhilaration Blaze was ready to make a pact. Perhaps not the brightest idea, but still, it was all a contagious momentum now and no one can get off a roller coaster mid-flight.

"We need to go back." Blaze was warming her freezing hands by the fire in the cabin.

"Did you forget your texts?" asked Daffodil as she thumbed through the wealth of information she was supposed to read.

"No, I mean tonight. We need to go back. Santu was right."

Jake was shaking his head. This wasn't right. "No," he said simply.

Annabelle was surprised that the challenge was led by poor deficient Jake. Blaze was Irish: she was naturally crazy. Not that Annabelle had any intention of going near the church ever again. If the stupid old woman had given up on them there was only one thing to do and that was to get out of here.

"Really?" Annabelle asked in delight. "Why Jake? Why shouldn't we go tonight?" her tone rang with condescension which made Daffodil furious.

"Because," said Jake, "*they* are coming to *us*."

Blackwater Herald Moon Tribune
Sunday, June 23ʳᵈ, 1941—
One penny

CURRENT WAR UPDATE
GERMAN ARMY INVADES SOVIET UNION

*O*peration 'Barbarossa' has Germany declaring war on the Soviet Union. Despite having signed a non-aggression pact with the Soviets in 1939, yesterday Hitler ordered an invasion from the south, the west and the north. Joseph Stalin has been taken by surprise and Hitler boasts it will be the greatest fight the world has seen. Italy, Finland and Romania join the German battle. The Red Army still outweighs the Nazis by millions with at least 9,000,000 men, but it is believed Hitler's military skill will overshadow the battle.

LOCAL NEWS HEADLINES
TOWN HALL MEETINGS A DISASTER

Amongst the horror of the Second Great War, disappointment has turned to fury as the recent Monday night meetings at the Blackwater Town Hall have fuelled more aggression than resolve. The pervasive sensation of fear has now taken over the town: The remaining residents are now deserting the settlement in droves.

"It feels as if a dark shadow has fallen across our once beautiful town and I am afraid for my life," stated Miss Thelma Adams of Lawrence Street who was finishing the last of her packing. "I am moving to Shrewsbury Creek. It's as far away from Blackwater as I can afford to go."

And this seems to be the sentiment of the majority.

"*The need to move as far away from this dark and dismal town is beyond my understanding,*" *said Mrs. March Greenwood of Lancaster Drive, "but I can feel something strange moving in the streets and it feels like it's coming for me.*"

There is no physical explanation for the anomaly but it is evidently affecting the mood of the remaining residents and they are now hurrying to remove themselves from the township. Even Bishop John Biggs has expressed concern. The Bishop has been caught having secret discussions with the Archbishop of Portachamps Cathedral. It is believed by many that he has requested that the esteemed Archbishop perform an exorcism at the Saint Catherine's Church of Redeemus. On questioning by the Herald Moon Tribune, the Bishop has denied this.

"*No,*" *said Bishop Biggs, "I have not requested an exorcism at all. I have simply asked the Archbishop to give us a sacred blessing. I do believe there is something wrong here in Blackwater and I do believe we need to be aware of the possibility that black spirits may have formed here due to the extreme and shameful reactions from a large section of the population. These masses laid blame on the Lost Children for the accidental burning down of our church: The devastating result of which has been a rapidly decreasing population and a malevolence that has pervaded the town to the extent of practical desertion. I am mortified that I cannot save Blackwater.*"

Additional comments made by Miss Grace Durand, an advocate for the Lost Children, follow those of the Bishop. "Because of the people's inability to come together as a community and their natural decline toward violence and hatred, we now face the fact that Blackwater has no future. Those left, are right to move on. They must make new lives in new places and begin again without this terrible blackness that plagues us here. It is a dreadfully sad time for us all."

It appears that the Bishop may be right. And it seems not just the town is being deserted; hope too, seems lost to us all now.

Please note the local school will shut its doors this Friday. Until further notice, any remaining students may take classes at Miss Durand's home in Marchenby Street. Miss Durand has opened her house to anyone in need at this terrible time. Please feel free to attend at your discretion. She also continues to call for any information regarding the Lost Children.

Blackout time: Zero Hour tonight until 5:03 A.M.

WORLD NEWS HEADLINES
HITLER AUTHORIZES KILLING OF THE IMPAIRED

It has been discovered that in October 1939 Adolf Hitler authorized the euthanasia (T4) program—of those whom are deemed 'unworthy of life' and 'useless' to society. Adolf has said that wartime is the best time for the elimination of the incurably ill. Doctors and nurses in psychiatric hospitals have cooperated and even supervised the killings. Now it has been discovered that groups of 'consultants' have been visiting hospitals to decide who will die. It is estimated that about 70,000 German and Austrian physically or mentally impaired patients have been euthanized so far. Handicapped infants and small children have also been euthanized.

German mobile killing squads—Called special duty units, these squads have been assigned to kill during the invasion of the Soviet Union. It seems all Jewish men, woman, children, Roma Gypsies and Soviet political officers have been shot without regard for age or gender.

Rudolf Hess—Deputy leader to the Nazi Party, parachutes into Scotland from his Messerschmitt 110, and says he wants to meet with King George to discuss peace terms.

Potatoes rationed in Holland—Food Rationings for Blackwater— Page 7.

"Captain America"—New comic strip has become popular very quickly.

LECTURES FROM CHURCH OF ALL SAINTS—*Where was the Garden of Eden? Who were Adam and Eve and the Tempest? What is the mystical significance of the Fall? These questions Bishop Geoffrey Horty will answer at the Church of All Saints. Sunday 7.15am. Admission free. Collection.*

~Brought to you by~

FLYING BOAT SERVICES—QANTAS EMPIRE AIRWAYS, LIMITED
A weekly service is being maintained on the London-Singapore-Sydney route.

OXO CUBE—Make it Beefy!

Static Recording No.1029—On Loop

BUGSY. 1910-1917. GHOSTED AGED 7.

H ello. I don't feel well. Oscar says I have to be strong but I just want to go to sleep. I think Bruises does too. But you can't sleep here. You can't do much to be honest. It would be boring but I've started to lose track of everything. Oh sorry, Oscar is reminding me to tell you about myself.

I am called Bugsy. That is because I like to play with bugs—all different kinds. I raise them and take care of them and play with them so they don't get bored. Bugs can get bored too, you know. I really like the Black-backed Meadow Ants. Even after they've ghosted they make little farms. I also like Crucifix Beetles (their claws are sticky) and Spotted Millipedes are very clingy. I also have Parasitic Wasps (which Bitsy especially hates), Devil's Coach Horse Beetles, Red-veined Darters, lots of different weevils and heaps of common grasshoppers. I've been trying to teach the grasshoppers to fly. All ghosted things can fly. They just don't get it. But my favorite is earwigs. I race them. Sometimes it gets our whole group together which Oscar really likes. We all barrack for a different earwig. These days we usually lose interest before the race is even finished though.

I ghosted when I was 7. When I first ghosted I was much happier than Before. Before was awful. I don't remember where I came from or when I was born or what my name was. All I remember was that I was in a home for orphans. We came in from all different countries like cattle being herded onto a slaughter truck. No one could understand each other. The home was a huge abandoned building which had rats. (Scraps says he ate one once you know.) There were no trees, and the playground was just a road.

We played a string game called Jacob's Ladder. And we also played cards. It wasn't as much fun as racing earwigs though.

There were bad people that came to that place. Some children got taken away but no one came for me. I was glad. I didn't know where they would take me. I knew no one wanted me anyway. So one day I ran away. And guess what? No one came looking for me. See, I told you no one wanted me.

I wasn't lonely. I didn't need anyone anyway. So don't think stuff that's not true.

After I ghosted Oscar found me. I tried to punch him. I wanted to be left alone. But Oscar just kept following me everywhere. He would say stuff like, "It's nice to meet you" and "you're a good kid". It felt really weird. I didn't know why he was doing that. And then one day he noticed that all these ghosted bugs were following me. Oscar laughed and said we'll call you Bugsy. And that's when I realized: I didn't have a name until then. And for the first time I noticed all these ghosted bugs hovering around my head. I started laughing and wondered if I'd done that before. Laughed, I mean. So Oscar said I could bring my bugs with me and said I could come and meet some other orphans that I might like. I thought that was weird too. I mean, why would I *like* someone?

But it turned out okay and I stayed. It's been a really long time now though and I have a growing feeling inside me that is scary. I feel like I'm being eaten up from the inside out. Lots of my bugs are disappearing too. I don't want them to leave me.

If Bitsy hadn't found the old wooden sound box and figured out how to make it go on we would never have been able to make these recordings. She's very clever. If Dog wasn't cruel to her all the time I think she would remember more.

I don't think that anyone hears our recordings but Oscar says we have to be hopeful. And Oscar is the only one who gave *me* hope. Ever. So I have to believe him.

Is anybody out there?

Do you want me?

~Present day~

~PLACES PLEASE~

Daffodil showed Jake how to use her watch. Along with the cleverly distilled crystals and crushed gems that she had hidden inside it, there were several dials on the back and sides which she had added a long time ago. She had created a kind of new age time device that she credited to her parents dying. Old things reminded her of the life she had lost.

It was only the day before Daffodil's parents died that her mother had passed on the watch. When her mother had placed the timepiece in her daughter's hands and told her 'it was as important as her future' and that she must always keep it close, Daffodil had started to wonder why she had been so specially chosen for its possession. Of course Daffodil had no brothers or sisters so she had never experienced sibling rivalry.

It would be only weeks later that Daffodil would hide under the staircase with her beloved keepsake, as greedy relatives with loveless eyes sorted through the house and its belongings. The watch was the only thing they didn't get—besides Daffodil of course. Daffodil was sent to a 'boarding school' called The Institution. It was at the ends of the earth, and a place where any practice of her gift was treated with ridicule. They could beat her as much as they wanted. They would never know what she knew.

On her first day they had shorn off her messy blond hair and taken nearly all the possessions she had brought with her—except the wristwatch.

She presumed they didn't want her to be tardy. That was one of their biggest mistakes.

Daffodil had treasured the antique as if it were Dorothy's slippers—every now and then she would tap it three times and close her eyes just in case it would take her to some magical place away from the awful life she had now been dealt. But all it gave her was dead-parent-ghosts.

As much as she longed to see them, their afterlife forms were not like having her mother and father back. They did not offer succor; they did not offer affection. They were like warning devices that appeared out of nowhere to tell her what was dangerous and what was bad for her. Yes, she could summon them, but what was the point really? They just smiled and told her to be careful. It was beyond saddening—it felt like she had lost her parents twice. So what about danger; what about love?

"But-I-need-static," said Jake breaking Daffodil's reverie.

"Right, so you need to turn it over. Think of it like a trick. The front of it looks, well, like an old fashioned watch," she nodded at the obviousness of it. "But if you turn it over it has most of the stuff we need." She pointed to a tiny side button. "This is for the radio—not that we'd be able to get a station here anyway." Daffodil shrugged. "Just press the end to adjust it." Holding the watch up to her ear she pressed the switch until she heard that midway life between stations. She passed it over to Jake. Jake's relaxed smile was enough.

"Thank-you."

"It's yours," Daffodil said without remorse. And suddenly she realized it was just a device that told time. It wasn't a conduit to Oz; it wouldn't bring her mother back and it wouldn't help her in this bizarre situation. "It's yours," she repeated more confidently, "you need it way more than I do."

Jake had chosen the right person to trust. Daffodil was pure in heart. He didn't know how, but he knew the watch was beyond important to her. No matter, when they got out of here he would give it back. He just needed his static. He needed to sleep in this strange place and he needed to trust. Daffodil had given him both. He would be eternally grateful.

"Okay," rallied Annabelle, "so who is the 'us' we are supposed to be waiting for?"

"Jake doesn't seem to know," Daffodil said with a shrug.

"Well, it better not be a friend of Madame Glizsnort," replied Annabelle with a threatening stare.

Blaze sneered. Who was Annabelle trying to threaten? "So do we just sit here and wait for them?"

"Well, I am thinking I might have to regurgitate dinner but otherwise, yes, we can just sit and wait." Santu was looking pale. "Do not eat the eggs."

"The flames are really going now," added Blaze, staring at the fiery demons. "I'm happy to wait."

And so that is what they did.

Duette seemed to have come to terms with her situation and tried to enter into the conversation as much as possible. She cursed her previous dismissal of the English language. Words had become her disability. Reading minds didn't require hard and fast language rules—it was more about the person's thoughts and feelings.

Jake paid little attention to the chatter preferring to rub Daffodil's watch between his thumb and forefinger as if he might wake a genie.

Santu pushed himself into the furthest corner of the main room and began to try to decipher the myriad of information Madame Glizsnort had given him. There had to be something in there.

Blaze and Daffodil found an unexpected connection. Having asked Daffodil about her suitcase full of crystals and strange looking stones, Blaze was surprised to discover some fascinating information. Blaze's request seemed surprisingly genuine to Daffodil, who had spent a lifetime with torment and skepticism at The Institution, from nasty, hate-filled girls that should have been focusing on more important things.

But then Daffodil noticed something else. The sleeve of Blaze's top had ridden up to above her wrist and it revealed her very damaged skin: Burns from long ago twisted across her pale flesh puckering its surface with ugly scars. Hoping that Blaze had not seen her fleeting look of horror, Daffodil questioned what else this girl might be covering up. But Daffodil knew that people only revealed what they needed to reveal, and they kept secret what they had to, to survive.

And so, together, Blaze and Daffodil sat cross-legged on Daffodil's bed discussing the magical properties of minerals and gemstones and the energies of crystals while Daffodil entwined some leather-clad crystals into her messy blond hair.

Blaze had never heard about how powerful crystals could be, but she was captivated by the intriguing explanations. Daffodil talked about the Kundalini and Kriya Yoga she practiced to increase spiritual ascension and began explaining how to grow crystals, spreading out the substances she would require to begin the growth process. Growing crystals, she told Blaze, gave her an extraordinary feeling of accomplishment.

When Blaze asked how she had gotten into the Secret Society, Daffodil explained, without hubris, that she had developed a method of chemically changing crystals. She had made astonishing strides with her creations and had completed some unexpected and highly sort after results that the scientific community had coveted. The award she had won had given her the confidence to ignore all the teasing and cruelty at The Institution.

Blaze's congratulations were genuine, if not filled with confusion. Blaze still had no idea how *she* had been chosen for this mission. A medal for ill deserved valor was just a torturous reminder of the truth.

Daffodil mistook Blaze's silence for apprehension.

"Here," Daffodil said as she twisted off a very special ring and handed it to Blaze. Blaze's eyes widened. The silver-green stone was mesmerizing.

"It's incredible. I didn't notice it."

"It's Chrysoprase. It's a very powerful ring that has been blessed by the Sisters of the North. This ring has been imbued with a spell that took a very long time and a great amount of energy." Daffodil looked Blaze in the eye. "The wearer bears its powers."

"And what powers are those?" Blaze asked excitedly.

"Each living human being has the ability to see ghosts. It is only because of other mortals, unbelievers in a cynical world, that people are deterred from being able to see and talk with them. The spirit realm *is* real. It exists. Most people are only open to sensing spirits when they are asleep—it's like a form of meditation—open access to the dimensions." Daffodil shrugged at the inevitable cycle of it all. "This ring opens the bearer's mind to the universe, to the spirits. It has bonded with me; our vibrations have entwined."

Those words immediately jolted Blaze from her fascination. Quickly she handed it back.

"It looks . . ."

"Alive?" asked Daffodil knowingly.

Blaze nodded. "I can tell it's powerful."

Daffodil smiled. It was the first time she had ever shared any of this information with anyone. Chemically changing crystals gave her the opportunity to talk with scientists about the structural changes but not about their spiritual qualities. Pulling off one of the amulets around her neck, Daffodil passed it to her new friend.

"You need this one," she said as she looked into Blaze's eyes. "And these two as well." Daffodil pulled two more stones from her menagerie and looped them onto a leather strap. "Protection." Daffodil said earnestly. "The banded agate is an ancient Sudanese stone. It's to protect you from the 'evil eye'." She made a mock ghostly sound. "Wooooo."

Blaze laughed. "What are the other two for?"

"The second is Peridot, to ward off evil spirits, and the third is ruby. It will warn you of danger." Daffodil had become momentarily solemn. She hoped her eyes impressed the importance of the stones.

Blaze accepted them gratefully. For some reason, time felt like it was standing still. It was only momentary, like a manifestation of moments, collided. How could Daffodil have known? Had she just guessed? No that was impossible. Blaze had never told anyone about those poor ghosts she left behind. The same ghosts she had felt trying to follow her all this time.

"Thank you," Blaze said simply. "Thank you." Maybe she had finally found someone she could share her secret with?

Annabelle had waited long enough. The kook and the ugly redhead were giving her the creeps. "I'm going to bed. If they're 'coming to get us', maybe they'll just wake me up." Her sarcastic tone was not lost on anyone.

"Maybe they will," replied Blaze coolly. "Maybe they will."

"They won't," whispered Daffodil to Blaze who winked back.

"I know," whispered Blaze. "Why would you wake the devil on purpose?" Blaze smiled. "*We* need to be awake for them right?" she asked. "I just hope I can stay conscious. I feel like I've just come out of a coma I'm so tired."

"Don't worry. I'm not going to sleep. I have some stones that will help me stay awake. You go to sleep though."

"Shortly. I just want to wait a bit longer." Blaze eyed the stones Daffodil was plucking out of perfectly shaped containers.

"Ahh," said Daffodil smiling. "You want an awakening stone! That's brave. But I'm sorry, these are for the experts only."

Blaze nodded, not sure she wanted to be forced to stay awake anyway.

"Then 'the experts' shall keep them."

Duette's ankles were sore. It was a strange sensation—as if dull pain was stretching underneath her skin like snakes. Instinctively, she reached down to stroke her fingers across the pain but that hurt even more. Pulling up the cuff of her wide-legged chinos, she peered at her skin. Surprise and confusion sullied her thoughts. It was as if her new found desire to talk had dulled her mind. Dark bruises had spread across the tops of her feet and around her ankles. She tried to remember when she had bumped herself. She tried to remember anything that would have caused such damage. But nothing came to mind.

Her brother, who had been trying to make sense of the texts, sensed her uncertainty and looked over. Following her gaze, his eyes met with the dark shapes on her shins.

"God what have you done to yourself?" Duel moved over to inspect the discoloration. Duette shrugged and looked up at him, her eyes full of fear. "It's alright Duette. There will be a reason for this. You probably just didn't notice because of the cold. Or maybe it's the cold that has caused this?"

"Cold can't do that." Daffodil was peering over at Duette.

"How would you know?" Duel gave her a stern look.

If Duel had known that Daffodil was a graduate in Acupuncture and Iridology and that she had certificates in Reiki, Naturopathy, Aromatherapy and several other holistic medicines, he may not have had such a retort. The trouble with mind-reading was that it was a very 'present' thing. It could not tell you about someone's past or their accomplishments, or necessarily what they did or did not know.

The tension was palpable. And Duette, as much as she tried to, could not keep their thoughts out of her head. This place had damaged her and there was no telling to what extent the damage would be her undoing. Quickly pulling down her slacks again, she covered her black and blue ankles.

"It fine. I remember now." Duette tried to control the tremor in her voice—another liability of talking. "I hit feet with luggage bag. Yes. It is bag."

No one believed her and Duette obviously knew that Duel had read her thoughts. But she pushed everyone out of her mind.

"I going to bed."

"Me too," muttered Duel, horribly confused. He really needed to read his sister's mind but she had shut him out. Again.

Annabelle, pretending to be asleep, was conveniently ignoring everyone. So Duette had a few bruises, they weren't going to kill *her*. Feeling her stomach, Annabelle wondered how long it would take: The icy pit inside her felt like cold hard crystal. Maybe Daffodil could analyze the manifestation after her demise. Getting out of bed, she made her way to the bathroom. She would shut the door and have a steaming hot shower. Perhaps it would give her a little extra time.

Daffodil noticed how tired Jake looked.

"Jake, you should get some shut-eye. I'm not going to sleep. I'm going to keep watch. I promise to wake you if anything happens."

Jake was grateful. He had experienced forced sleep deprivation many times in his short life but for some reason he was beyond exhaustion. At least he had his watch now: Static, sleep. It would be alright, he just had to keep going. Remembering the saying his father had taught him when he was very young: 'Every microsecond becomes a second, every second becomes a minute, every minute becomes an hour, every hour becomes another, and that's how you survive', he felt his body begin to calm. With a small nod to Daffodil he silently made his way to bed.

"Is he alright?" Blaze whispered to anyone who might be listening. "I mean, you know, in the head?"

Santu didn't want to reveal the boy's secrets but perhaps giving Blaze a clue would help her understand. The visions he had seen of the boy's mistreatment were horrible.

"I think," said Santu quietly, "that he is most insecure. He has had a very bad time of it." Santu tried to blink away memories of the visions. "Jake is just needing a bit of self-esteem," Santu shrugged, "and maybe a friend he can trust." His locks shook as he nodded and winked at Daffodil—brown eyes sparkling at her like the sea in sunshine.

The fire suddenly flared behind them. The others didn't notice but Blaze turned abruptly toward it, frightened.

"I'm already on it," whispered Daffodil with a sad smile. She had sensed something indefinable about Jake straight away. Although she could have pressed Santu for the information, she chose not to. Jake and Daffodil would make a friendship because they liked each other, here and now.

"How come he's here?" asked Blaze, turning away from the fire and back to Santu, hoping he would send her one of those glinting looks.

"I was recognizing him after seeing his suitcase," said Santu closing the ridiculous text that he had been trying to comprehend. "And then when he told us at the mess hall he was liking antiques, I am realizing who he is."

"Who is he?" asked Blaze.

"Did you not see all those pins on his case?" Santu gestured to the other room where Jake had gone to sleep.

"No," Blaze replied looking in the direction of Jake's room. "He said he won that Youth competition. Is that what you're talking about?"

Santu shook his head smiling. It seemed right that Jake was more proud of winning a lesser competition because he found the final pick much harder.

"No," replied Santu, "that is little baby stuff for him. When I am seeing that big red one with the green cross on it I am knowing who he is." He stretched his nose hoping that it would ease the pain. "That badge is from a really important competition called the Angus Goldmark Judging competition. I only know about this because my history teacher tried out for it. He was not even getting through the first cut of 20,000 and his knowledge on antiques blows me away like a bomb."

"So," said Daffodil trying to ignore Santu's strange sayings, "are you saying Jake's an antiques expert?" She looked at Blaze with raised eyebrows. "That's kinda cool and just a little bit weird."

Blaze nodded. "It is Jake we're talking about. So what happens in this competition?"

"They are getting all the best people in the world to join up and then have this month long tournament. Hundreds of people are chosen but they are slashing them down pretty quickly. Then they test them with some very rare and most difficult pieces. They are having to name and date the pieces and extra information gets you extra points. This contest goes seven days a week and it can really make you into gravy soup."

Blaze wondered if Santu was just making sayings up. "So he was in it? This competition? He got into it?"

Santu smiled. "He is not just getting into it. He is *winning* it."

"What? That's ridiculous," said Blaze. "He's the most stressed person I've ever met."

"Stressed if it is emotional, sure, but not if it is factual."

"Is that what he's doing when he covers his ears?" asked Daffodil amazed.

"Probably." Santu shrugged. "Cannot either of you remember hearing about the youngest winner of the trophy for the Angus Goldmark Judging competition? It was all over the news. He is the youngest person by about 35 years to have been winning it."

Blaze and Daffodil shook their heads.

"I guess it's not that big in Australia," said Daffodil.

"Nor Ireland."

Santu flicked a curl from his forehead. He was annoyed with them. It wasn't their fault but it didn't stop his irritation. He shook his head. What was the point?

Daffodil noticed Santu's irritation. "So, that was the accomplishment that got Jake into the Secret Society?"

"Yes," said Santu still looking peeved, "but you need something else as well."

"Like your visions?"

"My visions, you seeing dead parents, Jake's high noise thing." Santu shrugged. "All of us are having a gift."

"What about you? What was your accomplishment?" Daffodil was actually wondering what it was that got Annabelle admitted to the Secret Society but right now she needed to figure out how to get Santu on side.

"Glass," said Santu curtly.

Annabelle had returned from the bathroom and everyone stared at her. She rolled an eyebrow and went over to her bunk bed and sat stiffly on the hard mattress.

Blaze sniffed in Annabelle's direction. The room had suddenly cooled.

"So Santu," said Daffodil nudging Blaze, "how did glass get you into the Society?" Daffodil was tipping a bag of engraved jade amulets upside down.

Santu yawned. "I was helping to make a new type of orbital telescope. It can be viewing images over twice as far as the ones they have been using." Shrugging he added, "Won an award for it."

Blaze was feeling worried. Now Santu, Daffodil and Jake had all won awards for their work. Had there been some terrible error that had mistaken Blaze's 'bravery and heroism medal' for something important? Beads of perspiration formed on her brow. Maybe no one would ever find out about it. Perhaps she could make something up?

"That," said Daffodil, "is really amazing. You're very clever."

"Thank you." Santu was coming around again, his ego warming to the attention.

Daffodil took note: Santu was moody. He didn't like things that didn't go his way and he didn't like people disagreeing with him. And flattery got you everywhere.

"So," she said, her voice a little higher and brimming with enthusiasm, "how long have you been fascinated with glass?"

Santu brightened up immediately and began to regal stories of his youth and how glass had become so important to him. Blaze had cottoned on to Daffodil's ruse and joined in looking fascinated with every word whilst nudging her friend in delight.

As Santu continued, Blaze whispered to Daffodil. "I don't think he's the only one fascinated by glass around here." Blaze flicked a look over at Annabelle. "Have you noticed how many times she looks in the mirror?"

"Maybe she keeps forgetting what she looks like?" scoffed Daffodil in between her overly enthusiastic expressions toward Santu, who was pacing the room and gesticulating with relish.

"Yeah," said Blaze, "well I don't know *why* Miss Sleeping Beauty is here—unless it's to make us all miserable."

"She's not that bad," smiled Daffodil looking over at Annabelle's perfect face. "I just think she got some issues she needs to deal with."

Blaze shrugged. "We've all got issues."

"Ain't that the truth," whispered Daffodil as she contemplated an Indian moonstone.

"Can I bunk here?" The words just fell out of Blaze's mouth. Blaze was shocked at herself for showing vulnerability. "I mean if you're not going to sleep then it would be easier for you to wake me if something happens." Blaze hoped she had covered her awkwardness. But more so, she also hoped that Daffodil could be a trustworthy friend. Blaze would test her. If Daffodil let her down then it was an easy fail.

"Yeah," said Daffodil unfazed, as Santu droned on. "You want a pillow?"

Static Recording No. 5241—On Loop

Oscar. 1903-1917. Ghosted Age 14.

Hello. My name is Oscar. I chose my name because it has the word 'car' in it. I would normally tell you everything about myself that I can remember but I am running out of time. These recordings are taking too much energy and my memories are fading too quickly.

I have waited too long. I am afraid I am losing us. But I know if I do not try to do something straight away it is inevitable. I have already lost one. That was so awful. I wish I could remember all the details but it was so long ago that the thoughts have faded. I do not want that to happen to any more of us! And the Shadow is waiting for us. It thinks it has nearly beaten us. I have to stop it. I have to make sure we are saved.

There are so many lost ones here. I used to be able to find them easily—the newly ghosted—but there are other forces about now and they are disappearing before I can sense their presence. I am scared for them. I don't like the Shadow. It doesn't come near me but still, it threatens me somehow. I am worried about Dog and Bruises.

Dog has always been distrustful. He has forgotten most of the things that happened Before. And actually, I am grateful for that. The things he told me when I first found him after he ghosted, upset me deeply. At least he still remembers his family. I know he pretends he doesn't care but don't fall for that. He is deeply wounded. It is impossible for him to manage all that it is.

Bruises is almost lost to us now. She has sunken deeper into her own sorrow. She can no longer see what is good. Her hurts have manifested into large bruises—the bruises she proclaims to love—but it is just the familiar that she hangs on to. If she weren't a twin to Buttons I would relinquish my efforts. But Buttons has all the strength of a Model T Ford Speedster. Gosh I admire that. And with Melody (and Baby) giving us the music that fills up our lost souls, I think we can go on for a bit longer. Wonderboy holds on to his clue about the redhead and if Bugsy can keep that bevy of flying creatures swarming around him, we may just be able to fly away on their light. Plus, let's not forget about Scraps, who has single handedly impressed everyone with his confession of eating a rat that did not kill him but finding that a green potato did.

These are the lost children I must save. I don't know why. It is just what it is.

Bitsy says she saw something last night. It was a full moon and that usually gives us a bit more energy than usual. I hope she did. None of *us* saw anything. But, we were all playing our own games. Except Bruises and Bitsy: Bitsy was practicing screaming at the window—practicing like her mommy did Before. And Bruises was curled up in her favorite corner playing with her spiders.

I can't remember when Bruises talked to me last. That is very bad. I have always been the one who could remember when the others couldn't. I am going to try to get everyone to play charades tonight so I can go outside without them noticing. More and more, everyone is pulling away. It feels like we are many individuals on a leaking raft and everyone has already given up. We must fight. We must fight until there is no fight left in us. As surely that will happen.

I will go out tonight and try to find what Bitsy saw.

Time is running out.

I must go.

~Present day~

~FACE AT A WINDOW~

The only sounds Daffodil could hear were the crackling of the fire and the rasp of the cold air outside. Surrounded by protective amulets, she had been gazing out the window for so long she had completely lost track of time. She wasn't used to being without her watch and in this place darkness just meant darkness. Perhaps Jake had been wrong. Maybe there wasn't anyone coming at all? One last time, she gazed out into the icy black void—and that's when she got the shock of her life.

A flash of white zipped past the window—it was so quick she couldn't be sure what it was. Again, it flicked past the other way. It looked like it was being pushed away from her like iron fillings from a magnet. Of course! The amulets! Quickly, Daffodil scooped them up and tossed them all inside the lead lined case and locked it down, leaving herself completely vulnerable.

And then it happened.

A sad ashen face flashed up to her window. The small luminous figure, dressed in some kind of military uniform, glowed like the moon and smoky wisps ebbed around him like shimmering breath. The boy's eyes were level with hers and he was trying to speak, to scream, to yell.

"I don't understand," cried Daffodil, her voice stirring the others. "I can't hear you!"

The boy looked confused. It tried to scream even louder. Then suddenly it stopped. Looking back over its shoulder, the boy looked afraid. Before Daffodil could even comprehend what had just happened, it vanished.

"No, come back!" Daffodil screamed as she ran and swung open the door. Icy air hit her face with the force of a slap.

But it was too late. The terrified face had dissolved into the freezing night. Daffodil was tempted to run out there. Maybe she could find it? But it was a foolish and dangerous thought. As she leant backwards on the closing door she saw Jake. He was standing at the doorway of his bedroom and he had an expression that she knew would stay with her for the rest of her life.

"Did you see it Jake?" Daffodil's voice trembled.

Jake was shaking his head very slowly. Daffodil didn't understand what was wrong with him. If he hadn't seen the ghost why was he so deathly pale? And then gradually, Jake's left hand rose from his side until his palm was level with Daffodil's eyes. In it lay her watch. It was screaming with static. Daffodil shook her head. She didn't understand what Jake was trying to tell her.

"I-know-why-I've-always-felt-the-need-to-hear-static." Jake's eyes were wide with alarm.

"Why Jake? What's wrong?" A chill ran up Daffodil's spine.

"They're-in-there. I-can-hear-them."

~Present day~

~V⊕ICES IN THE STATIC, CRY~

The commotion had woken everyone up. Annabelle was annoyed.

"You better have seen something—" Annabelle stopped mid sentence. Several horrified glares had turned in her direction. "What's going on?" she asked in confusion.

"I saw it." Daffodil's voice was chill and quiet. "I saw a boy's face at the window. He was screaming but I couldn't hear him." Daffodil looked over at Jake who was still standing wide-eyed and holding out Daffodil's watch.

"And . . . I . . . heard . . . him." Jake held out the hissing watch as if it would prove his claim. Everyone was silent. What can be said after announcements like that?

Daffodil realized that Jake's words weren't running on in a staccato-like rush. She was about to ask him about it when he interrupted her thoughts.

"What did he look like?" Jake asked.

In her mind Daffodil saw the boy's face again. It was awful. She shut her eyes trying to rid herself of the vision. "Scared."

"Wait a minute, just wait a minute." Annabelle was remembering her own haunting vision. "What do you mean you can hear *them*!? How many are you talking about? And are they all here or are they from all over? And what do you mean you've *always* been able to hear them? And in that case why have you just realized now!?"

Jake was overwhelmed by Annabelle's barrage of questions. He was already dealing with truths he had always known but never faced before. Jake shut his eyes and began shaking his head all the while still holding the watch out in front of him.

"It's okay Jake," said Daffodil throwing a furious glance Annabelle's way. "Just maybe think about one thing." Her voice was calm and reassuring. "Do you remember what you heard tonight?"

Jake nodded slowly, his eyes still shut. "Yes."

"Well that's really good Jake. What did you hear?" Daffodil wished Jake would put the watch, with its accusatory crackling and hissing, down by his side.

"It-was-the-boy-who-likes-cars. He-is-a-ghost-now."

"The boy who likes cars?" asked Daffodil with a sigh. Annabelle's torrent had returned Jake's speech to a rushing jumble.

"Is this a joke?" chimed Annabelle suspiciously.

"Shhh!" shot an angry Duette. "You being quiet unless you say a bit intelligence!"

Everyone stared at Duette in surprise. Duel was starting to feel really proud of his sister. He had never heard her use such emotion in her voice.

Annabelle sneered and rolled her eyes.

"Just listen to me Jake, okay?" said Daffodil. Jake nodded. "So what did the boy who likes cars say?" She held up a hand. "And just speak slowly if you can Jake and you can open your eyes when you're ready."

"He . . . is . . . worried . . . about . . . the . . . others." Jake nodded and slowly squeezed open his eyes looking only at Daffodil. "There is danger coming to hurt them and he needs help."

"Did he say what kind of help?"

Jake wasn't sure how to answer this question. Hearing the voices in his sleep made it feel a bit like a dream that was quickly vanishing. He shook his head.

"I . . . can't . . . remember."

Annabelle sniggered. The poor boy had just had a bad dream. At least now she could push those other visions away again, push them deep down where they belonged.

"Okay, well I think that's a good start." Daffodil eyed the rest of the group avoiding only Annabelle.

"They in pain," added Duette, "I feeling it."

"Which doesn't make any sense at all," said her brother skeptically— Duette had never claimed to *feel* emotion from thoughts. Yes, she could sense moods but she had never actually experienced them. "I mean, if they're dead, why would they feel pain?"

Blaze shivered and fingered the amulets that Daffodil had given her. She didn't notice that the ruby was glowing.

Jake was nodding in agreement but didn't take his eyes off Daffodil. "The boy said some of them are hurting. But I don't know what that means." Jake was still holding the watch out to Daffodil. That gave Daffodil an idea.

"Jake, do you think you have to be asleep to hear the voices?"

Jake looked at the watch as if it were a crystal ball. "I don't know. I've only ever listened to go to sleep."

"Would you mind trying?" Daffodil didn't want to push him but it was the only idea she had. "Maybe close your eyes and relax and just see?"

Jake was nodding. He wanted to help—both Daffodil and these people in the watch.

"I think there's a reason why I have remembered that I've heard them before. I think that's why we're here. We have to save them."

Static Recording No. 5242—On Loop

⊕SCAR. 1903-1917. GH⊕STED AGED 14.

Hello. Can you hear me? I'm Oscar. You saw me! I know you saw me! I saw your face. Please can you hear me now? I cried out but you just shook your head. I need you to hear me. I have rushed back to make a recording. I know something of you! I know that one of you understands—one of you can hear these recordings. One of you can help. Please we are in very bad danger.

You must help us. We need help!

I am distraught now. Bruises must have followed me out of the church when I came to look for you. She shouldn't have done that! I had everyone playing and I thought they were busy but she didn't stay inside where it was safe.

I felt the Shadow when I was at your window. That is why I had to rush back. But I was too late! I was too late!

And now she is gone. Bruises is gone. The Shadow has taken her. And it's all my fault. Buttons will be devastated. She will try to come outside and look for Bruises. And then I will lose her too.

Please you must come. I know you can help us. We do not have much time. The Shadow is getting stronger and stronger. I felt its power when I came out to find you. Bruises must have distracted it. It has taken her instead of me! There are only nine of us left now.

This is all wrong. *I* am supposed to save all these ghosted ones. *I* am supposed to protect them. I haven't done that tonight. I shouldn't have left her.

Please you must hear me. You must help us. We have waited so long. I knew someone would come eventually. I knew you would come and help us.

You must come, but you must be careful. The Shadow is very dangerous. It will take us all—you included. It does not discriminate. It just consumes. You must be watchful. Do not go near the graves and do not move around alone in the light. It can see you better. For us it is the dark. We can no longer move when the light is out. The Shadow has taken the energy of the light from us. Now we need moonlight to move. That is good for us to meet though.

You must hurry.

Time is running out.

Time is running out for everyone.

Please! Hurry!

~WHICH DOOR SHALL WE OPEN TODAY?~

The shrill ring of the newly installed alarm shocked everyone from slumber. In the slipstream between sleeping and waking, imagined colors stirred in their minds, alleys of memory drifting forever away from their wakeful state.

"What happened?" murmured Daffodil to the slowly stirring group of people strewn across the beds.

"I fell asleep," said Blaze apologetically. "What happened to those stones that were supposed to keep you awake?"

"Oh, I threw them back in their case with all the others. The amulets were pushing that ghost-boy away."

"I'm so tired," yawned Santu as he got up to inspect his nose in the mirror. Black circles scooped his eyes. At least the throbbing had eased. "I need my Y's."

"Z's," said Blaze slightly frustrated. "You mean Z's."

Daffodil climbed off her bed to find Jake in the other room. He was sitting up and staring into space as if he were hypnotized.

"Jake? Are you alright?"

"I-fell-asleep. I'm-sorry."

"That's okay Jake." Daffodil managed a laugh. "We all did. Do you remember hearing anything else in your sleep?" She winked at him. "Slowly Jake."

Jake concentrated. "Something . . . about . . . a . . . shadow." Jake was trying to pull the words back. They felt like slippery eels, squirming ever harder the more he tried to hold onto them. "I think the Shadow can cause bruises." That didn't sound quite right but his brain felt like someone had rung it dry.

"Oh," replied a horrified Daffodil. "Let's just keep that between ourselves, hey?" She nodded encouragingly to Jake. "We don't want to worry Duette about that right?"

Jake nodded and then shook his head. He had forgotten about the bruises on Duette's ankles. "They need help."

"Yeah," smiled Daffodil, "I think we all might."

Santu's strident voice could be heard from the bathroom. "Well how we doing this then?" he asked. "Is anyone having any beaming ideas about how we deal with this?"

"Well," Blaze was stoking the fire as if she were jousting, "does anyone have any ideas if Madame Glizsnort is a part of this?"

"I cannot get any vision from her words. I always get the vision from people's words." Santu was washing his face.

Duel agreed. "And I cannot hear her thoughts," he said in annoyance. "Duette can't either."

"I can speech!" cried Duette.

"Sorry," said Duel in exasperation. He had been speaking for her for so long he forgot she suddenly wanted to change the rules.

"Not be rude!" Duette had not only felt his annoyance in her mind she also recognized his tone. That was a first for both of them. This was a whole new ball game.

"I'm sorry," he replied with a more apologetic attitude, his wide set hazel eyes reflecting his apology.

"That better." Duette was starting to enjoy this added aspect to language.

"Hey," snarled Annabelle, "could you little froggies calm down."

The fury that flew from both Duel's and Duette's minds nearly blew Annabelle backward. It was truly shocking. If the others in the room hadn't seen the burst of electricity soar across the air they would never have believed it. Blaze's eyes were lit with delight.

"Whoa," cried Santu, "let us *all* just take it easy."

Daffodil had just walked back into the room and felt the surge of wrath whiz past her.

"What the hell is going on in here?"

Duette and Duel turned their fiery eyes toward Daffodil.

"Nobody, calls us frogs!" Their voices were perfectly synchronized.

"Oh, that's just far about." Santu was crisscrossing his pointed forefingers at them as if he were deflecting the devil.

"*Far out*," corrected Blaze, still in shock. "And yes, it really is."

"Okay, okay," said Daffodil. "No one," she looked around at everyone determinedly, "will call you that word ever again." She eyed Santu, her glance questioning who was responsible. Santu threw a quick look at Annabelle. Of course, Daffodil thought, who else would it be? She eyed Annabelle with a warning.

Annabelle thought that the fact that a stupid hippy was trying to threaten her was almost amusing. If she hadn't been on the other end of that . . . whatever the hell it was, Annabelle would have been as cocky as ever. But the childish fear always echoed in the back of her mind: If they rejected her, she might be left alone in the dark.

"Fine. I didn't realize you would be *so* offended by that. I meant it *affectionately*." Annabelle raised two palms in a gesture of feigned innocence.

The squinted eyes of Duette and Duel stared at her for a second longer before deciding she had learnt her lesson. This was nice for Duel. They were back to sharing minds and feelings. It was the only way he had ever communicated with his sister until this place. Duette felt his relief. But she pushed her guilt aside. It was time she became an individual, and again, she shut him out.

Blaze had enjoyed the show but if they weren't at breakfast soon, the threat of Madame Glizsnort bursting into their room was looking likely.

"Do you think Madame Snotty will be there this morning?" asked Blaze.

"If she is," said Santu, "I'm ready for giving her a piece of my brain."

"*Your mind*," corrected Blaze. "And so am I. How about we go to breakfast and start trying to sort out a way to overcome her?"

"Thank god. Someone is having a good idea," replied Santu. "Let's hope there are no eggs!"

Blackwater Herald Moon Tribune
Monday, December 8th, 1941—
One penny

The 826th day of the Second Great War
CURRENT WAR UPDATE
JAPAN ATTACKS U.S.!

*A*t 7:35 a.m. yesterday, 361 Japanese bombers—their wings bearing the insignia of the Rising Sun—appeared over Honolulu and began dropping bombs. They were joined by 30 ships and 20 submarines. They attacked American airfields and shipyards and have killed up to 2,500 American personnel. The assault was made without warning, when both nations were at peace. Oahu Island was hit, as was Pearl Harbor; the latter having been engulfed in flames as an oil tank exploded.

As President Roosevelt replied to this declaration of war, Japanese paratroops were still bombing America's key Pacific outposts. Over 150 planes were still diving and releasing a rain of bombs despite the losses inflicted on them by the swarm of American fighters which flashed among them. Heavy damage and grievous loss of life are reported from the crowded city of Honolulu.

The President declared that Japan should now consider herself at war with America and Britain in the Western Pacific. Manila and Guam have also suffered bombings. Page 3.

LOCAL NEWS HEADLINES
CHURCH FACES MORE CONTROVERSY

The latest controversy to plague the Saint Catherine's Church of Redeemus is threatening to curtail worshipping once again. After thriving for the first few months, several members who previously denounced the church began returning. However, now some of these attendees are claiming they have seen visions whilst being inside the building and are adamant these visualizations are not figments. Some say they have seen a wicked version of Christ seething above them, whilst others have gone so far as to declare they have seen a 'ghostly looking duck'. Their fear has renewed doubt amongst the community and the doomsayers are again out in force. The Herald Moon Tribune is reminded of the feverish atmosphere of the Salem witch hunts.

Yesterday there were only a dozen worshippers and the Bishop is now considering using the building for other purposes as well. For those determined to keep the town functioning he is offering this opportunity to any businesses that are suffering from the sliding economy.

Please present your ideas to Bishop John Biggs by next Friday. "There will be no rent required," the Bishop has stated, "just a pledge to help maintain this beautiful building."

Due to the failing community, this paper is offering another free week of advertising to all the local Blackwater businesses.

For those of us determined to stay—Good luck Blackwater!
Blackout time is Zero hour until 8:23 A.M.

BUSINESSES STILL OPEN: More Adds—Page 9.

Mrs. O'Donnel's Sweet Shop—*Licorice, butterscotch, and rationed bags of boiled sweets—perfect at the end of a meal or to take the taste of dust from your mouth!*

Bertie's Butchery—*Your rationed meats all here.*

Clip Clop Dairy—*Milk is still being delivered by horse and cart despite rations.*

Sortium Apothecary—*Try our tonics and remedies at half price on Tuesday.*

Miss Durand's Instructional School—*Marchenby Street. All welcome!*

Blackwater Tobacconist—*For your sheer smoking pleasure.*

Candlesticks and Combs—From Hardware to Hair Care!

WORLD NEWS HEADLINES

Soviet Attack—*The German attack on the Soviet Union has lasted six months and killed millions on both sides. Story Page 6.*

More Japanese Attacks—*Today Japanese troops invaded The Philippines and Malaya, and attacked Hong Kong. Page 3.*

~Brought to you by~

His Masters Voice brings you Bing Crosby's "Silent Night" & "White Christmas".

~Present day~

~GHOSTS AT A GRAVE~

Arriving back at the freezing church, they found Madame Glizsnort waiting. It was as if she had been lingering for a lifetime. She wore the same gray skirt and woolen jacket with embossed looping 'G's' on the lapel. Daffodil surreptitiously checked her watch. They were early. Sitting silently she went over their plan in her head.

"You will be taking some unusual lessons today. It is to test both mind and body. It is to test your gifts and your willingness to grow. Do not be alarmed."

Immediately, everyone was alarmed. What did this skeletal woman have in mind? How much did she know about their individual gifts? How did they know she wasn't dangerous? Why hadn't she turned up yesterday afternoon? Would their plan to get the truth out of her work? Furtive glances danced around the room.

Santu was supposed to wait but anger was broiling inside him. He had only once known such fury and he had sworn never to let it overtake him again. But, Santu knew all too well, that promises were bankrupt.

"Madame Glizsnort! It is about time we were being treated with some respect. We are wanting to know wh . . ."

Before he could get the next word out Madame Glizsnort had crushed him back into his seat, his sinus's swelling with rekindled pain. The reflections of icy fury that initiated his restraint went flying across the cold church making everyone shrink in their seats. Fear ebbed in their chests and questions poured into their minds. Exactly what kind of danger were they in and how long would they be trapped here with this awful woman?

"You will listen to me and you *will* do as I ask." Madame Glizsnort's sickly features looked beyond desperate.

Suddenly, like the flow of water from an opened tap, everyone in the room could hear one thought: 'You have to do this, you have to help. If you want to get out of here you must try to understand. If not, you're lives will be in grave danger'. Had it come from the old woman or someone else?

"Now, prepare for your first test!"

Even in this bizarre situation, Santu's competitive spirit brimmed like the foam on furious surf. He couldn't help himself. And this room, this church, was making him more competitive and more heated than he could ever imagine. Something was influencing him. Or someone.

"You." Madame Glizsnort was pointing to Jake. "Everyone silent!" she eyed him carefully. "Close your eyes and tell me what you can hear."

Daffodil was angry. This woman better not put too much pressure on Jake or she would have to deal with a lot more than that interesting display Duette and Duel put on this morning.

"Silence!" Madame Glizsnort repeated looking directly at Daffodil. "Everyone close your eyes. See what you can hear."

The silence was deafening.

"I'm-sorry-Madame-Glizsnort-but-I can't-hear-anything-except-my-own-breathing," said Jake.

If Annabelle hadn't caught the vision of a little scruffy dog out of the corner of her eye, she would have been included in Madame Glizsnort's assessment of the hopelessness of the group. But Annabelle was confused. A dog had flashed past her but as she turned, it disappeared. Where had it gone? Was she going mad? And why could she hear a duck quacking? As she turned back to face the front of the classroom she caught the expression on Madame Glizsnort's face. It was one of disturbingly indescribable pleasure. Annabelle shook her head. She wasn't sure why. And then she realized that everyone was looking at her.

Duette was trying to concentrate but the pain in her legs was distracting her thoughts. The bruises had spread. But there was no reason why. At least tracing the pain with her fingers seemed to help. Everyone seemed very involved with Madame Glizsnort's demands. It was strange but Duette didn't feel any of it. All Duette wanted to do was to sit quietly in a corner and nurse her bruises.

"Stop!" screeched Madame Glizsnort.

"We shall *all* be involved in the next task."

Santu wondered why there was a next task when the first one had been such a failure. Anxiety was crouching inside him ready to leap. He was used to winning everything. And at the very least he was used to someone winning something. This was bizarre in the extreme. He felt like a little child playing musical chairs without any chairs.

"I am well aware of the abilities of this group. Why do you think you have been specially assigned here? This is going to push your personal quests to beyond the kind of boundaries you have been confined to. Here we will challenge you. Here you will find something inside yourself that you did not know existed. And here you will face fear. I know that there is dread within you. If you are afraid, you are smart. If you are smug, you are a fool. And I have no time for fools. Let me make that clear."

The outburst was obvious: For whatever reason, they were here to find out more than the truths they had brought with them, and with that knowledge would come jeopardy. Who could know how the gauge would slide?

"Now, close your eyes again and see what you can *hear*."

Suddenly the images came bursting at them from every angle. It was like a painting made of slashes and blobs and sound and hurt: Each indescribable moment was framed with pain. Every person in the room, excepting Madame Glizsnort of course, was either covering their eyes or their ears, or their head.

Madame Glizsnort heaved a sigh of relief. At last they could feel it. She would let the pain rise until they understood. '*Finally*,' she thought. There was so little time left. Inch by inch it was slipping away. At least now they all had a chance—If they could just find a way to fight the Shadow.

As soon as Madame Glizsnort had sensed the light, she released them from their duties and disappeared into the snow. Once again, the exhausted students made their way toward the mess hall. At least they felt like they had made some progress. What progress that was they weren't sure, but some strange merge had occurred and there was no going back.

"Everything is gray and gray." Santu was facing the same gray eggs he had eaten yesterday and his stomach squirmed. Everything looked inedible but he was starving. He couldn't understand why girls would want to diet.

"You judging us." It was Duette. She had definitely found her voice. "You fat too."

Santu was confused and then sorry. He had been thinking about fat people and wondering how they got fat when food could be so horrible.

"Whoa, I am not meaning to be judgmental, I am just thinking . . . hang up a minute . . ." Santu's palms were raised.

"*Hang on,*" said Blaze impatiently.

Santu ignored her. "Are you saying I cannot think without being in this trouble?"

"You can think many. But you not be mean."

"This is not what I was meaning to say . . . think . . . say," he said in confusion.

Blaze had no idea what Santu and Duette were disagreeing about but there was something she wanted to say and she couldn't wait for them to see eye to eye.

"You know, I think I could see a graveyard up on that hill over there." Blaze was pointing in the direction of the church whilst peering cautiously at a bowl of suspicious mash. "Way up behind the church. If you look hard you can see a whole lot of stones protruding from the snow. I'm assuming they're graves. It doesn't look that far you know." Blaze was faced with a sea of horrified faces. "What?"

"You want us to go to a graveyard?" asked Daffodil.

"Sure, why not?" said Blaze wondering why they weren't excited to go.

"Well," said Santu, "I guess *some people* do not like visiting a place of the dead."

"Who? Children and scaredy-cats?" Blaze replied.

"Alright," replied Santu knowing she had hit a sore point with him. "We take a vote. Who is *wanting* to go to the graveyard?"

Blaze raised her hand.

Daffodil had been thinking: Maybe the graveyard was the perfect place to find something out about the ghosts they were trying to sense? She raised her hand and nodded at Jake encouragingly. He raised a very stiff palm up to his shoulder. He had to trust someone and he had chosen Daffodil. Duel shrugged his shoulders and shot an arm in the air. It felt a bit triumphant. Then, very slowly, Duette raised her hand too. And finally so did Annabelle—she wasn't going to be left here alone.

Blaze raised her eyebrows at Santu. "Majority rules," she said victoriously, her green eyes glinting.

Santu shrugged. He didn't like graveyards. A feeling of foreboding wrapped itself around his chest. He took a deep breath. "Great. I am guessing lunch is 'to go' then," said Santu begrudgingly.

Blaze blinked in amazement at Santu. He got it right. "Yes, *to go*," she repeated cheerfully.

Santu had no idea why Blaze was so happy about their take-away lunch but he grabbed a stale piece of bread and slapped a gray piece of meat on it before curling it into a sandwich. He shook his head and made his way to the door. Each of them grabbed something off the table and followed Santu.

Blaze smiled. Even when Santu was the only person that disagreed with an action he was still the leader.

As the freezing air hit their bare skin, their faces began to numb. Daffodil pulled her multi-colored scarf tighter around her throat and tucked her hands under her under-arms. She wondered how long it would take before they all ended up with frostbite.

Annabelle marched up beside Santu and made a sad face. "Oh dear," she said in a baby voice as she rolled her bottom lip, "don't like being a loser?"

Santu smiled. The beautiful blond with the frosted-seascape eyes never missed an opportunity.

"Blaze is liking a challenge," Santu replied. "This is good in a woman." Santu watched Annabelle's expression turn into a scowl. A perfect strike. Annabelle flicked him a look of disgust and sauntered ahead of him on her long legs, still wearing a ridiculous pair of high-heeled boots.

'*Interesting*', thought Annabelle. She hadn't figured him for a game player. Still, no one had ever beaten her yet and his threats about knowing her story didn't discourage her. Annabelle planned her next move.

Daffodil checked that Jake could make the journey. Thankfully, his feet had improved with her special balm. There was no way he was going to be left out of this.

"I-didn't-see-anyone-in-the-window-of-the-church-today." Jake was concentrating on keeping up with Daffodil.

"Me neither. But I think I heard something weird." Daffodil was thinking about the shuffling noises coming from the ceiling.

"Me-too." Jake was glad. At least he could confide in someone. He concentrated on slowing his speech. "It . . . sounded . . . a . . . bit . . . like . . . scuffling. It could have been rats."

"Maybe," nodded Daffodil relieved that Jake had remembered to speak deliberately without her reminding him, "but I heard something like a hissing or crackling noise too. It made the hairs on the back of my neck stand up."

"I thought I imagined that." Jake often imagined the sound of static. It helped keep him calm.

"You heard it too?" Daffodil felt like something was creeping across her skin.

Jake nodded and shivered. "It was different from the static I like though."

"How?" asked Daffodil.

Jake thought for a moment. "It-was-cold."

The freezing air was biting into Duette's face. The pain she was now experiencing from the bruises was making it hard to concentrate on anything else. The graveyard had better not be too far away.

"What long to graves?" Duette asked through chattering teeth. Duel gently pushed the word 'how' into her mind. "Oh." Duette said surprised that her brother was helping her after her outburst that morning. The pain had allowed Duette's to let her guard down and unfortunately, in those flickering seconds, Duel had accessed her mind. Simultaneously she knew that he had felt her pain. "*How* long to graves?"

Duel moved over to her, worry written all over his face. But Duette dismissed him with a sharp shake of her head.

In his mind he heard the thought: 'I will tell you if it gets too bad. Please let me do this my way.' Duel wasn't sure what to do. Perhaps for now, he would let it go but he would have to figure out what was happening to her.

Annabelle wanted to be the one to answer Duette's question. "Twenty-five minutes," she said confidently.

"Perhaps though, only twenty," said Santu. Turning to nod in Annabelle's direction, Santu caught the look she gave him. "Already we have been walking for ten," he said with a shrug.

"Did you add *Jake* into your calculations?" Annabelle said curtly as she glanced at the hobbling boy.

"Did *you* add *Duette* into yours?" Santu didn't bother to watch Annabelle turn around to check Duette's progress but he knew she did. He smiled to himself.

Annabelle wanted to ask why Duette looked so pained and washed-out but she didn't want Santu to have the upper hand. So she just sniffed at him and quickened her pace.

For a time everyone was silent. The only sounds were shoes crunching on snow and the occasional ghostly swirl of icy wind. At least the trek was keeping them warm.

Suddenly Santu's voice struck the air.

"Hey!" yelled Santu, interrupting everyone's thoughts. "Look at that!" His tone made everyone look up. What they saw was indescribable. And chilling. Each and every one of them froze in their tracks.

Blackwater Herald Moon Tribune Friday, February 20th, 1942— One penny

CURRENT WAR UPDATE
JAPAN ATTACKS AUSTRALIA

Yesterday 188 Japanese warplanes, led by naval Commander Mitsuo Fuchida, attacked the Australian city of Darwin. Warnings—thought to be referring to the returning U.S. fighter pilots and their B-17 escort—were disregarded. With surprise on their side, the Japanese bombers quickly shot down all of the U.S. planes except one. Then 81 Nakajima B5N torpedo bombers attacked 45 vessels in the crowded Darwin harbor and 71 Aichi D3A dive-bombers, escorted by 36 Mitsubishi A6M Zero fighter planes, attacked the Royal Australian Air Force bases, civil airfields, and a hospital. The death toll is unknown at this stage. PAGE 3.

LOCAL NEWS HEADLINES
LOCAL CONSTABLE SAFE

After many months of worry the Herald Moon Tribune is pleased to announce the discovery of the whereabouts of our local constable and war hero, Macalister Glizsnort. After suffering several dangerous injuries he is now recovering in a British hospital in Holland. Grace Durand, his companion, finally received a letter from him and was so delighted, she allowed us to publish an extract.

EXTRACT FROM A HERO'S LETTER

"*My sweet, please do not worry. I fear you may have believed the worst as I have been unable to write to you. I am fine and convalescing in the hospital here in Holland. I will tell you what has happened but please know that the wound is healing although I do not believe my ears will ever improve. As you know I have been actively piloting B29's—although I am still a bit miserable about not being chosen as a First Class Radio Man (you know how I love radios—are you enjoying the old Radiola VIII I found for you?)—nevertheless, I love flying the B29's—they are very fast.*

So, we were flying over France ready to go into battle to do a bombing run with firebombs—they are in clusters and are dropped right over the stations—well I'd gone down to 2500 feet to drop lines and the enemy came at me right out of the black sky without warning. They shot about seventy holes in the rear wing and shot out one of the brakes on the left side and then I felt it. A .50 caliber bullet from a gun turret tore through my right thigh braking the bone and damaging ligaments and muscles. The pain was really quite terrible. But I had good men in the sky with me and they managed to shoot the bastards down.

In a way it was good that I wasn't flying too high. I managed to right the plane, which was still adequate to fly, and head back while the excruciating pain numbed my thoughts of what could have happened. I am not entirely sure what followed but the boys told me I made a good landing before falling unconscious.

I developed a bad fever from the wound and was quite delirious for a while but as you know, I would never leave you. I have been here for several months after being moved from the small clinic where I was treated initially. They are talking of an honorable discharge as the damage was extensive. As I am still having problems with my ears and the broken ear drum, I think they may send me home. It is a shame as I wanted to get some more of those damn Nazis but at least I will be able to see you again. You cannot image how much I miss you. I am also looking forward to returning to the police force. I will write as soon as I know what is to happen."

WORLD NEWS HEADLINES

Germany, Berlin—It is reported that Nazi Officials have held a conference in Berlin where they have discussed the implementation of their

'Final Solution'. The result of these talks indicates that the fate of 11 million European Jews is dire. Page 5.

United States, N.Y.—Father and Son Draught—Men between the ages of 20 and 44 began registering today in the nations 'father and son' services draft which is expected to add 9 million to the U.S. Armed Forces. The country's man-power is estimated at 40 million.

Indonesia, Bali—Japanese troops land on Bali. Page 9.

Men's Shirts Shorter—Men's shirts will be styled with shorter sleeves and shorter tail said a spokesman from the Drapers Chambers of Trade yesterday. Also at the meeting, women were protesting the poor quality of stockings available and refused to accept going barelegged.

WHY SINGAPORE WAS LOST—And the consequences for Britain now that it no longer holds any military position in the east. Page 7.

Blackout Time: Zero Hour until 7:34 A.M.

~Brought to you by~

With Wolsley Socks upon your feet, you'll be comfy, cool and fleet!

~Present day~

~THE SHADOW HAS A MOUTH~

In the distance they could clearly see the graveyard. But they could also see something much more disturbing: A solitary man was digging a grave. He was dressed all in black with a heavy black coat and a top hat and he seemed to be effortlessly hollowing out a grave in the icy hard ground with a long handled shovel.

There were several things wrong with this. He was all alone, in the middle of nowhere without even a vehicle nearby. There was also a very thick fog that ebbed behind him—the same mist that enclosed the entire area—which would have been impossible to penetrate without getting lost.

Everyone seemed to register this information at the same time. And, just as they recognized the incongruity of the scene, the man's face shot up to stare straight at them. Then just as quickly, his head shot around to look back over his shoulder toward the mist. In the next instant a huge black shadow began to rise from the ground. It spread around and above him. The man's terrified eyes followed its movements as if the strange dark shape had rendered him immobile. Within seconds, it covered the entire graveyard. An acrid smell filled the air making it almost suffocating.

This all happened in a matter of seconds; too quick to defend the tricks one's mind can play. And everyone's challenge is to trust their first instincts.

Abruptly the Shadow began to move toward them, and that's when, simultaneously, each of them realized how much danger they were actually in.

"That's not smoke is it?" murmured Blaze unnecessarily.

Everyone's eyes were transfixed on the slowly approaching whirlpool. No one could answer. No one could move.

And then the Shadow was upon them, its forces whipping at them, threatening to tear their immobile bodies to pieces. The charge of wind that soared toward them was astonishing in its power: Violent in its desperation for destruction, the strength of its hatred overwhelming.

Its many coils rotated inside the dark, fluctuating mass, whisking and thrashing as if looking for release. Whatever this thing was, it was full of conflict and loathing and fury. And the seven motionless teenagers would be caught and swallowed and obliterated if they didn't do something— quickly.

But one of them *was* moving! Moving the wrong way! Duette was being pulled toward the sinister spiral. Its outstretched arms were dragging her inward and upward, toward the dark vast hollow of its horrible mouth. It was gruesome and terrifying and hopeless.

Duel wanted to scream out but he had no voice.

The dark mass was hauling Duette in and she could do nothing to save herself. In his mind he screamed 'fight, fight, fight' over and over again but her mind was drained, blank, lost.

Just as the Shadow wrapped its smoky malevolent arms around her and opened its huge ugly mouth Duette managed a small apologetic smile for her brother: Her brother that had been there for her all her life; the one who had sat through experiment after experiment so that she could prove herself; the same brother who had stood up for her during the taunts about their deaf father and her bizarre talents; a brother that had protected her, always.

This had all happened too quickly. There was no chance of defense. It was a cruel and impossible situation with only one advantage.

Jake.

"No!" screamed Jake as he scrambled forward. No creature was going to curb his primal instinct to save.

While the others were frozen to the spot Jake began charging toward the ugly black mass. A surge of twisting winds hurled toward Jake, the pitching tempest gaining power with its impending victory. But Jake was thinking about Duette, and if running into a hideous and deathly tornado was the only way to try and save her, then that was what he had to do.

Disbelief, shock, fear and dread ran through the minds of the others. All they could do was watch. Jake was about to commit a fatal mistake. They knew that once Duette was gone Jake would be next and then the Shadow would come for them too.

Just as Duette began to disappear into the dark coil, Jake, with arms raised, smashed himself into the creature. As soon as his skin struck the shadow there was a massive explosion. Wails of agony soared through the cold, still air as the black mass ruptured right at the point where Jake stood: The Shadow was splitting into a million particles.

Instantly Duette was dropped to the ground from a height that should have broken her fragile legs. In the explosion Jake was ricocheted several meters away and flew through the air before landing with an agonizing thud. His muscles sparkled with burning electricity and his heart raced as if he'd run a marathon.

Able to move again, everyone ran toward Duette. The howls still trembled in the air as the creature began to reconfigure. It shot up high in the air and then blasted back toward the graveyard—and toward the motionless grave-digger. Soaring high up above him, it then swiftly bore down on the darkly clad man, its mouth devouring him in less than a second before disappearing into the earth.

Duel was hugging his sister as if she may dissolve into dust.

"I fine," trembled Duette as everyone flooded her with questions. "Please Duel, letting go."

"Are your legs okay?" he asked as he finally released her. Duette looked weak and pale—she looked like she had just been dragged into an unfathomable abyss by a wicked and hateful creature. He tugged at the cuff of her pants to reveal her dark bruises. They had stretched up to her knees.

"Oh god!" cried Duel as he saw the growing discoloration. Everyone was in shock at the sight of them. "I've got to get her out of here."

"We should *all be* getting out of here," said Santu. "Who knows when that thing is coming back."

Jake had hobbled back to the group and Daffodil turned and hugged him tightly. Jake's body stiffened. He didn't like being touched. He tried to squirm away but Daffodil didn't let go.

"Oh Jake, that was crazy!" she screamed at him. "I'm sorry, I know you don't like hugs but you saved Duette's life!" Everyone started to congratulate him. The attention was too much for Jake. He shut his eyes shaking his head.

"But-I-didn't-save-her," he said defiantly.

"Yes you did! Jake if you hadn't run into that thing . . ." Daffodil couldn't understand why Jake would be saying such a thing.

"It-wasn't-me," Jake insisted again. "It-was-the-watch." Jake was holding up the remains of the wristwatch, now a twisted mess of gold and parts. "I'm-sorry-Daffodil—it-was-the-watch-that-exploded-the-Shadow-not me."

Daffodil stared at what was left of her watch. It was smashed, almost melted. He handed it to her, his head hung low. She took the ruined gadget and gazed at it in astonishment.

"It's okay Jake. Really." She was staring at the remains of a life now lost: The last piece of her parents. "It was just a watch." Daffodil looked back up at Jake. "You won't have static anymore."

"And-you-won't-have-your-parents."

"You don't think I'll be able to see them anymore?" Small tears welled in her eyes.

Jake shook his head.

"It's okay." Daffodil blinked away a tear. "They can't help me anymore anyway." She smiled softly and tucked the broken metal into her pocket. Could all those amulets she encrusted the back of the watch with, have done this? It didn't seem possible.

Santu was about to ask how they were going to be able hear the ghosts without static, when he realized that one of them was missing. Quickly, his eyes roamed the area before finally locking onto the bright red hair of Blaze. She was waving frantically from the graveyard.

"What the hell is she doing?" cried Santu not sure whether to be furious or terrified. "Get away from there!" screamed Santu. But Blaze was shaking her head.

"You've got to see this!" Her voice was a mixture of excitement and terror. "You've got to see this!"

Everyone's adrenaline was still pulsing.

"I'll go," said Santu, "she's gone with the bananas." Santu twirled a forefinger at the side of his head.

"No way," said Annabelle against her will. "I'm coming too." What was wrong with her today? Why did she feel like she was in competition with Santu about crazy stuff like this? Oh well, better to die on the attack rather than run away in fear. Anyway, it was Duette the Shadow wanted, not her.

"I'm going too." Daffodil had nothing to lose. Not anymore.

"Me also," added Duette. She stood up with a slight wobble and reached for Duel's shoulder to steady her.

"No Duette. You need to go back and rest." Duel couldn't help but be protective.

Duette screwed her nose up at her brother. "No."

"This is stupid! You can hardly walk."

"Then is stupid," Duette huffed at him. "Longer we wait, more Shadow come back."

"She's got a point," said Daffodil with a shrug of her shoulders.

"Help me go!" Duette thrust out a determined arm at Duel.

He shook his head in frustration. "Alright but so help me god, if that thing comes back I'm going to push you straight in."

Duette smiled. "Fine."

Jake had already started hobbling toward the cemetery. What else was there to do?

"Over here, over here." Blaze's voice was getting stronger. Her red hair was visible over the top of an old curved headstone. "You see that mist."

Everyone turned to face the outskirts of the graveyard. The mist was so thick you would get lost in it within seconds.

"What about it?" asked Daffodil.

"Impenetrable," said Blaze matter-of-factly.

"What do you mean?" asked Annabelle.

"Just what I said. Haven't you noticed it? It circles the edge of this place. It's meant to be there."

"Blaze," said Daffodil, "are you trying to say that whoever has trapped us here has also made this mist barrier so we can't get out?"

Both Blaze's eyebrows rose. "Trapped us—exactly. That's not normal mist. And I can guarantee that if you want to go in there, it's a one way trip. Do you want to try it?"

Daffodil stared at the blanket of fog. She shook her head. "Not that desperate yet thanks."

"And look." Blaze made a large flourish. "These graves are all together in a row. This is the one where that gravedigger was standing." Blaze was standing right on the edge of a hole so deep you couldn't see the bottom. Everyone took a step backward which made Blaze laugh.

"Please just move back a bit Blaze," said Daffodil nervously.

"Just look. There are nine headstones here all exactly the same and listen to this." Blaze paused momentarily for effect which, under the circumstances, was absolutely unnecessary. "'Here stand the graves of the Lost Children. When we find their names we will honor their lives.'" She was reading from a white arched template that stood beside the first grave. "The gravestones are blank. See."

"Why is this one the only one to be dug up?" asked Santu as a shiver ran down his spine. For some reason he shot a look over at Duette as if she would know.

"Not know," she said shaking her head fiercely.

Jake took a step closer to the headstone. "I-think-that," Jake took a breath—he needed to stop speaking like a race-horse caller—"this grave has been dug for one of the children in the static." His voice was cold and measured.

"What do you mean?" asked Blaze.

"And I don't think that grave digger was alive."

"You mean the gravedigger wasn't eaten by that Shadow thing?"

"I don't think so." Jake had a lot more to tell but he wondered how much he should say. "I think that man was trying to bury one of the people in the static. I think it was helping the Shadow."

"How can you bury a ghost?" asked Daffodil in horror. "I mean we're assuming their ghosts right?"

Jake held up a hand. It was to silence everyone. He could hear something. He needed to concentrate.

"Did anyone else hear that?" Jake asked, his voice eerie and light and full of foreboding.

The icy winds were the perfect conduit for the cries of ghosts. Who could have known that?

Everyone's skin was crawling.

"What is it?" Daffodil's voice was a whisper.

"It's a girl," he said in a hush. "She's crying. She's scared and she wants her sister." Jake stopped and stared at Duette.

"What!?" asked Duette; the fear creeping up her neck.

"She says her name is Bruises."

Blackwater Herald Moon Tribune Monday, November 9th, 1942— One penny

CURRENT WAR UPDATE
GERMANY RETREATS IN DISORDER

Yesterday, the greatest Armada the world has ever seen launched a second front in North Africa. German and Italian troops have retreated to Tunisia where they have been surrounded by British and American forces.

Winston Churchill, with the help of Field Marshal Bernard Montgomery, determined that the Allies would win in North Africa and has crippled the Afrika Korps led by German general Erwin Rommel forcing him to admit defeat. Rommel's deputy has been killed and the African Corps commander, General von Thoms is now one of nine thousand prisoners.

British, American, Australian and New Zealand forces have managed to crush the Germans and Italians causing scores of thousands of casualties for the enemy. PAGE 3.

LOCAL NEWS HEADLINES
WAR HERO WELCOME

Captain Macalister Glizsnort will be welcomed home today at 4 P.M. at the town hall. After conducting research into the adventures of the ace pilot, reporter, Henry Frienly has discovered just how courageous this Blackwater resident and local constable, has been. In a brief interview with the pilot our reporter has also learned that he is humble in the recounting of details and offers much gratitude to the men at his side. Glizsnort also hopes the community will be keen to have him back on the police force as soon as his injuries allow him to return. Let's all welcome Macalister home!

LITTLE ORCHARD SCHOOL HOUSE

Bishop John Biggs has welcomed Miss Grace Durand and her pupils into the Saint Catherine's Church of Redeemus. "It is a delightful turn up of events," said the Bishop. "It is the perfect match: A school during the week and a church on Sunday."

The school has been named by popular vote amongst the children as the 'Little Orchard School House' and Miss Durand hopes that all her students continue to come to class even though she has moved the school from her residence at Marchenby Street.

"It was just too small in that little house," said Miss Durand. "At the church we have pews for seats and plenty of room for blackboards. It's wonderful!" Miss Durand also added that the children have started a plant cultivation class. "We are planning to turn the church grounds into a lovely garden with vegetables available for those who are suffering with rationing," she said yesterday.

Anyone interested in attending classes needs to arrive prior to 9:00 A.M. Monday. We wish the Little Orchard School good luck!

WORLD NEWS HEADLINES
ONLY ONCE 85 YEARS BEFORE

1915—When the English mother of 22 year old Second Lieut. Alexander Buller Turner, received the news he had won the V.C. medal of valor in 1915, she was grateful his death had not been in vain. 1942—But when the same mother was told her second son, Lt. Col. Victor Buller Turner of the Rifle Brigade, had gained the same V.C. award for valor against the same foe 27 years later, she could not contain her astonishment.

Her first son, dead from German bullets in the Battle of Loos, was not as lucky as her second son who, after receiving head wounds after a bitter battle with the Germans, is now recuperating in Middle East Military Hospital and is off the danger list.

Then the mother was told that only once before had two brothers won the Cross and that was 85 years ago!

Blackout time tonight is 6.57pm.

Germany, Berlin—*A radio broadcast to the people of Germany has informed them of a ban on all dancing—including the teaching of dance. Page 8.*

Rotterdam & Hague—*German occupiers confiscate all bicycles.*

Blackwater Theatre—*debuts Tweety Bird in: 'Tale of Two Kitties'. Session Times: Monday to Saturday—12:00, 14:00 & 16:00.*

~Brought to you by~

Yeast-Vite tonic tablets—*bring quick relief from Headaches, Nerves, Lassitude, Depression, Insomnia, Rheumatism, Indigestion and More!*

Milk of Magnesia—*for stomach troubles, indigestion, flatulence, acidity, heartburn, sick headache, and furred tongue—there is no other remedy the world over!*

~Present day~

~Winds of Ghosts and Memories and Tears~

D uette gripped Duel's shoulder tightly. It was all she could do to stop herself from fainting.

"This girl Bruises? Did Shadow take her?" Duette was swallowing back her fear.

"I think so," said Jake speaking as slowly as he could. "There's other voices too. But it's hard to understand them. They all seem to be crying out at the same time. It's like echoes. It's very strange." Closing his eyes, he tried harder to concentrate.

Suddenly Jake's eyes flew open in horror.

"What wrong Jake?" Duette's mind was filled with Jake's terror.

"I-just-remembered-what-the-boy-in-the-static-said-last-night." Jake was shaking his head back and forth, both hands tapping his ears.

"Jake, try to concentrate please." Daffodil spoke gently.

"He-was-warning-us-about-the-Shadow. I-got-it-wrong. The-boy-didn't-say-the-Shadow-could-*cause*-bruises . . ." his voice faded to a whisper, "he-said-the-Shadow-*took*-Bruises.

Duette threw a look at her brother. What were they talking about? Did her bruises have something to do with this Shadow? She couldn't understand them.

"What are you talking about!?" Duel yelled out accusingly.

"Duel, just be waiting for the minute," Santu said. "We are needing to hear what Jake is remembering. Keep going on Jake, you are doing very good."

Jake wasn't listening to any of them. He was concentrating on trying to express what he had heard. Slowly. It was really hard when his brain just wanted to rush it all out.

"The boy in the static said the Shadow was coming to get them and that we must help but he also said we shouldn't go near the graveyard. The Shadow has more power here." He shook his head. There was something else. "And we should never walk around alone in the light. It can see us better."

Wide eyed expressions followed; not one of them free of panic.

"Everyone, get out of here now!" yelled Santu.

There were no questions, debates or challenges. Duel grabbed Duette and everyone began to run for their lives. Not even Jake's damaged feet could stop him from keeping up.

Back in the cabin they all collapsed on the beds. Duette was beyond exhaustion. She curled up in a ball and closed her eyes. Duel sat at the end of her bed. The worry he felt was excruciating but he didn't know what to do. How would he tell his father if something happened to his only daughter? His father could see no wrong in Duette. In his eyes, everything she was and everything she did was perfect. Duel understood: Duette had given them all a way of communicating without the need of spoken words, but still, there was a sense of fallibility on Duel's part. Although sure that his father loved him, Duel did not ever sense the joy that came from his father's interactions with Duette. Duel threw the thoughts from his mind before Duette could take hold of them.

"We need to figure something out," said Duel. "Duette can't go on like this."

Daffodil grabbed her case. "I'll make her some lotion and I've got some really strong amulets she can have. At least it might help for now." Daffodil started pulling out all sorts of bottles and balms and gems.

"Thanks," said Duel unsure of all this hocus pocus stuff. "I guess if it delays the bruises from spreading . . ."

"It will help," said Daffodil as she began mixing St. Jonhswort—a herb used for internal bleeding, healing wounds, banishing evil and fighting battles; Sandlewood—a protective agent which also calmed the mind and Agrimony—an essence used to protect the wearer and reverse evil incantations. Mixing these with the energies of Obsidian, Rutile and Smoky Quartz, she could create a powerful unguent for Duette.

"We're due back for lessons," Blaze said abstractedly.

"I'm not going to lessons!" cried Annabelle a little too aggressively.

"What else are we going to do?" Blaze had collapsed on Daffodil's bed, her wild red hair falling about her.

Santu exhaled. "What can we do with this Madame Glizsnort?" His visions had left him and he felt lost. "I cannot fight her."

"I don't know if she's got anything to do with the Shadow but I don't think we can trust her," said Blaze.

"I don't know," said Daffodil as she blended powders and liquids. "I think she is trying to help these ghosts but I don't know if that means sacrificing *us*." She nodded as she tapped a tiny mixing spoon on the edge of a small marble bowl. "Mixture's ready." She climbed off the bed and moved over to Duette.

"Then," added Santu, "until we are sure what this crazy old lady wants, we will have to go."

"Perhaps we should play dumb? Maybe she will be forced to tell us the truth?" suggested Blaze.

"Well," said Annabelle with a cold stare toward the redhead, "that shouldn't be too hard for *some* of us."

Blaze's face flared. "At least it might take *some* acting talent. And you have to have *emotion* for that."

Santu sighed. Why couldn't girls just punch each other like boys? "Well," he said with his smooth tones, "at least Blaze is *having* an idea."

Blaze's fury softened to a smile. Santu was amazed that she could look all fiery one minute and the next, look like a she couldn't hurt a bee. It was confusing and fascinating. Santu wondered what a stranger might think of those green eyes sprinkled with golden specks like dancing fires. Would they see what she was capable of? Santu hoped Blaze would confide in him about the fire, perhaps unburden herself of the fears that had kept her running away from herself. But he did not see how that was likely, not under these circumstances. Still, her allure was captivating: Wild and wonderful; childish; and afraid. A heady combination.

Envy flew into Annabelle's heart. Why did he always treat Blaze like she was perfect? Annabelle was a hundred times smarter than the stupid Irish girl. There were her excellent grades, her revered musical talent and, of course, her perfect features. What was wrong with the stupid boy? No matter, Annabelle was used to playing emotional games. In her mind she imagined the final win. It would be delicious to watch Blaze cry.

Although Jake hadn't understood what had passed between Annabelle and Blaze, the familiar smack of those particular emotions had pulsed around him. Anger and jealousy had been his mother's companions for a long time but he had never understood where they came from or why. At least these two girls were not aiming it at him. Instead he concentrated on the facts.

"At least I think we're safe in the church." Jake was speaking to his hands. He had discovered that it helped him focus on his speech.

"Why, what do you mean?" asked Daffodil as she gladly centered her attention on the only person in the room who wasn't focused on their own feelings.

"I think that's why the ghosts are staying in there. I don't think the Shadow can get to them while they're in there."

"*Perfect.*" Annabelle's sarcasm was becoming tiresome.

"No, that's good! That makes sense," said Blaze enthusiastically. "Why do you think they're safe in the church?" Blaze decided to fight the tall blond's scorn with sassy eagerness. *Good luck blondie*, she thought.

"The boy said that he shouldn't have left the church. There was something about that girl called Bruises following him out. I think that's why she got taken."

Everyone turned to look at Duette. Daffodil was gently massaging the lotion onto her bruised legs. Duette looked terrible. Perspiration covered her face and her contorted expression revealed how much pain it caused her to have Daffodil touch her skin—Daffodil was apologizing the whole time.

"I don't think Madame Glizsnort is going to fall for us pretending to be stupid," said Duel. "She seems to know us more than we'd like to admit." He was looking at his sister. "And I don't know how long Duette has got."

"Maybe *one* of us," Annabelle was eyeing Blaze, "should try to find a town and get a doctor?"

"Did you *see* a town on the way here?" Blaze's eyes were fire-flecked emeralds.

"Anyway," said Daffodil, "this is not something a doctor could fix." Seeing the look on Duette's face she apologized immediately. "Sorry Duette. Don't worry we'll figure this out. I promise."

"Promises," said Annabelle, "are hard to keep—especially when they're not true." Her cold, blue eyes stared at Daffodil as if she were a fool. But in that moment, Annabelle had let her guard down. For it was a broken promise that had destroyed *her* life and in the fleeting moments that she took to choose her words so carefully, she forgot that there were people in the room that could read minds.

"You have ugly mouth!" Duette's expression was full of hatred. The pain was making her angry and vengeful. "No wonder you mother left you."

Annabelle couldn't keep the shock from her face. "How dare you!" How had she let the frog-girl into her mind? She had been so careful to protect herself.

"Okay, okay you two! Don't be blowing up your cool." Santu had felt Annabelle's vision in the same moment Duette must have read her mind. He was surprised. He didn't think Duette could access Annabelle's protective screen—a moment of weakness on Annabelle's part. So the cool blond was vulnerable. And apparently, Annabelle thought as much of promises as Santu did.

"Some of us are having mothers that are leaving us, some of us are having mothers that *died*," Santu was tripping his gaze from Annabelle to Duel and Duette, "some of us are having mothers that are haunting us," he nodded at Daffodil, "and some of us are having mothers that are still alive and don't give a damn." He blinked cheerlessly in Jake's direction. "And some of us are using this pain as an excuse to be heartless." Santu knew all about those devoid of mercy. He stared in Annabelle's direction. "And some of us are having mothers that are murdered. But we try not to let it turn us into a frozen fish."

Indeed, Santu's mother had been the victim of remorseless cruelty just because she was different. Suspicion of all things unusual was customary when she grew up. Yet the shock of her death had never left him. What they had done to her—a single mother in a town devoted to religious fervor—had been brutal and beyond redemption. At ten years old, Santu was left with a deserter for a father and a mother who was murdered: And all because she carried the gift of vision—the very same gift Santu had inherited. In Santu's mind, it meant that he would never be able to allow a relationship into his life. But *that,* was nobody's business.

"*Cold fish . . .*" said Blaze in a whisper that trailed off. Santu's revelation had come without warning. Nothing in his demeanor gave any clue to such a trauma. Was his confidence just bravado? And why hadn't he mentioned what had happened to *her* own parents? Perhaps had hadn't seen the truth about her at all.

Annabelle's face was burning with rage. So concerned that her spell had been broken, she barely heard Santu's confession. Instead, she glared at the boy with the suntanned skin and shining curls as if it were his fault her mother had abandoned her.

"And *some* of us," Annabelle replied in her composed manner, "just might die for it." Storming into the bathroom, she locked the door.

The room was silent but eyes were making contact in all sorts of meaningful waves.

"I'm so sorry Santu," said Daffodil, her dark brown eyes resting sorrow upon him. "That is truly awful."

Santu didn't want to discuss it. Enough had been said for today. He shook his head and held up a dismissive hand. Daffodil nodded in understanding.

"You don't think she wants to make one of *us* die do you?" asked Blaze, her mischievous eyes dancing.

"Just let her be," said Daffodil. "She just needs someone to trust."

"She be waiting long time," said a gruff Duette who was actually starting to look a bit improved. "Legs better pain," she nodded at Daffodil. "Merci. C'est un soulagement."

"She says it's a relief," Duel said feeling a great deal of relief himself. "Thank you so much Daffodil."

Daffodil shook her head. "That was just a bit of a quick fix. I'll work on something more powerful." It was just a mainstay: Something to tide Duette over for a short while. But Daffodil understood that a bit of hope never hurt anybody. Daffodil nodded and patted Duette's shoulder. "Don't you worry Duette, okay?"

Duette *was* worried. She was worried because she was going to die. She could feel it. That would mean leaving her brother and father all alone. It was her father who had inspired her desperate need to read minds. Her mother had died on the day of their birth. She had suffered severe contractions and copious hemorrhaging. When the ambulance hadn't arrived for over an hour, he had, in a frenzied attempt at saving her life, madly driven her to the hospital, speeding all the way. But he hadn't heard the horns. Or the sirens. The 'jaws of life' would not be so named that day. At the hospital, the doctors had been able to save the babies—but not the mother. He had never forgiven himself.

Both Duette and Duel had been the neonatal unit for several weeks before the final reality of the situation hit their surviving parent. He would have to take home two little babies and no mother: Two little babies he couldn't hear crying; two little babies he couldn't hear laughing.

And so Duette, without even understanding what she was doing, began to use her mind to communicate. Early on she found it easy to exchange thoughts with Duel, for Duel had no barriers. But her father was more difficult. Decades of impediments competed against each other, their walled fortresses not easily brought down.

Duette had no idea how long it took for her father to feel her thoughts, but by the time she was in preschool, he was adept at receiving her attention. It made him feel worthy again and, after a long while, he began to be able to express his love more easily. This made it all the more effortless for him to pick up Duel's thoughts. He began to feel whole in a way he could never have imagined.

But now, thought Duette, *he would have to deal with devastation all over again.* A small tear trickled down her nose. Knowing Duel could feel her pain, she let it go to him: It was too much to fight.

"Oh god, Duette's giving up! But I thought she was feeling better?!" cried Duel. "I'm not going to let her die!"

Santu was back in the present. "What can we do?"

Duel shook his head. "Anything. Everything. *Something.*"

Santu suddenly had a very weird feeling. "What is the time?" It was a rhetorical question. No one had a clue. The only watch they had was a melted mess and the alarm Madame Glizsnort gave them was just that: An alarm without a clock face.

"Is that supposed to be funny?" Annabelle, having decided to come out of the bathroom, looked as unblemished and stonily beautiful as ever.

"No." Santu sounded urgent. "Seriously, what is the time?"

Suddenly everyone noticed how dark it was.

Blaze was stoking the fire. "I don't know. I've already put a couple of logs on and that seems like ages ago now."

"Santu." Daffodil's voice was eerie and confused. "It looks nearly as dark as when we first arrived here. But that doesn't make any sense. That would mean it's about . . . maybe, midnight?"

A cold chill ran through the room.

"Then-lessons-are-over." Jake's voice sounded strange like the words were strangling in his throat. "And-Madame-Glizsnort-didn't-come-for-us."

"And," added Duel in an unswerving voice, "we *need* to save Bruises."

~Present day~

~In Decisions~

"We've-got-to-go-now!" For some reason urgency had replaced uncertainty.

"Go where?" asked Blaze as she looked out into the dark.

In the past, Jake hadn't had too many people listen to him. That wasn't very surprising. But right now he had a dozen eyes on him wondering what he was about to say.

"Santu-understands." He threw a sharp look Santu's way.

Santu nodded. "The church for a start." He hadn't picked it would be Jake but there you go. Even Santu's visions couldn't stop him from misjudging people. Since Santu's nose had been broken, the images had become confused. It was difficult to be sure of what he should be feeling but for some reason he trusted Jake, and for right now, that was enough.

Annabelle was shaking her very beautiful head. "I don't think so!"

"That's okay," said Daffodil, "you stay here with Duette."

Annabelle was not sure how horrified to be. What was worse: Being left alone with a dying girl or being left with a dying girl in the dark?

"That is absolutely . . ."

Santu cut her off. "Thank you Annabelle," he said with the most genuine tone he could muster. "You are truly being worthy of all your accolades." Blatant flattery. It hurt Santu to say it but he was well aware of Annabelle's response to praise. And it was not necessarily untrue—just redundant given Annabelle's attitude. But Santu knew how difficult life had been for Annabelle. He understood that deception had facilitated a life of emotional conflict—so confusing for someone so naturally self-determined. Every syllable of admiration aimed at the broken girl gave her a second of recovery, a moment of smothered self-hatred. Still, he could not concede that it was an excuse to be malicious.

"Then," announced Blaze, "it is to the church we shall go." They steeled themselves.

"Daffodil, I am understanding you have amulets that can protect us?" Santu had been paying attention even when absorbed in other matters.

"Yes, but they repel the boy ghost. Perhaps they're too strong?" Daffodil thought about this for a minute. "Of course! I am such a fool. I'm giving them the wrong information." Daffodil decided to change her focus. Inviting good spirits was more important than repelling bad ones. "Just give me a minute."

While Daffodil fiddled with crystals and gems, Jake became more and more anxious. He tried to calm himself by reciting all the antique coins from the 1800's that he could remember. His favorite was the 1871 French Gold 20 Franc coin which was named the 'Lucky Angel' for the guardian angel it was embossed with. In World War 1 French pilots always flew with a gold angel coin in their kit believing it would protect them from the German Red Baron Ace. In World War 2, Hermann Goering hoarded them, only giving them to those German Aces that made their fifth killing.

"How," said Blaze, "will we find them?"

"Well," replied Santu, "we know Daffodil can see at least one of them and Jake can hear them."

"I-could-only-hear-them-in-the-static," added Jake nervously.

"And in the graveyard." Annabelle was checking her cuticles.

"Jake's not going to stand in the graveyard to listen to ghosts!" Daffodil glared back at Annabelle.

"Wow," Annabelle sighed condescendingly. "Calm down hippy-girl."

Duette shot a fiery thought at Annabelle. But it zapped what little strength she had left. Duette couldn't understand what Annabelle's problem was. After the electrical mind-storm that the twins had hurled at her that day, she was surprised Annabelle hadn't run for her life. Duette herself was stunned by what had happened. At least, Duette thought, give credit where credit is due. This girl had the resilience of a mastermind—or a really dumb cow. Duette was still to decide which.

"Let's just everyone be concentrating on what we are going to do." Santu didn't tolerate any emotional self indulgence. "Let's get us some *positive* ideas. Hit it into the park."

"*Out* of the park," said Blaze abstractedly.

"Out?" asked Santu. "No, no, we don't want our ideas to be going away. *In* the park. *In* the park." Blaze shrugged. Santu had a point.

There was teeth grinding and forehead rubbing, chin tweaking, and a reasonable amount of squinting, but not a lot of ideas. Jake couldn't wait any longer. He didn't know why he had been taken over by this urgency but he couldn't resist its pull any longer.

"Let's-just-see-if-we-can-get-into-the-church-first," said Jake, his rushing words strained with anxiety.

"Blaze nodded. "I think we should wing it too." Now she was starting to talk like Santu.

"Okay!" cried Daffodil finally. "I'm done. Could everyone please take one of these?" She was holding up multiple silk sachets that clanked as she waved them at the group. "I have mixed some gem stones, crystals and herbs that should protect us without repelling the ghost . . . or *ghosts* as the case may be."

Each of the concerned party accepted their small packet from Daffodil.

"Thanks," said Blaze. And then in a whisper: "Do you think I need the others you gave me as well?"

Daffodil smiled. "You're the last one they'll come looking for, I promise."

"So," said Santu, "what do we do with them?"

"You don't *do* anything with them." Daffodil couldn't believe none of these people had any idea about crystals. "Okay, when we are in the church, I want everyone to be very aware of how they feel."

"You-mean-like-sick-or-something?" asked Jake feeling a bit overwhelmed.

"Well, yes, that's an indication of a presence definitely. But I'm thinking more of your senses. For example you may feel a sudden really cold chill."

Annabelle rolled her eyes. "Yeah, a cold chill will be quite a shock."

To Annabelle's surprise, she was completely ignored. It was a simultaneous reaction that came from the unexpected bond that the rest of the group had inadvertently formed.

"Now," continued Daffodil as if Annabelle had not spoken, "we may not be able to see them. I am bringing some concoctions that may help, but be aware of any extraneous emotions. Please, try to keep all this in mind—it's really important."

Annabelle felt suddenly frightened and it had nothing to do with ghosts. She was being left out. *No one* ignored her. Ever. It was almost terrifying to her and it stunned her into silence.

"Alright," said Santu, "are we ready?" Everyone nodded. "Right then, let's get out of here."

Opening the cabin door brought the reminder of just how excruciatingly cold it was outside. The whole idea seemed suddenly outrageous. The frozen earth and subzero temperatures made hesitating an instinctive reaction. Blaze stared into the dark icy night, immobile.

"Come on Blaze." It was Santu. "I am right beside you. We have got to be doing this for Duette."

Blaze held onto her silk sachet of amulets and forced herself to move one step at a time. Who did she need to trust more?

Annabelle was fuming. She flung the door closed, as if to severe a lifeline of impossibility, and moved back over to the fire.

"You know," muttered Duette, "he not like you." It didn't take a mind-reader to be able to see the expression in Santu's eyes when he looked at Blaze. "I wonder why is?" she added sarcastically.

"You better not die while everyone's gone or they'll blame me." Annabelle's face was burning. She turned toward the fire so Duette could not see her tears.

"Well," said Duette with her last ounce of energy, "I certainly try not die. I not want anyone blame *you* for anything."

Annabelle knew Duette knew. Hopefully Duette was too sick to care. If the dying girl had only briefly read her thoughts, it would be the one she was reminded of everyday. Santu had also picked up on the images. Nevertheless, without understanding why, Annabelle knew Santu would never betray her trust. It was more to do with his own mind-set than being a custodian of truth for truth's sake. But Annabelle knew that Duette had no such qualms. And if Duette revealed the facts, there would be no more pretence; Annabelle's life would fall apart.

Annabelle felt the icy pit in her stomach spreading again. It was as if fear was making it grow. The pain was terrible and terrifying but she still was not going to tell. Maybe if Duette died she would think about the consequences of her own dilemma.

Or maybe she would just let it take her too.

Blackwater Herald Moon Tribune
Wednesday, February 3ʳᵈ, 1943—
One penny

CURRENT WAR UPDATE
GERMANS SURRENDER AT STALINGRAD

*O*nly weeks after Hitler declared 'Total War' and ordered Nazi troops to fight to the death at Stalingrad, the Fuehrer has had to face the reality of the situation as Commander Friedrich Paulus surrenders. It appears Hitler's obstinate refusal to give in has lost him an entire army. After being encircled by the Soviet Union's forces, German troops were forced to fight hand to hand combat in the streets in a bitter and exhausting battle that should have ceased sooner. Reports indicate that 91,000 Germans have been taken prisoner by the Russians. Page 4.

LOCAL NEWS HEADLINES
MARRIAGE ANNOUNCMENT

The Blackwater Herald Moon Tribune is pleased to announce the official engagement of Miss Grace Durand to our local war hero and police officer, Constable Macalister Glizsnort of Westbury Way.

Miss Grace Durand of Marchenby Street, is a most admired teacher at the Little Orchard School House and is well known for her unfailing determination to uncover the truth behind the group of missing children now named the Lost Children.

Constable Glizsnort is of high reputation as a hard working police officer who, prior to his war efforts, was awarded the 'Most Helpful Resident' for three *years in a row. He and Miss Durand have tried to discover the truth regarding the Lost Children for several years to no avail.*

This is an auspicious time for the couple as their engagement coincides with the Constable's promotion to Sergeant, effective Wednesday 15th of February. It is well known to all of us in Blackwater that Constable Glizsnort is an awarded war veteran and his return to the police force has been a welcome episode amongst the local turmoil here.

The wedding date is set for May 2nd this year and will be conducted at Saint Catherine's Church of Redeemus which is also where Miss Durand teaches during the week. After their marriage Miss Grace Durand plans to move to Westbury Way.

The ceremony is at 2pm and will be followed by afternoon tea at Pettigrove Atrium. Any interested members of the community wishing to attend the wedding ceremony are invited to the Cross Roads Church site. Please announce your intentions to Bishop John Biggs and sign the register.

MARCHENBY COTTAGE—UNDER THE HAMMER

Now that Miss Durand is getting married, she hopes to pass on her beloved cottage at 132 Marchenby Street, to someone who will love the old house as much as she has.

The property, owned by three generations before her, was left to Miss Grace when her adoptive mother passed away several years ago as there were no other living descendents.

Miss Durand would therefore also like to announce the sale of the property.

"It is an exciting time and also a time of sadness. To say goodbye to this home will be difficult but it will be wonderful to start a whole new life with Constable Glizsnort."

For any inquiries regarding this sale please see our local real estate agent Mr. Peter Potsbury who shares a shop at 133a Main Esplanade.

"The house is an absolute gem!" added Mr. Potsbury. "It will not last long!"

WORLD NEWS HEADLINES

United States, Washington D.C.—*The world's largest building has been completed in Washington. It has been named the Pentagon and has* taken 1,000 workers just to complete the air-conditioning system. *More Page 9*. **United States**—*The sale of pre-sliced bread has been banned due to war demand for metal parts.*

North Atlantic, Newfoundland—*Four United States chaplains have drowned after giving up their life-jackets to save others. Their ship, the Dorchester, carrying 900 others, was torpedoed by the German submarine U-223. The chaplains joined arms, said prayers and sang hymns as they went down with the ship.*

Germany, Munich—*A professor and five students charged with treason for making graffiti and leaflets will all be executed by beheading today.*

~Brought to you by~

BOVRIL—Salutes the women of war and supplies them with a ready source of strength and energy that will help them through!
BEAR BRAND STOCKINGS—Active ankles need them!

~Present day~

~Edge Meets Periphery~

By the time they reached the church, each of them was shivering. Much to Jake's unease, they were huddled together for protection, desperately checking for invisible shadows in the yawning darkness. There was just enough light from the moon to form silhouettes from the tall trees, mystery and fear.

Standing before the large entry door they paused preparing for whatever was next.

Blaze took a deep frosty breath. Wrapping her palm around the frozen brass handle she said a prayer. The handle moved with her wrist. Relief and trepidation flooded her body as she heaved the door open. Everyone crowded around her not sure what to expect. Would Madame Glizsnort be lying in there in a pool of blood? Would the Shadow be hiding ready to leap out at them and steal their souls? Would evil ghosts try to drag them into limbo?

But nothing happened. The angel statue looked down upon them, her frozen arms reaching toward them as if they were in need of redemption; the air still. So they crept past her into the dark of the church. The gas lights along the walls had been extinguished and Santu's pen torch was of little help.

"A glow bug would be of more help than that," whispered Blaze anxiously.

Santu shrugged his shoulders and shook his dark curls. "Well I apologize for not carrying these glow bugs with me."

"Shhhh." It was Daffodil. "There's something upstairs."

A chill ran down everyone's spine.

"Daffodil's-right." Jake was moving over to the staircase that was half hidden by the altar. "Upstairs."

Daffodil stayed close to Jake as they headed the team up the stairs. A groaning creak from the the wooden steps nearly sent Blaze jumping into Santu's arms but Santu managed to prevent her from falling backward and spun her back around into position. She wanted to say sorry and thank you but there were no words in her freezing, numb, terrified body.

Jake arrived at the top of the stairs first. The moonlight was streaming in the long arched windows, stretching dark forms across the floor.

At least there was enough light up here to distinguish shapes.

Daffodil was next. She was almost disappointed when she couldn't see anything except piles of moonlit boxes and old chairs stacked like kindling. Comics and newspapers were strewn across the old oak floorboards like they were waiting for some invisible reader to come to their rescue. What were comic books doing up here anyway?

"There's nothing up here," Daffodil said to those behind her.

A wave of disappointment hit as they all stood at the top of the stairs and peered into the nothingness.

"AAHHHHHHH!" screamed Blaze as something scurried across her feet. Her shriek made others nearly jump out of their skin. They huddled closer.

"What is it?!" cried Daffodil.

"Something ran over my foot!" Blaze was stamping her feet. Why was waiting for disaster to happen so excruciating? Blaze had negotiated flame-driven smoke to save children, she had climbed out on lofty roofs, she had thrashed her way through massive surf, but she had always gone head first to attack the danger; she had never crept slowly toward it waiting for it to attack her first.

"Perhaps it is just a little rat," said Santu as he aimed his small flashlight at Blaze's feet.

"Yuck!" said Blaze stomping her feet again.

"No," said Santu, "no rat." Everyone's eyes had followed the light: No rat, no evil creature; nothing at all.

Raising his torch back toward the interior Santu made an involuntary gasp.

"What are *they*?" asked Duel as he squinted into the light of the torch.

Everyone's eyes had followed the beam of the torch and now they were trying to figure out what they were looking at. All around the end of Santu's pen torch, at least a dozen or so flying bugs hovered. But these weren't ordinary moths or insects—these bugs glowed like the moonlight itself: Transparent and iridescent. They were mesmerizing.

"You are wanting glow bugs?" asked Santu as they all stood transfixed at the sight. "Will these do?"

"They're not glow bu . . ."

A scurrying noise over to their left distracted them.

"Over-there," said Jake.

"Why can we see these . . ." Daffodil didn't know how to end that sentence, "whatever they are, but not the ghosts?" Straining her eyes, she tried desperately to see something other than glowing bugs. "Can you hear anything Jake?"

"I-don't-think-so." Jake sounded disappointed. He had hoped he would hear *something*. He didn't like the idea of having to traipse all the way to the graveyard in the dark. But it seemed that might be the only way. Jake turned to Santu. Santu shook his head.

"Not yet Jake. We give it a bit longer. Yes?" Santu nodded encouragingly at Jake but his apprehension was hard to hide. Daffodil had been right: The temperature in the room had dropped remarkably. But it wasn't just the cold that concerned Santu; it was the sorrow within the frosty air that made him feel sick. Santu was experiencing something strange. Visions had come to him all through his life—they had often been sporadic and vague and, except for recently, they had only ever been initiated by a person's words—but now he was feeling something else and it was making him very uneasy. It was as if he could sense a presence—not quite whole but apparent just the same.

Duel could hear everyone's thoughts: Fear; trepidation; disappointment; curiosity. It was all surging through his mind with desperate energy. Duette had always been able to buffer the information. Why hadn't he paid more attention to her instructions on how to shut thoughts out? There was something else too: The thoughts were coming from beyond the group around him. That was unusual. Typically Duel could only hear the thoughts of those close to him but he knew there were definitely others in this extraordinary and unsettling place.

"We are not the only ones here," said Duel. "I can hear thoughts but they are not making any sense to me. It's as if they are all muddled and confused. I cannot understand."

"Yes," agreed Santu, "I am agreeing that there is something up here too but it is weird, like they are and they are not here."

Blaze shivered. "What if they're not ghosts? What else could they be?"

"Maybe there's something else up here that will give us some clues?" Daffodil was looking around at the sparse room. "What about all these boxes?"

"Over-here," said Jake to Santu. "Shine-your-torch-on-that." Jake was feeling calmer now, even in this crazy situation. He knew his speech was still rushing out of him like Morse code but he could feel something else slowly taking over.

Santu followed Jake and held up the pen light (still encircled by shimmering bugs) over the contents of one of the boxes. Jake started to rifle through the contents.

"Blaze-was-right," said Jake. Everyone listened intently as if something profound was about to be announced. The tension was unbearable. "Glow-bugs-are-better-than-a-pen-torch."

"Jake!" whispered a half horrified half amused Daffodil.

Jake wasn't sure why Daffodil was mad at him. The glow bug things were actually much brighter than the small torch. "There's-just-really-old-newspaper-clippings-in-here." He moved to the next box and Santu followed. "Same-in-here-too."

Just as Blaze was about to suggest they try going back down the stairs again, a sudden blast of noise made them all jump in fright.

"What is that!?" As Blaze cried out if fright, a burst of light radiated from the same area the noise had come from.

"Oh, wow." Jake didn't feel the fear in the same way as the others. He saw problems and solutions. There wasn't a lot of gray area to worry about: what he had gone through had taught him to think of things as good and bad, black and white. And right now all he could see was good. "That's-an-old-Radiola-Super-VIII! Amazing! It's-from-1924." Jake was getting really excited. He seemed to be missing the point that it had just started up all by itself. "It-has-everything-that-counts-in-a-radio! Quality-of tone, distance-reception, selectivity-and-beauty! With-the-remarkable-invention-of-the-Super-Heterodyne-built-into-it! It-was-only-a-year-after-this-little-baby-was-invented-that-the-first-television-transmission-took-place! They-called-it-Radiovision-back-then. Look-at-all-those-dials!"

"Great," said Santu drolly. "He has turned into an infomercial for the antiques." Daffodil drove a hard elbow into Santu's side. "Ow! Geez." Santu turned an undeserving expression toward Daffodil who threw back a look that clearly told him not to make fun of Jake. Santu made a girly face at her and formed a love heart with his forefingers and thumbs. Daffodil glared at him and moved over to Jake's side.

Jake was standing in front of the huge wooden device and was patting its sides as if in congratulation. It was a massive piece of antique craft, as tall as Jake himself, with several dials and a face of timber-framed glass. Staring into the light of its front panel, Jake listened intently to the buzzing noise it was emitting.

"Um," interrupted Blaze, "you did all notice that it turned on by itself?"

"Yes, Blaze," said Santu. "We all notice this." Santu was wondering how they had missed the thing. It was enormous. It was like a radio on steroids: Lots and lots of steroids. "It is half the height of the wall! You saying this is a radio? With stations?"

"And . . . with . . . static." Jake was smiling now, he was in his element. Static was comfort, safety, something he understood. "*This* is how the ghosts made the recordings." He looked confidently over to Daffodil. "I've got static now."

Daffodil could see the change in Jake's face. He looked like a different person; calm, assured. And his speech sounded as normal as any teenage boy. That's when she knew.

Jake was fiddling with the dials trying to find a voice amongst the aggressive hissing that the machine was making. They were all watching him as if he were about to predict the winning lotto numbers. But as they waited and watched they saw Jake's face turn to confusion.

"Maybe-I-need-to-be-asleep?" Jake asked in obvious distress.

"Maybe," said Duel, "we just all need to calm down." Duel was feeling as much anxiety as anyone, and he knew if they didn't all try to relax, they wouldn't be able to help his sister.

"Wait." Jake held up his hand. His eyes were squinting in a desperate effort to capture some thread of decipherable noise. His face was looking hopeful again.

The moon had moved too far across the sky now and the last bit of moonlight was almost gone. Patience was being stretched tight and anxiety and all its forces had taken over.

Just as it seemed time to give up, Jake made a noise of sudden understanding and his eyes lifted up to look at the group. His expression was filled with confusion and concern.

"What's wrong Jake?" asked Daffodil as gently as possible.

"It's-a-baby." Jake looked shocked. "I'm-hearing-a-baby."

No one knew what to say to Jake. They could tell it was disturbing to listen to, but what other choice did they have?

"Jake," said Daffodil, "you don't have to do this. We can find another way."

"No," said Duel, "he has to listen . . . Duette . . ."

Jake looked lost. "It's-just-that-it's-a baby. I-didn't-think-a-baby . . ."

"Jake, turn it off." Daffodil moved over to the huge radio and reached out to turn the knob.

"No . . . wait." Jake was alert again. Shaking his head he started to smile. "It's . . . not . . . upset." Jake started laughing, his face relaxing again. "It's . . . weird. The baby is just talking gobbeldy-gook. It doesn't sound afraid or anything but I can't understand it."

"Do you think it's a ghost from *here*?" Daffodil asked.

"Definitely. It's definitely from here. I don't know how to explain how I know that. It just is."

Everyone accepted Jake's word. There was no reason not to. It was just frustrating: Duel and Santu could feel their presence; Jake could hear a baby; Daffodil had seen the boy's face the night before; there were otherworldly glow bugs still flitting around Santu's pen light; and the radio thing had turned itself on; yet they couldn't see or hear anything of any help.

"Why can't I see the boy ghost?" asked Daffodil. "I could see him last night."

Blaze remembered all the crystals and stones Daffodil had been playing with. "I know you said you shoveled all your stones back into your case so that you could see him but was there anything you may have left out?"

Daffodil shook her head.

Duel thought some more. "Are the amulets you gave us stopping them?"

Daffodil had a lot to take in. It seemed now everyone was expecting her to figure this out. It was a nice change from being belittled and abused at The Institution but it was also an extremely different situation.

"I'm going to have to go back to the cabin and . . ."

A rising noise stopped everyone. A lilting melody was growing around them; the minor chords of a forgotten tune running through their blood like a lost memory.

"Can you hear that?" whispered Blaze staring wide eyed at everyone. Their reactions answered her question.

"What is it?" asked Daffodil.

"Sounds a lot like a church organ to me," said Duel, "but it's coming from far away."

"Maybe a cry for help, yes?" said Santu.

"But the organ is downstairs," said Daffodil.

"You mean a ghost is playing the organ downstairs?" asked Blaze.

"That would be what I mean," said Daffodil.

"Then," said Blaze, "some of us need to go downstairs."

The music suddenly started to slow. The notes were becoming quieter and the mood drifted away like a tide.

Santu checked his torch. The glowing bugs had disappeared. He looked out the window: Light was ebbing at the horizon.

"We're too late," Santu said. "The light is coming in."

"And," said Duel in a dark tone, "the Shadow will be waiting."

Static Recording No. 5243—On Loop

OSCAR. 1903-1917. GHOSTED AGED 14.

Hello my name is Oscar. This is an urgent recording. I am in charge of all the ghosted ones here. I have been making these recordings for a long time but this is the most important one I have done. I have seen you!

You came! You came to see us! We are so excited!

We can see you . . . why can't you see us? Baby is upset. Melody knows you heard her tune but you left us anyway, and Buttons is crying all the time now. She wants her sister, Bruises. It has become torture—now that we know you can save us. But you do not seem to know it. You have to believe! You have to trust. You have to stop being afraid of things that you don't understand.

Please come back. I cannot leave now. Buttons will not let me go outside. She is terrified she will lose me too. And if it weren't for Baby, I think Melody would let go as well.

Dog has taken the place of Bruises. He just sits in a corner and won't talk to anyone. He is even ignoring Scruffy and poor little Scruffy is terribly upset.

Duck has lost his sense of direction. That may not seem important to you but you must trust me, it is awful for Duck. He waddles off towards Scraps to bite his ankles and then does not know where he was going and ends up wobbling around in circles.

I know you saw the bugs. We were watching you. Bugsy was very clever. He sent them to you. Their radiance might make them more nimble and more free . . . but do not be fooled, they are still of divinity and all its weight; they are just less burdened by it. Bugsy told them to go to the light. Of course the bugs thought it was a different kind of light, the light we are all waiting for, but they went anyway. It was funny that they stayed, as if that silly tiny light was going to take them to the afterlife.

When the darkness ebbed and the sun came, they knew Bugsy had lied to them. But they still love him and are hanging around his head like a darn halo. Well, they are bugs.

I do not know why you cannot hear us in our transmitter contrivance. I have been standing right beside it the whole time. It is where we record our dialogues. For some reason we can hear you and we can see you. That has got to be important. Don't you think?

Oh that's right. Melody just reminded me you could hear Baby. Baby doesn't normally do recordings. It's just because his baby voice is on a different transmitting signal and we have to record it differently. It must have been a very old recording still playing on loop that you heard. Melody said that's why she started playing the organ—she was playing notes that were similar to baby's pitch.

But then the light came. Melody tried to keep playing, she tried really hard, but as we have said, the light makes us motionless now. Melody is still stuck sitting at the organ in this way until the darkness comes again. It is cruel because I can tell she is worried about Baby but she cannot go to him. She sacrifices this to help us all.

Wonderboy is telling me he has something important to tell one of you. He won't tell me what it is but he says it will change one of you. Well, he is Wonderboy you know.

We are buoyed with hope now that you have come to our safe place. We are praying and hoping that you will find us, in truth and in light. We are praying we can go home, we are praying as we have done all these years for good to find us. Maybe, in this small church, you will be our saviors. Maybe losing Bruises will not be entirely hopeless. There are eight more to save if you can find a way.

Please, try to find a way!

Blackwater Herald Moon Tribune
Friday, September 10ᵗʰ, 1943—
One penny

WAR UPDATE
ITALY SURRENDERS

*U*tterly defeated in air and sea, Italy has laid down her arms to the United Nations in unconditional surrender. Seven million Italian Soldiers have ceased fighting against the allies and now, the birthplace of fascism will be the first of the Axis pillars to fall. The Allies offered Italy's new military leader, Badoglio, every assistance and expressed the chance for Italy to take vengeance on the German oppressors. Page 4.

LOCAL NEWS HEADLINES
NEW INFORMATION ON LOST CHILDREN

Blackwater journalist, Mr. Henry Frienly has made inroads into the case of the Lost Children. With new information coming to light several actions have been taken.

Amazing articles have been found from The Blackwater Herald Tribune (before it became the Herald Moon Tribune) that are almost 25 years old. They were only discovered when Mrs. Grace Glizsnort was cleaning out her home in Marchenby Street in preparation for sale. We remind readers that Mrs. Glizsnort married Sergeant Glizsnort in May and moved to Westbury Way after their wedding. Although it took Mrs. Glizsnort some time to go through the many boxes before discovering their worth, the papers appear to be well preserved and, although somewhat aged, are in excellent condition. When

163

asked why she thought Miss Germaine Durand (Grace's adoptive mother) would have kept all these articles, Mrs. Glizsnort stated that her mother had never divulged ownership of them but now she wondered if it had something to do with her own adoption and missing brother.

Readers, be aware that we are about to quote from one of these articles and some may find the information controversial and upsetting in nature. If you are of timid heart we ask that you do not read on.

Blackwater Herald Tribune—November 19th, 1919

'The ghostly sightings have disturbed the neighborhood. With over half the population being observers of this anomaly, the questions are less and the regard greater. This is an issue of unforetold horrors. The sightings are very real to those who have encountered them. Many are adamant that the children's faces cry for help and a few witnesses are tainted with suspicion because of the worrisome images. It was clear to one onlooker that a particular child clearly carried the markings of inflicted hatred—her bruises were gruesome to the extreme. Yet still she walked amongst the living, although living she was not. Some community members in the area have reported high pitched screams being heard late at night and yet others have given testimony that these figures have hovered outside their windows with desperate and howling faces.

Bishop Paul Augustus O'Connor says that the only hopeful sign in this whole debacle is that as time goes on the children seem less orientated; less focused in their directive to terrify the occupants of Blackwater. We can only hope that these misguided, passed-on children will find their peace and stop disrupting the community.

Prayers this Sunday will include the judicious words of God and of course there will be prayers for these children, lost and without direction. We commend those that guide them toward Heaven. As usual, the service will be at dawn.'

Due to these articles, the Blackwater Herald Moon Tribune in accordance with the laws of the guardianship of the community, and the word of Bishop Paul Augustus O'Connor, would agree that it is time to put this matter to rest.

Although we cannot locate the bodies of these Lost Children it has been agreed that gravestones should be erected to mourn their passing. The gravestones will remain unmarked until such time (as is hoped by Mrs. Glizsnort) that their names are discovered.

Mrs. Glizsnort has organized a fund raiser to afford these children the memorial they deserve. Bishop John Biggs is fully invested in these proceedings and will be asking for voluntary donations this Sunday. If you would like to donate, the Bishop is offering specially imported Chinese Tea (a gift from

Archbishop Broadley) for coin donations. For all those that choose not to donate, free tea will be available as usual.

"It is the Godly thing to do," agrees the Bishop. "And our community needs to put this matter to rest also. Perhaps these children just need someone to grieve for them. And I and Mrs. Glizsnort will be the first to take this step. We hope and pray that others follow."

We too, at the Blackwater Herald Moon Tribune, hope that this is the end of the matter.

Blackout time: 7:45 P.M.-6:48 A.M. Moon rises 8:43 P.M.

WORLD NEWS HEADLINES

Italy—*Believing he needs Germany's protection from his own people,* **Benito Mussolini** *visits Hitler and allows Germany to take military control of Italy. Not long after, Mussolini's fascist collaborators get* **King Emanuel's** *support and turn against him, arresting the dictator and forming a new government headed by military leader* **Marshal Pietro Badoglio***. On order from* **Hitler***, German paratroopers seize the imprisoned Mussolini from detention in the Abruzzi Mountains before Germans begin an attack at Salerno.*

Tunisia, Africa—*Over 250,000 German and Italian troops are captured and Allies prepare to invade Sicily and Italy.*

Italy, Sicily—*Over 250,000 American and British troops land in Sicily in the largest amphibious invasion in history. Germans and Italians escape to mainland Italy.*

Germany, Hamburg—*Operation Gomorrah: The British bombing of Hamburg causes a firestorm that kills 42,000 German civilians. Soon after 1 million inhabitants flee Hamburg.*

German occupiers forbid flying of kites (6 month jail sentence).

~Brought to you by~

MENTHOLATUM BALM—*Keen journalists have a nose for news but they still need it for breathing and smelling! But not if your nose has catarrh! This balm clears catarrh and colds quickly!*

HOE'S SAUCE—*In the words of a housewife who really knows,* "*It's the best!*"

BLACKWATER PLAZA: The First Technicolor Musical! Bing Crosby and Dorothy Lamour in 'DIXIE'. Sessions 10:00 A.M. & 2:00 P.M. A Paramount Picture.

~Present day~

~The In-between~

The decision to go back to the cabin was led by Daffodil. Knowing how powerful and difficult the potion was that she had to make, she encouraged the others to return with her. The group was already split—with Duette and Annabelle still back at the cabin—and Daffodil wanted to keep everyone together as much as possible. There was no way of knowing if either the cabin or the church was safe but at least if they were together they had a chance to help each other.

Jake had not wanted to leave. He had wanted to listen to the garbled baby talk to see if he could eventually understand it. But thankfully, Santu had agreed and insisted they all return together.

Quickly, they raced away from the eerie light of the church, away from the deathly angel that beckoned them at the entrance, and away from the murky daylight that hid the Shadow.

On arrival, their dire situation was obvious. Duette was looking grave and Annabelle was huddled in a corner seeming lost. Not exactly what the team facing an angry Shadow and desperate ghosts were expecting as a welcoming party. Most of them gravitated toward the heat of the fire but Duel and Daffodil moved over to Duette.

On seeing the way his sister looked, Duel was distraught. "Daffodil, please get her some more of that ointment."

"Of course. Can you check her bruises for me please? I need to know how strong to make it." Daffodil quickly checked her bed for any crystals she may have left out of their case. "You were right Blaze." Daffodil smiled at Blaze as she held up a bag full of crystals. "They didn't get put back in the case. It's so obvious I can't believe I didn't think of it before. These are very special shamanic Quartz Crystals. The shaman's use them to help mediate between worlds. As soon as I make some more of this potion for Duette I will be able to make an elixir that will, hopefully, help us to see the ghosts." Daffodil pulled out her case and spread her wares onto the bed.

"That's amazing," said Blaze, "do you really think it will help us see them?"

"If we are in the correct meditative state—which I think Santu and Duel can help us with, then yes, I do."

"Anything you are needing Daffodil," said Santu, "just let us know. Yes?"

"How is she?" Daffodil asked Duel as she measured and mixed.

"It's worse but the bruises don't seem to have spread as quickly since you put the lotion on her." Duette groaned as Duel inspected her legs.

"That's good. I might make this one a little stronger."

"I don't mean to be selfish here," announced Blaze, "but I'm really starving. Time feels like it's moving quicker than it should. My body is feeling weird. And we should try and get Duette to eat something too."

"Also me," said Santu. "I could eat a pony."

"Argh," said Blaze, "that's disgusting."

Santu shrugged. Irish people must revere ponies.

"But," said Daffodil, "we can't risk going outside in the light. And anyhow, how do we know anyone has put food out? If Madame Glizsnort is gone maybe everyone else is gone too?"

"This is true, but Blaze is right," said Santu. "We are needing to get some food for all of us."

That was it for Annabelle. If she heard Santu praise the redheaded freak again she would lose it. And the fact that everyone had ignored her was completely unacceptable. She raised her head and stared at them as if they were aliens.

"And I'm a ghost too am I?" Annabelle's voice was seething.

"Well that would be explaining why we are not seeing you." Santu's patience with Annabelle was shrinking with every pitiful statement.

"You left us all alone! You left us to go off on your stupid . . ."

"Shut it." Santu was all for interrupting rubbish. "Just shut it Annabelle, I am not listening to this rubbish."

Annabelle was shocked. And the shock made her even angrier. The worst part was that the anger made her talk—and that's always when secrets escaped.

"Well I'm glad you found your little ghosts because they've been screaming for help for way too long!"

Blaze rolled her eyes—she knew she was going to go hungry now that Annabelle's little attention-seeking revelation had occurred. Annabelle was going to drive everyone away from their goal—and she was probably going to make it all up anyway.

Duel was enraged. "What do you know Annabelle!?" Her thoughts had been closed to him and now he was feeling infuriated by his incompetency. "I swear if you know something and you don't tell us I will damage you—I will damage your stupid little brain in a million ways."

Annabelle's alarm was veiled. "Well maybe if I had a 'little brain' you might be able to do that." She was smiling politely. "But you forgot my brain is quite the enigma." A cold, hard stare followed. "Can't we read my thoughts? Awwww. Can't do it without your dying sister's help?"

Santu had had enough. "Your brain is not being an enigma, Annabelle. Playing music, getting the good scores, these are not things making you interesting! I know. I know about you. Do you want me to be telling all these people—these people that we *all* have to trust? Are you wanting me to tell them!?"

"No Santu," Annabelle felt the bile rising in her gullet. "No I don't want you to think you are responsible for telling the world what has happened to me in my life. No."

"Then, I am suggesting," replied Santu, "that you are trying to keep yourself in check." Santu had to give her some credit: Annabelle was one hell of a girl to keep down.

"Honestly," said Duel, "I do not care what happened to this horrible girl." Duel was frustrated beyond belief. "But DO YOU THINK YOU COULD CONCENTRATE ON MY SISTER!"

Everyone cringed. Even Blaze's hunger pains were momentarily quashed.

Earlier, as they had run back to the cabin, Daffodil had had an epiphany, but she had waited until she had been able to assess her collection before making any promises.

"Duel there's a special mixture I could make that may help Duette."
Daffodil sounded hesitant.

"But?" Duel could tell there was a catch.

"Because you and Duette share thoughts, you could take some of the
burden from her." Daffodil's mouth was twisted in uncertainty.

"Just tell me Daffodil. Please."

"It's very powerful and it can only be used by people with natural
strength. It could be very dangerous if used without respect." Daffodil
paused. "Do you understand what I'm saying?" Daffodil looked at
Duel. It was a moment of uncalculated symmetry: He understood; she
understood.

"Do it." Duel was gritting his teeth. "Please, just do it."

If Annabelle knew anything, she wasn't offering it. She sat in the corner
and scowled. Except for Santu, no one believed there was any truth to her
claims. If she had known something, why wouldn't she just spit it out? But
Santu knew what was happening to Annabelle. And he knew, if she didn't
confess her truths soon, she would be overtaken by that icy cold growth
inside her, and then *she* would be in the same situation as Duette. The only
difference would be that the group's level of concern for Annabelle would
be as cool as the air outside—and that would be Annabelle's demise. Being
hateful didn't get you liked *or* saved.

Daffodil handed Duel more of the lotion for Duette's legs and began
working on the tonic that Duel would need if he wanted to help his sister.
Using this type of concoction was a huge risk. If Duel wasn't strong enough,
it could potentially make Duel as sick as his sister. And he didn't seem to be
as resolute as Duette which was also worrisome. But Daffodil knew, if she
had a brother or sister, she would willingly take on whatever she could to
try to save them too. Everything in life was guess work and sometimes you
just had to take a leap of faith. That gave Daffodil another idea.

As she worked on the tonic, everyone else discussed the strange music
they had heard in the church, the huge radio that had turned itself on,
and the garbled baby voice that Jake had heard. It was all extremely
overwhelming.

Then someone thought to ask about Madame Glizsnort.

"Where is the old hag? Do you think she got taken by the Shadow?"
Blaze was rifling through her bag hoping to find some kind of snack.

"How will we get out of here if we don't find her?" asked Duel as he
gently rubbed Duette's ointment on her bruises.

"Actually," said Jake who had been wondering about all these questions too, "I'm not exactly sure that we are on the map if you know what I mean?" He seemed like he was in a trance: His eyes were gazing at nothing and his speech was slow and monotone.

"What do you mean 'on the map'?" asked Blaze who, after finding no food, now sat poking at the fire and staring at the twisting flames.

"I am agreeing," said Santu. "Are you thinking *time* or *place*?" Apparently Jake and Santu were having their own discussion. The others listened trying to comprehend what they were saying.

"Both," replied Jake. "I think we're in some kind of limbo." Jake was really just thinking out loud—something he had never done before: It was strange to let his thoughts out before reciting them in his head.

"Yes," agreed Santu, "I don't know how it is possible, but I am thinking we are somehow in-between."

"Uh huh, but I think this is or *was* a real place. It could be somewhere in real time but it's not *our* time if you know what I mean?" Jake suddenly understood what it was to talk freely. It was like a switch had been turned on—or off, he wasn't sure. But for the first time in his life he felt like speech could free him rather than restrain him. With no one to judge him or threaten him, he began to feel like words had become a facilitator rather than an impediment. It felt liberating and, well, really good.

"Yes, I am understanding exactly. It is like we have entered a time-free zone. Like time is moving forward, yes, but also, we are perhaps stuck between the past and present." Santu was nodding as if the information was dropping into his head with each dip.

"It's strange though," said Jake as he stared into space. "Time doesn't seem to be passing in the same intervals." Jake shook his head. There was no rational way to explain what he was feeling.

"I am in agreement," said Santu. "It is very odd." He shrugged his shoulders. "There is no scientific explanation. We are, say, sailing between the waves. You know?"

Blaze did not like what she was hearing. "Are you saying we do not exist in our own time anymore?" She stabbed the flames a little too vigorously and they roared back at her as if they had been hurt. "How is that possible?"

"It's not so much that it's possible rather that it is *not impossible*." Jake said.

"Um," replied Blaze, "could Confucius please explain—in normal English?"

"We are not trying to be confusing you," said Santu offended.

Blaze sighed. "No, I didn't say you're confusing us, I said 'Confucius'." Blaze shook her mane of red hair. "But yes, you *are* confusing *me*."

Jake smiled. Blaze and Santu were funny together. "I think," Jake said slowly, "that we have been brought back to a mid-time to connect with the ghosts—*and* Madame Glizsnort."

"What?" asked Blaze. "Now you're saying Madame Glizsnort is a ghost too?" And with those words Blaze suddenly realized that impossibility was purely an afterthought for those who were prepared for anything. "Oh my god. She's a ghost isn't she?"

Daffodil was still mixing. "But why can we see her and not the others?"

"Could she be in a different time too?" said Blaze trying to put the puzzle pieces together in her mind.

"I do not think that is it," replied Santu. "But she is definitely tied to the other ghosts somehow."

"She's a mean old angel—if that's what she is." Blaze was imagining all those strange religious beliefs suddenly being true. "Maybe she's trying to get them to heaven?"

"Well she's not doing a very good job of it," grunted Annabelle.

Daffodil tapped the final measurement of liquid into Duel's potion. "Maybe she can't see them either? Maybe she needs people that are alive to help her."

"Or," Jake added, "maybe *they* can't see *her*."

Static Recording No.575—On Loop

Dog. 1906–1918. Ghosted Aged 12.

Hi, my name is Dog. I have decided to do a recording of everything I can remember about the other ghosted ones; you know, put it all together. Everyone is losing their memories quickly now and I wonder how long we have here. I have always been so angry about everything but today I feel that even being angry is too much effort.

I guess Oscar is our captain—not that *I* need someone in charge of me, but the others do. I don't really care what happens to me now. I have been here too long and all I want is to stop existing. That may happen yet, who knows?

At the moment Oscar is playing Whispers with Bitsy. We had a bit of a fight and he's ignoring me. That's alright. I don't feel like talking to him anyway. He was mad at me for being grumpy with Bitsy but she was so annoying. I guess I shouldn't have told her to get lost—I mean, seeing that she already is. Anyway, Oscar will get over it and when he's not looking I'll say something nice to Bitsy. She's a good kid really, she just talks a lot, you know? Girls.

So I guess I'll start with her. Bitsy lost her mommy at a train station but at least her doll came with her when she ghosted. I guess dolls ghost too?

And Oscar, well he does love to talk about cars. When he does recordings he always talks about the war. He fought with soldiers and everything—he was just a kid when he went to the frontlines. It must have

172

been terrible. Some of the stories I've heard him record are darn awful. I generally try not to listen.

Who else? Well there's Scraps, he's French and he died because he ate a green potato. Crazy huh? He ate rats and other stuff but he died from a potato. The world is stupid. Life is stupid.

Um, then there's Melody and Baby. Melody plays the organ here. She says she used to have a really big piano but after the war started, it got taken away. When she was alive she got polio and now that she's ghosted she still has calipers. I've tried to get her to take them off but she says she can't. Baby was found in a field and now Melody takes him with her everywhere. I think it keeps her from wanting to disappear like me.

Buttons and Bruises are twins but they are really different. Buttons is happy and Bruises is sad: Sunrise, sunset. Bruises used to be funny but she lives in her own little world now and it makes Buttons confused.

Then there's Bugsy. He's a good kid. Loves bugs. The darn things float around his head like a hat. We have earwig races and Bugsy's earwig always wins. It's pretty funny.

And of course, Wonderboy. There are lots of comic books up here and he has spent all this time trying to figure out how to flip the pages. Bitsy does it for him—he still can't do it. He doesn't remember much except something about a redheaded girl.

Then there's me, Dog. My story is long and I don't want to tell it anyway. All you need to know is what I've told you because you need to save them. I don't care what happens to me. There's nowhere for me to go anyway.

I don't know what's going to happen to them. I don't think anyone is listening to these recordings. Are you? Are you listening? God damn it . . . .

Just help them! It's like watching your family slowly die. Oh, you don't think I know what that's like?! What would you know anyway?! You're just sitting there and not doing anything. I hate you. I hate everything—alive, dead, ghosted; everything—you included.

I hope you die and get stuck in oblivion forever. Go to hell.

~Present day~

~In the Slide~

Everyone had agreed that a few hours of sleep whilst there was still light was probably for the best. Blaze had found plenty of snack bars after riffling through Annabelle's pack and had given them out to everyone. For some reason, Annabelle had packed enough protein bars and snacks to feed a family for weeks. A fleeting thought ran through Blaze's mind: Could Annabelle have been planning to run away? Blaze decided she didn't care. Quickly she ripped off the wrapper of a strawberry meal-replacement bar and bit into it.

Annabelle watched Blaze raid her luggage. It didn't matter. Annabelle figured if the growing cold inside her body continued to accelerate she wouldn't need any of that stuff anyway. Instead, Annabelle concentrated on the potion Daffodil was making for Duel. Perhaps as a last resort she could ask Daffodil to help *her*. Of course, there would have to be niceties exchanged first—a bartering of the soul, if you will. And so, Annabelle, in her most manipulative dogma, decided to be nice to Daffodil.

Daffodil was using her awakening crystals. There was lots of work to do and to be able to do it in peace and quiet, while everyone slept, was perfect. It would be impossible for her body to keep using them, in fact, it could be extremely dangerous, but for right now it was imperative. Sleep would come later.

By the time she was ready to wake everyone, both Duel's potion and the elixir to help them see the ghosts, were prepared. But before Duel could consume his liquid, Daffodil needed his help to put everyone in a meditative state so that they could fully absorb their ghost-busters tonic.

Daffodil had gone over the method in her head many times before committing to it. She wanted it to be exact. Normally she would have called on her parents, but of course, they were gone now. She reached into her pocket to feel the remains of the broken watch. At least she still had part of it to cherish.

It was dangerous to be mixing such strong potions. They were made for experienced shamans, not teenagers lost in the icy forest of no-time. But there weren't a lot of suggestions being buffeted around. And time was running out. It felt like the threads of her soul were slowly untangling. If they didn't hurry up and do *something* they may all end up like Bruises. That was not on Daffodil's agenda. Through all the awful times, through all the impossibly painful moments, Daffodil had refused to give up. She had always prided herself on self-worth and she wasn't going to stop now. There were too many people counting on her.

"Wake up everyone," Daffodil cried out. "Come on, things to do, places to be!"

As everyone forced themselves from the world of dreams and nightmares Daffodil prepared her speech.

"Duel, you will need to help us as a group before we all take our elixir. Then you will be able to take your potion to help you fight for Duette."

"Of course." Duel was ready for whatever Daffodil had in mind.

"Right, then do I have everyone's attention because you need to understand both *what* we are going to do and *how* we are going to do it."

Annabelle gave an enthusiastic nod: She had begun her plan.

"Okay. Please, if I'm not making sense, let me know. I can't tell you how important it is that everyone understands."

Annabelle forced herself not to roll her eyes—as if the hippy girl could say something that *she* wouldn't understand.

"Go ahead, Daffodil," Annabelle's saccharin voice rang out, "we're listening." Curious looks turned toward Annabelle. That's when suspicions began to grow. They were just icicles now but they would grow into stalactites before Annabelle would have a chance at implementing her 'sincerity'.

"Okay." Daffodil ignored Annabelle's fake smile. "This elixir is bound by spirit. By that I mean it is an ancient and rarely utilized mixture, usually only made by the most powerful shamans to mediate between two worlds. This blend uses some very ancient quartz crystal I have sourced from India. It is known as a 'living stone'. Shamans believe that the material and spiritual nature of it is united. They believe it is of insight and vision: Solidified light. It works in a threefold manner. First, we each depress a quartz into our forehead, just enough to make an impression in the skin—it is said one gains the ability to see through the essence of things. It will give us power. Second, we rub a mixture of crushed quartz on our bodies, the more, the better. Third, we imbibe a liquefied quartz drink. It will give us the ability to see ghosts." Daffodil waited for any questions. There were none.

"The quartz crystal is like a guardian to the spirit helper. It is said that after death the shaman is merged with the quartz: It forms his light, his sun. It is also unique in that the shaman's soul can come back to earth from Heaven in the form of the very same crystal, and so, the cycle of life and death, the rotation of sun and moon, the journey from earth and beyond, is capitulated." There were several nods.

"Good," said Daffodil feeling like she was explaining herself well. "Now everyone has to wear these." Holding up a handful of blue Celestite pendants she went on: "Celestite has been referred to as the 'Stone of Heaven' because it can be used to channel Angelic Wisdom, which just means it is used to contact the angelic realm. Wearing it around the throat will allow the amplification of our meditative state and give us heightened intuition." Daffodil took a deep breath. "Lastly, I want everyone to take one of these bags. Just put them in your pocket. There is a mix of gems and crystals. I've made a different one for each of you, to hopefully, suit your needs. Please don't lose them or get them mixed up with anyone else's. It's important."

For some reason Jake wanted to clap. So he did. It made everyone want to join in. And so for a brief moment Daffodil's felt the warmth of congratulations: Congratulations for a feat not yet accomplished.

"Thank you, I think." Daffodil was trying to keep the worry from her expression. "I'm all for optimism but I've never done this before. As far as I know it's all just hearsay."

"I am liking hearsay," said Santu nodding, his black curls swinging.

"Me too," said Blaze. "Let's just try to do this . . . *together*." She was looking at Annabelle whose face was stony. All that sweetness must have sucked her dry, Blaze thought.

"Okay," said Daffodil trying not to hesitate. "Duel you need to push away everyone's thoughts and feelings. You need to access all our tired, meaningless, meaningful fears, our questions and distrust. You should be able to use Santu to help you with that. We must be all on the same vibe. We must all be calm but rational, we must all feel safe but aware of fluctuations, and we must have faith that we can do this." Daffodil paused. She wanted everyone to take in her words because there were more issues to come.

"The quartz crystal is important in so many other ways as you obviously know from science. A large crystal can release hundreds of thousands of volts." Daffodil looked directly at Jake as the recognition took hold. "Quartz is the major component of radio transmitters and receivers."

Jake knew that, Santu knew that, and so did Duel and Annabelle and even Blaze. But the information was somehow incredible considering its context. Confidence in their challenge was growing by the minute.

Duel had a brainstorm. "I am sure we all agree that the church is the safest place to be. So I want everyone to gain confidence from that. We must remain positive." Everyone nodded.

"Unfortunately it's also the coldest." Blaze was still hovering close to the fire, poking and prodding it as if it were a sleeping child needing to be awakened.

"Well," said Daffodil, "believe it or not, cold is just a state of mind."

"If that's true, then how come my state of mind is focused on freezing?" Blaze was all-for this 'shamanic' view on things but the fact was: Cold was cold.

Daffodil eyed Duel. She raised her eyebrows as a 'get started' signal.

Santu wanted to help but in truth he didn't have a clue about how to help Duel. He had only just started to sense peripherals in the church that day. With no idea of what to do, Santu just stared at Duel with wide brown eyes.

But Duel had already taken over. Gently, he was pushing Santu into a wave of calm. To Santu, it felt like the seas of reason: Pushing out was the emotion of fear and apprehension and being drawn in was positivity and understanding. Realizing that Duel was somehow using his visions, Santu gave him full access. It allowed Duel to encompass and protect the emotions that created each of their negativities. Now Santu understood. Daffodil had chosen a wise partnership: Together they could do this.

When Santu and Duel had done their job and Daffodil could tell everyone was ready she took the largest and strongest hexagonal prism of quartz, the crushed crystal and the tonic of quartz liquid.

First, she impressed the crystal into each of their foreheads. Then she rubbed their skin with the glittering particles. Then, after giving them each a vial of liquid to imbibe, she tied the pendants around each of their necks and gave them their customized sachets. Everyone felt relaxed yet purposeful.

"Okay, Duel," Daffodil said gently. "Now it's your turn. You need to take the potion that will help your sister." Daffodil stopped herself from saying 'hopefully'. She eyed Duette who was still looking pale and distressed. Daffodil thought how unfair all this was for her new friend. This strange situation had given Duette the chance to finally discover the joy of conversation, but the very same circumstances had now rendered her mute. Daffodil could tell the pain Duette was experiencing was awful and she hoped desperately that Duel could help.

Duel accepted the potion. "Thank you," he said earnestly.

"Duel," Daffodil continued, "I think we need to take Duette to the church with us. I know it will hurt her to be moved but we all need to stay close to each other. Santu should carry her. You will need all your strength to concentrate. This potion should work pretty quickly."

Duel hesitated. "Alright," he said throwing a nod at Santu. If he was going to help Duette he was going to have to trust others. Santu's face was filled with assurance.

"Everyone will need to take their blankets and whatever else you need to keep warm." Daffodil had left the last statement until everyone was calm. "Because we're going to be staying in the church."

Everyone knew this was the safest and smartest option but, even in their newfound composure, it did feel a bit like they were creating their own trap. The unusual part of this was that they could all sense each other's reactions. It was like their minds were all floating in the same emotional atmosphere, as if one grand intuitive path had blended all seven of them together: They felt equalized. It would help them function emotionally as a whole: The same mind-plane attuned to the same vibration.

Blaze was taking a last longing look at the fire. "I'll pack the snacks."

"Everyone ready?" Santu asked. Small quick nods followed. "Alright then, let's go." Carefully, Santu picked up Duette and they moved toward the door.

Outside in the falling darkness, wrapped in blankets and covered in quartz dust, the group moved swiftly toward the old church.

They looked rather like the creatures they were seeking.

Arriving at the church this time, they found the door wide open: An invitation or a trap? Unfortunately, the only way was forward.

Blaze was first, the beam from Santu's pen torch giving her a narrow tunnel of vision. Putting all thoughts of rats out of her mind, she tiptoed past the grieving angel and made her way into the murky darkness. In her mind, she believed she could protect them if something bad were to come at her. It would give the others time to get away. In their spherical state it was natural to let each person's emotional strength come forth. Following her was Jake and Daffodil, and then came Annabelle and Duel, and lastly, Santu carrying Duette.

Blaze checked the area. "There's nothing down here."

"Let's move upstairs and find somewhere for Duette," said Duel. The potion was starting to take effect. His body felt tired, pain was seeping into his legs like icy dripping water, and his heart felt like it was going numb. The sensation was daunting and Duel realized it was going to take every ounce of energy to keep them both alive.

"Let me take Duette." Duel reached over to Santu. "I'm going to need to be close to her." Santu sensed Duel's discomfort but his flutter of concern was equalized by the rest of the group. Santu knew that the brother and sister would need to find a place inside the depths of their minds to fight whatever was happening. Santu did not envy Duel one bit. He knew those kinds of journeys rarely led to joy.

"Good luck," Santu said to Duel as he gently handed over Duette. "Stay strong. If I can be helping . . ."

"Thanks," replied Duel but both of them knew that was impossible.

Santu nodded and followed the others up the stairs. Duel summoned all his mental strength and followed.

Blaze passed the pen torch to Santu who pushed ahead to the front of the group.

"Let us see if we can be attracting some more of these glow bugs we like so much."

As everyone rounded the top of the stairs, a dozen or more glowing ghosted bugs flickered into vision and hung like Christmas lights around the end of the torch. For a few brief moments, everyone's attention was drawn to the winged luminous creatures, but a gasp from Daffodil reminded everyone that they were here for a greater purpose. As they each looked up they were faced with a vision that was truly haunting.

Blackwater Herald Moon Tribune Tuesday, December 7ᵗʰ, 1943— One Penny

WAR UPDATE
MEETINGS OF LIKE MINDS

*C**hurchill, Roosevelt* and *Stalin* declare they have agreed on plans and timing for the destruction of the Nazis. This comes after a purposeful meeting with Generalissimo **Chiang Kai-Shek** where aggressive plans for the defeat of Japan have been decided. PAGE 2.

LOCAL NEWS HEADLINES
MARRIAGE AT THE OLD CHURCH

On Sunday afternoon at 4 o'clock, before more than 30 guests, Miss Eunis Butterly of Pilturn Drive, daughter of Mr. and Mrs. Morris Butterly, became the bride of Mr. Henry Frienly, of Tunstill Road. The ceremony was held in Saint Catherine's Church of Redeemus, and was performed by Bishop John Biggs who has known both bride and groom since their births.

Mr. Frienly, of course, is the well known correspondent of the Herald Moon Tribune and is the son of the late James Morris Frienly, noted attorney at law of Blackwater.

Following a honey moon in Scotland, they will return to make 'Strawberry Cottage' in Berry Lane their home.

We wish them well and look forward to the very fine articles that Mr. Frienly contributes to our dedicated newspaper.

LOCAL LAD DECLARED MISSING-IN-ACTION

One of Blackwater's most jovial lads has fallen victim to this terrible Second Great War. First-Lieutenant Bert Haffey of Tumblestone Grove has officially gone missing from the U.S. raid on Munster. He had conducted several raids including the Regensburg attack earlier this year, and his Fortress was the only one which successfully followed its group leader all the way to Africa. Bert is the son of 'Bertie's Butchery' owner, Robert Haffey. Lieutenant Bert Haffey was a popular bus driver in town before going to war and is just 20 years old.
Blackout Time: 6:24 P.M.-7:01 A.M.

~Brought to you by~

HEINZ—*Basic English for Basic Foods! English will be the International language of tomorrow and we have beat them to it! Beans, Soups, Mayonnaise.*
VIM—*Get at that grease! Works in cold water to remove grease!*
IMPERIAL TYPEWRITTERS—*For better letters.*

~Present day~

~Put on Your Ghost Faces~

Several ghostly images were floating right in front of them. The luminous bodies shone as if a moon hung inside each of them: Opalescent figures that appeared to be more like reflections than anything solid. And, although glowing like the incandescent bugs still hovering around Santu's torch, their faces were drawn, their large eyes filled with sorrow. The smoky haze that stirred around them looked like warm breath hitting icy air.

Disbelief careened back and forth across the room and then, with only a curious second following, the radiant creatures abruptly vanished. Before anyone could register what was happening, they immediately reappeared in rearranged places. Then, once more, they flickered into nothingness—their bizarre actions being repeated again and again. Each time, the shimmering reflections moved closer and closer: A cautious study of the interlopers.

Each human blink saw a new and unearthly face peering straight into their eyes. The closer they came, the more astounding the apparitions appeared—the misty circle of light surrounding each of them, a refracted glow that seemed to expose their very souls.

Wide eyes met wider ones, but none of the group moved as the images flashed and flitted around the room with a speed and agility that was beyond imagination. It was impossible to tell how many of them there were. They spirited and shifted in strange static like movements, continually appearing, disappearing and reappearing all over the room.

There was something distinctly unsettling about watching these vaporous images flick in and out of sight and there was no mistaking the melancholic air that hung heavy around them.

Duel could tell he was draining the energy of the group. Slowly, he moved backward into in a darkened corner near the top of the stairs, and, laying his sister down, tried to concentrate on Duette.

At last, feeling as if she were being pulled toward one of the spirits, Daffodil moved forward. The others stood and watched, silently transfixed.

The ghostly form stopped still, hovering just above the floor, it's moonstone-translucency smoldering in the dark. The creature wore a long white dress but Daffodil could see there was something attached to the bottom of her legs. The girl seemed just as fascinated by Daffodil as she was by it. As Daffodil moved forward, she noticed the figure drawing a heavy bundle in close to her. Daffodil slowly turned back to the others.

"I think she's holding a baby?"

"The baby I heard?" whispered Jake as if loud noise would frighten the figures away.

"It must be." Daffodil turned back to face her floating companion. "Hello, can you hear me?" The figure laughed and flickered in and out several times, but when it moved its mouth, no sound came out. Daffodil shook her head at the small excited ghost and turned back to the group not knowing what to do next.

Suddenly another little girl suddenly appeared in front of Jake's face. The shock made him jump backward. This made the little girl laugh. As Jake composed himself she nodded at him and then disappeared again.

Figures of all sizes were still darting around the place.

"Is that a duck?" asked an incredulous Blaze. "And that's a dog."

Annabelle knew it was a dog. It was the same dog she had seen on their first day of lessons. But Annabelle was trying to stay quietly resolute. Could these ghosts divulge her truths? Again she was reminded of the vision Madame Glizsnort's icy stare had given her before she fainted: That dark abyss gaping below her; symbols circling her falling body . . . Quietly she tiptoed backwards toward the staircase.

Suddenly the Radiola burst into light. Loud static hissed from it accusingly. The same little girl appeared and beckoned to Jake but Jake was immobile.

"Go Jake, just try," Daffodil said over the horrible noise the radio was making.

Hesitantly, Jake walked toward the huge transmitter as the dials twisted and turned all by themselves. It was as if they were searching, crossing each hissing wave like a boat until finding something solid to anchor to. As Jake got closer to the device, the harsh crackling gradually smoothed.

"It's the quartz," cheered Daffodil, "the quartz is refining the search to correspond with us!"

And, as Jake stood in front of the oversized radio, the hissing eased and a cool, long wave of sound hummed around him.

"It's me, Bitsy! Can you hear me now?" The little girl's voice vibrated from the depths of the wave and sang out toward them. Her short, flouncy, white dress shivered and streams of hazy mist exhaled from her periphery.

Everyone stood still in shock.

And with all those stunned looks, the ghosts realized that for the first time in decades, their voices were finally being heard. Flickering images of ghosts and ghosted pets soared around the room. For a glorious moment in this awful place there was hope.

"Hello Bitsy," said Jake leaning toward the radiola. "I'm Jake and it's very nice to talk to you. Can you hear me?" Jake felt none of the anxiety that had always made it difficult for him to talk. In fact, he felt right at home.

The look on Bitsy's face was enough to bring tears to Daffodil's eyes. The little girl was so excited and surprised that it looked like she was hearing a human voice for the very first time.

"It's my sound box. I fixed it to make it work." Bitsy was looking both proud and delighted. "We've been recording into it for such a long time but you're the first voice I've heard come out of it."

Jake laughed at her excitement. "Well I think you are very clever Bitsy," he said looking over at Daffodil for a clue as to where to take this.

Daffodil just shrugged her shoulders. Who could answer that? "Introduce all of us to them."

Jake nodded. "Well Bitsy, and everyone else, our names are:" Jake pointed around the room as he introduced everyone, "Daffodil, Santu, Blaze, Annabelle, and back there, is Duel and Duette. They're not feeling well at the moment but you can talk to us."

"Oscar!" yelled Bitsy into the device. "Come here!" Bitsy disappeared and another boy appeared beside the machine.

"I am Oscar!" he announced. "I can't believe you finally came!" Oscar was looking around the room as if he were at the circus. "Thank you for coming, thank you for coming to help us. We are running out of time." Daffodil knew immediately that this was the same ghost she had seen at the cabin window. The boy's face was ashen and he wore the same glowing military uniform, hat and all.

"Why do you need help?" asked Jake speaking into the yellow light of the old radio.

"We are stuck here. We have been for a very long time. We don't seem to be able to find home. We don't even remember how to get there. Or who we are. We have to remember so that we can go home. And the Shadow is coming for us. Just like it came for Bruises. It is getting stronger all the time and we are getting weaker. We lose more and more of our memories the longer we are here. I don't know what happens when the Shadow takes you but I know it's bad. When it gets near you it feels like your soul is being pulled into darkness." Oscar wouldn't normally have said this loud enough for those he protected to hear, but it was beyond important that the danger they all faced was clear. "Each time it takes one of us we can feel our time here getting shorter. It's as if we are stepping closer and closer to a cliff edge. We have become desperate." Oscar's ghostly aura was fading, as if he were being drained of his ability to be. Decade upon decade of calling for help in this state of limbo had taken its toll. "There were others that came," his voice was almost a dull whisper now. "But they couldn't see or hear us," he shook his head. "They ran away in fear." He looked ashamed. "Once, a long time ago, it got one of them and we haven't seen anyone since."

Jake swung a look of shock toward Daffodil who reflected the same look toward Santu. Was it the Shadow the boy was talking about or something else? Whatever it was, it had already taken a human and no doubt, it would be coming for them too. But how were *they* supposed to help lost ghosts: Ghosts that had lost most of their memories; ghosts that didn't even know how long they had been in limbo? Where were they supposed to start?

Jake heaved a sigh. He looked over at Daffodil and motioned for her to come over to the radiola to help him. Daffodil threw a querying glance at Santu who nodded encouragingly.

Santu was thankful to have Daffodil here. She had proved to be powerful in their dynamic. She also had a lovely calming voice. Santu feared his voice may give away just how worried he was. Immediately, he had felt the distress from the ghosts. It felt like hundreds of layers: Frustration, anxiety and deep dark pain all crushed together. The experience was making it difficult for Santu to breathe but he tried to temper the nauseating feeling with positivity. If he allowed all this tension to spread amongst his collaborators, they could all sink into defeat.

Daffodil took a deep breath. A million questions were fighting to be asked first. Leaning toward the radiola, she spoke softly. "Perhaps you could just tell us whatever you do remember?" She looked at Oscar's ashen image. "Perhaps everyone could take turns?"

Oscar seemed pleased with this idea. He nodded to Bitsy who seemed terribly excited: Bitsy was about to tell her story to a real person, a person that could hear her *and* talk back. She was beside herself.

"I'm Bitsy," she said breathlessly. "I'm eight. I like to collect things." She was thinking hard. Oscar leant over and whispered in her ear. "Oh," Bitsy looked momentarily confused, "but I don't know if I remember much about that." Oscar whispered something else to her. "Oh, well, um, I remember the war?" she said looking hopefully back at Oscar. He nodded encouragingly. That seemed to help.

Oscar smiled at the new listeners trying to convey Bitsy's stage fright. Daffodil remembered how Jake had clapped when she was clarifying their plan. It had felt good. So Daffodil started to clap. The others followed. Bitsy's eyes lit up.

"Go on," said Daffodil, "you're doing a wonderful job."

And suddenly Bitsy could remember more than she had for a long time.

"My dolly! My dolly's name is Poppy!" Bitsy hugged her dolly tight. "I'm sorry I forgot your name," she whispered to it. She thought hard. "Poppy was with me when I lost my mommy." She looked excitedly toward Oscar who looked very proudly back at her and nodded. "I remember again!" Bitsy squinted, searching for more information. "My mommy was on the platform at the train station. I remember her face. Everyone was running. I got lost in a group of people and mommy was screaming." Bitsy was getting upset now. The memories she had desperately wanted to retrieve, she now wanted to give back.

Oscar pulled her away from the radiola and held her tightly whilst he directed another small girl to take her place. The girl looked very lost and unsure. But this wasn't stage fright.

"Hello. I'm Buttons. Bruises is . . . was my sister. We were very hungry. We are . . . were . . . are ten." Buttons looked desperately at Oscar who shook his head and waved for her to come and stay by him. He then motioned for a boy to have a go. The boy seemed very annoyed and shook his head. Oscar was talking to him but the boy looked adamant, even creating aggressive staccato-like movements with his head. It was a disconcerting visual: His body kept its translucent glow but his head was switching on and off like a light bulb. Oscar gave up on him. A little girl was tugging on Oscar's arm. It was the one with the baby. A long dress flowed to the girl's shins, and now it was apparent to all of them, that she wore some kind of metal devices on her legs. Oscar nodded to her.

In an instant she was at the radiola smiling at everyone. Melody was trying to make up for Dog and his bad behavior. She hated it when Dog was rude to Oscar. If it wasn't for Oscar they would all be inside that ghastly Shadow.

"Hello, I am Melody and I am eight," her heavy voice was cut with an unfamiliar accent—deep and clipped. "This is Baby." She held up the bundle as proof. "I am sorry but I have forgotten nearly everything except that I had polio and I once had a piano that my papi bought for me."

Everyone realized that this must be the one who had played the church organ.

"You play beautifully," said Daffodil realizing that the devices the girl wore on her legs must have been calipers. Did ghosts remain crippled in the afterlife? Daffodil shook the thought away.

"Oh, thank you very much," Melody said rapidly looking shy. "Oh! I remember that my mami and papi were teachers! Well papi was before he went to the war . . ." Melody's thoughts had come and gone in a swirl. Now her emotions were on the downward slide.

Daffodil felt Santu, Jake, and Blaze encouraging the little girl. They all seemed to be sensing that positivity helped these lost souls remember.

"You're parents were very clever then," added Daffodil. "Teaching is a very important job."

"Papi didn't come back from the war and then mami died too." Melody looked forlorn, her accent getting stronger and harder to understand.

"Oh," said Daffodil trying to keep her voice level. This was a desperate situation. Daffodil knew that her thoughts were being understood by the rest of her group. They must find out as much as they could and try to piece it all together. "I'm very sorry Melody. But I'm sure you're glad you have Baby to take care of. I can see you love Baby very much."

The little girl immediately cheered up. Santu was impressed. He threw congratulations out to Daffodil who smiled involuntarily.

"Oh yes, Baby and me have been together the whole time. We found Baby in a field all alone. We don't know how old he is."

"Do you know where you come from Melody?" As soon as the words had come out, Daffodil regretted them.

"I do not know." Immediately Melody looked upset. Clutching Baby even tighter, she shook her head and looked to Oscar for help. Oscar reached out an arm beckoning for Melody to come join Bitsy and Buttons by his side.

"What a help you have been Melody. Thank you so much." Daffodil was trying not to think about how impossible this situation was. Relying on the emotional support of the group, she put on a cheerful face.

Melody was replaced by a small energetic boy.

"Hello," his voice rang out over the radiola like a song. "I am Scraps. I am French, yes a froggie if you like." He shrugged.

Daffodil shot a look toward the dark corner where Duel and Duette had taken refuge. She couldn't feel them anymore but she hoped they could feel this little burst of French energy—and she hoped Annabelle would keep her mouth shut about frogs.

"It's nice to meet you Scraps. Is there anything you can remember?"

"My papa was a pilot I am remembering and my mamma was a nurse. Oh yes. It was a nice childhood but then my papa went to pilot planes for the war but I don't think he was there very long."

"He came home?"

"Oh no, no, no. He never came home."

Daffodil was wondering if there would be a light at the end of the tunnel: Any light in any tunnel. This was beyond difficult to listen to. Remaining bright she said, "And your mother?"

"Mamma was a nurse for infectious patients, yes?"

Daffodil knew where this was heading. "Yes, I understand."

"Yes. She got, how you say, tuberculosis." Scraps nodded. "And then I ate a green potato."

"Oh dear," said Daffodil wondering why that bit was important. "Did you like green potatoes?"

"Like! Non! I have eaten rat that taste better!"

Oscar sensed that things had taken an unfortunate turn. He thought it would have been because someone would have made a 'frog' comment but it was the green potato that did it. It seemed that all these conversations were ending in misery. And that was not where they should be headed.

And then Oscar felt it: The desolate wind was stirring.

The Shadow was coming for them. Now. There would be no time to introduce Bugsy or Wonderboy. And Wonderboy had a clue for one of the newcomers. It would never happen now. They were done for.

~Present day~

~THE SHADOW'S DAY IS NIGH~

D uel was now connected to Duette like he had never been before. This wasn't just a joining of minds and thoughts—this was like being immersed inside a person's soul. He could feel everything that Duette had ever felt, could understand everything she had ever thought. He knew all her memories—and in the way *she* remembered them. It was like being injected into someone's body but without any control.

Pain was rising up through his legs: Clotted blood trying to get through arteries. His heart felt like it was gasping for oxygen, and he was beginning to lose his grip on reality. There were voices around him, strange voices, voices he didn't recognize. They sounded trapped and damaged. But there were other voices too: Distant slingshots of hope that spun toward him; doves in the dark mess he now found himself in. These voices sounded lighter, kinder—further away, yes—but hopeful. He concentrated on their tone: Something good to grab onto before he drowned in Duette's agony.

But just as Duel managed to make a connection with them, a thunderous, rushing crash boomed all around him. '*Oh god*,' he thought, '*here we go*.' He grabbed his sister tightly and concentrated on those distant, buoyant voices.

✳ ✳ ✳

Santu felt the surge just before the noise came.

The wall of stained glass windows downstairs rattled violently before a huge roar of energy exploded through the church like a herd of angry lions. The building was struck with such fierceness that each and every window in the upper storey was blasted inward, the glass shattering across the length of the area, the room inhaling a rush of freezing cold air. The powerful vortex swirled around the perimeter of the building threatening to destroy everything in its wake. Its force seethed with hatred and anger, they could all feel it. And it was hungry. The Shadow had come and it wasn't going to leave without being satiated.

In the sudden attack, the ghosts had been caught off guard. In a lifetime of expectancy they were facing a moment of unanticipated menace. Oscar was furious with himself. He had felt the pain in each of their speeches and let them keep going: A stupid mistake; a selfish mistake.

The violent winds were roaring, battering the outside walls of the church in frustration, but each of its attempts to reach through the splintered windows was somehow being thwarted. Rage spun through its currents as it threw all its energy toward the old stone walls. Excitement increased its might.

Heaving itself against the church, it managed to focus its supremacy at the broken windows. From there it could see them all. Delight. Soon souls would be scrambling inside its dark mass, their sicknesses and weaknesses, tender morsels to be savored. It must have them, consume them, destroy them.

In the roar of the winds, Daffodil was screaming something to Jake. Jake couldn't understand her. They had been plunged into the depths of darkness as the scrolling twist of the Shadow curled at them trying to drag them back through the broken glass. The moonlight had been almost obliterated, the radiola had gone dark and the ghosts had disappeared.

Had the Shadow taken them already?

Santu had known that they were walking a fine line. As much as he appreciated Daffodil's positive spin, he had felt the darkness coming for them. It was like a slow burial. The dirty whirlpool would suffocate their minds and their bodies would follow. Oscar had said the Shadow was getting stronger. He was right. Since they had seen it in the graveyard it had almost doubled in size and might.

Blaze and Annabelle had been able to hold onto the stair rail to keep from being pulled into the whirlwind but Santu could see they could not last. Moonlit glimpses of their horrified faces tortured him as he struggled to protect them. In that bizarre moment when you recognize really hellish things are about to happen, Santu felt strangely calm. Equally committed to saving both Blaze and Annabelle, his mind churned. 'Here we go,' he thought. 'Here we go.'

Daffodil had managed to force her way, cross winds, toward Jake. She was pointing to the dim corner where Duel and Duette had been concealed: Their two figures were being dragged toward the smashed windows.

"It's come for them!" Daffodil was clutching Jake's arm.

Jake had anchored himself to a section of the radiola, but Daffodil's extra weight was unbalancing him. He could just make out Daffodil's voice but he had no idea what to do. If he let go, they would both end up going out the window with Duel and Duette.

"Why aren't they struggling?!" screamed Jake.

"Because they've been broken! I shouldn't have given Duel that potion!"

Everyone watched as Duel lamely tried to hold his sister back. The Shadow had come for her and this time it would get what it wanted.

"No! Duel!" Santu was screaming. He could see Duel being pulled toward the window. Santu needed to do something but if he let go he would end up going in the same direction—then perhaps the girls would follow him. What could he do? Ferociously he scrambled through his options: They were all deadly. He shook his head. The effort of trying to hold onto the balustrade, shielding the two girls, and thinking of something to do, was impossible. Something had to give.

Santu had no choice. If the stupid Shadow wanted blood so much it could have his. Maybe if he was inside it he could fight: Kill it from the inside? Quickly he pulled off his belt and lassoed Blaze to the stair rail.

"Sorry Annabelle," he shrugged as he let go of her. "All is fair in love and war."

"I wouldn't know," she yelled against the winds.

Before Santu had time to comprehend why he was not moving, Annabelle gave him a last smile. Suddenly, he realized she had buckled her own jeweled belt around him, tethering *him* to the handrail, and now Annabelle was now being dragged toward Duel and Duette and into the blasphemous winds.

Santu had been surprised in his life. He had never been this surprised. Annabelle—the most scared of all them, the rudest, the most inconsiderate, the most selfish, and the most filled with self-hatred—had surprised him like no other. She was about to sacrifice herself . . . for what? To save him? It didn't make sense.

"Jake," screamed Daffodil, "what did you do last time?"

"Nothing! I just went in holding onto your watch!"

Daffodil looked at Jake with an expression of apology.

"No!" Jake screamed. "No! Don't let go of me!" But Daffodil already had. She didn't see that there was a choice. Jake had never screamed in his life but now he screamed in fury, he screamed in wrath, he screamed with a passion he never knew existed.

And then *he* let go too.

Blackwater Herald Moon Tribune
Tuesday, June 6ᵗʰ, 1944—
One penny

WAR UPDATE
D-DAY INVASION!

A llies have used an immense armada of 4,600 ships with several thousand *smaller craft to invade German occupied France. Over 50,000 British, Canadian and U.S. troops have landed on the beaches of Normandy which Mr. Churchill says is the first in a series of forceful attacks determined for the European continent.*

Major John Locke, who was leading a squadron of Thunderbolts said: "I have never seen so many ships in all my life. The constant flashes from enemy guns meant that the beach was getting a heavy pounding but behind the allies there seemed a never ending stream of cruisers, destroyers, corvettes, L.C.T.'s and P.T. boats." Page 3.

LOCAL NEWS HEADLINES
BIRTH ANNOUNCEMENT

Sergeant Macalister Glizsnort is proud to announce the arrival of twins. On June 3ʳᵈ, his wife, Mrs. Grace Glizsnort recieved treatment in the medical rooms at Minchinbury but has been reported as healthy after the births.

Mr. and Mrs. Glizsnort were furthering their investigations regarding the Lost Children last Friday when Mrs. Glizsnort suddenly went into labor a good 100 miles east of Blackwater.

Although slightly premature, the babies: A boy and a girl, are both well.

"We will wait until the Christening ceremony before announcing their names," said the very proud father yesterday.

Both Mr. and Mrs. Glizsnort thank everyone for their good wishes and hope to be home soon to show off the newcomers.

WORLD NEWS HEADLINES

England, Bletchley Park—Decryption Machine conquered! *Named the Colossis II, the decoding machine—discovered by the code-breaking facility in England—is so efficient that it has decoded the German Navy's Enigma messages almost in real time.*

London*—'Daily Mail' has become the first transoceanic newspaper!*

New York City*—A bodily substance has been discovered by Oswald Avery. Abbreviated to D.N.A., it is said to be a major breakthrough in the study of genes and their development.*

~Brought to you by~

Sorry if you can't always get SANATOGEN NERVE TONIC FOOD! Their ingredients are in high demand to help the war effort! KILLS PAIN QUICKLY!

PEPSODENT—Furry teeth? We use Irium! Stains disappear for good. Take old tube back to the shop!

~Present day~

~Night is the Shadow's Day~

D uel's back faced the broken windows and his attempts to push his sister away from the rushing winds were ineffectual. A few more seconds and they would both be gone. The icy cold air was at least numbing the pain in his legs and the black nothingness that was pulling him in, was effectively suffocating him anyway. Duel's mind had fallen into a pit of empty night: His only thoughts were of a dead mother and a deaf father full of grief. Falling backward into the anesthetic of oblivion, the pain was leaving him. Everything was leaving him—including life.

The ferocious winds were tearing at the inside of the church now, yet the full force of its energy was outside the building. The old cardboard boxes holding the newspaper articles were being shredded and the yellowing stories from so many decades ago were being thrown around the room like unwanted memories.

Rapidly rotating currents pulled in their prey: Delicious broken souls that had been abused, hated, tormented and ridiculed. It was too excruciatingly wonderful. Nothing could save them now. There was time to relish each and every one of them, savor the myriad of weaknesses and pain. The exhilaration was almost too much.

"Hold on to him!" screamed Daffodil as she felt herself slide across broken glass toward the windows. Coming up behind Duel and Duette, Daffodil tried to sway herself toward anything that would give her some

197

leverage. Jake was following quickly behind her. But, moving in these swirling winds made it impossible to negotiate direction and Daffodil was getting away from him.

Annabelle gave Daffodil a lovely smile as she was dragged into the pathway of Duel and Duette. "Aim for the beam below the window," Annabelle screamed at Daffodil.

"Aim!?" Daffodil was trying to get away from the window, not aim *for* it.

"Do it!"

It was the first time in her life that Annabelle did not enjoy barking orders. Daffodil couldn't understand it but Annabelle seemed to be the only one in control. Jake suddenly understood what Annabelle was thinking. When he finally got close enough to clutch Daffodil's many layers of clothing he grabbed on and decided to never let go. If Daffodil was going into the dark and freezing abyss that swirled beyond the window, then that's where he was going too.

One after the other, they hit the wall below the largest shattered window: the shards of glass tearing their clothes and ripping at their skin; the icy cold air streaming down on them, freezing any thoughts of escape. Annabelle's plan had given them a few extra seconds. But, anchored only by Duel's weak grip on her ankles, Duette was being lifted in the air.

"Jake!" cried Daffodil. "Throw in your crystals."

Jake fumbled in his pocket trying to reach for the crystal bag Daffodil had given him earlier.

The Shadow was shrieking now, a noise that was hideous and all consuming. It could sense Duette, so close now, so close. The whipping winds sucked in the delicious taste of her impending defeat.

"Duette!" screamed Daffodil. "Duel!" Daffodil's feet hit the wall below the sill and she felt her legs being pulled upward toward the open window. Quickly she scrambled to wedge her feet under the butt of the ledge.

Just as the defenseless bodies of Duette and Duel were disappearing into the vortex, Daffodil managed to get out the remains of her watch. Risking everything, she reached her arm above the window sill and threw her crystals and her watch into the swirling draft, her feet lifting from their hold.

Jake had finally found his crystal bag and threw the entire thing in as Daffodil felt the darkness of the Shadow graze her skin. Then something grabbed her around the waist.

It was Jake.

But it was too late. The coiling winds had pulled Daffodil's feet away from the wall and now she headed upward and into the dark mass—with Jake attached.

No one heard Jake scream out Daffodil's name. Instead, their ears were struck with the blast of a huge explosion which was followed by an enormous crack of lightning. The zigzagging light shot through the sky like an arrow from God and immediately the winds grew suddenly weaker.

As the suctioning currents died, everyone dropped to the ground.

The static electricity from the explosion sent a jolt that flared through every one of them. Duel, although virtually unconscious, felt the rip of voltage shoot through his body. It was like a charge of energy—exactly what he needed. In the strange state between death and light he understood. Crying out to his sister he passed all those thoughts to her. And then the voices sang. The sound was incredible and powerful, their words would be forgotten but their meaning would stay. Somehow they found Duette and somehow she heard their song.

Annabelle felt the explosion too: It was just in time. The Shadow had reached for her and she had felt the hideousness inside it. She had never feared death, in fact she had wanted it to come, but not like that, not inside that awful mess. Yet, even in the relief she felt to have been saved, she would never forget that, in the final moment, Santu would have sacrificed her over Blaze.

As Daffodil collapsed back to the ground—still joined to Jake—she saw something extraordinary fill the blackness of the night sky: A bright white beam burst into light at the apex of the vortex. The light seemed to be fighting the dark mass. The Shadow, now half its size, and finding itself in a furious fight for its own existence, turned away from the church. Its currents had fired up again but, like a flailing child, it could not dislodge the monkey on its back. Twisting and turning, the black dusty turmoil tried to rid itself of the white light.

"Where's Duel and Duette?!" screamed Daffodil looking around the dark room desperately. Shock trembled through her body. Trying to comprehend what had nearly happened was overwhelming. Santu had undone his belt and was helping Blaze with hers. Annabelle seemed quite calm. She was leaning out the window looking down.

"They're down there," she said simply.

Daffodil jumped up and stuck her head out one of the broken windows. "Oh God! They look dead!" Daffodil went to run back down the stairs but felt herself being held back. Without taking his eyes of the struggling Shadow, Santu had shot his arm out to stop her.

"You cannot be going anywhere," Santu said. He sounded perfectly calm but he was not about to have anyone else be taken tonight.

Angry, Daffodil began to yell at Santu to let go. Carefully he twisted her back around toward the window. Daffodil could only watch.

The dark whirlpool was retreating backward, toward the graveyard, and inside the swirling blackness, hundreds of tiny explosions were going off, each one reducing its size. The white light was still crowding the sinister currents but, just as it looked like the dirty whirlwind may have fought the white light off, the glowing radiance tripled in size and then exploded around the black mass, encompassing it. Yelping, as if it had been struck, the whirlpool immediately shot into the ground, disappearing completely.

"Is it gone?" asked Blaze uncertainly.

"For now," said Santu. He motioned to the horizon. "This might be why." The sun's fiery corona was spilling a sickly yellow light across the horizon.

"Now can I go?!" yelled Daffodil a little too loudly.

"We can all be going," Santu replied releasing Daffodil.

Running, Daffodil made a quick exit, followed by the others—Annabelle trailing at the rear. The twins were lying beside each other as if they had been laid out for burial. Shaking horror from her thoughts, Daffodil knelt beside them and was surprised to see her broken watch lying on the ground beside them. She flung it in her pocket before scrambling to check their vital signs.

"Are they dead?" asked Blaze as she overlooked the lifeless duo.

Daffodil shook her head. They were alive—just.

"Santu," Daffodil's voice sounded strangled. "Look at this."

"How is this possible?" Santu asked, disbelief ringing in his tone.

"Duel must be stronger than I gave him credit for." Daffodil was smiling now. 'Well done Duel,' she thought. Somehow, Duel had used the potion and fought for his sister, and somehow he had managed to heal Duette's bruises. She was truly impressed. "I guess you shouldn't underestimate people." Daffodil gave a fleeting look of recognition to Annabelle.

One of Annabelle's eyebrows rose. She smiled back at Daffodil. "Ditto," she replied. "Good job with the crystals." New doors had opened and appreciation for what had passed, now buoyed their connection.

"What happened to the ghosts?" asked Blaze as she nudged Annabelle out of the way to reach Santu.

"I don't know," said Daffodil. "I don't think the Shadow came for them. It seemed to be focused on Duette and Duel. Maybe taking a life is more important than taking a ghost?"

"Oh, yeah," added Annabelle. "Thanks for sacrificing me Santu."

"I am only having one belt." Santu shrugged casually. "But your diamond belt is very much more to my tastes." Santu's voice was teasing but his eyes told her the truth: He had finally found some respect for Annabelle.

"They're diamantes." Annabelle's piercing stare was disconcerting. "It looks better on you than me. Keep it." Annabelle's cool blue eyes danced mesmerizingly toward Santu.

Why did she have to be quite so good looking?

"Does anyone have an idea on what that white light thing was?" asked Blaze trying to avert the newfound camaraderie between Annabelle and Santu.

"I have a theory." It was Duel. His voice was croaky and he hadn't yet managed to open his eyes.

"Duel!" cried Daffodil. "You're awake!"

"Well I do like people stating the obvious," murmured Duel.

"And sarcasm!" added Daffodil. "What more could we hope for?"

One of Duel's eyes squinted open. It rolled around for a moment before landing on Daffodil. "Nice potion by the way," he said as he motioned to sit up.

"Bit too strong?" asked Daffodil with a grimace.

"Not for a 10 foot bear." Duel winced as pain shot through his back. "Nice fall too for that matter."

"Sorry Duel," said Daffodil awkwardly. "I probably should have warned you about how strong it was. But I didn't want you to go into the experience already afraid of what might happen." She paused. "You fixed Duette you know."

"I know." Duel looked down at his sister. The moment he had freed her had been incredible. It was like a million exploding stars lighting his mind like fireworks. When he discovered that not only had the potion allowed him to enter Duette's mind, but that it also allowed him to remove himself from his own body, he knew how to fight. Reading minds without a body was the most extraordinary thing Duel had ever done—explosive to say the least. And when he realized that the black mass was focused on all the negativity that had created Duette's bruises, Duel knew how to let the hideous thing consume the harm done to her first before consuming their souls. The tactic gave them just enough time before the Shadow was struck and spat them out. And then of course, there was that one voice that called out to him. They were lucky though. Another few seconds and they would both have been devoured. At least now Duel knew why his sister had taken on the bruises of the ghost girl.

"She's an empath you know," he stated blandly.

Duette began to stir. "Who a what?" Her voice sounded far away.

"You are an empath. You feel other people's emotions and you can take on other people's pain. Probably why you never felt the need to use conversation." He smiled. "I think the name I'm looking for is 'know-it-all'."

Daffodil smiled. "I believe it is."

Duette was forcing her eyes to focus. She felt like she had been dropped from a large height. Oh wait. She had. But the fall had happened just as Duel had found her. In her mind it was like someone had found the key to all her pain and had opened the door to release it. She scanned her legs.

"They okay," Duette said delightedly. "You save me brother." A small tear tumbled down her cheek. "Merci." She wrapped her arms around Duel. "You allowed to read my mind when you like." Duette knew she would never feel the need to shut him out again.

"Ah," said Duel, "but I think I have read enough of your thoughts for a lifetime."

Duette laughed but it felt like her chest was ripping in half. A cry of pain escaped.

"Broken rib," said Daffodil. "That's going to hurt for a while."

"Broken rib nothing to bruises." Duette smiled at Daffodil. "You, merci too. You did good thing to give Duel potion. He a very strong boy. No one give him enough credit. Now he know. Merci." Duette's face then wrinkled up. "I not like being empath. You give me potion to stop this?"

"That," said Daffodil shaking her head, "you have to live with. But celestite will help. It will ease the way you absorb other people's emotional friction and stress. You know Duette, now it makes sense that you have always isolated yourself. It was probably instinctive to protect yourself from other people's turmoil. Don't worry I'll organize something for you." She smiled at Duel. "It's just lucky that Duel is so strong." Daffodil knew that if he were not, the twins could both be dead. Daffodil nodded thankfully.

Duel shrugged in a very French way. "What can I say?" he said feigning nonchalance.

"Right," said Annabelle, "Now that we've all discovered how amazing everyone is can we try to figure out what happened?"

For some reason Duel laughed. "What is it that you want to know Annabelle?"

"What was that white light thing?"

Duel shook his head "When we were in the Shadow—not nice by the way, I do not recommend it—we could feel all the angst and torment that the blackness had absorbed: Maybe all the souls it has swallowed? Anyway I could hear lots of voices: Distressed ones and good ones." He paused for effect. "I heard Madame Glizsnort's voice telling me to fight."

"Do you mean she was inside that thing?" asked Blaze confused.

"No," Duel shook his head. "I think *she* was the white light."

Static Recording No.5243—On Loop.

Oscar. 1903-1917. Ghosted Aged 14.

H ello? I hope you can hear me, I have to whisper and I must be brief. We are all shocked at what the Shadow did to you. I am so sorry. It has gotten so strong now that I fear we shall never make it. We had to leave, I'm sure you understand. We could do nothing to save you, you see. We could do nothing to protect ourselves either.

I have slipped back into the church while it still hedges between daylight and dark, before I become still with the light. I came to talk to you but you had all run away. Just like the others. I want you to know that I don't blame you. In a way that is exactly what we did when we came and hid in this church. We ran away from the Shadow in fear. We never even thought about facing it. I mean what would we have to fight it with anyway? Perhaps it was for this reason that we have not been able to find our way home. Maybe fear has consumed hope and possibility. Perhaps if I had taken us all away from here long ago, we would have found another journey. Maybe that journey could have guided us home. I try not to blame myself but you understand that I am responsible for everyone. It is just how it is.

And my calls for help have now gotten you into trouble. I am so sorry. I do not know what I expected you to do.

It was Dog that compelled me to take everyone and leave. He was going to sacrifice himself you know. He was going to just fly straight into that disgusting cavernous mouth and disappear from being. It would have taken his existence-time with him too. That would have left us with no time to try to save ourselves. You see, the Shadow swallows our time as well. When Bruises was taken it felt as if part of *our* lives had been sucked out of us too. The light comes faster now also. It is terrifying because we can't move in the brightness anymore. Have I told you that already? I'm sorry but I can't remember so many things now.

It's not Dog's fault. You shouldn't judge him. He has had terrible things happen to him. He is in such a state now that he thinks going into that thing will stop his pain. He can't understand why he cannot go home. And he has lost his view of what is right and what is not. Most people would if they had lost all their family members one by one including his three sisters, his brother, his mother and father.

I didn't let him though. I mean I didn't let him go into the Shadow. I just couldn't. It won't be less painful for him in there it will be worse. Much worse. He doesn't believe me but I know it's true. I can hear a voice you know. I can't explain it but I can hear a beautiful songlike voice. It can't save us. I understand that now. But it is nice to know it's there. I try to hear it when I'm worried but sometimes it gets very faint. Perhaps you can hear it too?

Anyway, I must go now. I have to hurry because the light is getting stronger. You will probably want to know where we have gone but it is not a place for you to follow. I have been there once very briefly. It is very dangerous. It is a place where it feels like you are walking along an edge: On one side is a black gaping hole and on the other side is a gray gaping hole. One looks scarier than the other, but the truth is, they are both gaping holes into the unknown. Surely the Shadow would not be able to exist there? Perhaps we shall not exist for long either. It is worth the risk. I will not let any of us fall victim to that swirling hatred.

I wanted to thank you for trying but you must not try anymore. I don't want you to go into the Shadow either. There have been too many lost to that beastly thing. We must risk the move. It is unfair to threaten any more beings by asking for help. You may never even hear this recording. And for that I am very sorry. I will still look for a way to save us and get us home but I am finding it harder and harder to believe. I wish there was more time.

Pray for us, especially Dog and little Buttons. I fear she will be next. She misses her sister so. I wish you more luck than we have to give but still, I offer it in earnest.

May *your* journey take *you* home.

~Present day~

~JOINING FORCES~

B ack in the warm cabin they inspected their wounds and tried to regroup. Several of them had lacerations from the broken glass and Duette and Duel had received nasty injuries from their fall.

"Is it safe here?" blurted Blaze. "I mean if the Shadow can get us in the church it can surely get us here." Blaze was rubbing her stomach where Santu's belt had restrained her against the thrashing winds.

"Actually it was not actually coming inside the church," Santu corrected her. "It was using its force to suction us out." Santu's thoughts were forming out loud. "But if we could be applying some sort of force field—"

"Um, sorry to interrupt," returned Blaze annoyed at being contradicted, "but we are in the cabin *not* the church and anyway I don't think that the science of matter and energy and all their interactions apply to a human-swallowing Shadow!" Blaze's face was bright red with fury. Being brave was one thing. Throwing your life into the jaws of death was quite another. Plus, Santu seemed to be standing awfully close to Annabelle.

Evidently, their combined meditative state had worn off.

"Then no," replied Santu. "I am thinking that we are not safe here. We are not safe anywhere." Blaze crossed her arms and heaved out a sigh. She already knew that.

"Blaze," Daffodil said gently as she threw a harsh look at Santu, "I think we'll be safe for now. I think what Santu was *trying* to say was that we should consider some options that might protect us from that monstrous thing."

"Thank you Daffodil," said Santu nodding in his very expressive way.

"But," added Daffodil rubbing her forehead, "we also need some ideas on how to help these ghosts."

"So you think the ghosts are still there?" asked Blaze. "You don't think it got them?"

Daffodil shrugged. "Did anyone feel like the ghosts got taken?" She looked around the room. Everyone was slowly shaking their heads. "Alright then," said Daffodil, "let's assume the ghosts are still there."

"Alright," said Santu, "then I think we are needing to split into two groups and throw away some ideas."

"*Throw around* some ideas," said Blaze tediously.

"Yes!" said Santu looking oddly confident. "Let's throw them everywhere! Daffodil you go with Jake, Blaze and Duette. And my team will be with Duel and Annabelle."

Blaze didn't like this new game Santu was playing. He was teasing her, she was sure of it. Well he and Annabelle could play all by themselves. Enough was enough. Blaze turned on her heel and sidled up to Daffodil.

"Let's bring on some ideas to blow everyone away . . . *like a bomb*," Blaze said smiling at Santu with a renewed vigor. She was ready to take bravery to a new level.

The two groups threw out ideas at a furious pace. Daffodil was shocked at the plethora of thoughts. But she was finding it hard to concentrate. There was something very real troubling her and it had nothing to do with the Shadow or the ghosts. As the members of her group talked over the top of each other, she sat and rubbed her broken watch between her fingers. It was like a kind of meditation. The tangibility of the object had become a genie's bottle of possibility. Not that it could bring her parents to her anymore—that was over—but it could help her forge new thoughts. How the watch was not shattered to pieces was bizarre. The metal even seemed to be stronger.

Daffodil was only half-listening as the suggestions poured out: Blaze insisted that she return to the graveyard; Duette suggested that she use her empathic skills on the other ghosts—an idea that was quickly rejected because it seemed she absorbed their pain and not their memories; and Jake proposed that he sleep next to the radiola and let the static whisper into his dreams. But Daffodil felt consumed by the watch. She scratched at its insides sure there was something more to its structure.

Santu was experiencing the same explosion of thoughts from his group. Duel had noted that to deflect the Shadow they needed to understand what it was. Santu agreed but he also thought that there must be some kind of device to hinder the whirlpool's ability to pull them toward it. Annabelle wondered how they could summon Madame Glizsnort's white light without actually having to summon her.

By the time everyone had joined up again there were lots of ideas but not many of them were feasible.

Of course ideas are just estimates that, without being tested, are just proposals. Still, a theory is really the only place to start if you want to accomplish a task that seems unimaginable. So they followed in the footsteps of the greats and did not let the small box of truth, as they knew it, restrain them.

After listening to everyone's final thoughts Santu contemplated the essentials.

"There are three definite facts that will be helping us figure out who these ghosts are. As Blaze has reminded us, those unnamed gravestones are being there for a reason." Santu cleared his throat. "Each of the ghosts we talked to through that big radio . . ."

"Radiola VIII," said Jake firmly.

"Yes, thank you Jake. They were all saying something about war. We are not knowing which war, but this we will figure out. Secondly, we all agree that they are seeming to be orphans before they . . ." Santu hesitated, "before they died." Why was that so hard to say? "Plus, as Jake says, those boxes full of old newspaper articles may be having some clues in them. If we can be getting any details about which war they are talking about we will at least be having a time-frame."

Daffodil motioned to speak but at that very moment she felt a click under her fingers. She shook her head to deflect the conversation while she looked at the broken metal of the watch. A tiny latch was jutting open from underneath an embedded ruby stone.

"I am thinking," Santu went on, "that our presence, and especially Daffodil's way of talking to the ghosts, is helping them remember."

"I agree," replied Daffodil as she kept fiddling. "We are like anchors to them. It's like we secure them to existence. I don't know how much we can get them to remember though."

Santu nodded at everyone as if it was their fault he had to say it. "Our next problem: This Shadow." Santu sighed and shook his head. "I would like to be making a device to deflect it but there is nothing out here except old timber." Santu saw Blaze raise her hand. "And no Blaze, no one is thinking that going to the graveyard is a good idea."

"Well," announced Blaze, "who made you king of the decisions?"

Santu knew Blaze was angry at him but anger was not a decision maker. Not here anyway. Blaze was just annoyed because he had been giving Annabelle attention. Well he was not into playing games. And he wasn't into relationships. They were the last thing on his mind. Eventually they may understand. If not, then so be it.

"No one is making anyone king, Blaze." Santu shrugged his shoulders. "We can take a vote, yes? Who is thinking Blaze should go back to the graveyard? Move up your hands."

Blaze looked around the room. No one raised their hand—not even Daffodil. Santu had made Blaze feel like a fool. She blushed furiously, golden flecks sparking in the deep green irises of her eyes.

The fire behind them swelled suddenly with flames—a log had fallen from the top of the pile pushing heat outward. The warmth from the surge expelled itself across the room. Jake had been sitting closer to the fire than the others. His old worn clothes were not keeping the cold out and he knew if he didn't at least try to regain some heat he could get deathly sick. But now he was too hot, even in just his favorite ghost-busters tee shirt. He jumped up, patting his back as if he was on fire, and moved over to the door.

"Right then, my idea is stupid and I take it back." But Blaze didn't take it back. She was going to sit and stew on it until she found her opportunity. Blaze knew it was important to revisit that graveyard. There was something about the burial site: the hole; the strange grave digger. It may take some maneuvering but there would be a chance and she would just have to wait it out.

"No Blaze," said Daffodil, "ideas can't be stupid."

"Just wrong then." Blaze wouldn't make eye contact with Daffodil.

Santu was wondering if Blaze and Annabelle had changed places. He flicked a look over at Annabelle and caught her unawares. Annabelle was delighting in Blaze's embarrassment. Santu grimaced. Girls were impossible to understand. One minute they were unbelievably brave, the next they were disappointing. He tried to focus on the task at hand.

"We are all agreeing that when the ghosts remember, they are feeling sad, and that sadness lures this Shadow." Santu was pacing now. "So, we must be positive and fight. And we must not be ducks!"

"*Chickens!*" said Blaze, her voice full of anger. "And I think we've proved we're not *chickens.*"

"I agree," said Duel ignoring Blaze's outburst. "When I focused on the voice inside that mass, I'm sure it helped. But I wouldn't have liked to be in there for a millisecond longer."

Santu now looked at Daffodil who didn't seem to be paying attention. She had been fiddling with that broken watch the whole time they had been thrashing out ideas.

"Daffodil, what are you thinking?" Santu gestured toward her hand. Daffodil didn't answer and everyone turned to look at her.

Santu was interrupting Daffodil's moment of discovery. She had just managed to lift the latch inside the watch without breaking any more parts. She could see a small cleft filled with a minute piece of scrolled up fabric. It looked very old and incredibly fragile.

When Daffodil's eyes rose from her discovery they were wide with shock and confusion.

"Daffodil?" Jake was worried. Why was she looking so frightened?

Daffodil was staring back at everyone perplexed. "Does anyone have a magnifying glass?"

The look on Daffodil's face was enough for Santu to know she had found something significant. Santu had brought several glass samples with him. He loved glass—concave, convex, mirror, you name it. It was pretty much a given. Rifling through his case, he found the most powerful one.

Daffodil carefully unrolled the scroll. It was torn in half. The first explosion must have ripped it as the watch snapped. Piecing it together, it measured about as long as one of her small tabular crystals. The print was miniscule and the script was old fashioned and hard to read. Some of it had been scorched and tiny bits had broken away. She read out loud.

"Binding Love is wrapped seven times around this medium with the positive energies of our 3 generations which augments when you find no-time. Join the 'S' bold and envisioned and the 'J' who you will always trust. Befriend the fiery 'B'. Do not let her blast her bravery into oblivion. Save the two 'D's with our potion and all together there is hope for the little girl 'A'. She needs love the most. Again our love is bound by ribbons of giving and caring and hope. You are the finders and so it shall be. With love, from Daisy for daughter and granddaughter."

"My grandmother wrote it." Daffodil was looking at the rest of the group in confusion. "It's about now." She realized how obvious her statement was but it was all very strange. Daffodil's grandmother had died several years before she was even born. How had she known all this information and how had she managed to get the watch to Daffodil? How long had the message been in there? Memories suddenly flowed back to her. "When my mother gave me the watch she said it was 'as important as my future'. It didn't really mean anything until I saw my dead parents. I thought that's what she must have meant." Daffodil felt very strange. A time warp had closed and trapped her inside its bubble. There seemed no escape.

"Is this some kind of joke?!" Annabelle's attempt at sweetness was long gone now. "What did you mean by 'the little girl A'?!" Annabelle was quite obviously furious. How would anyone know what *she* needed? And she certainly was no longer a *little girl*.

"I am thinking," said Santu knowing he would touch a nerve, "that this is about what was happening when you were a child." Much to his discomfort he looked her in the eye.

Annabelle was horrified. "That was just a dream," she lied.

"Annabelle," Santu's voice was touched with pain. "I know this was not a dream." He wanted to go on but he had no right.

"Let's all stay calm." Daffodil had no idea what was going on with Santu and Annabelle but this was not the time for it: Again Annabelle had managed to shift the focus.

"No," said Santu. "I am very sorry. There is no need to bring more negativity. Your watch, we will take as a positive sign, yes?" Santu shrugged.

Daffodil was wondering how else to take her grandmother's words. This was enormous, overwhelming: A prophetic note from the past filled with generations of love.

"I think I know why the watch had such a devastating effect on the Shadow the first time." Daffodil looked at Jake. "The watch has been bound by three generations of love: It's an inimitable tie. It's everything the Shadow hates. Not to mention all the protection stones embedded into it." But Daffodil wondered why the watch had not had the same effect the second time round.

"Well," said Santu hoping his confidence level sounded high, "then I think we are in the best of company—grandmother included." Santu could see how much this meant to Daffodil but he couldn't understand how it would help their cause now.

The rest of them smiled at Daffodil. Daffodil was grateful for the support but she knew they didn't fully comprehend how powerful this new find was. No matter, she had taught herself everything she knew and now she would just have to figure this puzzle out as well.

"It's getting dark again." said Jake. "We need to figure out what we're going to do." It was strange but he was feeling stronger with every difficulty they faced. Obedience had always been a foolproof survival method but now he was beginning to understand what it was to think and speak independently and it felt good.

With no sleep and no real intentions they gathered themselves and made a choice. They each understood if they failed at this then they failed at their life; and the consequences of that went beyond their own egos. The fact that they were responsible for children of war, orphaned in tragic circumstances, and desperate to be reunited with something that resembled 'home', gave them all some kind of motivation. Even Annabelle found voices in the call.

And then Daffodil understood why the watch had had no effect when she threw it in for a second round. There was something she would need to do to give the watch more power but it was dangerous and the effect probably wouldn't last long. But what was life if it was not challenging? Daffodil knew what to do—she just didn't know how many others she would be putting in danger to do it.

And without understanding exactly what he was seeing or how it found him, Santu was hit with a vision that was both alarming and disastrous.

Blackwater Herald Moon Tribune
Thursday, September 7ᵗʰ, 1944— One penny

The 1831ˢᵗ Day of War
WAR UPDATE
8000 FLYING BOMBS DESTROY LONDON

*E**ight-thousand of Hitler's specially designed long distance rockets and bombs have been bombarding London for 80 days. Hitler has had prisoners working on his V2 rockets that can be fired from great distances and carry 2,000 lbs of explosives on board. Devastation has ensued, and London and its surrounds have suffered terrible damages. To meet this new form of attack, additional guns were sent to the Thames Estuary and intruder squadrons have been sent out to patrol over the Dutch and Belgian coasts. An average of 100 flying bombs a day, have been launched at London. Page 4.*

LOCAL NEWS HEADLINES
LOCAL CHURCH LOST TO BOMBS

In a devastating blow to the remaining members of the Saint Catherine's Church of Redeemus and the children of The Little Orchard School House, one of Hitler's 'flying bombs' has flown off its course and struck Blackwater. The bomb damaged the bluestone building so badly that it is unlikely to be fixed. With little materials available and so few people left in the neighborhood, the future of the church seems grim.

It is the final blow for a community that has struggled with disaster since the church was burned down in 1939.

213

Bishop John Biggs is at a loss as to what to do. *"I cannot accept that those who did not believe in our church were right to do so. I am devastated that this has happened and I fear that Blackwater shall fade away now."*

Mrs. Grace Glizsnort has also asked to add to the article by saying that she is greatly saddened by the destruction of the church and school but while the weather is still warm classes will now be taken in her garden at Westbury Way—the house she shares with her husband, our local sergeant. As the weather cools she will try to reassess the school's location.

Mrs. Glizsnort also wishes to remind everyone how lucky they are that the church's graveyard was unaffected by the bombing. She does however, plead with the remaining residents to leave the unmarked gravestones, set aside for the Lost Children, alone. Several have been maliciously vandalized which, she says, not only shows lack of respect for those who have passed on, but also denigrates those who have donated their precious money to have them erected.

And so, the Herald Moon Tribune, ends this with a prayer for the future. Let us hope this is not the end of Blackwater.

WORLD NEWS HEADLINES

ROMMEL COMMITS SUICIDE*—Eight German army officers have been hanged, with piano wire, for their part in the attempted assassination of Hitler on June 20. It is believed that Field Marshall Rommel, whom was suspected of involvement, was given the choice by Hitler to either commit suicide with cyanide or face the murder of his family and staff. Rommel has since been found dead by cyanide poisoning. Page 7.*

D-DAY ATTACK*—Although heavy casualties have been suffered, the Allies have been able to retake Paris.*

THE MINISTRY OF FOOD*—As a woman, it is your instinct to give the lion's share of the larder to the man of the house and to give the tasty bits to the children. But without **your** rations 'nerves' are bound to result. Your family would rather you be cheerful than take your rations! So don't go without!*

~Brought to you by~

PHYLLOSAN*—Revitalizing Tablets for every man.*

ROBBIALAC PAINTS*—Today WAR WORK Tomorrow PEACE WORK.*

FRY'S COCO*—And all is well!*

~Present day~

~If you seek the truth you may lament the past~

D affodil had treated everyone with quartz and celestite and they were all lulled back into a meditative state. Thankfully Duette was helping this time because it was a lot harder to get everyone to emotionally connect. Blaze was especially difficult to compose.

As they ran to the church in the dimming light, the bitter, cold air bit at their skin and snowflakes fell upon them: burning ice that gouged at their exposed faces. Skeletal black trees towered over them tracking their pursuit with unseen eyes and the frigid ice crunched beneath their feet as if trying to eat them in the chase.

"Is it getting colder?!" asked Blaze with exasperation as they ran past the angel and tore up the fragile stairway.

"I am afraid this is so," replied Santu gravely.

"What do you mean by that?" asked Blaze accusingly as she climbed the highest step. In the dim light the room looked daunting: The moon was rising casting an eerie glow through the smashed windows; huge shards of broken glass glinted with the secret light of hidden knowledge; gray shadows slung their slippery silhouettes across the aged floorboards as if they could creep away and hide at any moment; and freezing gusts of air swirled around the room, keen to play with its prey before their ultimate destruction.

"I am meaning that every day we get closer to whatever this is, the colder it gets. You have not noticed this?" Santu pulled his blanket tighter around him.

"I thought it was because I hadn't eaten very much. No fuel, you know?" Blaze shrugged as a shiver ran through her body.

Santu shook his head.

"But," interrupted Daffodil. "*Why* is it getting colder? I mean, are we making that happen?" Daffodil threw down her sack filled with crystals and gems.

"It is not us," said Santu, "and I think it will change the closer we get."

"The closer we get to what?"

Santu shrugged. That was a conversation for later. "We are not in control until we understand." He swiped a look at Annabelle who seemed to have grown even paler. She knew that he could tell something was wrong but still she would not let him, or any of the others, in. The visions Santu was having of her were getting more and more real. Annabelle's insides were hardening. And her mind was following. Each cruel jibe, each taunt, each nasty thought that filled her head was twisting into an icy solidity inside her. Before long the cemented hatred would consume her and she would join the Shadow willingly.

Sometimes Daffodil found Santu infuriating. His words circled around meanings that he wouldn't commit to. And if he checked out Annabelle one more time with those all-seeing, brown eyes, Daffodil thought she might hit him. She sighed—she could never hit anyone. And Santu was alright. Why was she feeling so edgy? Oh that's right, they were all going to die.

Santu busied himself with a pile of kindling. The decision to bring the iron tray and several logs from the cabin was a great idea by Daffodil—although Jake was sure the grief-stricken angel guarding the entry did not approve. Once the kindling was stacked, Santu carefully encouraged the growing flames with gusts of oxygen. Once the flares finally took hold, the very power of making fire ignited everyone's energy.

As an added attempt to thwart the Shadow, each of them wore a twisted bed sheet tied around their middle. When they were all in position they would be secured to a sturdy post or heavy object to help protect them from the violent suctioning winds.

Duette and Duel had been chosen to stand as guards. Together their minds were so strong now that they believed they could join forces and create a barrier that would at least deflect the advances of the Shadow for a short time. Daffodil had yet to prepare the perimeter of the room with her crystals and gems that would ensure their protection, positivity and strength but she had given Duette a mild potion to help with her empath skills. Daffodil hoped she wouldn't regret her timidity with its potency.

Wrapped in blankets, the twins stood at opposite ends of the church's second floor, and, with the new and enhanced control of their minds, they kept vigil, swapping ends every now and then to ensure that they both felt a bit of warmth from the fire.

Duel's feelings of concern about his sister were still strong, and so, trying not to infiltrate her thoughts too much, he kept guard. And Duette let him. There was a newfound respect between them that had solidified their connection: They understood each other without threat; they were individuals but bonded; they were one plus one equals two. It made them both feel stronger, more independent and more capable of being leaned upon by the other.

Jake had only one mission in mind. "Well I'm going to try to see if I can hear something in the Radiola's static. Maybe I will be able to find some really early recordings that have more information about the ghosts. They said they're all on loop." He crossed his fingers in the air like a wave goodbye. It made Daffodil feel strangely sad. Jake had come into his own. It was an incredible adjustment in the very short time they had all been together but she hoped he would still look to her for support.

"Santu," Daffodil turned away from Jake, "how about that torch? It's getting a bit dark in here?" Santu switched on his pen torch and aimed it at the boxes of old newspapers.

"No bugs," said Blaze disappointedly.

"They'll come back," said Daffodil without conviction.

"I guess we are needing to do some reading," Santu said tiredly. He heard his own voice. "Remember, we must be staying optimistic. We do not want to be testing our new ideas so soon." He eyed Daffodil. "Are you needing help to set up all the protection devices?"

"I'll be fine." Daffodil's voice sounded flat. She mustered a confident smile. "I'll be good," she tried again.

"Right," continued Santu. "Let's all take a box of newspaper articles and drag them over to the windows." Santu was faced with looks of horror.

"Of course," said Annabelle, her voice heavy with sarcasm, "there's no point in making the Shadow struggle to get at us, we should just wait for it at the window. I mean, that is where it came for us, isn't it?"

"I am believing it is!" Santu said jovially.

Blaze sniggered. "Yeah," she said, "it's also where the moonlight is." Blaze was moving around the room collecting all the old articles that had been strewn everywhere by the lashing winds.

Annabelle sneered at Blaze and followed Santu's orders. But the box she had begun to drag was so old that it split in half and the huge pile of papers slid out of their ancient container as if in protest.

Blaze gave Annabelle a dazzling smile and peeled several editions from the top of her slurry before idling over to the main window—the exact window where Duette and Duel had been pulled through.

The twins exchanged glances. Neither of them wanted to be involved in the dispute between the two girls. Duette thought it was especially futile to carry on like this over a boy. Sure Santu was good looking—in that obvious kind of way—but he was just a boy. The twins grabbed some papers and followed Blaze to the window. They all tied themselves to an appropriately sturdy object and began to read.

Jake was trying to figure out how Bitsy got the huge, old radio to work. He moved around the bulky piece of equipment looking for a switch. Right at the back, under a pile of decomposing comic books, he found an unplugged electrical cord.

"Anyone seen a socket?" he called out into the darkening room.

"There's one over here." Daffodil was pointing to a crumbling hole in the wall opposite.

"I've got to get this thing near that thing." Jake gestured toward the disintegrated part of the wall that Daffodil had pointed out.

"Ah," replied Santu, "we are using technical terms."

Jake didn't get the joke. He was busy trying to push the massive transmitter toward the power socket. Santu moved over to help him. The machine was heavy but not so heavy that the two of them couldn't slide it along the floor quite easily. As they shoved it across the floorboards something slid off its top making a loud clattering noise which startled everyone.

"Nobody should be panicking," said Santu, "something fell. It is looking like normal human matter. Do not be worrying. It was on top of this ridiculous thing."

Daffodil went over to see what it was. "I can't see behind here. It's too dark in this corner." Santu stopped pushing and passed his torch over to her. The light from the torch revealed a dust cloud filled with a whole cluster of items. The objects ranged from piles of letters wrapped in ribbons, to old tins filled with war medals, and even baby mittens.

"What are you finding?" asked Santu as they pushed the radiola into place.

"It looks like someone's personal effects," said Daffodil as she sorted through the dusty pile.

"Santu?" Is was Annabelle using her sweetest voice.

"Yes, Annabelle?" Santu was checking the dangerous looking socket. He whispered to Jake. "Maybe we should get Annabelle to be plugging this thing in?"

Jake laughed and whispered back. "Aw, but she's so much fun to have around."

Santu looked at his new friend in surprise. "Well I am the uncle of a monkey! You can be throwing out sarcasm too now?" He smirked up at Jake's pleased face. "Already you are being around Annabelle too long."

"Actually I think I've been around *you* too long." Jake was surprised at himself too. Something new was happening to him, something good. Slowly he was beginning to understand how to be sociable, how to joke, how to laugh. Briefly, the strange sensation of confidence washed over him. He had never felt anything like it. It was amazing.

"Me!?" Santu said with mock insult.

"Santu?" Annabelle sang. "What are we looking for *exactly*?"

Santu took a deep breath and plugged in the radiola. His hand paused waiting for the inevitable electrocution but nothing happened. He breathed out in relief and motioned for Jake to try the switches on the front of the contraption.

"Well," Santu replied as he threw a curious look at the socket, "anything to be doing with war for a start. How old are all these articles?"

"These ones start from 1914. This article is about the assassination of Archduke Ferdinand in Sarajevo," replied Annabelle sweetly.

"I've got some here that are dated from 1898," said Blaze more insistently.

Jake started fiddling with the dials and suddenly the light came on. He listened closely trying to find any kind of voice in the static. Every now and then a hideous screech from the machine blared at everyone making them wince. Daffodil managed to tie a makeshift knot with Jake's bed sheet around a part of the radiola while he was testing the dials.

"1914," said Santu trying to ignore Jake's attempts at tuning the radiola, "is when the World War One started. That assassination started it. You know, 9 million people died on the battlefields, and the same on the home fronts because of the food shortages, genocide, and ground combat. It was a terrible war. What is the article saying?"

"Um, *Two bullets were fired on a Sarajevo street on this sunny June morning killing both Archduke Francis Ferdinand and his pregnant wife. The conspirators were: The assassin, 19-year-old Gavrilo Princip whose Slavic nationalism burned deep within him for he believed that the death of the Archduke was the only way to release the chains binding his people to the Austro-Hungarian Empire; and Independent Serbia who provided the ammunitions.'* Annabelle face twisted as she read on. "There is an account by an eye witness. It says: *As they were returning from the Town Hall after their official engagement the car slowed down and Princip drew his pistol firing two shots. The first struck the wife of the Archduke, the Archduchess Sofia, in the abdomen. She was an expectant mother. She died instantly. The second bullet struck the Archduke close to the heart. With his last breath he called to his mortally wounded wife, 'Sofia' before his head fell back and he collapsed. His death was almost instant. The officers seized Princip. They beat him over the head with the flat of their swords. They knocked him down; they kicked him, scraped the skin from his neck with the edges of their swords, tortured him and all but killed him.'* Annabelle looked up at Santu.

"Oh yes this is true," said Santu as he walked toward Annabelle. "This Balkan Region of Europe was seething with political angst. This death of the Archduke was setting in motion a series of events that changed the world."

"Why was he so important?" asked Blaze trying to deflect Santu's attention.

Santu tied himself to a section of railing near one of the boxes. "This Ferdinand, he was being heir to the throne of the Austro-Hungarian Empire. When the Serbian assassinated Ferdinand, Austria-Hungary was then declaring war against Serbia. There were alliances with each side formed of several countries and from there it just was growing."

Suddenly a massive burst of static screamed out from the transmitter.

"I've got it!" yelled Jake, "I think I can hear something!"

"Yes," yelled back Santu, "we are all hearing *something*."

"Sorry," said Jake as he turned down the volume. "These dials are so dust-filled that they are kind of hard to get right."

"Just so long as the Shadow is not attracted to loud static." Santu smiled. He liked Jake. Jake was a straight up kind of guy: A 'what you see is what you get' character. Santu knew only too well how rare that was these days.

"Ah, guys?" Daffodil's voice was strangely calm. Everyone except the preoccupied Jake turned to face her.

"What is being wrong Daff?" Santu asked.

"These letters . . ."

With Daffodil's words, a chill ran down Santu's spine and he was struck with a strange vision but it was clouded in white and impossible to make out.

"What are you finding?"

"These letters, the ones that fell behind the radiola, they are from . . ." She looked up at Santu with big, brown, confused eyes, her blond messy hair like a halo in the darkness. "These letters are from Macalister *Glizsnort* to his *fiancé* Grace Durand." Daffodil held one up for the others to see. The notepaper was yellowed and moth eaten. The looping letters were beautifully scripted with some kind of flowing ink pen.

"The date is September, 1941. And in this one she says she is 30 and she thinks she is too old for him to marry her. He is away fighting in World War 2. He says he doesn't care how old she is."

A numbing cold swelled in Santu's chest. "Perhaps it is Madame Glizsnort's grandmother?"

"Maybe," said Daffodil dubiously. "If it wasn't for the swirling double G on Madame Glizsnort's collar . . ."

"She could be having the same initials as . . ." but every word Santu pushed out seemed to move further away from him. "What are the other letters saying?"

"They're all love letters." Daffodil was both charmed and repulsed simultaneously. Someone had actually loved Madame Glizsnort?

"Um," interrupted Annabelle, "are you claiming Madame Glizsnort, the frozen old witch that has been giving us grief since she came on board that bus, was apparently a fiancé in 1941?! If she was 30 years old in 1941, that means she would have been born in 1911! We have been talking and conversing and *seeing* a person that is apparently over 100 years old!"

"And she is being good at math," said Santu drolly.

"Listen," said Daffodil holding up an enormous pile of notepapers and ignoring Santu's tendency to self-amuse. "There are lots of letters where he is begging her to marry him but she won't commit until she can try and '*help the Lost Children*'." Unexplainably, Daffodil felt nauseous. "Macalister was an awarded war veteran. Look at all these medals." She held up a handful of ribbons and medallions. "But she wouldn't give herself to him until she believed she had done everything she could to help these Lost Children." Daffodil lifted a pile of dusty newspaper articles that had been added to the wrapped up letters. "According to these, he was a great man." Daffodil dropped the pile back on the floor.

Everyone felt the hairs on their arms stand up.

"The lost children?" asked Santu.

Daffodil nodded and went on to read one of the letters.

"'SAT 28th September, 1941.

My darling Macalister, my love for you is endless and the kindness in my heart for such a man is bound by true desire and willful extremes yet I must follow my heart in other matters as well. You know I have had grave fears in the two years gone by for those lost souls, the ones I call the Lost Children. You know I must quest for more knowledge to help these little children with no homes. I cannot do this with a husband that belongs to the harsh realities of war.

Fleet Street got hit yesterday and the damage was shocking. Here in Blackwater we were privy to a dreadful showdown. I should think there were at least 60 planes in the sky and I saw 6 shot down. We had to spend several hours in the shelter at Warwick Street. While we waited, I confess to grieving for being without you. I worry so terribly about your wellbeing and what you are experiencing. Please do try and be as careful as possible.

I have so far, made no progress on the matter of these Lost Children—even with the help of all your contacts—except that I believe that all these children perished in the First Great War. I fear they have been roaming the afterlife for a long time and I truly believe that if I cannot find a way to send them to God, that their sorrow will have grave repercussions for everyone.

The mood in the town has grown heavy and dark. People have turned against each other. There is a foreboding here now that weighs upon us every day. I fear, the longer these children are left to suffer, the more imminent the danger of malevolence shall be. Our lovely Blackwater shall be disturbed beyond redemption. I do not fear the children. They are absolute innocents. It is the length of time they linger between worlds that concerns me. I believe something vengeful is growing and it is not just focused on the children but our entire Blackwater community. With the acceleration of our Second World War, many of the people have become grief-stricken and inconsolable and it is another issue which compounds the apprehension of our residents.

It is Myrtle's birthday tomorrow—I am sure you know your own sister's birth-date! She has chosen not to celebrate this year but Harold insists that we all have a picnic. Perhaps some tea and cupcakes with the children will be just what she needs to cheer up a little. We will be praying for you and all the troops.

My sweet, do not idealize me. I do not deserve such a gentleman as yourself, so kind and loving. There is much before us that must be dealt with. I honor your service to this country. But let us always be honest with each other. I am too old now for you to carry on a life and we must be realistic in all matters even those guided by our hearts.

If I have let you down it is my greatest sadness but my endeavor must be met and it seems I am the only one that has the will to discover the truth without succumbing to the terrible hatred that pervades the issue of the Lost Children.

Your love for me has made me stronger and for that my gratitude is boundless. My faith is also fortified and it is this that encourages me to forge on. My respect and utter devotion to you is too strong to allow you to become entangled in something so unnatural. I will be too old for marriage by the time you return from war. You deserve a young and vibrant soul who can immerse herself in your duties.

My apologies run deeper than blood and God and all his obedience. Forever yours, in the stars and moon, God bless you and keep you.

With my greatest love, Grace Durand.'"

"So these lost children are our ghosts?" Santu was squinting into the air as if he was looking for something. "What does this boyfriend say?"

"Fiancé," corrected Daffodil unsure of why she felt so protective towards two strangers. "Well there's one here that was written not long after." Shuffling through the dusty pile Daffodil found the one she wanted and began to read.

"29ʰ October 1941.

Grace, my darling fiancé. Your letter, although filled with the sadness of the times, buoyed my spirits. I know everything is uncertain at the moment but I truly believe, my love, that peace will come to us and the world. I understand that you will only make our sentiment official when I return to you, which I believe is of a superstitious calling by yourself, but I understand and will hold you to your agreement on my assured homecoming.

This Second Great War now gains momentum and it seems evil is compounding the days into long dark nights. After the Italian troops took 155,000 men and invaded Greece via Albania, we were put on alert. We were told that the Greeks could field 420,000 men and that the Italian troops were hindered by bad weather but this also stopped us from providing air support for the Greeks. We are told that German troops may also be provided to assist the Italians and so our forces have now landed on the Greek Island of Crete to begin mining the waters off the coast. I am ready to do what I can. I do not know when you shall receive this letter but I pray it will be before Christmas.

Do you remember 2 Decembers ago? We snatched an hour together and walked across the freshly fallen snow to attend the Christmas dance? I remember our first kiss as if it were yesterday. I should have wed you that very day. I wish with all my heart I had convinced you that our marriage could unite us in our quest for truth regarding the Lost Children. Instead I let you forge on with your refusals. My foolishness is with me daily.

I know you fear for the Lost Children but, with my hand on my heart, I promise to pursue this with you when I return home. Do not give up hope for them; do not give up hope for us.

Please do not let the numbers of age instill doubt upon our love. There has never been any uncertainty in my mind that our future will be as happy, if not happier, than our past.

Oh, I do so long to begin our life together. We certainly should make a real success of it and I'm sure we will. There are many things of which I cannot be sure, but of you, I am absolutely certain. I know the quality of your heart, I know the goodness that guides our spiritual map, and I know what is right and true. Nothing can part us. Sweet one, I look to the future.

I understand that you do not want to be idealized but it is hard not to sing the praises of such a wonderful woman with a heart full of goodness and faith. My sweet, we are a part of eternity. Darling, there is no more precious gift than the sure love of a good woman. I am going to treasure that gift all my life.

Well, Beloved, I must go to sleep now, our troops face a long battle ahead.

I love you with all my heart.

By the Grace of God go I.

Adoringly yours, Macalister Glizsnort.'"

The words brought Santu unwanted visions. They had piled on top of each other fighting for dominance. It was as if his mind was the battleground for the love between Grace and Macalister and the Lost Children. There *had* been true love between the two but the future took Macalister's dream of a happy marriage to a dark place. His wife, so consumed with the mystery of the Lost Children, had taken him to the brink of loss many times: Loss of wonder, loss of joy, loss of intimacy; but never the loss of his love. The man stood tall and strong and never gave in to anything—including his wife's eventual madness. The pieces were starting to fall into place.

"The First Great War," said Santu, "was being from 1914-1918. So these *Lost Children* were being ghosts a long time when she wrote this letter in 1941."

"So I guess," said Daffodil, "we can concentrate from 1914 on?"

"Do you think," said Blaze, "that the Second World War could have revived the ghosts' torment?"

Santu nodded, his mouth turned down. "Well she says she is having grave fears for them for the last two years. This corresponds with the beginning of World War 2 in 1939. Maybe they are going through everything again?"

"So," Annabelle was flummoxed, "no one is at all concerned that we have been seeing a woman that is apparently over 100 years old and quite evidently dead?"

"Not really. It is different, yes, but no, not really," said Santu enjoying the moment just a little bit. "Blaze has already guessed she was a ghost."

Static Recording No.5244—On Loop

Bugsy. 1910-1917. Ghosted Aged 7.

Hello. I am called Bugsy. That is because I like to play with bugs—all different kinds of bugs. I don't feel well. I started feeling even worse when Oscar took me to the other place. I almost forgot about my bugs!

Oscar took us away in such a hurry. He said we were all in very grave danger. But he didn't say why or where we were going. We left in such a rush that I had no time to think. I felt very strange. Everyone looks really bad. I didn't like it at all but I couldn't remember where we came from.

I asked Oscar where we were before and he said we were in the church. And then I remembered! My BUGS! I left my bugs! And when I first met Oscar, he said if I wanted to come with him I could bring my bugs. But this time he forgot them. That's like forgetting Bitsy or Melody or even leaving Baby behind.

It made me start worrying and I can't think about anything except my bugs. They have been with me my whole ghosted life, you know. They were with me *before* Oscar. But I was afraid that if I told Oscar I wanted to go back he would stop me. He is very good you know, but he is very powerful too. Much more powerful than any of us.

So I turned to the only one here that wouldn't care about leaving: Dog. Dog is okay. He acted really furious when I told him but he's going to help me find my bugs. I don't think Oscar would understand but I am nothing without them.

Dog did a swell job. He found our church. I am trying to make a recording but I'm not sure if it's working—I usually get Bitsy to make it go on. It's moved too. The recording thing we use. It's moved to the other side of the room. I don't like it there. I've been yelling at it but I'm not sure it's recording. It's all lit up like it is when Bitsy turns it on but I can't see anyone or anything. Where are my bugs!?

Dog says we have to stay dormant until we are sure the bugs are here but I'm so worried about them. I feel really sick. I don't like feeling like this. I want my bugs. I want to scream out 'Bugs!' But I don't want to frighten them either.

Dog and I have made a decision. It is very important. I know that now. Dog and I have decided that if we can't find my bugs, we will not go back to the other place where Oscar thinks he can save us.

No. We will go into the Shadow. Bruises is there after all. And Dog says there's another way home. We have to go through the Shadow which is scary but he thinks that it may be the only way. He's got a point. We've been trying everything to go home and it hasn't worked. Maybe we should try this?

First I need to get my bugs.

Second, I need to make sure this is recording because I don't want Oscar to think I just left without a reason.

Thank you for helping me Oscar. You're a 'good kid' too. But I have to find home; I have to find some place other than here. I have to find someone or *something* that wants me. To do that, I have to take my bugs and keep looking. I never thought I could like anyone, ghosted or not, I guess I found out I could.

Please Oscar, take care of Bitsy. I miss her already.

~Present day~

~Documents in the Attic~

B laze had been thinking about the little ghosted girl with calipers on her legs. "What do you make of this?" she asked. "It's dated November 17th, 1916 and it's from the Daily Express. *Polio Epidemic Affects Travel Rules For Children and those with Infantile Paralysis. On this day in 1916, the following has been issued by the Seaboard Air Line Railway, concerning the South Carolina quarantine against infantile paralysis. Railroad tickets will not be sold to children under 16 years of age unless a certificate is furnished by the local Board of Health, where one exists, and where no local Board of Health exists, by family physician residing in the locality showing that the child has not been in contact with any case of Infantile Paralysis and has not had the disease of Polio this year.'*"

"What this polio?" asked Duette flicking her angular fringe from her face.

"This is a highly infectious viral disease," said Santu.

Annabelle rolled her eyes. Did Santu have to know *everything*?

"I am thinking too," he went on; "that there are two kinds, but the worst is being the paralytic one. It is attacking motor neurons in the spinal cord, and is causing paralysis in your arms and legs and it can even affect your sight and taste. It can paralyze your lungs too. That is what iron lungs were used for; they pushed and pulled the person's chest muscles to make them breathe."

"They live in iron lung?" asked Duette absolutely horrified.

Santu nodded. "It was infecting lots of children."

The stories from the articles that they swapped were difficult to listen too. Each of them was distressing in their own way. Whether they were about bombs killing civilians and children, about the many fatal diseases that had taken numerous lives, or about stories of lost soldiers, they all ended miserably.

Continuing to immerse themselves in the task at hand they plowed on in the belief that there would be something that could prove useful later. What else was there to do?

Jake was still listening intently, trying to find a vibration for the voices they sought. Disjointed words called out to him but they jumped and switched owners. Frustration was starting to sink its teeth into his optimism.

Both Blaze and Annabelle continued to ignore each other until Blaze found a bizarre article that, if anything, would at least give everyone something to think about other than doom and disaster.

"Hey listen to this. It's from May 5th, 1916, and it's really bizarre." She had their attention. "*Horace Thole, deaf and dumb, has been presented with a chauffeur's license. He depends on his sensitive skin to detect sound.*"

"One of your relatives Jake?" asked Santu. But Jake wasn't listening.

The others smiled but this was all very peculiar and adding to the weirdness didn't help.

"Maybe," said Daffodil, "we should just try and focus on the important stuff. Otherwise we'll be here forever." Daffodil was still thumbing her way through the amazing wealth of love-letters and articles from the box that had been left on top of the radiola. Could these papers really be about the skeletal, gray skinned woman who had terrified them with her icy stare? And why would such important keepsakes have been left in the church attic to turn to dust?

"Sorry," said Blaze tugging on the sleeves of her cardigan. "It just seemed so . . ." she shook her head. "I don't know."

Annabelle couldn't resist such an open invitation for ridicule. "It was 1916 Blaze. That guy wouldn't have been allowed to fight in the war. Obviously. They were probably desperate for chauffeurs. Great time to be deaf and dumb." Annabelle was the only one who thought her sarcasm was amusing.

The fire from the burning logs was stretching thin wisps of flame upward in the cold, still air, trying to extend its warmth all the way to the ceiling. The curling flares formed strange shapes around the dark room, elongating and contracting like life forms. But the heat that the fire produced was barely significant in the freezing temperatures. Still, the orange glow brought the observers some comfort.

And there were more observers than the human eye could see.

"Anything Jake?" asked Santu over the crackling static.

Jake shook his head. "Maybe I can't do this."

"Whoa," said Santu, "don't be shooting yourself down. No negativity, remember?"

Jake nodded and turned back to the radiola.

Santu looked out into the dark night and searched anxiously for a sign of the Shadow. But the world beyond the broken church windows was motionless and silent. There were just the bare bones of trees lit by murky moonlight and lots of white, sound-deadening snow. Defeat loomed all around him but he wasn't going to let it beat him.

"Alright! We need to be focusing." A bit of energy was needed to revive everyone's lassitude. "Is anyone remembering anything about the ghosts mentioned that can be helping us?"

Daffodil tentatively raised her hand, but just as she did, Jake cried out in excitement.

"It's one of the looped recordings! I can hear it!"

Immediately everyone's attention turned to Jake. The only sound *they* heard was the mind numbing hiss of static. Jake was waving a hand, palm down, to quiet everyone.

"Don't be stopping reading," whispered Santu, "this could be taking a while."

Returning to the piles of insurmountable information, they periodically glanced up at Jake. His concentration levels looked immense.

"It's really dark now," whispered Daffodil. "Why do you think the ghosts aren't showing themselves?" Daffodil peered around the room as if squinting would make them appear. As she shone the torch into a far corner she jumped with fright. One glowing bug suddenly appeared in the torchlight. As her eyes grew big, another one popped into sight. And then another and another. "Um, guys . . . I think we've got lift off."

"Oh wow," cried Blaze, "they're back." But although the ghosted bugs turned up, there were no other spirits to be seen.

"Can anyone see any of the ghosts?" Daffodil was getting really worried now. Foreboding loomed. Something had gone very wrong. "I don't know how to explain it but it feels different in here now."

Santu was nodding. For some reason Daffodil always turned to Santu for assurance. This time there was none and her senses sent up emotional flares.

Suddenly Jake's sharp tone penetrated the silence.

"I can hear a boy . . . he's calling himself 'Bugsy'. He says Oscar took them all away just as the Shadow turned up here. But Bugsy forgot his bugs." Everyone looked at the torch in Daffodil's hand. A dozen bugs were fluttering around in its beam.

"But," said Daffodil looking desperately around the room, "where is *he*?"

Jake shook his head but kept going. "He doesn't feel well and he doesn't like the place Oscar has taken everyone. He's *really* worried about his bugs." Jake's face turned white with panic. "And he says if can't find his bugs, he and another boy called Dog will go into the Shadow."

Daffodil jumped up. Love letters flew amongst dust clouds. "We have to find them!"

"Maybe," thought Santu quickly, "Bugsy cannot see his bugs? Hold up the torch, Daffodil, and go over to the Radiola."

Daffodil moved as quickly as she could without disturbing the glowing creatures. "Jake, try to talk into the Radiola like we did last time."

"It was on a different wave-length!" Jake was horrified. How would he ever find the right frequency without the ghosts actually helping him? "Bitsy moved the dials last time." Jake had started twisting and winding frantically but his anxiety was making him clumsy.

Everyone was on their feet. It is almost impossible to stay still under such circumstances. In the next moment Daffodil saw a flicker.

"Jake slow down!" She moved closer to the transmitter. Jake was looking at her with a horrified expression. "Just go very slowly Jake," she said, her voice was low and toneless. Jake followed her instructions watching her wide brown eyes for any indication. As Jake's hands gently moved the dials left Daffodil saw another flicker. "There Jake! Right next to the radiola! Go really slowly . . . now go just a bit left."

The flickering gradually got stronger until they were faced with the ghosted images of two little boys. One looked about the age of six or seven and the other one looked about ten or eleven. The littlest boy was moving his mouth. It was easy to see what he was saying. Daffodil held up the torch for him.

"Jake that's nearly perfect. Just turn the left dial a tiny bit to the right."

As Jake twisted the dial they were all hit with an excited shout.

"My bugs!!!" Bugsy at once flashed over to the torch and scooped them into his arms. He then dashed straight back to the Radiola. "Look Dog, my bugs!"

The other boy shrugged his shoulders and nodded his head. It was the body language of distrust. It was the same angry boy who had refused to speak into the radiola last time. Daffodil knew cynicism and suspicion to be a cover for hurt. She had even gone through a stage that had rendered her a master of that type of behavior. It didn't take long for her to realize that it generally turned people away. Involuntarily she threw a glance at Annabelle, but Annabelle looked quite interested in the new development.

Jake was the closest to the two boys and the obvious one to try to communicate with them.

"Hello to both of you. We're so glad you came back for your bugs. We've been really worried about you."

"Yeah, my bugs," Bugsy said. "I'm named after my bugs. My name is Bugsy. This is Dog." Some of the bugs were fluttering around his head like a halo and several were in his hands and a few were sitting on his shoulders. He reminded Santu of a Spanish statue covered in pigeons. "I forgot my bugs." Bugsy was trying to smile at each of them which was difficult because the ones flying around his head kept moving.

Daffodil decided to tackle the one called Dog and leant in close to the radio. Jake wrapped a supportive arm around her shoulders before moving away. Daffodil's heart beat a little faster. Jake didn't like to have people touch him and he certainly didn't like to touch others. This was momentous. But there were other things to take care of right now. She threw a kind smile back at Jake but Jake was concentrating on the ghostly figures.

"Hi Dog, I'm Daffodil. I think it's great you came with Bugsy to find his bugs. We really want to talk to you. And we really don't want you to leave, okay?"

"Yeah," started Dog, "well we've got the bugs now so . . ."

Daffodil's thoughts were charging. If she let them go now they were all doomed, she was sure of it.

"We know something," she tempted him. "We'd like to tell you but you'd have to stay here if we tell." Daffodil tried to appeal to the child in him—she hoped there was still one in there somewhere.

Bugsy was delighted. "Is it about my bugs?"

"Well," said Daffodil slowly and enticingly. "It's definitely about your bugs and your duck and your dog." She was winging it and it was risky. But, so far, except for Scraps, they all seemed to be named because of their ghosted selves. Why else would the other boy be called Dog?

"What about my dog!" The boy was immediately defensive. Daffodil was right: Dog was worried about his pet but he didn't want to admit it.

"I don't think your dog likes the place that Oscar has taken it to."

Dog shook his head. "None of us likes it." Then suddenly he looked suspicious. "What's my dog's name?"

Everyone panicked. They knew Daffodil had just been trying to maneuver Dog into staying. What would she do now?

But Duette and Duel were all over it. Together, after their terrible experience in the shadow, their abilities had gotten stronger and more absolute. Ghosts were just another entity to penetrate. They pushed the thought to Daffodil.

"You mean Scruffy?" Daffodil asked nonchalantly.

Dog was astonished. "What about Scruffy?" Apprehension was bulldozed by hope. Was that what it was? Dog couldn't remember feeling that before. But to feel hope about saving a stupid, annoying dog was unsettling. Anger brewed inside him. How dare this stranger make him feel like that. Who the hell did she think she was?

"We can keep Scruffy safe here. And we can make sure everyone finds their way home." Daffodil hoped she wasn't lying.

"We gotta go." Dog looked fiercely at Bugsy.

Bugsy was about to follow Dog's orders when his bugs started to fly away from him. They flew over to Jake and pinioned themselves to Jake's eyebrows. Jake wasn't sure what to do: Ghosted bugs attached to your eyebrows can be very disconcerting. Obviously the bugs didn't want to go wherever it was that Oscar had taken the others.

Jake threw Daffodil an urgent look. Daffodil tried to think of something that would have gotten through to *her* when she was angry and upset.

"Well the bugs obviously trust us not you." It was hurtful, and for that, Daffodil was sorry, but if she could get Bugsy on side, maybe Dog would follow. Just maybe.

Bugsy was devastated. His eyes filled with luminous tears and he reached out his arms as if that may make the bugs return to him. But he didn't move away from Dog.

Dog hesitated. He was strangely affected by what had happened. He didn't understand it and he didn't want to try. For the first time in his existence he decided to chance it. This was the end anyway. And there was no reason to take Bugsy into the Shadow if there might be another way home. The dim-witted dog could come with him if it really wanted to. He kind of missed it following him around all the time anyway.

"Alright then," Dog said warily. "Tell us your stupid secret."

OBSERVER

VOL. 5, NO.175 London, Friday, August 31, 1914   3S

GERMANS DEFEAT RUSSIAN

UGUST RESULTS SO FAR - Germany declares war on Russia an nce - Britain declares war - Germany invades Belgium - Austria-Hungary lares war on Russia - Serbia declares war on Germany - France invades Al eat Britton declares war on Austria-Hungary - Austria invades Poland - Aus ngary invades Serbia - France declares war on Austria-Hungary - Russia in

st Prussia - Russia vades Galica - Japan ares war on Germany- stria declares war on elgium - Russians invade Konigsberg - Germans occupy French city of iens - and TODAY - ERMANS DEFEAT USSIANS AT TANN- BERG. Page 2.

HEP! HEP! HEP! LONDON KIDS MARCH OFF TO "BATTLE"—THAT'S WAR FEVER IN ENGLAND

War Scene in London—Group of Boys, Engulfed by the War Wave, Marching Through Whitehall. Note the Dinner-Pail Drum.

Austrian Troops fighting on the Danube

DRUG PRICES RISE 20 PER CENT BECAUSE OF WAR

he United States it is Reported that sh Supplied Opium has made a leap ice of 55 Cents on the Pound. The as also Halted Supply of Quinine t is Mainly Produced in Hamburg, rmany. Page 7.

Paris - Archer M. Huntington, the pres dent of the American Geographical Soc ety, and Mrs. Huntington, were held for uestioning before being arrested under he charge of Spies. Full story Page 8.

Germans march near Liege. See Page 3.

~Present day~

~D⊕G DAY AFTERN⊕⊕N~

D affodil and Jake took turns trying to explain the circumstances of why they were here. By explaining that the ghosts had been watched over by a woman called Madame Glizsnort during her lifetime, curiosity took over from suspicion. Daffodil explained that they believed this woman may have spent most of her life searching for the truth of what had happened to those she called the Lost Children. They even explained that this woman had put off her marriage in her effort to discover their truth.

"And her letters indicate that you may have all ghosted during World War I."

The two ghosted boys flashed in and out. It was as if the information was too much to bear: Had someone cared about them all these years? And then Dog had a sudden and intense memory. Quickly, he began to talk to Bugsy. Dog's mouth moved so rapidly that it was impossible for the spectators to tell if it was good or bad. Bugsy was the first to mouth the words into the radiola.

"We remember a woman called that."

Emotions swirled around the room like a whirlpool. That was an impossible answer. But this was *all* impossible.

"What do you mean you *remember* Madame Glizsnort?" asked Daffodil.

Bugsy and Dog exchanged glances. "She wasn't called Madame she was just called Misses. She was the teacher at this church." Bugsy looked excited with himself. "I can't believe we remember that. Maybe being near you helps us?"

"Oh," said Daffodil. "I'm sure it does." This was a bonus she hadn't expected. But she was confused. She reminded herself to ask one question at a time even though thoughts were filling her head like a rush of water. "But this is a church not a school."

"Oh no," replied Bugsy, "this was a school for ages. She always seemed sad but I liked her. We learned a lot."

"Why was she teaching in the church?"

"I don't think there was anywhere else to teach. And she loved the church so much. She used to tell us about the history of the windows and . . ."

Dog elbowed Bugsy. Bugsy elbowed back.

"They don't need to know that!" cried Dog.

"But I'm remembering heaps of stuff. It's really swell to have memories come back!"

"Okay, that's really helpful Bugsy, thank you." Daffodil was pleased: Bugsy was capable of defiance. Daffodil paced herself; she was one question away from understanding. "So did Madame, sorry, *Mrs.* Glizsnort *know* you were in the 'classroom'?"

Dog and Bugsy exchanged worldly glances.

"I think so." Momentarily Dog's defenses were down. Resistance just didn't seem necessary. "She looked for us. She talked to us when no one else was around but she definitely couldn't see or hear us—we yelled a lot trying to get her attention." Dog shrugged. "But she didn't answer." Dog looked at Bugsy with an immense sorrow that held an unforgiving life. "I wanted her to know. I was so angry that she couldn't hear me or see me." Dog looked around the room as if he were looking for someone that might judge him. "And then she disappeared."

"She disappeared?"

"We just couldn't see her anymore," said Dog. "And all the children in her class disappeared too."

"That was when Oscar started getting worried," added Bugsy. "She had been acting weird though, hadn't she Dog?"

Dog thought for a moment. "I guess she was, well . . . kind of scaring the students."

"I see," said Daffodil wondering what that meant. Perhaps Madame Glizsnort had died and the school had died with her? But what most concerned Daffodil, was why Madame Glizsnort had not been able to find the ghosts after she passed away. Surely, she would still have sought them?

Suddenly it occurred to Daffodil that Madame Glizsnort must have been the one who initiated the Secret Society for Gifted Teens. How she could have been involved was beyond Daffodil's understanding but how else could this all tie together? Daffodil turned to Jake whose eyebrows still fluttered with translucent wings. Unable to move his face, he shrugged his shoulders. Her look followed over to Santu.

"Daffodil," began Santu, "ask them if it is dangerous where the other ghosts are hiding out."

Daffodil asked the question. The answer wasn't what she wanted to here.

"It is very dangerous," said Dog slowly.

The yawning blackness of the night became overwhelming. The small slither of orange light from the fire was waning but shifting might disturb what was going on. One false move and both Dog and Bugsy could disappear again.

"Then," said Santu knowing the ghosts couldn't hear him, "I think we are having to to do something pretty drastic."

"What have you got in mind?" asked Jake raising his butterfly eyebrows.

"I am thinking we should be sending Dog back to get the others and we should be concentrating on Bugsy to try to find a way to send him home."

"But," said Blaze, "forcing him to remember his life *before* will make him upset."

"And," said Annabelle, "that's sure to bring negativity into the mix." She blinked twice, "And the Shadow."

"Yeah," said Santu, "I think I am knowing what I am implying." He looked momentarily annoyed and then stopped himself. Everyone had a right to be worried. "I am sorry but we may have to be facing the Shadow again." Santu shrugged. "Unless someone else is having a light-globe?" He looked around the room. A sea of perplexed faces stared back at him.

Bugsy was starting to panic. He couldn't hear what the humans were saying and he knew Dog was getting suspicious again.

"What's going on?" Bugsy cried into the radiola. "You're not going to leave us are you?"

Daffodil was quick to reassure him. "Oh no, Bugsy! Of course we're not going to leave you. We are just trying to figure out the best way to get you home quickly."

"You mean," said Bugsy feeling numb with excitement, "you can take me home?"

"I'm sure we can Bugsy," replied Daffodil. "No, I know we can. We just need to figure out the best way to help you." She wiped the slick of cold perspiration from her brow. Her body was running on overtime. The awakening crystals she had used had taken their toll. With little sustenance and hardly any sleep she felt like she was about to crumble into a thousand pieces. Biting her lip she tried to stop herself from fainting.

Jake saw her falter and looked desperately at Santu. Santu nodded back at Jake. Santu's visions had returned to him but they were not the kind of visions he was used to. Daffodil was in real trouble.

"Daffodil," Santu said, "you are needing to rest."

Daffodil was annoyed at herself. For the first time in her life she was truly needed and now she was falling apart. "I'm okay Santu." She showed him an appreciative smile. "I need to do this."

Santu recognized that tone. It was one of necessity and complete awareness. Daffodil was not going to give up or give in. Santu respected that. She knew what was happening to her body and she wanted to keep going. He nodded appreciatively.

"Alright, Daff." Santu gave her a serious stare. "But please, if we can be helping, you must say this."

Daffodil didn't expect that from Santu. It made her emotions chug into gear. She pushed them to the periphery. *Not now*, she thought as she threw an assertive nod in Santu's direction. Then she gave him an expression that was hard to misread. Santu nodded.

"Right," Santu said, "I am saying this on Daffodil's behalf because if she is saying this, the ghosts will obviously be hearing her." He took a deep breath. "We are needing to encourage Bugsy to remember his story. Anything that is sounding familiar with something you have read, no matter how unimportant, just be speaking upward. The first is always being the hardest." A sad smile swam across Santu's face.

"But," said Blaze, "what about the Shadow?"

"I know." Santu didn't know what to say to her. He couldn't tell her it would be alright. "Look, we have been fighting it twice already. Now we are having Daffodil's protection stones and Duette and Duel's shield. Who knows, maybe Madame Glizsnort will be helping us too?" He paused knowing his speech was minimalistic. "You are brave Blaze." Santu gave her a meaningful look. "People think that because someone is brave, they are *not* scared. These people are wrong. We are all scared. This, I *can* promise you. I am thinking that I can also promise that if we are not doing this, we might be finding ourselves lost in limbo too. So, we are ready?" Everyone returned a rapid, 'let's get on with it' nod. Santu turned to Daffodil.

Daffodil took a deep breath. "We want to help you very much." Looking from Dog to Bugsy, she said, "but we need you to help us to do this."

Suspicion brimmed in Dog's sad face. The humans had been talking amongst themselves for a long time without directing any looks toward himself or Bugsy. Dog was feeling a strange mix of emotions, emotions he hadn't remembered feeling until now. He wanted to trust what they were saying but he just couldn't.

Dog remembered when he'd first met Oscar. In hindsight it was almost funny. He had put up such a fight. Oscar had just let him go until exhaustion took over. Then Oscar grabbed Dog and Scruffy and brought them to the church, where surprisingly, it had felt safe. Slowly Dog stopped jumping at every sound and settled in with the others. Never once had he admitted to Oscar how terrible it had been after he ghosted: There were awful entities out there. And Dog was just glad to be away from their greedy need-driven fears. And at least in the church the stupid dog, Scruffy was safe with him too. Not that he would ever admit that to anyone.

Dog whispered something in Bugsy's ear. Bugsy looked horrified.

"What are you going to do with us?!" Bugsy cried into the radiola.

Daffodil was taken aback by the alarm in his voice. "Oh Bugsy," she replied in the most sincere tone. "We just want to help you. We hate the Shadow and we don't want it to take anyone else away. We want you and your bugs to find home. Isn't that what you want?"

Bugsy was confused. He looked up at Dog and whispered something to him. Dog nodded and, uncharacteristically, wrapped an arm around his companion. Dog moved over to the radiola.

"I don't trust you," Dog stated. "But I don't trust anyone." He thought for a moment. "And maybe it's about time I did. There's not much to lose."

So serious for such a young thing, Daffodil thought. How awful to feel like that even after you've died.

"Thank you, thank you from all of us," said Daffodil. Emotion was building in her chest. "Then Dog, I trust you too."

Dog hadn't expected that and it disturbed him.

"Dog," Daffodil went on, "I need you to go back to Oscar and tell him what you have seen here today and tell him he needs to bring everyone back. She looked him hard in the eyes. "All the animals too." Daffodil knew that Dog would understand she meant Scruffy. "*I* trust *you*. Dog, I cannot tell you how important it is that you remember everything you have experienced here now. Please whatever you do, don't forget."

Dog couldn't remember anyone trusting him with anything. This was really important and *this* was beyond the faith of good. All of it grew inside him like a tree.

"I'll do it," he said carefully. "I'll do it if you promise to help Scruffy before me."

That was an easy answer. "We absolutely promise to help Scruffy."

"Before me," Dog added defiantly.

Daffodil swallowed. She scanned the rest of her group. They were all nodding. "Okay, Dog, we promise to help Scruffy, *before* you." Was that even possible? They couldn't talk to a dog. What if they couldn't help Scruffy? Then Dog wouldn't go either?" Daffodil decided to worry about that later—if there was a later to worry about it.

"Alright then," said Dog, "I'll go back to Oscar."

It was a horrible moment. Bugsy was holding onto Dog's arm desperately. White, pearly tears were rolling down his cheeks and he was begging his wary friend to stay. All Bugsy kept saying was 'if you go I'll never see you again'. It was heartbreaking.

Dog started to reassure Bugsy. He pointed to the winged creatures still dancing on Jake's eyebrows and that distracted Bugsy for just a moment. By the time Bugsy had turned around, Dog was gone.

INFORMAL TRUCE FOR FRONTLINES AT CHRISTMAS

in the freezing, wet conditions of No Man's Land on the front-lines, the German and English troops have agreed to stop the gun fire. The waterlogged trenches, at just 50 yards apart, are close enough for the opposing men to hear each other and even smell their enemy's food. Curiosity has pushed them to begin talking to each other and this has led to the truce which has seen them bury their dead together and talk like comrades. P2

A Letter Home - Our reporter has found a letter from one of the English troops of this truce: "In the darkness of Christmas Eve I saw lights twinkling and realized the German troops had put Christmas trees in front of their trenches lit by candles. As they sang Silent Night, we applauded and began to sing too. A meeting was called between us & the Germans -our captain returning with a German cigar! Many of us swapped addresses with the 'enemy' and talked of our loved ones at home, We swapped goods and newspapers. One can not help but wonder what would happen to us all if the spirit showed here were caught by all the nations of the world." PAGE 3.

~Present day~

~One Goodbye too soon~

If Bugsy's distraught tears weren't enough, his bugs were expressing their angst too. They flitted into everyone eyes, they swooped at Jake's eyebrows as if their nesting place had become contaminated, and they scuttled in the dark shadowy corners of the room away from Bugsy. Bugsy was inconsolable. He flashed and flitted after them never moving quickly enough to catch them until finally he gave up. His bugs did not want him anymore. He slumped to the ground. Duette gave up her post to try to console him but she had no idea how to do that. And then she wondered, if with all this new found talent, she could push positive thoughts into a ghost. It was an interesting premise. Duette opened her mind.

"What do we do?!" cried Daffodil after watching Bugsy chasing his bugs around the room.

"Now," said Santu, "we invest in Bugsy." He stared at the little boy hunched at Duette's feet. "What are you thinking, Duette, Duel?"

Duette spoke softly as she stared at the sad little boy. "He need encouragement. Everything have left him. His little bugs need to trust him again." She knew what to do. As Duette concentrated, the bugs came flying toward her before suddenly making a circle near her chest. Duette pushed the circle, like a thought, towards Bugsy. Obediently, they encircled Bugsy's head.

Bugsy was amazed. His bugs had come back to him.

Daffodil spoke into the radiola. "Bugsy, they're relying on you now. Your bugs need you to find home." She paused. "Do you want your bugs to find home?"

Bugsy nodded.

"Then come on over here and talk to me." Daffodil motioned for him to speak into the radiola so that she could hear him. In a flash, Bugsy and his halo of bugs were at the old transistor.

"But I don't know what to say to them," Bugsy said sadly.

"Bugsy, just tell your bugs that they are safe with you. Tell them that we will find a way to send you all home."

"But what if their home is somewhere different to my home?"

"I think you will find that it's the same Bugsy."

Bugsy cheered up a bit. "But what about Dog and Oscar and everyone else?"

"Yep," said Daffodil, "same place." With a gentle smile she added, "You may all go there at different times but you will all arrive at the same place. You will all be together. But you won't have to be afraid anymore. There won't be a Shadow and you will remember everything."

That pleased Bugsy enormously. "That's good because I was worried no one was going to be waiting for me there."

Daffodil felt her heart drop. If this poor little boy didn't even remember his own parents, how were *they* going to help him?

But that wasn't what Daffodil should have been worried about. In fact that wasn't what she should have been thinking at all. Neither should any of the others: Especially not Duette and Duel who should have been guarding the building with their thought-force-field.

As the distant echo of a thunderous roar came surging toward the church they simultaneously realized that the whirlpool of hatred was coming. Again.

In the charge of panic that seized her, Daffodil managed to tell Bugsy to hide behind the radiola. "Don't leave Bugsy. Don't go away. I promise we will help you, just don't leave."

Bugsy was terrified. But he had also spent his whole life being told what to do. All those orphanages had manipulated his tired little soul. He followed Daffodil's orders and, with bugs still circling madly around his head, he flashed all of them behind the huge old wooden radio.

Duette and Duel were feeling the draught swirl toward them. They were furious at themselves for having been caught off guard. Concentrating hard, they tried to regain their force-field.

Santu was pushing the boxes back toward the wall as far as his bed sheet would let him. Blaze and Annabelle were doing the same. The moonlight disappeared: The dark vortex of the Shadow was getting nearer. The thin wispy flame, which had been virtually insignificant before the Shadow's impending arrival, started burning with a supernatural force. The flares were rising higher and wider and making a hideous roaring noise that made Daffodil tremble. Knowing it was very possible for these ferocious flames to burn the church down—and all of them in it—she decided to do something quickly.

Intentionally, Daffodil had not anchored her bed sheet to anything solid. Quickly, she unfurled it and folded it, and running toward the burgeoning flames, she threw it over the fire. Then, grabbing the iron tray underneath the burning logs, she swiftly flipped it over and on top of the blaze. The tray was searingly hot and Daffodil felt the skin on her hands immediately blister and peel. The pain was excruciating but there was no time to consider it.

The thrashing winds were close now and the noise was deafening. The others were screaming at Daffodil but she couldn't hear what they were saying. She didn't need to. She was doing what had to be done.

Daffodil readied herself for the moment when the Shadow hit the church. It would unquestionably be made weaker by all the positively charged crystals that encircled the room, but she was sure it wouldn't stop the hideous mass from doing some serious damage. For that part she had another preparation. If it worked, it would be magical. If it didn't, she would surely die. Squeezing her eyes shut, she prayed to her lost relatives as she held her ground and waited for her moment.

The Shadow was now soaring around the outside of the church. Its winds were blasting at the building in a temper tantrum of rage and hatred. Newspapers were lifting out of their boxes: swirling paper tornados. The crystals were preventing the wild suctioning gusts from coming more than a few meters inside the church but Daffodil wondered how long it could be held off. Right now though, that didn't help Duette and Duel. They were being buffeted around like kites. At least their sheets were holding up.

Now the Shadow was upon them. Its ugly funnel mouth was surging and heaving just outside the windows desperate to get to its victims inside.

Black-dust arms were reaching, getting stronger with each rotation; the noise of the hissing spiral becoming more and more deafening, as if loud noise would make it all the more destructive. Then, with a vast rush of air, its dark breath tore through the windows.

Daffodil felt herself being pulled toward the violent windstorm. It was time. As she slipped closer she threw an apologetic look back at Jake. The sight of his frantic expression was awful. But her guilt and primal fear only encouraged the Shadow's strength. It made a massive whip toward her and she felt herself being lifted off the ground.

Voices yelled at her from around the room but they were distant echoes over the force of the winds. Unable to regain the concentration needed to recreate their force-field, Duette and Duel were being bashed against the walls around the windows, their natural instinct to protect themselves, causing their hands and arms terrible damage. How long could they have held it off for anyway?

Daffodil was nearly there. The force was really strong now and it had pulled her up to the windowsill. Her body was fighting against her will. Her autonomic sympathetic nervous system was trying to save her from danger, throwing intensive warning signals through her body. With a fleeting prayer, she forced herself to stop struggling, and grabbing the overhauled watch, she threw it into the dark swirling currents.

Suddenly, a great explosion erupted and blasted Daffodil backwards with a force so strong she was thrown half way across the room. Poor Duel and Duette were also thrown backwards so vigorously that their sheets were torn away from the window-railing and they too ended up in a crumpled heap on the other side of the room. Others smashed their heads against walls and crashed their bodies into the floor.

Daffodil didn't stay still for long. Immediately, she ran back to the window to see what had happened. Unsure of what she would face she gazed at an incredible sight.

The explosion had stopped mid-blast and a brilliant white light now hovered at its middle like a half-opened surprise. And, inside the white light, two lovely women floated mysteriously. The Shadow had shrunk back and was frozen on the fringes of the bright glow, unmoving.

Most of the others were untying themselves or had already joined Daffodil at the window. What they saw was both miraculous and surreal. The many gaping mouths stared at the sight in utter silence. Only one voice spoke out.

"Mom? Granny?" Daffodil whispered. "I don't understand."

"Child, it is not for you to understand right now, just accept." The soft tone of Daffodil's grandmother rang out toward her.

"But . . ." Daffodil quickly scanned the faces beside her. It was quite clear that the others could also see her dead mother and grandmother.

"Sshh," Daffodil's mother said, "you have done so well darling. I am so proud of you. We are all so proud of you." It was the first time since her mother's death that Daffodil had heard such reassuring words. This conversation was nothing like the simplistic, disappointing dialogues the apparitions of her dead parents had carried out.

"Why are you here?" Daffodil asked, still very confused.

"Darling," said her grandmother, "you have used your knowledge well. You have used my scroll just as it was intended. I have always known you would face this ordeal. I made sure I would be able to help you. I knew you would understand your calling."

"Which," added her mother, "you have done and more." Daffodil's mother smiled softly as she looked at her daughter. "Yet, there are still many more secrets to uncover."

"I have so many questions," Daffodil replied.

"I am sure you do darling, but I am afraid we do not have long."

"You have to go?"

"Yes my beautiful daughter, but we must first take them back with us."

"The ghosts?" Daffodil looked around frantically. Where was Dog? Why wasn't he back with everyone else? "But there is only one here at the moment! You have to come back and take them all." Immediately, Daffodil ran over to the radiola and called out to Bugsy who appeared beside her, his bugs resting on both ears.

Bugsy stared at the hovering white light just outside the window.

"It's so beautiful," he said before disappearing and reappearing at the window ledge.

Daffodil stood beside him. "This is Bugsy," she said to her mother and grandmother. "Bugsy doesn't remember who he is and we haven't had time to figure it out. And there are others that need to remember who they are too. We don't know how to find out and we don't know how to send them home. The other ghosts are coming back. If you could just wait or come back? Please don't leave yet."

"You will have to find another way," said Daffodil's mother. "These children must come home. The cycle must be completed. Look beyond your fears, all of you, and you will find new truths." Her eyes danced from Annabelle to Blaze. "Secrets are closed doors. You cannot achieve anything if you hide behind them."

Bugsy was waving at the two ladies in the white light. Without understanding why, he knew he needed to be with them.

"Hello Bugsy." The gentle voice of Daffodil's grandmother reached out to Bugsy and he realized he could hear her without the sound box. Immediately, Bugsy turned to Daffodil and began jabbering away to her, his bugs bouncing with every word. Daffodil smiled at him. *She* couldn't hear *him*, but she didn't need to, his excitement was all too clear.

"Daffodil," continued her grandmother, "it is good that we have Bugsy here. We know you will find a way to help the others cross over. We can see how your spirit has grown. And you have all these other clever people to help you." She swept an arm out at the shocked faces of Daffodil's companions. "We can't stay and we shall not be able to come back. I'm afraid the spell on the scroll has been used now—by all three generations. When you are older you will make another watch and it will be passed on to *your* daughter." Her smile was warm and kind and wonderful.

"But . . ." Daffodil didn't want them to leave. They couldn't leave, not yet.

"Darling," her mother said, "we cannot stay any longer. You must always trust your instincts and you must continue your work. You are going to be very well known you know. We love you so very much. And we will see each other again," she smiled, "but not for a long time."

"I love you both too. And dad, tell dad." There was nothing Daffodil could do.

Both the women laughed and nodded.

"Now, Bugsy," said Daffodil's grandmother. "Would you and your bugs like to come home? I promise you will be safe and loved. And don't worry; you will see your friends soon." She winked at Daffodil.

Bugsy was nodding so enthusiastically that his bugs were having trouble staying on his ears. He turned to Daffodil to tell her how happy he was. Daffodil couldn't read his fast moving lips but she understood what he was saying.

"Mom, granny, Bugsy can't hear me, could you tell him we will make sure his friends will follow him soon and that we think he is wonderful and that we will miss him and his bugs terribly." They passed the information on to Bugsy who flickered in and out quickly in his excitement.

"Come now Bugsy, come to us." But Bugsy didn't move. Daffodil's grandmother looked at Daffodil sadly. "Bugsy is worried about the others."

"Please," replied Daffodil, "tell him that his friends would want him to be the first to go so that he can be waiting for them when it's their turn."

As the words were passed on to Bugsy, his face lit up. He smiled a long awaited smile and glided into the light. As he did he began to glow with brilliant, bright, yellow light. Turning to face Daffodil, Bugsy raised a small hand and waved. Everyone waved back.

Daffodil's mother took Bugsy's right hand and her grandmother took his left.

"The Shadow," said Daffodil's fading grandmother, "will be inert for a time. We have reduced it considerably so you will have some time to save the others before it is strong again. But remember: You must destroy it. When all the others have passed over, you must make sure it is annihilated. Find out why it began, you will discover a way to exterminate it. Goodbye my precious granddaughter."

"Goodbye my darling daughter."

"Goodbye mom, goodbye granny. Thank you. Bye bye Bugsy." A tear rolled down Daffodil's cheek as the image of the three of them faded into a burst of white light.

Blackwater Herald Moon Tribune Monday, April 30th, 1945— One penny

THREE LEADERS DEAD
ROOSEVELT BRAIN HAEMORRHAGE
MUSSOLINI EXECUTED—HITLER SUICIDE

*A*fter President Roosevelt died suddenly from a cerebral hemorrhage in his sleep at West Springs, Georgia on April 12th at 63, now two other leaders have died. After being captured in Lake Como, Benito Mussolini, his mistress, Clara Petacci, and 17 of the Italian leader's henchmen, were executed in nearby Guilano di Mezzegere on Saturday, 28. Crowds gathered to revile his body.

And now, Adolf Hitler, leader of the Nazi Reich since January 30, 1933, the world's chief criminal, is also dead at the age of 56. It is believed he and Eva Braun married in a bunker in Berlin before committing suicide under the Reich Chancellery—he with a shot to the head, her from cyanide poisoning. Then, by previous instruction from Hitler, the bodies were burned to prevent the Russians from access to the remains. P4.

LOCAL NEWS HEADLINES
BLACKWATER'S DEMISE

Several years have passed since the last reporting of the Lost Children. We have had to repress our reports due to the surge of doomsayers. But it is apparent that the distress in the community has caused such great disturbance that we will all have to lie down.

The town struggles beyond hope now and our once thriving settlement seems destined for failure. The situation is dire.

After the bombing of the local church, the town has, again, fallen into contest: There are those that believe the Lost Children are responsible and will continue to perform evil acts, and those that believe they are innocent. The former agree that the children were the cause of both the church burning down, and now, it's bombing—they cannot believe God would have done such things to His house of worship.

And then there is the 'foreboding' that has permeated the streets with a sense of evil. Many claim to have seen dark shadows lurking behind them on the streets in both day and night.

"It is as if I am being hunted by something malevolent," said Mrs. Blakber of Shrine Street, just near the Cross Roads site of the church and its graveyard. "I know it sounds rather strange but I just know there is danger waiting here. I don't know where it has come from or why it is here but it is rather frightening." Some suspect that this disturbance has been caused by the doomsayers and their negativity—their hateful thoughts somehow manifesting to become a very threatening entity.

Many people, whose families have lived here for generations, are now moving on. The population of Blackwater has almost halved in size and businesses are suffering.

The remaining community has rallied together to try to halt the reducing numbers. All community members are asked to attend the meetings at the Town Hall every Monday evening at 6pm sharp.

PROMOTION FOR OUR SERGEANT

Our local Sergeant, Macalister Glizsnort, has been promoted again for outstanding service. On Friday 29, he was given the new title of Inspector. Although being offered an even higher position at a police station in far off Willow Lakes, Inspector Glizsnort refused. He has chosen to stay on at the Blackwater Station. "In this time of war and with the town diminishing, I want to stay and help in whatever way I can," said the Inspector. "This town has been my life and I will not leave until I find that I am the last man on the ship." And of course, there is my wife who feels she cannot move on without resolving the issue of the Lost Children.

He has a positive message for Blackwater though: "I believe there is also a good force here. A force that can fight the darkness we all feel. We just have to have faith, and of course, as always, we have to fight."

WORLD NEWS HEADLINES

Duisburg, Germany—*Duisburg is a dead city, but it has not been killed in the same way as Cologne. It has not been battered to extinction but it has had the life drained out of it. You wonder how the civilians existed in a city which had no life left in it; destroyed by itself; fallen victim not just to bombs but also to providence. How many cities have been destroyed like this? Page 8.*

Red Army reaches Auschwitz—*The army of the Soviet Union has discovered the Nazi concentration camp in southern Poland where they estimate the numbers murdered range from 1 to 3 million.*

Berlin, Germany—*Russians take German capital.*

Death Marches—*As allied arms close in on Nazi concentration camps they have discovered that the Germans have frantically tried to move the prisoners to forced labor camps. The prisoners have been made to walk very long distances in bitter cold with little or no food, water or rest. Those incapable have been shot and many have starved or died from exposure or exhaustion. PICTURES TRANSMITTED BY RADIO—PAGE 7.*

New Fuehrer—*Admiral Doenitz, spent time in a lunatic asylum in Manchester as a prisoner of war during the First Great War.*

~Brought to you by~

*PHOSFERINE—**The greatest of all tonics**—For Depression, Brain fog, Influenza, Indigestion, Sleeplessness, Debility, Headache, Neuralgia and More!*

*SOLIDOX TOOTHPASTE—**We use Ricinosulphate to give you dazzling white teeth!***

~Present day~

~WHERE DID ALL THE CHILDREN GO?~

As the white light shimmied into the sky above them, the dark mass of the Shadow was again revealed. It was half the size it had been, and it hovered, perfectly still, in some kind of stasis: There were no swirling winds, no growling thunderous roars.

"What do we do with it?" Blaze asked.

Daffodil picked up one of the protective crystals that lined the walls and threw it into the black centre of the immobile tempest. Instantly the Shadow made a dreadful yelping sound before stirring back into motion and quickly shooting off in the direction of the graveyard.

"Ahh," said Santu as he patted Daffodil on the back. "I am preferring to see this thing running away."

"Well," said Daffodil, "now you've all seen my dead ancestors. You're all as nutty as me."

"Good company then," said Santu with a relieved smile. "I guess our task is not impossible."

"Apparently not," said Daffodil feeling relieved. "But if they'd all been here . . ."

"Daffodil," said Blaze, "don't do that. It wasn't anyone's fault." Blaze reached out to grab her friend's hands and immediately noticed the burns on Daffodil's palms. "Daffodil," Blaze cried, "oh my god. Look at your hands." Daffodil looked down at them. They were bright red and large pieces of skin had peeled away.

"Yeah, they hurt."

"We need to go straight back to the cabin. Annabelle has a first aid kit fit for an ambulance in her pack," said Blaze also remembering all those snacks in Annabelle's bag.

"But what about the other ghosts?" Daffodil asked.

"I tell you what," said Santu. "I will be staying here in case they come back. Everyone is needing to get some sleep. We are not ghosts. We are needing to rest. Besides the light will be coming up shortly and the ghosts can't move in daylight, remember?"

Santu was right. Everyone was exhausted. He was also right about the ghosts.

"Then you should come back to the cabin too," said Daffodil. "I'll make sure I'm awake before it starts getting dark again."

Gratefully, Santu nodded agreement.

After Blaze handed out snack bars she began gently rubbing cream on Daffodil's damaged hands. The concoction that Daffodil had got Blaze to make from her collection was rather complicated but she felt her new friend had done as well as possible.

Luckily neither Duette nor Duel had broken any bones. They were badly bruised but Duette had quite clearly claimed them nothing to the discolorations Duel had saved her from.

"So Daff, how'd you come up with the idea?" Blaze's creamy skin looked almost translucent in the light of the waning fire which Santu had begun to reignite. It fascinated Santu that Blaze's features were in such contrast: That flaming wild red hair and such a soft, creamy complexion. But he knew not to stare. Girls didn't understand it when boys wanted to look at them. It made them either suspicious or conceited. He flicked a glance at Annabelle. The best way to get the girls was to make *them* come to *him*. Still it was difficult not to study her. He stabbed the fire a little too hard and embers spilled forward, extinguishing themselves like suicidal fireflies.

As Daffodil explained, the others watched Santu's attempts at stoking the dying fire. Jake had already gone into the other bedroom and climbed into bed. Being as tired as he was, he hoped he would be able to sleep without static *and* without nightmares. He closed his eyes, listening to the conversation in the next room, and waited for nothingness.

"I remembered that the white light, the one Duel believes was Madame Glizsnort, helped wreak havoc on the Shadow. After I read the scroll inside the watch I thought, if I could manage to fix the scroll and douse the watch with protective spells, it might bring some of the light from my ancestors. And, if I threw the watch into the Shadow, that white light would be even more powerful." She shook her head. "I had no idea it would bring them back. I had no idea we could have used them to save the rest of the ghosts. I'm so sorry."

"Heavy handed with the potions again?" asked Duel with a smirk. "You really need to work on that." Duel was lying on his sister's bed, his eyes closed and his elbows bent behind his head leaving Duette only enough room to sit on the edge at the bottom of the mattress.

A half smile crossed Daffodil's face before her head fell in disappointment. "I didn't think."

"It is alright Daffodil," said Santu. "None of us has been sleeping or eating properly in days. Nobody has been thinking right. Maybe you can be fixing the watch again?"

Daffodil looked out the cabin window shaking her head. "No, the spell has been used. Didn't you see? It exploded into light."

"Well," said Blaze, "those crystals you used around the perimeter of the church walls helped too. The Shadow definitely had to struggle harder to get to us this time."

Daffodil nodded. "Yes, but I think we will need more of them now. I've been growing them since we got here so we should have plenty."

"You are grow them?" asked Duette as if she hadn't understood correctly.

"Yes, it's not so hard if you know how. I'll explain it all later. Right now I think we need to get some sleep."

Duette snorted in her brother's direction. Duel was already snoring. And he was on her bed. She rolled her eyes and went into the other bedroom. Most of the others were already on the rock hard mattresses. Blaze was just wrapping the last bandage around Daffodil's left hand.

"You're very brave," said Blaze. She was supposed to be the brave one but she had not even thought about doing anything to protect anyone else. So far everyone appeared to be more courageous than her; including Annabelle. The bravery medal sat in her mind like a lead weight.

"Blaze," said Daffodil. "Heroes are made from hearts, and trust me, yours is as big as the moon. You just have to trust someone." Daffodil lay down on the hard bed trying to pull up her scratchy blanket with bandaged hands. "You know how to do it; you just have to take the risk."

Blaze didn't have a clue how to open herself to chance. Giving Daffodil a half smile she climbed off the bunk bed and lay down on her own. Sleep would bring her some rest but it would also bring back the dreams: Dreams of fire and screaming children; dreams of award ceremonies that ended up burning her alive; and a dream of a lost little boy standing beside a fire hydrant.

Daffodil was the first to stir. Why did she feel like she had been hit by a bus? Why was she so cold? She reached down to tug on her familiar patchwork quilt but the pain in her fingers reminded her that she was not in her own bed. As much as she hated the Institution, at least she had warm bedding there. The plight of their situation came rushing back: They were in the middle of nowhere, in freezing cold tundra, trying to save children that had ghosted a hundred years ago. Her head throbbed.

Daffodil squeezed her eyes open in the murky light that streamed through the cabin windows. The heavy breath of sleep had fogged all the glass: crystalline surfaces ready for a rewrite. Daffodil traced Bugsy's name through the slippery condensation. It was strange feeling sadness for a ghost that had finally found a home after so very long. But it was even more confusing feeling sorrow because she was not going *with* that ghost to be with her parents and grandparents. Daffodil swallowed the cruelness. She was still alive and she wanted to *want to be* alive. It wasn't that she had ever wanted to be dead, although it had occurred to her many times, it was just that the thought of not *being* at all had always been so much more desirable. It was hard to explain—even to herself. Perhaps it was because Bugsy's plight had touched her so? He had been so sad himself, and when she saw his delighted expression as he waved goodbye, it somehow made her feel remorseful.

"Daffodil," murmured Blaze, "is that you making squeaking noises?" Blaze was rubbing her very tired eyes. "Because if it's another ghost I'll . . ."

"No Blaze," Daffodil managed to smile at her new friend. "I guess I was just making a kind of eulogy to Bugsy."

"We still don't know who he was."

"I know," said Daffodil. "And I think we're supposed to honor them by putting their details on those gravestones."

"Do you think we'll ever get out of here?" asked Blaze wearily.

The chatter woke Annabelle. "Maybe we are already in hell? Maybe we're supposed to take the place of the ghosts?"

"Ta Gueule!" screamed Duette loud enough to wake anyone else that may have still been asleep. "You very horrible. C'est vraiment des conneries!" Duel shot a look at his sister. He had never heard her swear before.

Annabelle rolled a wrist. "Je vous demande pardon." She was a little bit apologetic and a large bit sarcastic.

Even in their wakening dazes everyone was surprised: Annabelle could speak French.

"Um," said Duel. "I believe you have just confessed to a truth that you have been hiding. When did you think it would be a good time to tell us you spoke French?"

As soon as the words had escaped, Annabelle regretted them. In her attempt to forever have the upper hand she had revealed herself. Fury burned inside her but it did not quench the frozen growth that was slowly taking over her body.

"Petit quantité," she said, knowing the reply should be 'un peu'. If she could pretend her knowledge was limited there would be no more questions asked.

Both Duel and Duette looked at her suspiciously. But Duette wanted to trap the girl.

"Duel happy to teach you," Duette said as she eyed Duel. He received his sister's anger and angst and everything else she was throwing at him. Duel threw some thoughts back. Duette turned up her nose at him and went to the bathroom.

"Well," said a blurry eyed Santu, "it is so nice to know we are not having any secrets with each other." Santu was feeling his nose. The severe pain had mostly gone now, replaced by a bass note throb that kept beating the middle of his forehead.

Suddenly, Jake grabbed everyone's attention. His loud jabbering was incoherent.

"Jake," said Santu, "slowing down, slowing down."

Jake took a deep breath and tried to calm himself. "I-remembered-stuff-when-I-was-dreaming! And-they-weren't-nightmares. I-mean-I-remembered-things-I-must-have-heard-whilst-I-was-sleeping-before-you-know-with-the-static." Jake was struggling to explain and the nerves and confrontation were confusing him.

"Jake," said Daffodil in her calmest voice. "You just need to calm down a bit. Just talk to me."

Jake took a deep breath and focused on Daffodill. "There are eight of them left. That doesn't include Bugsy or Bruises."

"That's great Jake," said Daffodil. "At least we know how many Oscar needs to bring back." She hesitated. "We don't really know how much Oscar remembers either."

Santu agreed. "You are being right Daffodil. Just because Oscar is in charge, it does not mean he is remembering any more than the others. Maybe he is in just as much trouble as the rest of them."

"Actually," Jake hesitated, "I think he's in more trouble."

Santu trusted Jake but this comment really worried him. "Jake, what are you meaning?"

"I mean, Santu, that Oscar is in as much trouble as the others, but he's putting himself last, like he's not as important. And I think he's more important than any of them—if that's possible."

Daffodil was hit with a sudden surge of panic. "We've got to get back to the church." She looked past the window she had marked with Bugsy's name. "And we have to hurry. If Oscar comes and no one is there to greet him—like we told Dog we would—we may have lost them all."

Santu twisted his nose. "Right then. Let us be flying there."

BATTLE OF GALLIPOLI DISASTER

Since Landing On The Wrong Beach At Gallipoli, Turkey, Allied Troops of England, Australia & New Zealand Have Faced Disatrous Casualties In The Thousands.

On the 25th April, the arrival of the 3rd Australian Brigade, the 9th, 10th, 11th, and 12th Battalions and the 3rd Field Ambulance at Ari Burni Point, faced strong Turkish counter attacks. Despite very heavy losses they have managed to hold a narrow triangle of land but have been unable to make headway. By April 26th over 1700 casualties were evacuated from the area nick-named ANZAC Cove (Australian New Zealand Army Corps). The Gascon hospital ship carrying the wounded, arrived at Heliopolis, where Sister Constance Keys states the greatest number of men at Gallipoli are either dead or wounded. Still, the Turkish attacks have failed to drive the remaining troops back into the sea. Full History Continued on Page 2.

PRISONERS TAKEN

The Australian submarine, AE2, was sunk by a Turkish torpedo boat, the Sultan Hissar in Erdek Bay in the sea of Marmara. It is believed the crew have been captured by the Turkish and taken prisoner. FULL STORY PAGE 6.

GERMANS USE POISON GAS

In the second battle at Ypres the Germans have begun using poison gas against allied troops. In a devastating move, they have developed an explosive project- ... which burns its victims, causing potentially fatal injuries ... only bone.

~Present day~

~W⊕NDERB⊕Y LIKES C⊕MICS AND GAMES~

"Where's Bugsy?! What did you do with Bugsy?!" Dog's glowing figure was screaming into the transmitter. Oscar was just floating beside him not knowing what to do. There was only one other boy with them looking petrified.

"Wait," said Jake as he twisted one of the dials a little bit to the right. "Okay, that should be right." He was motioning to Santu. Daffodil was quickly replacing some of the crystals around the edge of the room. Her bandaged hands made her feel clumsy and frustrated but she was more worried about how they were going to convince Dog that Bugsy had finally gone home.

Santu moved over to the radiola. "Dog, please, just let me be explaining. We did not *do* anything to him. Don't go to the bananas. He is okay, I am promising this."

Dog looked simultaneously furious, frightened and confused. It was his fault. He was supposed to take care of Bugsy. Oscar would abandon him for sure now. "I left him with you because I trusted you!" Dog yelled at Santu.

"And," said Santu, "you were right to do so. We found a way to get Bugsy home."

Oscar had pulled himself together now and had moved in front of Dog with a reassuring nod. "What do you mean 'home'."

"That is what Jake says you call it. In your recordings you are all saying you want to go home. Yes?" Santu asked.

Oscar nodded. "You mean he's gone to his family?"

"Well," started Santu wanting to be very careful with his wording, "We are sending him into the light with Daffodil's mother and grandmother. They are promising to take care of him and they are saying he will be waiting for all of you when you go into the light too."

Dog and Oscar crossed suspicious glances. This couldn't be right. Oscar couldn't have spent all this time desperately trying to get help and then have a ghosted one go into the light without even a goodbye.

"But," said Oscar, "Bugsy wouldn't have left without saying goodbye to me."

"I am sorry Oscar, I am sorry Dog." Santu didn't want to mention the Shadow—it would only bring more suspicion to the table. "Daffodil has been finding a way to bring her relatives here. They are being dead you know. There was no time. We hoped Dog would bring you all back before it was too late—they could not wait. Bugsy did not want to go without you but he was so happy in the light. I am wishing you could have seen his face."

Oscar said something to Dog. The third little boy was hanging on tightly to Oscar's arm.

"I guess," began Oscar, "that there is no reason for you to harm Bugsy. If I had not taken everyone away maybe we could have all gone together." Oscar looked miserable.

"Do not be worrying Oscar, we will be finding another way to get all of you home."

"What was it like?"

"The light?"

"Yes, what was it like for Bugsy?"

"It was wonderful Oscar. Bugsy and his bugs were all lit up with bright yellow light like the sun. His bugs were also looking very happy. Bugsy's smile was being huge. Once he felt it, he had to go."

Oscar's eyes were wide. Could it be true? Could they really have a chance at going home? He flickered in and out which at first made Santu panic. If they disappeared now they may never come back. But Santu needn't have worried. Oscar was just saying goodbye to Bugsy. Dog did the same and then the little boy followed.

"Thank you," said Oscar. "I am so happy for Bugsy." It was hard for Oscar. If he had just believed in these people he would never have taken everyone to the other place and now he could only bring back one at a time. Dog had been able to contact Oscar from the outskirts but now Oscar would have to ask him to go back and mind the others.

"We are being happy for Bugsy too. Now that you are believing us, you must be bringing the others back, yes?"

"Sadly, I cannot," said Oscar. "To keep the balance in the other place I cannot take them all at once. If I try, they will all be consumed. It is a difficult place but now it seems it is the only place the Shadow cannot touch us." Oscar's expression was earnest and grave. "I can only bring one at a time and I must wait until the balance readjusts before I can remove another."

Santu looked around to find Daffodil. Her expression reflected his. This was really bad news. Everyone was thinking the same thing: How were they going to bring the white light *eight* more times? The first time had been a fluke and Daffodil had completely destroyed her watch. It just wasn't possible.

"Alright," said Santu trying to think quickly, "well, let us just deal with what we can be doing now."

Oscar nodded and said something to Dog who returned a confused look to Oscar. Dog began shaking his head. Then Oscar said something else and Dog's eyes widened and he began to slowly nod.

"Dog is going back," said Oscar, "to take care of the others until I can bring the next one here. He doesn't want to go, but I reminded him about Scruffy. Scruffy is the reason he is called Dog you know. We can't move on without the ghosted creatures we are attached to you see. So he is going back."

Daffodil shook her head at Santu.

"Perhaps," said Santu, "Dog could be getting Scruffy now?"

"He cannot. Dog will have to go inside the balance-area to get him. He will have to wait until the others can find home before he can come out. The last to enter is the last to leave. I would offer to take his place but some of the others do not trust him. I'm afraid they trust me instead." Oscar was not proud of the situation he had put everyone in.

Santu was really worried. What kind of place had Oscar taken the ghosts to? But he didn't want any sadness at the moment. They were just getting over their last visit with the Shadow. Even though it would be dormant for a time he didn't want to do anything that may encourage its recovery.

"Well, I think I can be speaking for all of us here," said Santu looking directly at Dog. "That is a very brave thing to do. It takes a lot of stomachs and we are being proud of you. We expect to see you very soon with Scruffy."

Everyone in the room clapped. Dog could only hear Santu's claps but he could see what the others were doing. Oscar and the other little boy joined in. Although the boy wasn't really sure why he was clapping, it was fun all the same. Dog had a strange feeling inside his stomach. He wasn't sure what it was but it felt almost good and slightly warm. He couldn't remember ever feeling warm like this before but it was a powerful sensation. He thought about Scruffy and for the first time he felt like laughing.

Amongst the clapping, Dog lifted his head, waved goodbye and flickered a few times before disappearing.

The clapping went on after Dog had gone. It felt like if everyone stopped, the truth would set in.

"Santu," said Jake, "ask Oscar who the little boy is." Jake had started another fire on the iron tray which was now glowing with some degree of heat. This time they had made sure there were two pails of water beside the fire in case it went wild like last time.

"Oscar are you going to be introducing us?" Santu pointed to the ghosted one beside him.

"Oh yes, of course. This is Wonderboy," said Oscar. Wonderboy was floating up around Oscar's ear and whispering to him. "He likes comics and games." Oscar was distracted by whatever Wonderboy was saying to him. Wonderboy started pointing across the room and Oscar tried to focus on what was so important to his ghosted companion. When Oscar saw the redheaded girl he understood.

"Wonderboy is a bit shy but he says he knows the girl with the red hair."

"Blaze?" asked Santu turning to look at her.

"Me?" asked Blaze looking back at Santu. "How can he know me?"

Wonderboy was now pointing to the fire Jake had made. The long stretching flames were twisting and curling on the breath of oxygen.

"Um," said Oscar, "Wonderboy says that he knows you from the fire."

Blaze went sheet white. She felt sick enough to vomit. Shaking her head she bent over to stop the wash of nausea from making her faint. She rubbed the sleeves of her top feeling the ribbons of scars beneath the fabric. Which fire was the little boy talking about?

Santu knew the true reasons Blaze had kept the inferno hidden from everyone. As soon as he met the redhead with the gold-flecked, green eyes he had been hit with visions: Everywhere she went she was surrounded by flames. Blaze had never dealt with the whole truth herself. Winning a bravery medal for trying to save children from a fire that you started wasn't an easy thing to deal with. And if Blaze had told the truth he knew she would have been in serious trouble. But none of that explained how this little boy could know her. Didn't they conclude that all these children ghosted in World War 1? Santu turned away from the radiola and faced Blaze, who was looking completely stricken.

"How could he know you from the fire?"

Blaze couldn't speak. Gripping her stomach she crumpled to the ground, sweat dripping from her freezing cold skin. In the darkened room, lit only by moonlight, her red hair seemed all that much more lurid against her sickly pallor.

Wonderboy flew over to her and knelt beside her. His smile held a kind of apologetic look as if it was his fault that she felt so sick.

Blaze looked at him with utter horror. "I'm so sorry, oh god, I'm so very sorry."

Although Wonderboy couldn't hear what the pretty redhead was saying, he knew what an apology looked like. But the little boy wasn't looking for a confession from her. It was *he* that needed to make amends. Reaching for her face he knew it was the same soft face that he remembered so well. But something wasn't right. The memory he had held onto for so long was changing: It wasn't through the fog of a steam engine that he had seen her; it was amongst the smoke of the fire. And then, shockingly, it all came flooding back.

The mouth of the little ghost was moving with ferocious speed, impossible to lip read. Blaze was crying now and shaking her head with disbelief.

Oscar couldn't tell if what was happening was good or bad. He flew over to Wonderboy to console him. All anyone could see was Wonderboy jabbering away to Oscar and Oscar's slowly emerging expression of understanding, and then amazement. Gently, Oscar tried to encourage

Wonderboy back to the radiola. But Wonderboy wasn't moving away from the sad redheaded girl.

"Wonderboy says he knows about the fire." Oscar was back at the radiola and was looking both sorry and confused. Wonderboy gave Oscar an encouraging look. "He says that he knows that she started the fire. And he knows that some children died."

Everyone in the room looked appalled.

Daffodil was shaking her head. "No, that can't be right."

Blaze held up her hand and shook her head. "Listen to Oscar, Daffodil. Please."

Daffodil felt sick. This couldn't be happening. This couldn't be true. Blaze couldn't be a murderer.

Oscar went on. "Wonderboy had been following you for a very long time. It was only when the fire took off that you saw him. He was trying to help you save those other children."

Santu could see Blaze was in no state to go through with this. "Why was Wonderboy following her?"

Oscar asked Wonderboy, who floated at Blaze's side.

"Wonderboy says he used to play tic-tac-toe with a redheaded girl at school. He has remembered that it was his sister. He says you look just like her. That's why he followed you." Oscar was about to continue but a thought interrupted his speech. "Oh, now I remember Wonderboy! It was that girl you tried to help after she ghosted."

Wonderboy was nodding furiously.

"Oh," Oscar went on, "yes but we couldn't save her could we?" Oscar didn't want to bring it up again. It was awful at the time. "She was Wonderboy's younger sister who had ghosted when she was very young. Even though he could still see her, she didn't want to play with him anymore. Wonderboy was heartbroken." Oscar remembered the look on the ghosted girl's face. The darkness had infused itself upon her and there had been nothing Oscar could do to save her. He was too late and it had troubled him greatly.

Now, however, Wonderboy's faith was renewed.

Oscar looked perplexed. "Wonderboy says he understands that your friend is not his sister but he has also discovered something else."

"What is this?" asked Santu intrigued.

"Wonderboy feels the connection," said Oscar quietly. "This girl is related to him somehow."

Wonderboy then explained to Oscar that this was why he had disappeared from the church all those times—to follow this redheaded girl who seemed so familiar. Oscar was truly surprised: Wonderboy hadn't been playing hide and seek at all, he had been remembering.

For Oscar it was overwhelming. This news meant that the girl in front of them, now slumped on the floor in the dark, was the great great granddaughter of one of Wonderboy's brothers or sisters. That also meant that there had been other siblings that Wonderboy had not remembered: Other siblings that had lived and that had produced children that had brought this sad-faced, redheaded girl here.

"I am sorry," replied Santu, "but I am not understanding."

"This girl," said Oscar, his voice filled with gravity, "is Wonderboy's descendent."

Oscar's fears about upsetting Wonderboy were unnecessary. The look on Wonderboy's face was, well, wonderful. Who knew how many other brothers and sisters he may have waiting for him on the other side? Wonderboy flew to the radiola.

"I knew you were special to me. I knew you. I knew you."

Oscar was starting to enjoy Wonderboy's excitement until he took a look at the girl called Blaze.

The revelation had Blaze in tears: Relief mixed with sorrow: Finally her secret was out but the disclosure brought with it, the flood of torment that had plagued her all these years.

Daffodil tried to comfort her and the others rallied to her side. But Wonderboy was confused. Didn't she want him to be her relative? Santu could see the uncertainty in Wonderboy's eyes and as Blaze began to talk, he went back to the radiola to relate the information to Wonderboy and Oscar.

Blaze tried to explain it all to them. "I didn't do it on purpose, I had no idea I could do it at all." Blaze had discovered her power one night in the old boarding house where she was being schooled. It was where all the orphaned children went to school—a place filled with cruelty and hatred toward those less fortunate. Students already saw her as a curse. After what had happened to her family, how could they not? The day it had happened had been a terrible day; a day of incessant teasing by the other students and when Blaze had fought back, the teachers had forced unjust punishments on her. The fury had been building for a long time but that day she was at boiling point. In one of the red-carpeted, teak-walled, study rooms, Blaze had hid all alone while the older students ate and the younger students got ready for bed.

Staring into the open fire, Blaze had wished the world would just swallow her up. When the flames exploded in front of her, she thought it amusing. Perhaps someone had left something in the fire to cause such a reaction? But, in her solitude, she had stared into the flares willing them to do it again. She felt the anger build inside her, felt it peak at her chest and then felt the rage burst from her.

When the flames jumped out toward her, she stood paralyzed and unable to shift. The fire had moved impatiently toward her, eating the old, worn carpets as it propelled itself forward. Soon flames were eagerly jumping over each other to get to her. Blaze's shock finally broke and as more explosions thrust live flares onto the old drapes and dusty books, she managed to run.

Already, thick smoke was pouring from the room and the flames were licking the grand old door as if it were an appetizer. The fire was her vengeance and it would take no prisoners.

As her face hit the cold night air she realized she must go back in: she had to save them—it was her fault. There was no time for comprehension, no time to change her mind. She ran back in and crawled along the floor to get to the children.

Blaze was mortified now. The knowledge of the bravery award hung heavy in the air but Blaze couldn't stop. Now the story had begun it had to be finished. Memories racked her body with grief and horror and her voice shuddered with pain.

As she scooped gasping children from the smoke more and more had succumbed. By the time the older students in the dining hall saw the flames it was too late. Their only choice was to evacuate the building.

The fire brigade had saved her. If they hadn't found her when they did she would have surrendered to smoke inhalation and inevitable flames. She had been going back in for a fifth time. Many times since then, she had wished the firemen had left her there. Instead, they gave her a medal for bravery. And Blaze had stayed silent.

Blaze looked exhausted. "But, there is something else. Something worse." Blaze bit her lip and closed her eyes. The truth was the truth and there was nothing she could do about it. If the truth could kill you then let it do so now. "When I was eight years old . . ." Blaze's voice sounded hollow, as if she might fall down an abyss never to return. Slowly, she pulled up her sleeves and showed everyone her shame. Scars ribboned her pale flesh.

"Most of my skin is like this, but it's not from the fire at the school." A tear swelled and then fell. "I look like this because when I was eight our house burned down. My parents and my baby brother were killed. The neighbors rescued me and my other little brother Aaron. They took him away and I have never been able to find out where he is." Blaze was shaking her head now. "I must be responsible for that fire too. I was asleep. I don't remember. I didn't realize until I started the fire at the school." The iron weight of guilt was too heavy to tolerate. The unbearable truth was that what she had done had destroyed so many lives—the lives of her own family. "I killed my family."

After the school burned down, Blaze had closed her eyes to the incident and instead, had forged into dangerous situations trying to save others in an attempt to right her wrongs. Risk had become her savior. If death came, then so be it.

Santu realized now, that that was when Blaze had lost her perspective. It meant they had a liability on their hands. They couldn't have her running off to graveyards trying to fight the Shadow on her own. Here, there was no victory in hell.

Wonderboy was tugging on Oscar's arm. He wanted to talk to the redhead. Oscar tried to reassure him but it is impossible to quell impatience when it is so young.

"Excuse me," Oscar said into the yellow light of the transistor, "but Wonderboy is wondering why your friend, his friend too I guess, is so upset to be his relative?"

Oscar's words had brought everyone back to the reality they were facing right now. Santu had let Blaze pour her story out aware of how important it was to set secrets free. But time was running out. The light would be coming soon and they needed to send Wonderboy home. At least now they had some kind of direction. Santu shook his head in incredulity—after all Blaze was a relative. How much closer did they need to get?

"I am sorry Blaze," Santu said, "but you are needing to concentrate."

Surprisingly Santu's words were like a life-raft pulling her in from a fierce ocean of uncertainty. "What should I do?" asked Blaze wiping away falling tears.

"Can you remember anything in your family history that could be helping?"

Blaze was trying to pull herself together. She looked over at the little boy hovering beside Oscar, her watery tears bringing a distant vision to her mind.

"Wonderboy," Blaze said, a faint smile passing her lips, "I've just realized how much you look like my father when he was young." The familiarity brought newfound buoyancy to her awareness. Trying to plough back through the years of memories, Blaze felt like life was recoiling away from her. The years were being stripped away second by second. She was sitting in her mother's lap being shown albums of the past: A past that framed peculiar looking children in odd clothing and old scripted text; stories of distant and extraordinary happenings that made no sense in the world of the young Blaze. It was all strangely disturbing and even more bizarrely compelling. But now the memories were faded and murky and impossible to revive.

"Blaze," it was a gently spoken word from Jake. Blaze looked up at him hopeful that he could help her. "Blaze," he repeated quietly, "you're very wound up." Jake made a motion towards the dials of the radiola.

Blaze understood immediately. Jake had done so much to help their group and he had done it calmly and without any fuss knowing that everyone had been expecting him to be able to do it. The ghosts needed to have confidence in them.

"You're right Jake, thank you," Blaze said as she took a deep breath and tried to fall back into the dark abyss of her childhood.

Making her way to the radiola, Blaze's concentration drove her into a forgotten place: A place where lost things belong. Looking down on herself and her young life, she watched the scenes flick by like a comic book.

It was childhood history in reverse and it was bizarre: explaining the history of your family *to* the history of your family. She began shaking her head as if it was all too long ago.

"Blaze," it was Jake, "you have to try to remember." He tried to offer up a warm and comforting smile. "Just try. Please."

Blaze knew she had been under more pressure than this. Why couldn't she concentrate?

Daffodil understood the demands that Blaze must be feeling. Carefully she reached in her pocket. The stone she pulled out was a personal one, one she wouldn't ever have revealed normally. But these were not normal circumstances. Daffodil moved over to hug Blaze, gently slipping the powerful stone into her pocket. Daffodil didn't see it as deception, she saw it as assistance: It was time for Blaze to stand on her two, very strong, feet.

Blaze felt light headed for a moment—then she felt very strange. Images began to sprout in her mind, growing like organic entities.

"I'm remembering stuff." Blaze's eyes were crushed shut with focus. "I remember my grandmother talking about what a great beauty *her* grandmother was—she would be my great great grandmother. Apparently she had a mane of red hair just like mine. We had a really old black and white picture of her in our house." *Before it burnt down*, thought Blaze wiping more silent tears with her sleeve. "She had lots of suitors. I don't think she married until quite late in life though." Blaze shook her head in confusion. "I'm not sure but I have a vague memory that her first suitor may have died?" Blaze opened her eyes and seeing the audience staring back at her, she quickly shut them again.

"I think she had a sister." Blaze shook her head as if it were covered with seawater. "I think the sister died quite young. It might have been the girl you played tic-tac-toe with?

Everyone looked directly at Wonderboy. His face was contorting as he tried to remember. Suddenly his eyes lit up. He whispered something to Oscar.

"Wonderboy is saying something about a rabbit? You tell them Wonderboy. Just speak into the yellow light." Oscar gave him an encouraging smile and Wonderboy leaned forward.

"Well," began Wonderboy before flashing back to his position behind Oscar—the sound of his voice in the machine was horrible.

"Don't worry," said Oscar, "how about you tell me again and I'll pass it on? You know, like when we play Whispers?" Wonderboy nodded and began murmuring in Oscar's ear.

"Wonderboy says his sister got eaten by a rabbit." That didn't sound right. "A rabbit, Wonderboy? Are you sure?"

Bewildered looks glanced around the room but for Santu Oscar's words had brought the images. They were of Wonderboy's sister dying. It wasn't difficult to put two and two together. He moved over to the radiola and spoke as gently as he could.

"I am thinking," said Santu, "rabies. It was not uncommon in those days." Santu gave Wonderboy a nod. "Perhaps your sister was getting *bitten* by a rabid animal, not so much getting eaten by one?" Wonderboy nodded slowly.

"He says," replied Oscar, "that's what he meant."

"You have done so well Wonderboy. This is very helpful."

Wonderboy moved out from behind Oscar's shoulder. Remembering things felt strange and a bit frightening. Oscar held Wonderboy's hand and they both flashed in and out: Light, dark, light, dark, light.

This was all taking too long. Panic was drumming in Santu's chest.

"Blaze, do you remember what happened to the other children?"

Blaze shook her head. "It is so annoying," said Blaze. I can see it all in the periphery of my mind but I can't make it come into focus. After losing my family I tried really hard to remember my history."

And then Daffodil had a thought.

"Duette, Duel, can you help Blaze remember? I mean if you can read minds maybe you can read memories?"

Both Duel and Duette were shaking their heads with equal measure of disappointment.

"Unfortunately," said Duel, "we are only able to read the present mind—the immediate thoughts going through someone's head. We cannot read what is not remembered."

Everyone had stopped moving—it was as if the room was on pause.

Annabelle took a careful step forward. She had been observing every measure of each reaction since their return to the church. Now she knew what she would have to do. It was primarily annoying that she would have to divulge one of her secrets, but it also went against her better judgment. Still, if this didn't start going somewhere soon, the Shadow would be back and they'd all be dark mush before breakfast. *And* Annabelle had had enough. She just wanted out. Maybe it would be the last great thing she did before she died? Even if she did still run away, there was nowhere to go. It was only then that Annabelle realized just why she had been 'invited' on this ridiculous mission. She was not only going have to *use* her gift, she was going to have to *admit* to it.

"I think I can help." Annabelle's voice was monotone. Faced with a sea of suspicious expressions she rolled her eyes. "Yes, it's true!" she said in mock surprise. "Annabelle wants to help." Annabelle thought their reactions were rather harsh. After all, she did nearly sacrifice herself to help Duette and Duel when they were being dragged into the Shadow. "But I have to go back to the cabin first."

More distrustful looks arose.

"Why?" asked Jake. "If you can help why do you need to go back to the cabin?"

Annabelle heaved out an irritated sigh. "Well," she said with an Alice in Wonderland pitch, "because that's where I keep the photographic paper."

This didn't meet well with an already doubtful group.

"*And,*" started Jake again, "*why* do you need photographic paper?"

Annabelle's mouth twisted. This was it. She was about to commit the truth to a bunch of misfits that had no idea what they were doing. The only truth she knew was, that as dumb as most of these people were, she believed that they wouldn't try to use the truth against her.

"*Because,*" Annabelle stared coldly back at Jake, "I am a memory-grapher." Now she was faced with a wall of blank stares. She blinked slowly trying to quell her annoyance. "A memory-grapher can make visuals of memories." Annabelle shrugged her shoulders. There was no point in trying to explain it with words. "Look, if I get the photographic paper I can show you."

"You mean," started a very angry Blaze, "you could have just used this gift with the ghosts earlier and they could all have gone into the light by now? You mean you've just been risking our lives with that Shadow-thing when it could all have been solved?"

Annabelle exhaled. She should have known that the stupid redhead couldn't understand anything without a map and a compass.

"No," Annabelle replied coolly through gritted teeth. "I cannot do it for the ghosts because they don't *remember.*" She threw out a frustrated smile. "Understand? Does *everyone* understand now?"

Santu had understood from the moment she had called herself a memory-grapher. He had seen the images in her hands develop like old-fashioned photos. It was an incredible sight.

"Annabelle is telling the truth," Santu said at last—much to Blaze's disgust. "We need to be hurrying." He thought for a moment. "I will be going back to the cabin with Annabelle and Daffodil you can be taking over on the radiola. Explain to Oscar. This might just be getting Wonderboy home."

The trek to the cabin was both interesting and surprising for Annabelle. When Santu had admitted to being really intrigued by her ability he had also unwittingly admitted to being intrigued by Annabelle. And having Santu by her side made her feel all that much more irresistible. And of course Annabelle couldn't help but enjoy the fact that Blaze would be steaming back at the church. Even Blaze's dramatic retelling of her fire-starter story couldn't keep Santu by her side.

The tasty thought lingered in Annabelle's stomach for just a moment too long. A sharp, icy twinge plumbed her insides spiking up into her throat and piercing the back of her neck. Bitter bile rose in her gullet. Momentarily she froze on the spot.

Waving Santu's concerns aside, Annabelle pushed on again knowing that the icy formation inside her was getting stronger and knowing that *she* may not have much time either.

Blackwater Herald Moon Tribune
Wednesday, August 15th, 1945—
One penny

PEACE AT LAST

*J*apan finally surrenders! Only President Truman's decisions to drop the first atomic bomb, 'Little Boy' on August, 6th, killing 80,000 in Hiroshima— the majority being civilians—and then the second 'Fat Man' bomb on August, 9th, killing 75,000 in Nagasaki, has resulted in the surrender of the Japanese to the Allied Powers. Emperor Hirohito has announced that this new warfare could lead to the total extinction of human civilization and has agreed to peace, provided the monarchy not be abolished. PAGE 3.

LOCAL NEWS HEADLINES
REDUCED CIRCULATION OF PAPER

The Herald Moon Tribune is sad to announce its reduced circulation. Due to the current circumstances of Blackwater, this paper has had to decrease its run. We apologize to everyone fighting to keep Blackwater functioning but the costs have become increasingly difficult to maintain. You will find your copy of the Blackwater Herald Moon Tribune available every Wednesday from now on at the local grocer.

It is also time to say goodbye and congratulations to our dedicated journalist Mr. Henry Frienly. Henry has been offered a prestigious job at a popular London newspaper which, he says, although making the decision to leave Blackwater was difficult, he looks forward to life in London with his wife.

Henry says: "With the paper's reduced circulation, I felt at a loss to achieve all my goals but now have new opportunities to pursue. I wish to thank all our readers and I shall certainly keep in touch and let you know how we are doing in the big city."

We wish him well and will be watching his career attentively. Good luck Henry.

FURTHER EDUCATION FOR LOCAL TEACHER

Although local school teacher, Mrs. Grace Glizsnort has been educating the children of Blackwater for some years now, she was only doing so to aid the community. Now, however, since the bombing of the church and school, her pupils have decreased to a total of three. Mrs. Glizsnort, therefore, has decided to further her studies and become a fully qualified teacher.

Mrs. Glizsnort says: "We have finally organized for the building to be rebuilt—just in hardwood this time—but in the interim I will study further and come back to Blackwater a more competent educator."

For the next year, The Little Orchard School House will go without tutoring whilst Mrs. Glizsnort studies in London. Current students will be advised where they can be schooled during the year of 1946.

Inspector Glizsnort will still be protecting Blackwater even though he will be taking several extended leaves to spend time with his wife and children in London.

Constable Thomas Davidson is our eager new police officer who is to assist at the Blackwater Station and will available to take queries this Saturday morning.

MORE BUSINESS CLOSURES

***BLACKWATER MIDHILL BANK**—This branch will cease trade from Friday 17ʰ August.*

***MRS. O'DONNELL'S SWEET SHOP**—Sadly closing its doors next Thursday.*

***CANDLESTICKS AND COMBS**—Will be staying open until stock runs out.*

***BLACKWATER TOBACCONIST**—We regret to inform our loyal customers that we shall be closing at the end of the month. Tobacco can still be purchased at Bailsbury. Thank you to all our wonderful customers who, over* *the years, have provided a good dose of humor in these difficult times. May peace be with you.*

LAST MONTHS OF WAR

May 7—V-E DAY—*The German Government issues unconditional surrender to the Allied Forces.*

April to June—**OKINAWA**—*Japanese suicide bombers sink over 30 American ships and, fighting from caves and bunkers, the Japanese inflict 80,000 losses on American troops. At least 150,000 Japanese civilians have died—at least one-third of those have committed suicide. At least 100,000 Japanese soldiers have died, many also by suicide.*

July—*General MacArthur retakes the* **PHILIPPINES** *after Japanese cause 60,000 American causalities.*

August 15—ALLIES CEASE FIRE.

~Brought to you by—

CALOGEN—*For expectant mothers. The only calcium that allows the vitamin to be absorbed by adding phosphorus and Vitamin D!*
OXYDOL—*We've won the battle of washing!*

~Present day~

~The Memory Effect: Catch it Before it Freezes~

Annabelle kneeled beside Blaze. On Blaze's outstretched palm Annabelle placed the light-sensitive photographic paper before laying her own palm on top.

"Right," said Annabelle as she began to concentrate, "try to remember the memories you talked about earlier—if you can remember anything with old photographs or documents."

Annabelle could feel Blaze trembling. Was Blaze still shaking from her earlier revelations? Annabelle found that strange and a little bit self-indulgent. No matter. It was only Blaze's focus that Annabelle needed from her.

Annabelle tried to push the reminders of her first experience with memory-graphing away. She had been too young to find another difficulty to deal with and so she had hid it from everyone. Practicing on animals helped her discover which type of paper rendered the most distinct representations. Oh, and there were some small, confused children. But Annabelle's demanding tone usually resulted in their tearful silence. Annabelle sighed. She didn't even know why she had brought the paper with her on this awful trip.

As everyone stood waiting, not knowing how this was going to work, beads of sweat began forming on Annabelle's brow. She had promised herself that she would never do it again. But promises were just expectations waiting to be dishonored. Annabelle had known *that* since she was a small child. Why should she be the one to change history?

Delving deeper into her trance, Annabelle pushed all peripheral thoughts aside. The blackness moved in swamping every part of her body and her conscious mind. The familiar feeling began to take hold: Icy-cold strands moved inside her like hundreds of tiny glaciers and her mind began to turn. It was a daunting sensation and one she had never managed to overcome. It felt as if she were being crystallized, turned to stone, but it was working. All she could see was the pin light that would take her to the next photographic image.

Blaze was doing well. She was managing to center her attention on the family album. The images were fuzzy but Annabelle knew what to do. Each time she felt a new image emerge on the photographic paper she quickly pulled the piece from between their palms and replaced it with another. By the time Blaze's mental effort had waned Annabelle had what she needed.

But coming back was always extremely difficult. It was like thawing a cadaver and expecting life to flow through its body once again.

When Annabelle finally opened her eyes she found that she had been wrapped in blankets and dragged close to the fire. Annabelle had no idea she had been unconscious—the subconscious cares not for time.

"She's awake," Daffodil said quietly as she gently rubbed Annabelle's arm.

Annabelle cracked open her eyes. She felt like she had been buried alive in a snowstorm.

Santu was looking down at her, his face full of emotion. "No wonder you are keeping this a secret. It was not looking like much fun at all."

Annabelle didn't want his, or anyone else's, pity. "It was fine," she lied. "No problem." Annabelle threw the blankets off as if they were an insult and lifted her chin toward the photographs Santu held in his hand. "How'd we do?"

Blaze was sitting very still. What she had felt as Annabelle had drawn the memories from her was indescribable. Arctic hands had reached into her mind and pulled out thoughts like they were mucus. It had left Blaze feeling both afraid of Annabelle and amazed. It was a frightening combination: To revere something threatening was more than confusing.

Annabelle wasn't just mean: she was also very clever, very brave, extremely sad, and very, very dangerous.

Santu handed Annabelle the photographs.

"They are good. Whatever the hell it was that you are doing, they are good."

Annabelle nodded. "Got what you wanted?" Annabelle stood up trying not to show what a toll it had taken on her. She looked at the photographs.

They were perfect replicas: well focused images and clean lines of text. She handed them back to Santu trying not to look exhausted.

"Have you shown them to Wonderboy?"

"We are waiting for you." Santu's gentle smile reached out to her but that was the last thing she wanted. Kindness and compassion belonged in another world and Annabelle wanted no part of it. It was too late now.

"Look, I did my bit. I don't need to be involved in the love-fest. Just show them to him."

Santu didn't try to hide his disappointment. There was no point. Annabelle had made herself as hard as diamonds and this good deed wasn't going to change that. Santu moved over to the radiola where Oscar and Wonderboy were still hovering. He showed the first image to Wonderboy knowing that the best was yet to come.

When Wonderboy saw the first image he grabbed Oscar's shoulders in amazement. The image reflected a lovely round-faced woman with flowing red locks who was smiling sweetly at the baby in her arms.

When Jake had seen it, it had reminded him of Raffaello Sanzio's beautiful painting of the Madonna and Child. It had always made Jake feel overwhelmed with both awe and sadness. But in this picture the baby was Wonderboy and the redhead must have been his mother.

Wonderboy had remained transfixed for a time before he could respond. Leaning in toward the radiola he whispered one very slow word.

"Mamma."

Santu leaned in too. "There's an even better one here Wonderboy. Would you like me to read it?" Wonderboy made measured nods as if he rushed it might all disappear.

"This one is a . . ." Santu hesitated before realizing that the truth was all they had. "This one tells us how you died. Are you ready?"

Wonderboy nodded furiously. It was the information he had been trying to remember in this eternity of waiting.

"It says . . ." Santu swallowed. *"The orphaned Benjamin Oisin Walsh, born 1910 to Mr. Darragh Walsh and Mrs. Ciaran Walsh in the city of Dublin at 6.05am on the day of November 19th, has been found deceased on the day of December 27th, 1918 aged 8 years and 1 month old.*

The child has been found to have a tragic history.

Doctor Patrick O'Sullivan has validated that Benjamin's mother, Ciaran Walsh suffered from a long term nervous disposition that rendered her house bound. This depressive illness began when her third child, Sarah, died after contracting the acute viral disease of rabies.

Mrs. Walsh was found deceased on December 1st, 1916 after imbibing a large amount of amphetamines prescribed for depressive sickness. She left behind, her two other children: a son, Benjamin, aged 6 years, and daughter, Grace, aged 5 years. Both were older siblings to the deceased Sarah.

A short time after Ciaran's death, the husband and father, Darragh Walsh was charged with desertion. The 28 year old volunteer Private from Dublin joined his battalion toward the end of the Gallipoli campaign and it is understood he attempted to desert to get back to his children after being informed of his wife's death. Private D. Walsh was charged and sentenced to death on the 12th of November, 1916—the day before the battle of Ancre—and was held in confinement. It is noted by the Court, that this confinement probably saved his life as his battalion was effectively decimated during the Ancre battle. His sentence was finally commuted to four years penal servitude to be served on the frontlines. He was killed in action on the 24th of April, 1917 at Gaverelle.

It is understood that neither Benjamin nor Grace had any one to take care of them. Presumably, Benjamin spent time on the streets before being taken in by the reclusive and renowned newspaper cartoonist, Kenneth Connolly, who was well known for his comic strip stories.

Accordingly, Benjamin lived with this artist for about six months before Mr. Connolly was overcome by the influenza and died. It appears that Benjamin stayed in his house until the body was found but escaped before officers could catch him.

It is recorded that Benjamin was seen absconding with some of Connolly's artworks, however Officer Shane Kelly has stated that the works seemed very important to the boy and, probably believing he only had a short amount of time to flee, chose these artworks over his shoes [which were left behind at the scene]. It is a concern that the officer supposes the boy may think incorrectly that he is responsible for Mr. Connolly's death and is therefore unlikely to return to the sight."

Wonderboy was filled with amazement. He leant into the light of the radiola and whispered. "That's why I like comics so much! That man gave me those comic books. He wrote them for me. They were called Wonderboy! They were mine. I didn't steal them! And I'm glad I didn't kill him. He was so nice to me but I thought everyone who I loved must die because of me."

"No," said Santu. "This was not your fault."

"And I had another sister?"

"Yes Wonderboy, oh, I am meaning Benjamin. You are having two sisters," said Santu. "Sarah and Grace." Santu flicked through the images. There were family photos from a hundred years ago and several documents—all perfectly replicated by Annabelle. There was even an adoption certificate for his sister Grace. She had been taken on by a French woman called Germaine Durand who had moved her to England to start a new life.

Oscar was in a state of shock. These people really could help. He was so proud of Wonderboy it was beyond words.

"Wonderboy! Guess what!?" Oscar didn't care that he was interrupting the information that would take his charge home. This was a really important moment. "Wonderboy, you were named for your life Before and you didn't even realize it. It's wonderful, no it's Wonderboy!"

Wonderboy was laughing now. He couldn't believe all this was happening for him. "I am Wonderboy! I am!"

Oscar smiled at his little companion. Maybe this awful abyss *was* going to end.

"Go on, please keep going, this is very good," said Oscar.

Santu nodded. The rest of the police report was harder to read.

"Unfortunately officers found Benjamin too late. Medical reports from Bride Street Hospital revealed that he died from the Influenza evidently caught from Mr. Kenneth Connelly. Benjamin was found alone and disheveled on Blackrock Road, only meters from the house he grew up in.

It is noted that Benjamin Walsh may have been saved if he had received medical attention."

Santu decided to stop reading at that point. They had enough information.

Daffodil wanted to congratulate Wonderboy but it was all very messy and horrible. Even Santu, who always seemed so collected, was showing his fragility. Holding back her tears, Daffodil tried a determined smile for the little ghosted boy who had finally found a name. Moving over to the radiola, she leaned into its light.

"Your name is Benjamin! Wonderboy we've found your family."

As soon as this information struck Wonderboy, a magnetizing yellow light burst out around him. It was at once powerful and magnificent and complete. Wonderboy was going home.

Just as everyone realized that the truth could, in fact, set these ghosts free, a burst of warm bright light exploded behind them. Shielding their eyes, everyone stared into the bright glow waiting for something to happen. Was Wonderboy supposed to go in there all by himself? The seconds felt like hours but as they ticked by they could all see something forming within it.

Oscar was struck with wonder and grief. Finally, he was going to have to say goodbye to one of his ghosted ones. His regret at missing Bugsy's farewell was crushing.

Wonderboy was holding Oscar's hand tightly. All he wanted to do was go toward the warm glow on the other side of the room but he didn't want to leave Oscar.

As Daffodil squinted into the light, a familiar figure began to emerge. It was such a surreal experience that Daffodil went to grab Wonderboy to protect him. As her arms flew through the ghosted boy, an icy chill filled her veins before a warm glow encompassed her entire body. She had never felt anything like it. It was love, it was compassion, it was everything kind and devoted. Momentarily, Daffodil stared in awe at Wonderboy. Wonderboy laughed. It was the first time as a ghost that he had ever felt the warm, sticky heat of a human life slice through him.

The familiar face in the glow smiled calmly at them, her silver locks flowing down her back. There was no hint of the sallow skin or harsh features that had become recognizable.

"Madame Glizsnort?" asked Blaze as she stared curiously at the glowing figure. A gentle smile radiated out towards everyone in the room. There was something about Madame Glizsnort's expression that suddenly looked familiar—that kind of familiarity that resides in a residual part of the brain, the part that holds your history.

Wonderboy also recognized her. She looked exactly as she had the last time he had seen her. Whispering in Oscar's ear, Wonderboy reminded him of the teacher they used watch in the church—the teacher that knew they were there, but couldn't see them.

"I'm Wonderboy," he said proudly. Oscar tugged at his arm and whispered something in his ear. "I mean I'm Benjamin!" Wonderboy laughed excitedly.

"Hello Benjamin. It's so wonderful that we can see each other now," said Madame Glizsnort, her tone much kinder than when she had been tormenting the children of the secret society. "I always knew you were there. I could see a flash of light every now and then. It was so disappointing not knowing if you could hear me. It was tragic that my passing did not help us. Then, even though I could see you, *you* could not see *me*."

That gave Jake a thought. "Why can we all see and hear each other now?"

"It is as simple as the purity of white light. Pure because it is made up of all the colors of the world and encompasses all matter, all form, everything. But this is also a very special moment for Benjamin and me. Very important indeed."

Questions were pounding Daffodil's thoughts. "What happened to you?"

"Ahh," replied Madame Glizsnort, "Earth does not suit me."

Daffodil went to question her further but Madame Glizsnort waved an impatient hand at her. Some things had not changed.

"I know I have given you cause to dislike me. But I am afraid I had no choice. Time is running out. You needed to accept your fate quickly and now you need to understand that you will not be going anywhere until you have accomplished your goal." A tremble of peril wavered in her voice.

"You mean," said Annabelle, "*your* goal."

"Please do not hold these negative thoughts inside you." Madame Glizsnort had resorted to the kinder, teacher-like voice she had used earlier. "You must release them now and find a way to send all these ghosted ones into the light."

Santu, seeing Annabelle's cold glare, spoke up. "The harm is yet to come I am thinking," he said, hoping Madame Glizsnort would understand.

Madame Glizsnort knew that Santu was alluding to both the Shadow and Annabelle's demise. If only Santu knew just what was in store for them. But Madame Glizsnort also knew they would each have to understand on their own terms. Ignoring Santu, she looked over at Wonderboy, her face immediately softening.

"Benjamin, there is someone here to see you," Madame Glizsnort's soft tone rang out as she looked back into the white light that encircled her. Holding out her hand they all saw another tiny hand take hers. Slowly a small figure emerged looking very excited.

Oscar, still standing over the radiola, cried out Bugsy's name. The echo bounced around the room giving Bugsy a grand welcome. Bugsy gave a slow sideways wave; each of his five fingers capped by glowing bugs that flapped as they whooshed from side to side.

"Actually," said Madame Glizsnort kindly, "thanks to Daffodil's mother and grandmother we can now introduce Adam Adams."

Wonderboy and Oscar laughed.

"Is that really your name?" asked Oscar trying not to laugh again.

Bugsy nodded and smiled proudly." Yes. Adam Adams. I like it. It's easy to remember."

"So do I!" said Oscar in delight.

"And guess what else Oscar?"

"What Adam Adams?"

"You remember everything when you get here. But it doesn't hurt like it used to. It makes you feel whole. And there's no cold and you can play games and everything."

"That is wonderful," said Oscar in earnest. "I am so happy for you Bugsy . . . I mean Adam! So happy." And he truly was. He had never felt so happy. It was a miracle *and* it was real.

"When are you coming Oscar?" asked Bugsy hopefully.

"Soon Adam, soon." Oscar didn't know if this was true but he hoped with all his heart and soul that it was.

Madame Glizsnort interrupted. "Please, it is important that you remember what I am about to tell you." Her sternness had returned. "You must discover each of the ghosted ones' truths. So listen carefully. Adam's father was Professor Hamish Adams, an entomologist who made great advances in the study of insects. His mother, Catherine Adams was his assistant. Adam was born on May 8th, 1910 and ghosted in 1917 aged 7. He was orphaned at age 2 after his parents inhaled the poisonous gases they were using to help the war effort. He was in a terrible orphanage for several years before he ran away. Adam was caught in a daylight attack by German Gotha airplanes on June 14th, 1917. Fourteen bombers attacked London hitting the Royal Albert Dock, Liverpool Street Station and a school in Poplar killing seventeen children. Adam was found near the school. He says he was lonely and was looking for someone to play with. The air raid killed 162 civilian Londoners in all."

Bugsy was making exploding motions with his hands and then pretending to look dead.

"You must," continued Madame Glizsnort, ignoring Bugsy's theatrical rendition of his death, "remember these details so that you may add them to his gravestone." Madame Glizsnort's tone impressed the importance of this upon them. "We must all be recognized for our existence on earth."

The group was nodding. Poor Bugsy had had an awful life.

"Bugsy!" called out Wonderboy. "You did remember Before because you brought bugs with you! I remembered too! I loved comics Before. We were both named for Before!"

Bugsy was looking very pleased.

"And I've got more bugs now," he said. "And you will be able to have as many comics here as you want."

With that Wonderboy let go of Oscar's hand.

Oscar felt Wonderboy slipping away from him. "Go Benjamin Walsh," Oscar said to Wonderboy with an encouraging nod. "Go."

Wonderboy hesitated. "But I want you to come too."

"I'll follow you soon, Wonderboy, I promise. But you know I can't go until I make sure the others are safely with you first."

Daffodil couldn't let this happen. She couldn't let Oscar stay here when the white light could take him too. "Please, take Oscar with you," Daffodil cried out to Madame Glizsnort.

Madame Glizsnort looked sadly toward Oscar.

"Daffodil. This is not 'Oscar' and I am not God. Oscar needs to find his truth too."

"But Bugsy was able to go into the light and we didn't know about his history." Daffodil was feeling desperate. She could see this was tearing Oscar apart.

"Bugsy kept his bugs and when your mother and grandmother came they picked up on his history immediately. With you they are very powerful. They knew where to take him. But that avenue is closed now Daffodil. They told you so themselves. I am just an instrument to facilitate their journey. I come with love but not with all-knowledge. I come because I must fulfill my purpose. I have no other means."

Daffodil wanted to push further but she could see it would lead nowhere. For now she must be happy that Wonderboy would be going into the light. She turned and smiled at Wonderboy and Oscar. Wonderboy was hesitating and Oscar was looking distraught.

Santu was noticing something too.

"Daffodil." Santu was motioning for her to look out the window. The darkness was lifting. Light would come soon.

Madame Glizsnort felt the pull. It was time to take her new charge into the light.

"We must hurry," said Madame Glizsnort. "It is time for the next ascension. Each time I come I will have less and less time, yet, I have much to tell you. For now, you must keep trying. Concentrate on the ones with pets. And remember the gravestones." She looked towards Wonderboy and beckoned to him. "Come child, come to the light."

Wonderboy turned to Oscar. Oscar laughed at him and gave him a little push. "Go Benjamin Walsh. Go home. This is what we've all been waiting for. I will join you soon. Now go!" Oscar was holding back his tears. He loved all his ghosted ones so much.

Wonderboy smiled at Oscar. "Thank you Oscar. Thank you for believing."

And then before they knew it, Wonderboy was entering the white glow. Suddenly a burst of warm light erupted, nearly blinding them all.

When Wonderboy turned around, his face was changed. It was fuller and softer and the serene look in his eyes was extraordinary. He looked like a happy little boy.

Wonderboy was amazed. The cold, the fear and the sickness he had felt before had all dissolved. Now he felt full as if the white light had made him whole again. And memories were filling up inside of him: sand in a sandglass: good and bad; love and loss; pain and wonder. It felt right and surprisingly it wasn't overwhelming. He smiled an enormous smile. Madame Glizsnort hugged Wonderboy delightedly.

"Finally Benjamin, finally!"

As the white light began to fade they saw the excited face of the little boy they had just crossed over. He was punching the air like superman about to take flight. The last word they heard was the cry:

"Wonderboy flies!"

NEW YORK DAILY NEWS

~ New Yorks Most Favored Newspaper ~

Daily Edition - Evening - May 5 1916   One Cent

Mysterious Rumors have been circulating amongst the labyrinthine trenches of No Man's Land. It is said that a roaming band of deserters and derelicts from both sides have turned into caninbals and now stalk the unsuspecting soldiers.

UNITED STATES POPULAR AMENDMENT

The Estimable Prohibitionists Seem Determined To Make It Read 'See America Thirst'. PAGE 9.

New York Theater has sparked rioting protests after the moving picture THE BIRTH OF A NATION was shown recently. The film tells of the Civil War and its aftermath and includes the secret vigilante group the Klu Klux Klan. There have been so many complaints that it is thought the movie will not be shown again. More Page 7.

HOUDINI

THE MAN OF MYSTERY

PALACE THEATRE
EVENINGS DAILY

BATTLE OF VERDUN

February 21st marked the beginning of the battle that would result in massive casualties. After Germany's similtaneous attacks on the Meuse: Bois Bourrus, and Le Mort-Homme - where the French initially defended well - another attack on Cote 304 proved to be too intense for the French: 500 guns thundering on a field of not even 2 square kilometers. Suffering terrible losses at Cote 304, the French then faced the same losses at Le Mort-Homme. The French look to concede this disastrous battle. FULL STORY PAGE 2.

FLYING ACE - DEAD

After several weeks of heavy air fighting, one of the great French pilots has been shot down. Francois Marcel Thenault - referred to as the 'Flying Ace' for his record of enemy hits, lost his last fight on May 3rd. Several French pilots have become victims of this terrible battle at Verdun. Known casualties PAGE 5.

Cincinnati, O., - Horace Thole, Deaf and Dumb, Has Been Granted A Chaufeur's License. He States That He Relies On His Sensitive Skin To Detect Sound.

Vicksburg, Miss. - Police Are Investigating the Identity Of A Woman Giving Her Name As Mrs. A. A. Thoms Who Is Dying From Poison.

Washington - Mr. and Mrs, N.P. Alley motored to Redmond on Saturday and reported fine weather.

Beeville, Ill. - Miss Josephine Marceau was delighted on Tuesday evening when she was the recipient of a surprise party for her 18th birthday. The young folks enjoyed games on the lawn after which dainty refreshments were served by the hostess.

New Orleans, La. - Police received order to compel all persons frequenting cabaret cafes in the 'tango belt' to register names and addresses with police.

Rochester, N.Y. - Contino Costa, 30, and 3 children found dead from asphyxiation.

DAILY EXPRESS

WORLD'S LARGEST DAILY SALE

Nightly Edition - New York, November 17, 1916. One Cent

CARNAGE AT BATTLE OF SOMME FINALLY OVER

Since the start of the Battle of Somme on July 1st, catastrophic casualties have bloodied the British and French offensive. From the first day, British and Irish volunteers fell in staggering numbers: 20,000 dead; 40,000 injured. Without a breakthrough, the following months turned into a bloody stalemate. In October, very heavy rain turned battlegrounds into mudbaths. Finally the attempt to alleviate the French Army at Verdun and the desire to inflict heavy losses on Germany has now ended with the Allies having advanced a paltry total of five miles. The British have suffered 360,000 casualties, the French nearly 200,000, and the Germans, 550,000. For each mile gained in the advance, 125,000 Allied troopes have died. One witness has stated that the dead looked as if they had been strung out like wreckage, the barbed wire of the trenches trapping them like fish caught in a net. Many looked as if they were praying, the bodies fallen against t

W TRAVEL RULES FOR CHILDREN UNDER 16

o Epidemic Affects Travel Rules For dren and those with Infantile Paral- s. On this day in 1916, the following een issued by the Seaboard Air Line way, concerning the South Carolina arantine against infantile paralysis. ilroad tickets will not be sold to child- n under (16) sixteen years of age unless ertificate is furnished by the local board health, where one exists, and where no **cal Board of Health exists, by a family** ysician residing in the locality showing at the child has not been in contact with case of Infantile Paralysis and has not **had the disease of Polio this year.** re onthe Polio epidemic PAGE 5.

~Present day~

~Fire Burning Bright~

B efore they had even had a chance to comprehend Wonderboy's journey, Oscar was frantically facing the emerging daylight.

"I have to go now or I will not make it."

"Go Oscar, go!" cried Daffodil with the same words Oscar had used to send Wonderboy into the light but they all knew Oscar was not going anywhere near the light. The place he sought was dangerous and unbalanced. For all they knew none of the ghosted ones would return. Oscar sensed the irony but had no time to consider it. In a flash he was gone.

"We go home now?" asked Duette, her voice ringing with sarcasm.

"Yeah," said Santu with his usual buoyant cynicism. "Let's all be going home." He threw out a blatant smile. "Is anyone having a way out?"

"Madame Glizsnort?" asked Jake with a twisted smile.

"Not being funny Jake," said Duette. "Death too grumpy."

"You think Madame Glizsnort is 'Death'?" asked Jake in surprise.

Duette shrugged. "She like dead things."

Daffodil was exhausted. "I don't know about being Death but do you think she has anything to do with that impenetrable mist surrounding us?"

"I think," replied Santu, "she is everything to do with it."

Madame Glizsnort was not letting them go anywhere until they had done what they were brought here to do.

Annabelle was furious. Why was everyone giving in to this woman? She was quite obviously lying about whatever she was doing with the ghosts. Yet everyone just conceded defeat. Not Annabelle: *She* was planning her escape.

Blaze should have been feeling worn out but her revelation had made her feel lighter. Under the weight of her secret, the past few years had taken their toll and exhaustion had become part of her daily reality. Blaze knew, if she did go home, that somehow the truth would have to follow her out of this icy wasteland.

"Should we get some sleep?" asked Duel as a huge rumble of thunder roared through the still air.

"I think I'm going to fall asleep before I even answer that question," said Daffodil as she tried to make a pillow out of a pile of ancient newspapers.

"You're not even going back to the cabin?" asked Blaze. "It sounds like a storm is brewing." A burst of fork-lightning cracked through the pale sky like it was an eggshell.

Daffodil shook her head and then rested it on her newspaper padding. She wrapped her scratchy green blanket around her tightly before closing her eyes to let the darkness of sleep take her.

Blaze looked around the room in surprise. Everyone was following Daffodil's attempt to make a cushion out of the papers. Shrugging her shoulders, Blaze did the same. Obviously no one was going anywhere. If a storm came, they'd wake soon enough. After all, there were no windows. The storm could come right on in. Blaze laughed at the craziness of their situation. As she closed her eyes, the flames of the fire flickered across her eyelids.

How was she to know that the orange and red glow of the firelight would lure her mind backward to the night she was always trying to forget? And how was she to know that the burning embers would wake her gift once more?

Jake was shaking his head. He had woken well before the others and was trying to find a frequency on the radiola that could receive the older recordings the ghosts had made. The fact that they were looped recordings meant they would carry on as long as there were airwaves. The earlier the recording, the more significant the information would be—surely the ghosts would have remembered more. He would just have to keep trying.

Outside, rain had started falling, softly at first and then with more intent: An ignored whiny child that craved attention. Jake was surprised that the thunder and lightning hadn't woken anyone else up. Still, it meant he was free to fiddle on the radiola.

Jake had no idea how far back these ghostly dairies began, but he knew if he listened long enough, without interruption, he would come across something, some historical information that could help. There repetitive words were a coaster, rolling on decades of sadness.

Even though the murky daylight was waning, it was impossible to know how long he had been working on the dials, and now his fingers were cramping from the infinitesimal changes he had been making. Just as Jake was about to give up, he heard something, something important: A boy with an accent was calling himself Scraps.

Jake listened to the recording trying not to let the noise of the blood pumping through his ears deafen him.

"Bonjour. I am called Scraps. I am the only one that remembers how I ghosted. That is how I got my name: I ate scraps. And a green potato. So stupid! If I could have had frogs legs I would have been so happy. Frogs legs are my favorite.

I cannot remember my real name or the names of my parents but I remember many other things.

I remember my school. It was a good place. It was called The Lycée Francais Charles de Gaulle and it was right near Victoria station in London. It was a French school so there were lots of children from Europe. I learned my English from there also. My words are not so bad that people laugh at me but I would like so much to do better. I do not learn here in this place wherever this is. I cannot keep the information. This makes me, how you say, sad.

My family came to England from France before the war started. I remember the war. It was most terrifying. So many raids and sirens all the time, even in the center of the night. People were dying every day. That is where my father went. To this war. He had been a pilot before. Papa flew one of the first passenger planes that had an enclosed cabin. Do you know that the passengers all sat inside the cabin while the crew was left in the open air? I think it is funny. My Papa said he loved being out in the sky anyway. I cannot remember what kind of plane he flew in the war. He told me in a letter once. It cannot have been a very good plane because he did not fly it for so long. Mama said it was the plane's fault that he fell out of the sky but I just think she wants to blame something.

Oh yes. My Mama was nurse. I remember that because sometimes she would have to take me with her to the hospital. What was the name of it? Oui! It was called The Grove Fever Hospital. That's because it was on Tooting Grove. [giggling] Tooting sounds like when air comes out your bottom! That is why I remember it! I also remember there was a discharge room, where patients who were leaving did bathe and change from their hospital garments to their own clothes. That room always smelled very much. I did not like it there. But the hospital blocks were always sunny. My Mama told me they were made to let lots of sunshine and air in. There were isolation blocks too—for really bad sickness—but I was never allowed to go there. I remember some names of sicknesses. There was scarlet fever, TB of the lung, Scabies, German measles (more than just German people get that you know) Typhus, Mumps and many others.

Then Mama caught this Tuberculosis. I forget which kind. One minute both my parents were there; the next minute they were gone. So that is how I ate a green potato. I had to steal food you see, because I could not find any work. I slept in some strange places too. And it always seemed to be so cold. I will not eat a green potato again. I will always remember not to do that.

Oh, and I forgot to tell you about my ghosted mouse. It is called Tooting because I really like that word. [giggles]

I cannot think of anything else to tell you so I will finish this recording. This is my second one. Oscar says he is proud of me for remembering so much. I told him I can do many recordings. Just you wait and see."

Jake was astounded he had managed to find such an early recording. With his ear glued to the radiola he waited for what came next but of course the message just repeated itself.

Hoping to find someone else awake, Jake turned away from the transistor to face a disturbing sight. Blaze was sitting upright, her green eyes wide open, and she was staring intently at the fire glowing behind him. A chill ran up Jake's spine. And then the shadows on the floorboards in front of him gave him even more reason to worry. As he turned toward the fire, he realized that once again, Blaze's powers were out of her control.

The memory of Daffodil's heroic battle with the last blaze came straight into Jake's mind.

As Jake screamed for everyone to wake up, he threw the water-buckets onto the wild flames but nothing happened. Flares spilled forward and upward as if they were desperate to break free. As Jake ran to get one of the blankets, Santu pulled himself from slumber feeling disoriented and confused. He had been back in Basque, chatting up a pretty girl, the ocean beside them catching sunshine shards from across the horizon. But the girl had kept looking over her shoulder as if something was coming for her. Buoying uncertainty had unraveled his dream. Now he was looking at burning flames that were rising toward the old rafters of the church ceiling.

Seeing that Santu was at least awake, although he looked thoroughly dazed, Jake screamed out Blaze's name as he tried hopelessly to dredge the flames.

In Santu's state it all took a moment to make sense. Jake was signaling for him to wake Blaze. But Blaze was awake—she was sitting up and staring wide-eyed at the fire. Then Santu realized what was going on: She was somehow fanning the flames. He ran to Blaze to shake her out of her trance.

"Blaze you'll kill us all! Stop it!" Santu screamed as he shook her. As Blaze came to, the vision of Jake, Daffodil, Duette and Duel all trying to fight the towering flames struck her in the most horrifying of ways.

"Control it!" screamed Santu. "For god's sake Blaze! Control the damn fire!"

Blaze was trying to but she didn't even know how she had created the flames in the first place, let alone how to make them stop. Concentrating on the growing bursts of firelight she tried to shrink them in her mind but the inferno continued to burn.

"I can't do it!" Blaze cried out. "I don't know how!"

"Well you better be figuring it out Blaze! If we have no church we have no ghosts!"

Duette was screaming. Her jacket had caught on fire. Duel was trying to rip it off her but his sister wouldn't keep still. She was trying to run away from the fire burning on her body.

Santu threw Blaze's shoulders backward in fury and ran toward Duette. He managed to grab the front of her jacket and rip it open. The heat was so strong it had nearly melted the zipper and the fabric just fell into pieces in his hands. As he threw the jacket down Jake jumped on the flaming material. Duette was still running around as if she were burning: The shock had dislocated her from reality. Santu grabbed her and twisted her away from the fire almost throwing her toward the stairs.

Daffodil was getting too close. The fire was licking at her layers of clothing as if teasing her to come just a little closer. Jake yelled at her but the shocked look on Daffodil's face told him that he was too late. Daffodil's skirt was burning. In her alarm and still with bandaged hands, she didn't know what to do. Unlike Duette she didn't move at all.

Jake charged. He flung himself at her, throwing her to the ground. He lay across the red hot flames until they were extinguished.

"Blaze," screamed Santu again as if this might miraculously change the situation. But Blaze was lost in a world of her own making. Flashbacks were taking her away from here and returning her to a place of horror; a place she would never be able to escape.

"This isn't working. We've got to get out of here," yelled Duel. "Now!"

"But, the radiola," cried Jake, "you don't understand. It can't burn the radiola!" Jake was frantic. They didn't get it: It was their golden ticket out of here. "I'm not leaving," he said as he continued to bash the remains of a burned blanket at the raging fire.

"Duel, get Jake." It was Santu and he had no time for heroics now.

Santu realized that the fire had gotten out of control. A few army blankets weren't going to save them. He threw Blaze toward the stairs and motioned toward Annabelle to follow.

"Let's get out of here now!" cried Santu. "Everyone! Get out now!"

Duel had grabbed Jake and was dragging him kicking and screaming toward the stairs. As the fire reached for the old, oak beams of the lofty church ceiling, even Jake knew there was no hope.

Outside, the darkness of night was falling around them and the rain was driving itself into the ground as if it were divining for gold. The heavy downpour had turned the icy ground into a slick messy ice-skating rink and several of them slid uncontrollably before tumbling onto the freezing earth.

Blaze was one of them. She felt her feet skid, twisting horribly beneath her. Her arms flailed as she crashed onto the frozen ground. Her chin struck the hard ice first and her head was knocked backwards before her face struck the ice again. Her crumpled body slid several meters before hitting a tree. In those few seconds that passed Blaze felt like a lifetime had been taken and given back. As soon as her face touched that ice she knew what to do and exactly how to quell the fire.

Blackwater Herald Moon Tribune Wednesday, October 16th, 1946— 2 Pence

NUREMBERG TRIALS UPDATE

Twenty-two prominent Nazi leaders now face justice after the Nuremberg trials have sentenced 12 to death while the rest are to be incarcerated in Spandau Prison in Berlin. Herman Goering has committed suicide before his execution could take place, but Von Ribbentrop, Streicher, Sauckel, Frank, Jodl, Frick, Kaltenbrunner, Rosenberg, Seys-Inquart and Wilhelm Keitel shall be hanged tonight. The bodies will then be taken to Dachau and cremated in the ovens of the concentration camp.

LOCAL NEWS HEADLINES
BIRTH ANNOUNCEMENTS

***Inspector Macalister Glizsnort** and Mrs. Grace Glizsnort brought a baby boy into the world on Monday. He will be named Benjamin Oisin Glizsnort after Mrs. Glizsnort's brother who died in World War One. Mrs. Glizsnort will take a short break from her studies to take care of her new son. The family will be returning to Blackwater to baptize Benjamin at the Church of All Saints on November 12th as the new church building on the Cross Roads site is yet to be finished. Benjamin is brother to twins Jemima and Eustace. All are healthy.*

NEWSPAPER ANNOUNCEMENT

The current owners of The Herald Moon Tribune have chosen to turn the paper's run over to the locals. "The paper is no longer profitable as there are too few to buy it," said the Editor yesterday. "And most of our staff have left town anyway. It seems inevitable that we must follow suit."

Mr. Walter Bailey and Mr. Thomas Bentley will be taking over the control of the weekly issue with several locals responsible for editorials and community interest columns. Address any social interest stories to Mrs. Agnes Underwood of Hawkesmeade Street.

WORLD NEWS HEADLINES

***FIRST COMPUTER**—'ENIAC' as it is named, is our first Electrical Numerical Integrator and Calculator general purpose computer. It fills and entire room and weighs around 30 tons. Page 4.*

***SIGNALS IN OUTER SPACE**—the U.S. Army Signal Corps have discovered that communication is possible between Earth and space by bouncing radar waves off the moon and back to Earth. This breakthrough has begun a new program called the U.S. Space Program. Page 7.*

***JAPANESE WOMEN VOTE**—For the first time, women in Japan are able to vote in parliamentary elections. Page 11.*

~Brought to you by~

Throat doctors pick Old Gold Cigarettes—not a cough in a carload!

Popular Science Monthly Magazine—Television reaches out!

~Present day~

~F is for Forgotten, Fire & Figment~

From the ground, they had watched the glowing orange light of the fire in the top story of the church. Most of the witnesses, having tripped on the icy ground, were lying on the ice, their eyes transfixed on the scene they had just left. Rain was tumbling down on them as if it wished to bury them from sight, but nobody moved.

When the force of the flames had suddenly turned blue, Santu had panicked thinking that there may be gas in the building. He had scrambled desperately to get everyone out of there: A gas explosion would have killed them all. But the people he was trying to grab were struggling against him. It was Daffodil that finally got him to turn around and look up at the church properly.

What Santu saw, was beyond his comprehension. The fire was no longer burning. The orange flames had turned blue because they were *repairing* the damage that the fire had caused. Finally, as they watched, the blaze exploded with a burst of blue light and disappeared.

"Oh my god," cried Daffodil. "You're not just a fire-starter!" She turned to face her friend. "You're a fire-healer!"

Blaze was confused. She thought she had only *stopped* the fire from burning down the church. "Fire-healer?" she asked.

Daffodil nodded. Respect was written all over her face. "Now *that* is rare!" Daffodil tried to sound excited but a cloud hung over her discovery:

This gift could only be acquired by someone who had faced the darkness of death. "I definitely want you to be my friend." The others laughed and circled around Blaze, who was still on the ground—everyone except Annabelle. Instead, she stood aside, her icy glare lost in the sinking gloom.

"Well," said Santu, pulling at the collar of his leather jacket. "That was being a little bit too close for comfort. I was sweating slugs."

It was all very country music for a minute before the pain jazzed up Blaze's legs—the adrenaline rush had worn off. Uncharacteristically, Blaze cried out with the sensation.

Suddenly Daffodil realized what a strange position one of Blaze's ankles was in. She shot a look at Santu who understood straight away.

"I am getting Blaze," Santu said. "Cabin." He inclined his head over to the dark buildings on the other side of the church. Daffodil noticed the cabin fire had gone out. Perhaps Blaze had put out all the fires everywhere? Just another obstacle now. There were so many more important things at stake.

Heavy rain thundered down on the cabin roof threatening to destroy it. Although everyone tried to ignore the noise, there were sporadic, worried glances directed up toward the ceiling. While Daffodil attended to the wounds, the others took turns washing and changing into dry clothes. At least the burns on her hands had healed enough for her to use minimal bandaging. The balm she had instructed Blaze to mix was incredible and she committed the recipe to memory.

In turn, she attended to Blaze's horrible injuries; cleaned and wrapped a deep cut on Duel's arm which really needed stitches but Duel absolutely refused; bandaged Duette's sprained wrist; attended to the cruel pain of Santu's frostbitten toes; and cleaned and dressed the deep gashes and grazes on Annabelle's beautiful face. Annabelle would be scarred but there was nothing Daffodil could do. Miraculously, Jake had escaped injury free. Finally, she dosed everybody with crystals again.

As she worked, only the sounds of heavy rain and the steaming shower—fuelled by the newly ignited fire—could be heard. The room was filled with palpable silence. It was as if quietude was an entity itself. The strange occurrence that they had just witnessed needed a time of stillness to be absorbed.

By the time all the wounds had been bandaged and patched, Jake could no longer stay silent.

"The-radiola-is-alright," he said with obvious relief. Jake was pacing the room. He had tried to wait until everyone was ready to listen. Each one of them had to deal with what had happened in their own way. But he was bursting to fill them in. He made sure his speech was unhurried. "I can't believe it's still okay."

"Yes Jake," said Santu with a smile—Jake made the radiola sound like one of their comrades. "The radiola is going to be fine." Santu raised an eyebrow. "It could be ending up in better condition than some of your companions." He looked across at Blaze.

Daffodil had managed to construct a splint for Blaze's broken ankle but she had first had to reposition the bone. The inhaling-anesthetic that Duette had found in Annabelle's first aid kit hadn't made enough of a difference to stop Blaze from screaming. At least her other ankle was only sprained. Daffodil managed to bandage it firmly enough to reduce the throbbing. When Daffodil had finished she mopped Blaze's brow.

"I'm sorry," said Daffodil. "But you did a pretty good job breaking yourself you know."

Blaze was looking very pale. "Thanks Daff. I know you had to."

"How bad is the pain?" asked Daffodil squinting into Blaze's eyes seeking the truth.

"It's bad but nothing I can't cope with." No pain could compare to the burns.

"Okay," replied Daffodil. "Then take these and get some rest."

Annabelle stroked the gauze bandage on her face. She would be scarred. Perhaps beauty needed to have a stain? People had always judged her by her looks but she knew it gave no revelation about the pain inside. Could a scar reveal a truth?

"Is anyone going to address the fact that we now know Madame Glizsnort is a ghost, or a spirit, or whatever she is?" No one answered her. "Really? Not even a shrug Duette?"

Duette glared at Annabelle. "You a salope! I not discuss anythings with you."

Duel threw an amazed glance at his sister. She had just called Annabelle a bitch.

"Um," said Daffodil trying to diffuse the situation, "I thought we had already gone over that?"

"Well," replied Annabelle, "I don't trust her."

"Well," Blaze intoned, "I don't think we have a choice."

Annabelle was annoyed with everyone. Well they could all be fools. At least she had made her point. She crossed her arms and went to the bathroom.

Blaze watched her go. "Her favorite place when she hasn't got a comeback."

Duette still looked angry. "Her favorite place because of mirror!"

Blaze couldn't help herself and burst out laughing. "Your funny Duette, you should talk more."

Duette raised her chin and looked down her nose. "You right Blaze. See Duel, I funny."

Duel rolled his eyes and shook his head. He didn't want to admit it, but his thoughts had already been read: His sister was getting to be more amusing every day.

Santu was looking outside. Darkness had bruised the sky once again. Oscar would be back at the church with another ghost. "Some of us should really be going back."

"Please," cried out Blaze knowing what everyone would be thinking. "I'm really sorry about what happened but you can't shut me out." She looked desperately at Daffodil who flashed a look at Santu.

"Well," said Daffodil while still staring at Santu. "I'm sure we could make a crutch or something to help?"

Santu was grimacing. He wasn't sure that bringing Blaze back into the church was a good idea. But she *had* managed to stop the flames and if it wasn't for her and Annabelle they couldn't have crossed Wonderboy over. He chewed the side of his cheek.

"You are right Daffodil. It is not safe to be splitting the group up." Santu turned toward Blaze. "But you have to be promising to anchor yourself down with a bed sheet. We can't be trying to save you all the time."

Blaze was hurt. "You don't need to save me Santu. I am quite capable of staying alive without your help."

Daffodil was annoyed at Santu. Why did he always have to come across as superior? "Look just everyone take it easy. I saw a couple of branches outside that would be perfect to use for crutches but we'll still have to help her a bit. That other ankle is sprained and it won't heal if she tries to use it too much for support."

Blaze was so grateful she would have agreed to anything. "Just help me into the church and then I won't have to leave." Her urgent smile was pleading.

Everyone nodded or shrugged their shoulders except Santu, who sighed deeply.

"Duel," said Daffodil seeing the French boy standing by the door, "can you come with me?"

Now Jake was hurt. He was dying to tell them all about the foreign boy's recording but he felt invisible. He knew he shouldn't be surprised by that anymore, after all, he had been invisible all his life. Even when his mother was destroying his soul by spilling her hatred on him and burdening his young spirit with those malicious treatments, he was still a nothing, a nobody, less than a bug: Invisible.

Jake was descending into himself again: Such a tiny trigger, yet such a powerful reaction.

The only person that felt the ripping pain in the atmosphere was Duette. She swung her head in Jake's direction understanding only too well what being invisible felt like. The difference between the two was that *she* had retreated deliberately.

"Duel," said Duette as her brother opened the cabin door and exposed them all to the bitter thumping rain that was falling outside. "I think Jake be better helper, no?" She threw Jake's thoughts at her brother. Duel felt like he had been crushed. In his shock he simply stepped away from the door and made room for Jake.

For a moment Daffodil was confused. "Oh yes," Daffodil stammered as understanding came. "Jake could you please help me? I'm afraid you're going to get wet." Her eyes moved from Jake to the rain and back again.

Jake wasn't sure what was going on. Duette had done something. Suddenly he didn't feel alone or invisible anymore. Unexpectedly, his feelings of abandonment had vanished. Jake nodded quickly. Throwing a curious glance at Duette—who pretended not to notice—he went out the door with Daffodil.

Duel raised his eyebrows at Duette in a knowing smile. She shrugged her shoulders and curled her bottom lip as if she had no idea what Duel meant. Duel shook his head. His sister had changed. She never would have interceded to help someone before. Duel liked his new twin. He had no idea what would happen when they returned to their normal lives but he would always remember the person she had become under these extraordinary circumstances.

As a crack of lightning struck the sky, Duel handed out fresh blankets and found new sheets which were gratefully accepted. Curiously, he had found them a cupboard that he was sure had been empty.

As the cabin door swung open and two very wet, shivering people dumped some sturdy branches on the floor, a very excited Daffodil was shouting at everyone. Jake was glad that Daffodil had reacted with such exhilaration.

"Daffodil," yelled Santu over the top of her ramblings. "Slow down! What are you trying to say?"

Daffodil tried to calm down. "Sorry but Jake heard a really old recording on the radiola. He found a frequency that had one of their first recordings on it and they remember so much more in the early ones and he heard one about a French boy," she checked Duette and Duel's reactions, "yeah I know, and he is called Scraps and he remembers his school and where his mother worked and he remembers dying from eating a green potato, can you believe it? No me neither. Isn't Jake amazing?" Daffodil took a huge breath. She had exhausted herself.

Everyone was regarding their two sodden, shivering companions with awe.

"This is incredible," said Santu, "and we want to be hearing about it but if you guys are not having a hot shower and changing we might have two more ghosts to cross over."

Everyone patted Jake on the back as he went to the bathroom to wash. It was the greatest day of his life.

The trip back to the church was difficult. The ground was slick with heavy rain making it slippery and unpredictable. Duel helped support Blaze as she hobbled painfully in the blackening surrounds, and Santu balanced one of the thin mattresses over their heads to protect them from the tumbling rain. Everyone else shuffled underneath trying not to bump each other.

The church was as cold as ever. The rain didn't seem to have thawed the icy temperatures at all. Santu and Duel debated whether they should make another fire. Blaze sat silent. Everyone would have to endure these conditions because of her. When Duel started building a fire on the old iron tray, Blaze sighed with relief. Maybe they thought they could trust her after all.

Santu was directing traffic as usual: Instructing Duette, and Duel, to guard the windows; Daffodil to check her protective crystals; Blaze to anchor her sheet to the railing beside her; and Jake to inspect the radiola for damage. It helped Santu feel more in control. It was enjoyable watching Annabelle's reaction to being ignored. He smiled to himself.

"The radiola is fine," reported Jake as he carefully held tight onto the left dial and delicately twisted the one on the right. He was sure now that he had figured out how to move the controls so that he could hear recordings that were just slightly forward in time from Scraps' last one. If he could pull it off, Jake would be able to hear all their memories.

"So are the crystals," added Daffodil.

"No Shadow," said Duette. "We guard this time—non distraction."

Duette's words made something inside Jake shiver. Her accent was just like the French boy, Scraps. Even the boy's speech mannerisms were like hers. Duel's way of speaking didn't make him feel the same way. Of course Duel had learned English very well at an American School but Duette hadn't learned at school. She had learned to speak English by listening to other people.

As a zigzag of lightning forked through the air, a strange thought struck Jake: Could Duette have been picking up English so quickly because of Scraps? Had she been using her empath skills without even realizing? She had learnt astoundingly quickly considering she had hardly spoken any English before she came here. Jake wasn't sure what to do. Should he say something? Was it even important?

Jake was about to ask Daffodil when he heard the faint hum of another recording. He focused hard and began the laborious process of trying to pinpoint the exact frequency.

"Daffodil," began Blaze as she thumbed through some dreadful articles about the devastating destruction caused in World War One. "What is a 'fire-healer' anyway?"

"Well," said Daffodil hesitantly. The truth was always around the corner, waiting. "The manipulation of fire is actually very rare. Only those with the powers of the spirit-realm are given an opening to that gateway." She stared hard at Blaze but Blaze was looking at newspaper articles.

"Usually," said Daffodil quietly, "a person must first die before they are capable of such a thing." Daffodil's sad eyes gazed at Blaze. "Or go to the brink of death where they learn to hover between the two realms."

Blaze looked up at her friend. "Die?"

Daffodil suddenly had a revelation. "Blaze!"

"What? What's wrong?"

"Oh my god Blaze. I've just realized something."

"What!?"

Daffodil had everyone's attention now.

"Blaze you didn't start the fire that killed your parents and brother. That fire was what *made* you like this—a fire-starter, a fire-healer." Thoughts were tumbling into Daffodil's mind. "That's probably when you started seeing spirits! Quite often, children don't realize they are seeing them. They manage to accept these visions as if they are everyday life."

"What are you saying?"

"Well," said Daffodil now seated beside Blaze and looking at her as if she were an extinct animal. "Shamans believe, that to become a fire-healer you must first undergo an initiation. Do you remember anything significant after that fire burned down your house?"

"I've only ever tried to forget."

"Blaze, this is really important. I want you to try to remember but make sure you recognize that the images are memories. Try to keep yourself removed. Otherwise . . ."

Everyone knew what Daffodil was thinking. And there were enough things to worry about without having another inferno to put out.

Blaze nodded. If she was truly going to control this 'gift' she would have to start learning, and quickly. For the first time since that fire burned down her house and nearly burned her alive, Blaze tried to go back to that day.

Torturous images flashed one after the other in her mind. She tried to hang on to them; let them flow sequentially, but it was horrible. They were so real she could swear the smell of burning flesh was all around her. Daffodil's soothing words kept her both in the present and the past. Finally one image glowed brightly. Immersing her mind and pushing all the other reflections away, she focused on it.

"There was a doctor," Blaze began, her eyes closed firmly. "I thought he was a doctor? He had such lovely dark skin and very large brown eyes. When he looked at me I felt safe and the awful pain disappeared. He was all lit up. I think there was one of those doctor's lights behind him. Everything was white except for his beautiful brown face. His eyes seemed too big. I can see him leaning over me now."

"Did he speak to you?" asked Daffodil.

Blaze nodded. "Yes," she said, almost trancelike.

"What did he say?"

"I can't remember. It was weird stuff."

"It's really important. Just focus on that moment."

Blaze concentrated. The images became more focused. "Oh, yes. I remember he said something about a choice." Suddenly her eyes lit up. "Oh my god, he said something about the spirit world. I remember. How could I have forgotten?"

"What did he say exactly Blaze?"

"He told me I had made my choice but I didn't understand what he meant. Then he said I had made the more difficult decision and that most people in my situation chose the peace of the spirit world. He said my life would be infinitely more difficult from now on but there would be privileges if I sought them. He said destiny should not be trapped by flesh." Blaze shook herself from the reverie. The otherworldly peace she had felt with his vision stayed with her momentarily. "What does it mean?"

"Well," said Daffodil smiling, "I don't think that was a doctor for starters. Not a medical doctor anyway."

"No," replied Blaze. "I don't think so either. Who was he?"

"I don't know but the shamans certainly have a theory."

"About the doctor or the fire?"

Daffodil laughed. "The shamans have theories for many things. But they believe to become a fire-worker you must take the first step, which is the destruction of the self or ego." Daffodil shook her head. There was no need to get technical. "Essentially they say you have to die and be reborn before being honored with the power of fire. They believe that when you are hovering between life and death you face a choice: The spirit guides ask you if you want to become a permanent member of the spirit world." Daffodil made a face. "Basically, death. Or, you can accept your new destiny as a fire-healer. If you choose to live, you will always be connected to the spirit world. In a way you have crossed the only barrier most of the living will never access—until they, you know, die of course."

"After my parents died I kept seeing images out of the corner of my eye but after the school fire I saw child ghosts everywhere."

"Maybe you had to deal with all the grief before you recognized them as spirits." Daffodil paused. "And I don't think it's a coincidence that it took the fatal fire of your home to give you these gifts."

"But why would I start the fire at the boarding school?! I didn't want to hurt those little children."

"I don't know," said Daffodil, "but I do know, if you deny your true self for long enough it will come bursting out with more ferocity than most of us can imagine." Daffodil glanced at Annabelle. She didn't mean to, it was the physical reflex of thought. On seeing the reflection Annabelle returned, Daffodil quickly turned away again.

If *Annabelle* had the gift of fire, they all would have been burned to a cinder.

TSAR ABDICATES

Russian Revolution Erupts and, it seems, everyone has joined in the chaos including 80,000 troops who have now mutinied from the army. The reasons are many but include; Ongoing resentment at cruel treatment from the upper classes; Poor working conditions; and a growing political awareness by the common people. In the disorder Tsar Nicholas II has abdicated the throne. **Page 2.**

International Woman's Day

Turns Into Demonstration. The city of Petrograd swells with protesting women as they leave factories to object to food shortages. Men soon join them. Story Page 5.

RASPUTIN DEAD

Russian Mystic, Grigori Rasputin is finally dead. After being unaffected by enough poison to kill 10 men; being shot in the back; then shot thrice more - Rasputin still lived. But then he was severly clubbed and thrown into the icy Neva River. Finally on 16th Dec. 1916 he was declared dead. Rasputin's story P8.

COMBAT IN NIEUPORT 17'S

IN THIS THE YEAR OF 1917 WE HAVE PROVED WE C TAKE ON THE GERMANS! ENGLISH FIGHTER PILOT THE FRENCH PILOTS AT ARRAS, 60 SQUADRON, F FARM AND TOOK TO THE SKIES TO BATTLE THE IN THREE ALBATROS DIII SCOUTS NEAR ST. LE SUCCESSFULLY MORTALLY WOUNDING THE EI THE NIEUPORT 17S ARE A DIFFICULT MACHINE FLY AND GIVEN THAT THE AVERAGE LIFE EXPE OF A PILOT IS JUST 11 DAYS AND GERMAN ACE BEEN SHOOTING DOWN BRITISH AIRCRAFT 5 TO 1 - THIS IS AN EXTRAORDINARY FEAT. FULL STORY PAGE 5.

IMAGES OF NIEUPORT 17'S IN FLIGHT ON THE FATEFUL DAY.

~Present day~

~I Miss Frogs Legs~

"**D**affodil!" Jake cried out. "Where's that Celestite!"
Whilst extracting the liquid vials and talismans from her crystal bag, Daffodil ran over to Jake. She threw the strongest amulet over to him before spraying everyone with a solution that had absorbed celestite during a full moon.

Immediately everyone was able to hear. Jake's desperate looks turned to amazement as he realized everyone was listening to the same recorded voice as him. It was the first time in his life that he felt normal. No it was the first time in his life he felt better than normal. A smile rocked across his face as he increased the volume dial just slightly.

"Bonjour. I am Scraps and this is my mouse Tooting. This is recording three. I am here because I ate a green potato and ghosted. I was just ten. It is stupid—I know that now—but Before I was hungry and did not know about potatoes like this. I was used to eating frog's legs, and rabbit and escargot— these are snails you know: Very delicious but quite ugly to look at. But with wine sauce they are very good.

My family was well off before the war but that is a long time ago now. I remember where I lived with my parents. It was on Upper Belgrave Street in London. It was such a grand house. My bedroom was very big too. I had many toys. I would like some of those toys now. It is very boring here. It is strange also. Time moves forward but it seems to move around also. It is impossible to tell how long we have been here but we make sure we remember how many recordings we have made. It is the one thing Oscar says that we must never forget.

Oh, I remembered the plane my papa used in the war. It was called a Nieport 17 C-1 biplane. It was very small and difficult to fly. I overheard someone saying that the lower wings were weak because of how it was made and sometimes these wings fall to pieces in steep dives. But it was good to maneuver and had a good rate of climb. Papa used to fight the German air aces that harassed the French soldiers and people on the ground.

But my papa was shot down two years before my mama got tuberculosis.

Mama was a nurse but she died just before the end of the war. I think she would have liked to know that it finished. But maybe she found papa and they flew to heaven together. They did not forget me. They just thought I would be alive for a long time and also when they got to heaven maybe they could not come back to get me?

It was a shame that my papa could not put a long poem in the newspaper when mama died. Mama put a very long poem in about papa in the 'Deaths' part. Everyone said it was very beautiful. Part of the poem had about him fighting the war in his plane but I cannot remember the rest.

I am sad I forgot papa's plane last time. It makes me worried. But I remember it now so I try to be glad about that. Oscar says we must record as much as we can in our first recordings because soon we will forget everything.

If we will forget everything will we forget how to speech?

I am frightened in this place but I do not know why. It is cold and dark all the time but that is not why. The fear makes me forget more. I wish I could find my mama and papa. I am very lonely. Sometimes it feels like I cannot breathe and I panic but Oscar calms me down. He says I am silly because we do not breathe anymore anyway. He laughs at me but I can tell he is worried. There is something here that makes me feel like I am about to be eaten alive. It is nothing I can see. Can you see it? Will it make me forget how to speech?

A colossal crack of thunder shook the sky dislodging the frequency of the radiola. Jake was straight onto it trying to find the recording again.

Duette was feeling sick and she was finding it hard to breathe. The feeling had been growing as she listened to the boy's recording. It felt like she was being buried alive. Starting to panic, Duette stuck her head out the window. Why was the air supply shrinking?

Duel was alarmed. It felt to him like his sister was suffocating. He ran to her and pulled her back from the window.

"Duette," he yelled, "what is happening?"

Duette was shaking her head and holding her throat. "No air," she gasped.

Duel knew exactly what was happening. "Duette, you're an empath remember?!" He shook her unnecessarily. "You have to control this. Just try to separate yourself from the feeling."

Duette threw him an angry look. She had no idea how to do that. His gripping hands were making her even more claustrophobic.

Daffodil rushed over. "Duel let her go!"

"But . . ."

"Let her go!" Daffodil pulled Duel's arms off Duette and pushed the struggling Duette away from the window. Dragging a potion made from Rutilated quartz, kunzite, malachite and tourmaline from her pocket, she managed to pour the liquid into Duette's mouth. Daffodil had made it when she found out that Duette was an empath and right now she prayed the quantities were correct. It was horrible to watch: Duette's eyes were screaming for help.

Duette could feel herself going. There was not much time now. The world was disappearing from her vision.

"It's okay Duette," soothed Daffodil. "It's okay. Look at me. You're not going to die. You're going to be fine. You just need to accept that."

Duette couldn't take her focus of Daffodil's dark brown eyes. Letting the the rest of the world go black, Duette concentrated on Daffodil. Whatever Daffodil had given her was helping. A calmness began creeping through Duette's body. It felt almost like a separation of spirit and body. Duette wondered if her soul was leaving. Was she dying?

But then, somehow air came into her lungs. Slowly, Duette realized that this wasn't death. One breath turned into two and with that her vision returned. Now, her mind, body and spirit were shared but still somehow disconnected. What had Daffodil given her?

Thankfully, Duette had no comprehension of what had passed. In her effort to refill her lungs, Duette had gasped desperately, her eyes swelling, fraught with her demise. The noise was shocking: The last gasp before death. The group had stood transfixed and horrified.

It was only Daffodil's potion that had prevented an unenviable end. Duette may be feeling strange but at least she was alive—well sort of.

"Duette," said Daffodil as everyone stared expectantly at the girl on the floor. "There's no need to speak or move just yet okay?" Daffodil looked up at Duel. "Duel, I don't want Duette to speak yet. Could you please relay her thoughts to us?"

Duel nodded. He could see something was clearly wrong with his sister. Her eyes stared lifelessly at the ceiling and a glowing reflection hovered above her. He could not, would not accept that she had . . . no he threw the thought away.

"Thanks Duel," said Daffodil in her gentle way. "Now Duette, I need you to go back to what you sensed when you couldn't breathe okay? Don't worry, it won't happen again. I promise."

Duel was sensing his sister's refusal. "She doesn't want to. She says she is perfectly happy as she is."

Daffodil was worried this might happen. The potion was too strong. She berated herself silently. Daffodil knew how dangerous it would be if she couldn't get Duette to do what she asked. Duette was hovering between life and death.

"Duette," Daffodil continued a little more determinedly. "I'm afraid what I'm asking is not a choice for you. I am happy that you feel calm and safe where you are but if you want to stay alive you have to do as I ask."

Everyone's eyes widened. Was Daffodil implying that Duette was both dead *and* alive? Santu and Jake swapped anxious glances.

Duel felt the change in his sister. "Duette is worried now. She's just realized she can't feel her body."

"That's what was meant to happen," Daffodil lied, concerned that Duette might panic and ruin her chances of uniting her divisions. "To sense your body you have to do as I ask. You have to go back to that feeling that made it hard to breathe. It won't hurt."

Santu leant down and whispered into Daffodil's ear. Daffodil suddenly understood. She nodded thanks at Santu.

"Santu has just told me that as he heard Scraps speaking he saw a coffin being closed on a little boy. Is that what you felt?"

Duel nodded for his sister. "She says he was still alive. It wasn't a green potato that killed him. It was being buried in that wooden box."

Daffodil was horrified but she tried to keep calm. "Okay. So now we know that's how Scraps really died. He may have replaced the memory because it was too difficult. And Jake says that the others don't remember how they died so that makes sense."

Duel felt Duette's words in his mind again and nodded. "She is ready to go back now."

Daffodil took a deep breath and winked a thank you in Santu's direction. Santu nodded anxiously.

As Duette drifted to the moment of suffocation she felt an eeriness that was neither good nor bad. It was like time travelling forward to go backward: Her body felt insubstantial at first; her spirit stronger; her mind unearthly. But as Daffodil's words penetrated her strange world, Duette felt each separate entity merging. The horror she had felt at being unable to breathe was dissolved, with just the memory teetering like a rocking weight.

Daffodil sighed with relief. Duette had brought herself back. By returning to the moment that had stirred her empath skills, Duette had effectively won the battle. The glowing apparition above Duette at once dissolved back into her body.

"Acceptance that these things will not affect you is the key," said Daffodil. "I know it sounds easy for me to say, but I can make a weaker potion for you to practice with." Daffodil motioned for Duette to see if she could move.

"Weaker?" Duette repeated as she weakly pushed herself into a sitting position. "You make too strong potion again crazy girl?!"

Daffodil pulled a face of apology.

Santu laughed. "Well it saved your life so I think we are forgiving her."

Duette shook her head with a wan smile. She felt a bit like she'd been hit by a bus. Standing up, she checked her arms, legs and torso to make sure. "No bus," Duette hummed to herself. "Just stupid empath gift."

Everyone was watching her as if she were about to break into a million pieces. But just as she was about to tell everyone to stop staring at her as if she were an apparition something caught her eye.

"Oh," Duette said finally, "they here."

The others turned around. Oscar and another little boy faced them. The groups waved to each other. Jake took up his station at the radiola and, having etched the dials with an old nail, quickly found the frequency on which they could converse.

Jake beckoned to Oscar and his companion. "Welcome, I'm Jake."

Oscar leaned toward the radiola. "This is Scraps."

To Jake, it was a miracle. It was the very same boy that they had been listening to.

Daffodil smiled in recognition. Duette had felt the boy coming. Her empath skills were stronger than they had realized.

Santu whispered to Daffodil. "How are we going to tell him how he actually ghosted?"

Daffodil's meaningful look told Santu she had no idea.

"It's lovely to meet you Scraps," said Jake. "Do you know we've just listened to one of your early recordings?" Scraps looked at Oscar in delight. "You remembered a lot of information. Would you like me to tell you some things about you?"

Oscar pushed Scraps toward the radiola.

"Oh, yes please," said Scraps before suddenly thinking of something important. "This is my mouse." Scraps held up the glowing, wriggling animal. "His name is Tooting." Scraps was giggling about this but he wasn't sure why. "In recording, did I say what my name is? My *real* name?"

Jake shook his head. "No Scraps, I'm afraid you didn't. But I'm very glad you brought your mouse."

"Oh Tooting! He always come with me. I wish I know my real name."

"You told us about your mama and papa. Would you like me to tell you what you said?"

Scraps nodded vigorously.

As the conversation began between the ghosted Scraps and Jake, Blaze suddenly remembered something that she had read. It would fit with the time Scraps had said his father had died and it would also fit in with his comment about his mother writing a poem about his father after he was shot down.

Having already untied her sheet-anchor when Duette was struggling, all she needed to do was crawl over to the box of articles that held the narrative. The movement thrust a sharp pain up her leg. It felt like her bones were shattering. The pain killers had worn off now and the incessant throbbing was making her tired. Busying herself was the only way she could cope.

Scraps was very pleased with the information that Jake gave him. His enthusiasm was infectious. Everyone was excited for this little French boy who had been orphaned and left all alone.

"You know," said Scraps as he leaned into the radiola, "I died of a green potato. It is very silly, I know but it is true. A green potato can be very strong." Scraps was nodding sadly. "I am the only one who remembers how they ghosted you know. The only one." He would never forget how he ghosted. It was strange though, because Scraps was sure he had mentioned it in nearly all his recordings. Why hadn't the boy called Jake pointed it out?

Jake hesitated. He looked across at Daffodil. Daffodil looked at Santu. Santu looked back at Jake.

"Well, actually," said Jake "you . . ."

"Wait!" yelled Blaze. She was shaking her head vigorously. There was no need to tell the boy he was buried alive. He seemed so proud that he could remember how he ghosted when no one else could. "I have it! I knew there was an article that I had read that was similar." Blaze was waving the newspaper around in the air for the others to see. Santu came and took it from her.

"What does it say?" asked Duel. "Maybe you should read it at the radiola?"

Santu nodded and walked over to the machine to hand it to Jake.

"It's a human interest story," said Jake. The little boy looked confused. "It's a story about real people and the things that happen to them." This was taking all Jake's concentration. He had to remember to speak slowly. "It's dated December, 19th, 1918. Just after peace was declared."

Scraps nodded. "Is it about me?"

"Actually, it looks like it's about your parents and you. It includes the journalist's original story and a follow up of how everyone has done since he first wrote it."

Scraps looked delighted. Oscar patted him on the back.

"The journalist," started Jake again, "says he wanted to write a story about foreign couples that had moved to England before the war. He specifically wanted to talk to the widows of those men that had died in the war so he could ask them what it was like for them in England now, being far away from home and being without their husbands. The journalist searched for widows that had composed eulogies for their dead husbands."

Scraps was confused. "What is a ulery?"

"A eulogy?" asked Jake. "Well, it's a message that you write for people that you love when they die."

"Did someone write me a ulery?"

"I'm sure they did," lied Jake. "But we don't have that one at the moment."

This seemed to satisfy Scraps. He whispered something to his mouse.

Daffodil was amazed. Jake was in his element. How could the distraught boy they had introduced themselves to in the mess hall just a few nights ago, and this friendly, coherent boy be the same? Watching him made her feel amazed. And there was that pull. There was no denying it. She wanted what she knew she couldn't have—to be close to him.

Jake had a quick glance through the article and found the section that must have struck Blaze's interest.

"This part is talking about the wife of a pilot named Francois Marcel Thenault. The woman's name is Antoinette. She says her husband flew one of the first passenger planes in 1913."

"That is my papa!" cried Scraps. "He did fly in the open air while passengers did fly inside the cabin. I remember this!"

"It says, that after several weeks of intense air fighting in the Battle of Verdun, Captain Thenault was shot down on May 3rd, 1916. The battle is known to be the greatest and lengthiest battle of all and it was fought in a combat zone of only ten square kilometers. The battle, which lasted from 21st, February, 1916, until 19th, December, 1916, caused over 700,000 casualties—dead, wounded and missing." Jake couldn't believe what he was reading. So many people.

Jake read the rest to himself. The letter of a soldier had been included. The information was gruesome but he felt compelled to examine it.

'It is the most appalling mass murder of our history. One of the trenches is so filled with wounded and dead bodies, the attackers have had to use the parapets in order to be able to move forward. It is impossible to endure the horrible stench of Verdun. Everyone who searches for cover in a shell-hole stumbles across slippery, decomposing bodies.

At the front, chaos rules: Men are buried alive, there is no food and nothing to drink for days in a row; the thirst is so unbearable that some men are drinking from a pond covered with a greenish layer near Le Mort-Homme. A corpse is afloat in it; bloated with water. Screaming wounded who cannot be taken care of are everywhere. There is an unbearable smell of decay; many men are turning insane. Hell will not be this dreadful.'

"Jake?" Daffodil was worried, Jake had turned sheet white.

"Sorry-I-can't-concentrate," said Jake shaking himself from the ghastly reverie.

Santu patted Jake on the shoulder. "Good job. Take a rest, yes?"

"Sorry," said Jake again feeling ashamed. He handed the newspaper over to Santu.

"Without you Jake, this would not be possible. Do not be sorry." Santu's intense stare got through to Jake. Nodding, Jake moved next to Daffodil who greeted him with an encouraging smile.

"Um," said Santu as he scanned the paper. "Oh here. It is saying this woman, Antoinette, is being a nurse at The Grove Fever Hospital." Santu looked amazed. This really could be about Scraps. He gave Blaze a big smile.

Everyone in the room could feel the excitement. It was incredible.

"Do she work in the infections ward?" asked Scraps looking thrilled.

Santu scanned ahead. "Yes Scraps! It is saying she started working in the Infectious wards after her husband died."

Scraps looked sad. "Mama."

Santu was worried that this still could be a coincidence, so he searched further in the article. But everything he read, fitted. Then he found something that gave him goose bumps.

"Scraps, it is saying that she is living in a lovely big house on Upper Belgrave Street in Belgravia in the city of Westminster, London, with her son." Santu looked up at Scraps who was now pretending to try to read the article over Santu's shoulder. "It is saying that at the time of the article, her son is eight and his name is Henri Emile." Santu smiled at the little French boy. "That is your name Scraps. You are called Henri Emile Thenault."

Scraps was bobbing up and down in the air. His glow was pulsating and he was holding his fidgeting mouse up high in case it needed to see the article too.

The editorial had more information but it was about how hard life had been for Scraps' mother after her husband had died. She could no longer afford the house in Upper Belgrave Street and she had had to work double shifts to meet the costs of everything, especially the upkeep of the house and Henri's schooling and private lessons. Her heart felt like it had broken in two the day she heard the news of her husband's death and all she had wanted to do was be with Henri. But the demand of her work left her with little time and what time she did have found her exhausted. Slowly the pain had seeped into her bones and she feared she would not survive either. At the end of the article the journalist went on to say that the fever had taken hold of Antoinette only months after the original article was released and only months before peace was declared. Henri went missing and it was unknown what had happened to him.

Santu was concerned. They didn't have birth or death dates for Scraps' gravestone. All they had were the names and the knowledge of how they had all died. Was that enough?

Daffodil saw Santu's expression. She was thinking the same thing. Duette and Duel also exchanged glances.

Silently, they waited, hoping for another miracle but nothing happened.

Oscar started to look concerned. He spoke into the radiola.

"Why hasn't Scraps gone bright like Wonderboy?"

"Santu," it was Duette. "I think know why." She moved toward the radiola and took Santu's place. Santu knew what she was going to do and he was glad it didn't have to be him.

"Scraps," Duette began, wondering how she was going to tell him. "Scraps, I afraid it was not this green potato that make you ghost."

Scraps shook his head. "But it was! I told you I am the only one remembering this."

"Scraps, I know you ate this green potato but this not what *make* you ghost."

"But if I ate this green potato and lived why I am ghosted now?" Scraps was very confused. The only thing he was sure of was how he ghosted and now maybe that was wrong too. He shifted closer to Oscar.

Duette sensed his confusion. "I very sorry Scraps but I have way of knowing. I would not lie to you. Crossing my heart, see." Duette made a cross over her chest. There was no easy way to do this.

Duel suddenly noticed how similar Duette and Scraps sounded. Smiling to himself he realized that Duette must have been an empath a lot longer than any of them had realized. She had been accessing Scraps since she got here. How else could she have picked up the language so quickly? And then another thought occurred to him. Had Duette remained mute as child because she had merged her feelings with their deaf father's? Suddenly it all made sense. Poor Duette had been feeling the inadequacies of their father which must have compounded her guilt. No wonder she had never wanted to speak.

"Scraps," said Duette finally, "you have been very sick or almost dead. In your time it was much difficult to make sure someone dead. And sick bodies very dangerous because of carrying disease." She paused hoping some of this would sink in. "Scraps I think they think you already ghosted but you not ghosted yet. Still they bury you."

Scraps didn't understand what the girl was saying. He looked at Oscar. Oscar's face told him what he hadn't understood.

"I got buried without being deaded?"

Duette nodded. "We all very sorry Scraps. But maybe this how you meet Tooting?"

Both Scraps and Duette felt tears come to their eyes simultaneously. Then Scraps felt the chill. "I was so cold. And it was very dark." Scraps was remembering the only thing he wanted to forget. He held onto Oscar's hand. "I was very much scared. I remember this. I did not want to remember this again but now I must. I was very sick and I think I went to sleep. I tried to remember mama and papa because I was so lonely. And I wanted a birthday present."

Everyone was upset by this. But Santu was concentrating on the boy's last words.

"Scraps what are you meaning, you 'wanted a birthday present'?"

"The day when those people found me. The ones that thought I must be deaded. It was my birthday. I wanted to tell them but I could not make my eyes open. Then it got very dark and cold."

Santu looked in amazement at the crowd. Did everyone realize what this meant? The sea of wide eyes told him they did.

"Scraps," said Santu. "This is very *good* news."

Scraps didn't understand. "It is?"

"Yes, Scraps. It is wonderful. Are you remembering when you're birthday is?"

Scraps smiled because Santu was smiling. He wasn't really sure why. Scraps concentrated very hard. "Oh yes!" cried out Scraps. "It is the first month in rhyme about so many days. My teacher taught it me!"

"You mean the one that goes: 30 days has September . . . ?"

"Yes!" Scraps was at full volume now.

"That is the ace of black cards Scraps! Are you remembering which day it was on?"

Scraps had a vision. It was a memory so lovely that all his sadness disappeared. "It is the oneth."

"Are you remembering something Scraps?" asked Santu as he saw the pain melt away from Scraps' sad little face.

"Mama. She would always point like this." Scraps pointed his forefinger to the roof. "Number 1. I am her number 1 because I was born on the oneth."

Santu pulled his head high. This was important. He took a deep breath.

"Well, Henri Emile Thenault, son of Antoinette and Francois Thenault." Santu's voice was deep and commanding. "If you were being 10 when you ghosted and the article says you were 8 before your mother got ill, and the war ended in November 1918, that means you were being born on the 1st of September 1909 and you ghosted on the 1st of September 1919. You are doing so very well to remember everything."

Scraps looked at Oscar for support. Oscar was looking very proud. He held Scraps face in his hands and smiled at him. No one could hear what he said but they didn't need to. Scraps was going home: Another one to leave Oscar.

Suddenly a bright yellow glow encompassed Scraps ghosted figure. They all turned to where Madame Glizsnort had shown herself last time hoping she would come again. At once the warm glowing light returned to the church followed by several relieved sighs.

The seconds ticked by before the same familiar figure emerged from the brightness. Madame Glizsnort appeared tired but she also looked more powerful, perhaps brighter and less insubstantial.

"I am called again," said Madame Glizsnort. "You have done well. Whom am I greeting this time?"

"Madame Glizsnort," said Santu, "this is Henri Emile Thenault and his mouse Tooting. And we are very happy to announce that with Henri's excellent help, we are having another to go home."

Madame Glizsnort could not help but show her obvious pleasure.

"This is wonderful news! Henri and Tooting, there are two boys I would like you to see." She beckoned into the misty light behind her and two faces came forth. Their features were familiar but now they carried an angelic glow; a calmness that was almost overwhelming. The little lost ghosts had become angels.

"Bugsy! Wonderboy! It is me Scraps!"

The three boys laughed and clapped together. Bugsy and Wonderboy motioned for him to come to them—Bugsy still had bugs attached to his nose which made him look cross-eyed. But Scraps hesitated. Oscar hugged him and nodded for him to go forward. But Scraps wouldn't move. Oscar looked confused. He pushed Scraps again. But Scraps shook his head.

Madame Glizsnort laughed. "Henri, this is Adam Adams," she gestured to Bugsy, "and this is Benjamin Walsh," she patted Wonderboy on the head." Her tone toward the ghosted ones had always been faultless in its benevolence.

"Oh," cried Scraps, "you have real names!"

"Yes they do, Henri. And they have mothers and fathers here too. Both your mother and father are waiting for you Henri."

"Mama and papa?" Scraps squinted into the light hoping he could see them. He couldn't get used to being called Henri. For some reason he didn't remember that name at all. But if it made him find home he would get used to it.

"Yes, Henri, they are waiting for you."

"Why they not here now?"

"Because Scraps, they have chosen the light. It takes a while to fully absorb but once it is completed you cannot merge with the earthly zone again. But I promise they are very excited about seeing you."

"Yes?" replied Scraps in confusion. He had no idea what the lady was talking about.

"Come now. We do not have much time."

"Oh," Scraps looked at Oscar, apology filling his eyes.

"I want you to go Scraps! This is what I have been trying to do since I found all of you. It is safe and you will see your mama and papa! I will come soon. You will see."

Scraps felt the pull. Pure white light was flowing through his veins pulling him in, filling him with love and warmth and kindness. It was true—he would see his mama and his papa again. Now he could tell his papa that he remembered what kind of plane he flew in the war. But still he did not want to leave Oscar. He grabbed Oscar's hand and Oscar felt the love and warmth of the light surrounding Scraps. It was incredible. Perhaps he could hold Scraps' hand just a little bit longer.

The other two boys began to glow very brightly. Sensing the light was opening up, both Bugsy and Wonderboy became very excited. Bugsy began pulling on Madame Glizsnort's arm. It was an extraordinary sight: The irritable old woman that had terrified them with her steely glances now appeared unperturbed by a pesky child-ghost.

Was what Daffodil was seeing real? Had Madame Glizsnort's heartache for these little children caused her such angst that her mind had become unsound? And if Scraps' parents had gone to the light and could not revisit the 'earthly realm', then why was Madame Glizsnort able to move between the two domains? Something was amiss but, Daffodil couldn't sense exactly what was wrong.

"Quickly child," Madame Glizsnort began, "come."

"Madame Glizsnort," Daffodil interrupted, "you must tell us about the Shadow. We need to know how to kill it."

"The Shadow," replied Madame Glizsnort, "is not a being. It is not something that can be killed. It is something you must *destroy*. You are thinking about its fundamental nature incorrectly. You are fighting it without a sense of its command. If you do not change your attitude, it will be like fighting blind and deaf." Madame Glizsnort looked around the room. Duette and Duel were in her sights. "It is an amalgamation of everything that is cruel and unforgiving. Never underestimate its compulsion."

"I'm sorry," said Daffodil. "But I don't understand."

"I am afraid, my child, that you will. And it is only when you do understand that you will be able to fight it."

"But what has happened to Bruises?"

"The Shadow will keep her in limbo, feeding on her as long as it can until it is ready to bury her ghost and takes its essence. Bruises' memories will be lost and she will feel confused and strange, living transiently. Until it buries their souls they live in torment. There is only one way to alleviate their state." Madame Glizsnort looked directly at Blaze and then to her bandaged feet. She shook her head. "Blaze chose to go to the graveyard but you all ignored her. Now it is too late." Madame Glizsnort's words were illusive but finite.

Santu couldn't help the suspicion that rose inside him. He tried to hold it at bay but it was crashing at him like a furious ocean. He was angry that he had never managed to pick up visions from Madame Glizsnort. What was the hold she had over his ability? He didn't know how to trust without his visions. Was that why she had caused him to break his nose? Had the damage he sustained been a deliberate ploy to prevent him from seeing her story?

"What about this place?" asked Santu. "How will we be getting out?"

"*This*," said Madame Glizsnort, "is not so much a place as it is a situation; a puzzle if you will. There is no escape until it is solved."

"But . . ." Santu was about to command an answer at the same moment that Scraps moved into the light.

A burst of white light exploded with such force that newspapers scattered everywhere and everyone was blown backward.

Shock silenced them but the beautiful and powerful sounds of chanting angels rose up, encircling them, numbing their confusion. The echoing hymn was like a growing life resounding around them as if they were inside a church bell.

When Santu thought about this later he wondered if he had been silenced on purpose.

"It is getting stronger," smiled Madame Glizsnort. "This is very good. You will notice the difference." She turned to Scraps. "Henri, say goodbye to your friends. We have no more time here."

Scraps waved enthusiastically at the room: The same room he had spent such a long time in; the same room he believed he would never leave.

Everyone was on the ground except Oscar. Oscar floated next to the radiola. He hadn't moved an inch. Scraps couldn't wait to see what it would be like to watch Oscar come toward them in the light. He looked forward to it already.

"Come soon Oscar! Please!" cried Scraps. And the three little boys waved happily at their friend Oscar.

Oscar now waved frantically back at them as if he would never see them again.

As a huge crash of thunder vibrated around them, the white light disappeared leaving them all to the sounds of emptying rain.

Blackwater Herald Moon Tribune
Tuesday, July 22ⁿᵈ, 1969—
Six Pence

MAN LANDS ON THE MOON

*N*eil *Armstrong walked on the moon yesterday in a historic moment for the world. After descending in the Apollo 11's lunar module and stepping onto the surface of the Moon, he spoke the words that will stay in our minds forever: 'One small step for a man, one giant leap for mankind.' Six-hundred million people watched across the globe. As both Buzz Aldrin and Neil Armstrong went on to take moon samples, Armstrong reported that movement was easy except for the tendency to slip on the fine Moon dust. PAGE 3.*

LOCAL NEWS HEADLINES
BEREAVEMENT NOTICE

Chief Superintendent, Macalister Glizsnort, mourns the passing of his wife Madame Grace Glizsnort, 57 years of age. Madame Glizsnort was born in 1911 to Mr. Darragh Walsh and Mrs. Ciaran Walsh in the city of Dublin. She is survived by her husband, Macalister, her twins, Jemima and Eustace and her second son Benjamin.

As a child she was exposed to the First Great War and suffered terrible family tragedy. After losing all her relations—including her older brother, Benjamin and younger sister, Sarah—she was adopted by Miss Germaine Durand (originally a French citizen before moving to Ireland in 1912) who took her in and moved her to England to start a new life away from the tragedy

323

Grace had endured. Interestingly, taking on her adoptive mother's French heritage honored Grace with the title of Madame later on in life.

Madame Glizsnort is well known by the locals for being an exemplary teacher here in Blackwater. She was also a popular member of the Saint Trinians Choir Group and much loved by the children of her school classes.

Her teaching history started in World War Two, when she began instructing at her home in Marchenby Street. When the town began to disband, Madame Glizsnort then took up her teaching rounds at the newly rebuilt Saint Catherine's Church of Redeemus. Unfortunately the church was bombed in 1944 by a German V2 bomb aimed for London.

In 1946, whilst waiting for the church and school to be rebuilt, Grace ventured off to London, with twins in tow, to further her education and during this time gave birth to another son. On returning to Blackwater, Madame Glizsnort began to teach at the newly constructed building that was meant to be both church and school but, due to the townsfolk's continuing suspicions, no one would enter the structure. Unfortunately, the building became derelict, but again, as was the case with the determined teacher, Madame Glizsnort became the prime contributor towards ensuring that another church was built on Strawberry Lane to replace the ill-fated Saint Catherine's Church on the Cross Roads site.

She then established the 'Large Orchard School House'—an addition to the Glizsnort residence—where she taught from 1947 until last year when she became too sick to lecture. Her unfortunate illness, caused by her obsession with helping the Lost Children had worsened considerably in recent years, making her lose touch with the world.

However, Grace will always be remembered for her strong belief in doing good for the community. Never once did she enter into the negativity that took over the town regarding the sightings of the Lost Children—whom she remained an advocate for until her death. Unfortunately, Mrs. Glizsnort never solved the mystery of the missing children even though she dedicated her life to trying to discover their identities.

Her husband says: "All she ever wanted was to put names on those unmarked gravestones. You know, I wouldn't be surprised if she keeps looking for them up there in heaven."

It is a sad reminder that not all God's beloved children are taken care of. From all the community of Blackwater: Godspeed Madame Grace Glizsnort, and thank you for all your contributions to this town.

***Brought to you by: Clearasil**—come out and battle like a girl!*

~Present day~

~Fury and Lore~

The sweet sounds of angels singing filled their ears, lulling them like a baby's nursery rhyme. No one had moved since the white light had taken Scraps: Henri Emile Thenault. It was a strange moment where peace, sadness, joy and hope all mingle together to remind you that you are human.

For Oscar it was different. He felt even more lost. Was he being selfish? Why didn't it all feel perfect? Had he waited so long that now he could not feel any delight at all?

"It is time for me to fetch another." Oscar was speaking into the radiola but it all felt wrong. When the white light was present no one needed the machine to hear each other. Why was that?

Santu turned, the first to break away from the spell of the angles' voices, and rose to move over to the radiola.

"Oscar, should you be making the journey now? Is it time?" Santu asked.

Oscar nodded not knowing whether he needed to go, to not stay, or because he needed to go, to go. In all these eons of time he had never been this confused. He could see the white light was giving his ghosted ones peace, happiness, home. He had felt it when Scraps had held his hand but for some reason it was becoming increasingly worrying. Why? Why couldn't he just be happy for everyone? Why did he always feel this unending doom?

325

"It is as good a time as any. I can wait on the ether."

"Alright Oscar." Santu paused. "Oscar, are you being alright?"

"I am not anything," said Oscar. "I am a ghost."

And with that he was gone.

Santu not only felt the chill, he saw it. It was different to the cold, biting winds of the snow and rain of this godforsaken place. It was the coolness of uncertainty; it was the icy refrain of looming pain. Santu's heart went out to Oscar. He suddenly knew Oscar had no intentions of finding home: Oscar had never had one. Santu understood how he felt— there was no reason to find one. Oscar had taken residence in ill fate. He believed the Shadow was his cruel destiny and each goodbye was exactly that: A goodbye forever.

Santu felt the visions even after Oscar was gone. Each word, however unrelated to circumstance, brought the images to Santu like a smack. They were harrowing and cruel: Death, tragedy, more death, interminable pain, and yet more death. The final vision of Oscar, just a young boy, marching at the frontlines with the soldiers was shocking. Even knowing that they needed their ghosts to remember the way they died, Santu hoped, against his will, that Oscar would never remember any of it.

Santu looked at the rest of the group. They looked hypnotized. He clapped his hands loudly and watched them all shake from their trances.

"Oscar has gone to get another ghosted one," said Santu trying not to reveal his anger. There was no reason for him to be like this. What they had witnessed was incredible. But somehow underneath his cool skin lay some kind of truth that was seething; desperate to get out. Santu had no idea what it was but he couldn't ignore it. Not anymore.

Jake didn't take a moment. He ran straight back to the radiola to search for messages. Santu laughed. In his head Santu nicknamed Jake, the Redeemer. In the scale of trust verses distrust, Jake was a high 10: Trust in bright green.

"Jake," said Santu, "aren't you wanting to get some rest? We cannot know when we'll get another chance."

Jake shook his head. "I've got to do this."

Santu nodded. He understood. "Go for it Jake. You are doing a swell job."

Jake stopped for a moment. That didn't sound like Santu at all. It sounded more like the way one of the ghosted ones would talk. Maybe it was rubbing off on Santu? He seemed to have stopped his strange turns of phrase too. That was good. Jake didn't understand half the things Santu said.

"What is everyone else thinking? Are we resting or not?" Santu was walking around the room, his arms crossed over his chest like a chieftain.

Blaze had shuffled back to her spot next to a huge box of newspapers. Her ankles were throbbing, invisible drummers keeping beat inside her legs. There was no way she could sleep and there was no way she was going to ask for more pain killers; not after everything she had put everyone through.

"I've found lots of good stuff in here," Blaze said as she riffled through the maze of history.

"Yeah," added Daffodil me too."

Annabelle was looking out at the torrential rain. Every now and then the sky lit up with sheet lightning before the ground shook with violent thunder. The rain had managed to pour through the broken windows covering a good deal of flooring with slick icy sludge. Every time a flash of lightning lit up the sky, Annabelle turned her face from it as if it hurt her.

Santu tried to ignore the tall blonde. Annabelle was not even fighting it anymore. He had hoped that by revealing her secret and performing the memory-graphing, she may have started to battle it. But that was Annabelle's last good deed. She knew it and he knew it. Now she would wait. There was nothing Santu could do. He rarely gave up and his will fought him hard but it was useless. Annabelle had nowhere to go either. She had no home and her resistance was waning.

"Um, excusing me." It was Duette. "I knowing we keeping guard but, if one watching, the other can read." She was holding up a piece of newspaper that had been specially cut out. "And I think this one important."

"Go ahead," said Santu.

Duette's voice was quiet and sad. She spoke slowly so as to make sure she read it all correctly.

"*London kids march off to Battle—That's war fever in England. The enthusiasm to join the battle has reached the children! Young boys and even girls cannot be stopped to enlist.*" Duette reversed the paper she was reading so that, as the orange flames of the fire charged, the others could catch a glimpse of the picture of little boys and girls marching valiantly off to war. She took a deep breath. It was important to read the words perfectly.

"Recruiting Officers turn blind eye as eager children show up to join their army. Many of them are aged between eight and fourteen. Some of them are orphans, many simply do not know where their parents are. They will be needed in the trenches of Belgium, France, Russia and Turkey. Lest they fight the great fight and not succumb to the cruelty of the war."

Duette's eyes were wide and cheerless. She looked at Duel passing him the exasperation she felt. Duel returned her worried look but nodded. She understood. Feeling ashamed of a history that you had nothing to do with was valueless. The fight they needed to battle was in the present.

Santu looked alarmed. The images he had seen when Oscar spoke were coming back to him like thrashing fish in the hands of their captor. "Give me that cutting!" Santu practically ripped it from Duette's hands. He stared at the photo in shock.

Duette heard what Santu was thinking.

"Is Oscar?" she asked, trying to understand.

"Look at him," cried Santu a little too loudly. "Look at this one." He thrust the article back at Duette pointing to a boy in the background.

Duette peered at the blurry picture. The boy looked about twelve or thirteen years old. Pushing the thoughts of horror away she tried to focus on the image. Wide-eyed she looked up at Santu.

Santu collapsed. The visions were getting stronger and stronger. Everyone watched in disbelief. Daffodil ran to his side. Santu, the one in control, the one who had not been affected by any of this, had finally succumbed.

"Santu," said Daffodil, "what is it?"

Santu shook his head. He had never had such powerful visions. They were blasting at him from every angle like detonating bombs.

"It is Oscar, he is being very angry. He is lashing out." Santu was rocking back and forth. "He is not with the others."

"Could he still be here?" asked Daffodil looking desperately around the room.

Santu shook his head. "Worse," he said. "Outside."

Horrified glances were exchanged before Daffodil ran over to the window. Annabelle was already there beside Duette. Duel had been on guard but he had seen nothing.

"Everyone," screamed Daffodil over the thumping rain, "tie yourselves down!"

When no one moved Daffodil screamed the command even louder.

Jake was still desperately trying to get a reading.

"Jake, give me a hand!" yelled Daffodil.

As everyone prepared themselves for the worst, Daffodil and Jake dragged the struggling Santu toward a back railing and secured him with a bed sheet. Daffodil threw another at Jake and then tied herself to an old gas pipe.

"Santu?" Daffodil tried. "Santu will you be able to stand it?"

Santu was under attack, the images were coming faster now as if building toward a crashing end. "Oscar is being reminded of his life. Losing his ghosts one by one is bringing all this pain back again. It is being the cause of all his distrust coming back to him." Santu couldn't understand how this was happening. Visions had only ever come to him via words. "Duette are you feeling this?"

"No," said Duette. "Nothing."

Daffodil didn't know what to do. She knew what was coming and had no idea how to stop it. The crashing thunder and fork-lightning were coming faster now giving rise to her panic.

"Santu," shouted Daffodill, "is there anything in the visions that could help?"

Santu was looking pale. He was holding his head in his hands as if it would explode. All he could manage to do at this stage was shake his head. When would this end?

And then the grave sound of Duel's voice told them what they already knew was imminent.

"The Shadow," yelled Duel over the rain. "It's coming." Duel had tied himself to a railing near the window. It was too dangerous but he wanted to be close when it arrived. He had an idea. It was doubtful at best but at least it was something.

Daffodil was lost. "We are never going to be able to save Oscar now." She looked around the room. It was that moment of stillness right before disaster hits. Everything was in slow motion. Adrenaline was pouring into her bloodstream by the bucket load. The Shadow was coming and she had no more aces up her sleeve. Were they just going to wait and die?

"Get ready!" screamed Duel over the sound of thunderous air expanding along the path of a bolt of lightning. "Here it comes!"

Everyone gritted their teeth not sure what to expect.

Duel couldn't take his eyes off the menacing vortex. Winds began to swirl maddeningly around the church. Even the heavy rain began to twist sideways as it was pulled into the ferocious whirlpool of the black mass.

Daffodil could feel the winds lifting her body from the ground. She held on tight to the sheet praying that the protective crystals would keep the violent windstorm at bay. But the current was getting closer and closer and soon it was pulling everyone toward it.

"What's happening Duel?!" cried Blaze as she clung to the railing. She didn't want to have to test the strength of her sheet if she could help it. She had been so glad to have been allowed to come back to the church with everyone that she hadn't mentioned her sheet had a rip in it.

"It looks extra furious," yelled Duel as another forceful crash struck the air. The thunder was now so close it felt like the earth was quaking every time it roared down on them. And again the dark sky was turned to daylight as lightning lit up the world.

Blaze felt her sheet tear. It wasn't going to hold. It didn't seem fair now. After a lifetime of guilt and self-hatred she had just discovered the truth about herself, and now she was going to be torn apart by more loathing. That was it! Blaze suddenly realized what and why the Shadow was what it was. She was just about to try to scream it out to everyone when her sheet ripped further. Her broken feet were in the air now, horizontal with her head. The tempest was getting more powerful. She scrambled up the sheet and wrapped her arms around the railing. Why didn't she just let go now? She wouldn't be able to hold on like this for long.

They were all struggling, trying to fight an unwinnable war. It had gotten stronger in its absence. How had it gathered such power? Had it been feeding off misery while it waited to launch at them?

Annabelle was the only one who wasn't battling. The rapid winds were tossing her around like a tissue in a dryer but she had no fight left. She had given up.

It made Daffodil angry. You have to fight right until the very end. They were the rules. She could see that Santu was still struggling with his visions but he was also trying to combat the winds. Annabelle didn't have the right to give up. Not when other people were desperate to live.

Duel had tied his feet to the railing by the window so that if he did lose the struggle, he would go face first—maybe zap it with positive thoughts. But it also helped him see what was going on. Half his body was being battered and rained on as he flapped around at the window, but Duel kept trying to concentrate on the Shadow, forcing his mind into the furious funnel. That's when he saw something strange. He couldn't make it out. There was something hovering in front of the violent windstorm and whatever it was, it was stopping the Shadow from coming any closer to the church. Then lightning struck and the shimmering object lit up like a star.

"Oh god," screamed Duel, as teeming rain slapped his skin and flying newspapers attached themselves to his wet body. "It's Oscar!"

"What!?" shrieked Daffodil trying to stop herself from being smacked against the floor. "Where!?"

"He's outside. He looks crazy mad but he's resisting the pull of the currents. I think he's . . . ." Duel didn't know what Oscar was doing. It was difficult to keep watch on something when your body was being ripped up and down by ferocious winds. Then Duel saw lightning go straight into Oscar. He winced thinking that the light-rod would rip him apart but the opposite happened: Oscar absorbed the electrical discharge. Another crash and more lightning and Oscar did the same, getting brighter each time. How long could he do this for?

"I think that's why the vortex is so powerful this time. It's feeding off Oscar's fury." Duel couldn't figure out how the Shadow was able to take the anger from Oscar without consuming him. "Oh god! I think Oscar's trying to catch the lightning." Duel knew that sounded ridiculous. "I don't know what he's doing."

At that moment Blaze's arms slipped. She tried to grab onto the sheet as she was pulled away but the sudden force of her full weight made it tear through. Blaze and her hopes, her broken feet and her fire-healing powers were all going to be ripped apart, bit by bit. As she tried to grab onto anything in her path, the others watched in horror as she was dragged toward the window.

Duel didn't see it happen; he was watching the miracle that was occurring outside. Oscar had caught the last blast of fork-lightning and was glowing like the moon. He pulled his hands across his body and then pushed them out as if he were thrusting a ball away from him. That's when Duel realized what he had been doing. Oscar had been gathering the light-strikes and storing them to then force them back into the Shadow. The positive charge of the lightning would . . . "Oh my god!" screamed Duel. "Oscar is using the lightning to fight the Shadow."

Blaze was clawing at the window-frame trying to save herself. Blood was pouring from her palms as the broken shards of glass sliced through her skin like butter.

But Oscar was at work and the second his lightning charge hit the tumbling whirlpool it roared with pain. Its winds exploded outward, the sound of a thousand crashes of thunder. In the split second that everyone rushed their hands to their ears to dull the sound, they were all thrown back in the opposite direction. They hit walls and banisters and Jake was thrown head first into his precious radiola cracking part of its glass surface and knocking him unconscious.

Blaze skidded across the wooden flooring bashing her bandaged ankles and collecting splinters as she was flung back toward the railing and the rest of her torn sheet.

The blast of wind had brought with it a stench that made them gag. It smelled like rotting carcasses, perspiration and sewerage. Before any of them could realize what had happened, the Shadow had spun away and was headed back to the graveyard.

Duel was soaking wet and leaning out the window screaming for Oscar to come inside. But Oscar didn't move.

"Oscar you could have killed us all! You must come inside now!"

Thunder was crashing all around them. It felt to Annabelle like they were in the middle of an orchestra's grand crescendo, Bach's cello suite No.1. Surprisingly, she felt a desperate need to play the piano. It was as if she knew she would never produce those perfectly formed sounds again.

Oscar had turned very pale now that all the lightning had left him. He couldn't hear what the boy at the window was saying but Oscar could tell he was annoyed. Seeing the havoc inside the church he realized what they must have all thought. It was time for the truth.

Oscar disappeared and reappeared inside the church hovering at the radiola.

Daffodil ran over to check on Jake. She was terrified of what she might find. Thankfully he was just concussed. Seeing Blaze's bloody hands she went over and sat down beside her, exhausted. Grateful that her own burnt hands had healed quickly, Daffodil attended to Blaze's wounds. The cuts were deep but there wasn't much Daffodil could do except use a tincture of rhondite from the satchel she had fastened to her skirt. Using bits of torn sheet, she bandaged her friend's hands and returned to Jake's side at the radiola.

Oscar spoke into the radiola but the settings had been disturbed by the fierce currents and no one could hear him.

Thankfully, Jake had started to come around and Daffodil apologized to him first before asking him to fix the dials. As he stood, dizziness overwhelmed him but he steadied himself on the ledge of the radiola before twisting the dials to their pre-marked spots.

"How are you Santu? Have the visions stopped?" asked Blaze.

Santu nodded. "They are stopping when the Shadow blew out." Santu walked over to the radiola. There were a couple of things he needed to deal with. He leaned into its light. "Oscar is remembering everything now, yes?"

Daffodil and Jake exchanged confused glances.

"What do you mean he remembers?" asked Daffodil. "How is that possible?"

"That is why I am having those visions isn't it Oscar? Tell them Oscar. They are needing to know."

Oscar leaned forward. "I'm not going into the light—I have no home, I never did. I have always been doomed. No wonder I forgot everything. And I dragged everyone else's memories away too. I didn't even realize what I was doing. I thought I was protecting them but I was doing just the opposite. Maybe if I hadn't taken them in they would have gone into the light by themselves. I wanted them to forget their sadness, their awful pain but I imprisoned them here. I'm a monster."

"Oscar, that is not true," said Santu. "You are saving them from the Shadow. And that thing, whatever it is, has nothing to do with what you have done. The reason that you are all ghosting instead of going into the light is *because* of all that pain. Forgetting did not make them stay, Oscar. Forgetting is just making the time dissolve. You all would have been forgetting anyway. Do you know how long you've all been waiting here Oscar?"

Oscar seemed surprised by the question. He thought hard before shaking his head.

"You are all being ghosted for one hundred years Oscar."

The shock was too much for Oscar. He shook his head. "That can't be right."

"It is Oscar, I am promising," said Santu. "You know I have no reason to lie."

"But . . ."

"Oscar, you have every right to be feeling the anger that you do. But anger is the result of pain. As soon as you recognize this you will be able to go into the light too. I am not believing that you don't have a home. Everyone, no matter what has happened to us, has a home in the light. And all your ghosted ones—the ones that you *protected*—will be waiting for you there. They are all waiting for you now." Santu didn't have time for his own reservations: Suspicion was just an unfounded feeling.

"But my sisters? I didn't even know they were my sisters." Oscar's glowing form had his arms crossed over his head as if this would make the truth go away.

"What does he mean, 'his sisters'?" asked Jake trying not to fall down from nausea.

Daffodil, now sitting on the floor beside the radiola, tugged on Jake's pant leg. She motioned for him to sit down too. Santu was doing a great job, he didn't need any help. Jake gratefully slid back down to the ground. It felt like someone had given him a sleeping drug. Trying to keep his eyes open was nearly impossible. And every time he closed them for just a few seconds Daffodil was nudging him awake. Why was she doing that?

"Tell them Oscar. Tell everyone about your sisters," said Santu. The visions had replayed the whole awful truth to Santu. But it must be Oscar that told the story. Words of truth were like stitches sewing up the past.

DAILY STANDARD

- Daily - London, October 15, 1917 One Penny

WORLD UPDATES

April 6 - U.S. declares war on Nazi Germany. *April 23* - Main attack on Gaverelle, France. *June 5* - 10 million US men register for draught. *June 13* - German air raid carried out on London with Gotha G Bombers. 162 civ-ilian deaths, plus 46 children killed and 432 injuries. Update Page 9. *June 14* - German air attack on England -100 killed. *July 22* - Britain bombs German lines at Ypres with 4,250,000 grenades. *July 31* - Third Battle of Ypres begins in West Flanders, Belgium-Passchendaele. *August 14* -China declares war on Germany and Austria. *August 17* - Italy declares war on Germany and Turkey. *September 6* - Georges Guynemer, French pilot, shoots down 54th German aircraft. Further stories Page 6.

EXECUTION OF MATA HARI

Dutch Dancer Mata Hari will be executed by firing squad today. The penalty for spying for Germany will be carried out at Vincenr Paris. MORE PAGE 6.

FATIMA, PORTUGAL

Three young girls have claimed to have seen the Virgin Mary as a vision from God. P9.

Battle of Passchendaele

Third Battle of Ypres

Germans use poison gas at Ridge of Passchendaele in the 'Battle of Mud'. General Douglas Haig's attack began on July 31st with a plan to sweep through Flanders to the coast of Belgium to destroy German submarine pens. But the soldiers have faced a myriad of issues: 1 - The Germans did not have low morale as was believed.

2 -A heavy artillery barrage laun at German lines on July 18th dest any chance of surprise. 3 - In Aug the area was swamped with the -est rains seen for 30 years, causi the area to become so muddy as impassable. And 4 - Now the Ge' are using poisonous gas at Passc' -daele Ridge. So far the battle su too costly: For the sake of a few n kilometres, so far, the British have lost nearly 300,000 men and losse the Germans are over 250,000 ¿ count. Haig has to answer to his

Express Post

Edition - Chigaco, April 21, 1918 One

Red Baron Shot Down

Manfred Von Richthofen known as 'The Red Baron', has been shot down and killed over Vaux sur Somme in France today. It was just yesterday that we were reporting his 79th and 80th kills but today the German Fighter Ace pilot will no longer be a menace to our men. Full Story on Von Richthofen continued Page

Full Story on Von Richthofen continued Page

Battle of Somme - Too Many Dead

Earlier this month we reported that the Battle of Somme was finally over - Now the figures of the dead and wounded give us reason to agree that the battle was a disaster. PAGE 3

BRITAIN'S NEW FUTURE

In February, Britian's suffraget movement has been surprised by the new bill allowing women of property, over the age of 30 to vote

"CYCLOPS" STILL MISSING

The US naval boat 'Cyclops' still has not bee found after it went missing in the Bermuda Triangle in February. Its mysterious disappe-rance goes on. The Full Story Page 6.

ELECTRICAL FIRE KILLS 38

Oklahoma State Hospital now faces charges over the deaths of thirty-eight mental patient who died in the disaster. More Page 11.

CHILDREN IN DANGER

With all the devastation across the world: Disease epidemics; poverty; loss of parents and starvation - to name but a few - have become the main causes for children to feel they have no choice but to end their lives their own hand. It is a tragic situation. P8.

BIZARRE WAR MIRACLE

As Canadian pilot, Captain Makepiece into a steep nose dive to avoid German -fire his passenger, Captain Sedly, fell of the plane.

When the pilot leveled off several hundred feet below, his free falling passenger landed on the tail of the plane, drawn in by the plane's downdraft. He scrambled from the tail into his seat, unharmed.

~Present day~

~Oscar Likes Cars~

The thunderclaps rolled on outside as if they were warriors battling for ownership of the sky. Rain poured furiously: a crying child trying to stop the fighting. Oscar glanced outside. He didn't like the downpour. It reminded him.

"We all left the United States of America to go abroad when I was ten. It was 1913. My father was a very important man at the Ford Motor company and Mr. Henry Ford was using the first assembly line to make cars. He was making the Model T's out of this special vanadium alloy, a very special kind of steel, really strong—used for race cars. My father was sent overseas to bring the assembly-line to other countries." Oscar shook his head. That stuff wasn't important. "We had only been in our new home for a few years when our house was hit by a mortar attack. I was thirteen. It was 1916." Oscar took a deep breath.

"Everyone died except me. I was exploring. I liked to do that. My mother told me not to. She worried. All she wanted to do was move back home. She would beg my father constantly to let us go back home to America. When the war broke out my father believed he had to put his skills toward the war effort and went into the construction of ammunitions. But there was an air raid. Our house. They all died." The grief was making it hard for Oscar to speak but he couldn't stop, not now.

"I was only 3 years old when my twin sisters were born. Sometimes they annoyed me but mostly they were fun to have around. When I saw them all like that—after the bomb I mean—I didn't know what to do. It was a mess. Outside was chaos. People running everywhere." Oscar shook his head. "And then I saw a group of children all dressed in dirty rags carrying flags and they were marching. It was very strange to see all these organized young children amid the disorder. I ran to them asking where they were going but when I got up close I saw that they were covered in dust and debris from the explosions and some of them were crying. They said they were marching to the war. Most of them had lost their families and had nowhere else to go. One little girl said she was looking for her daddy because everyone else in her family had died." Oscar shrugged. "So I joined them."

Santu could see it all again but now he could listen without the terrible agony he had experienced before. Trying to concentrate on Oscar's words Santu nodded for him to go on.

"Well, it was an awful journey and a couple of the children didn't make it because they got very sick. Only a few of us got all the way to the frontlines. The soldiers were very nice to us. One soldier, Private Tom, took care of me. It was 1916 and he took me with the rest of his battalion to the frontlines in France. I don't know what happened to the other children.

"Then there was the Battle of the Somme in the North-East of France. It must have been around July because the weather was warm but the battle went on for months. There were mainly British and French troops—not as many French because so many got killed in the Battle of Verdun." Silent tears were streaming down Oscar's face. It was like it all happened yesterday. "So many soldiers died there." Now Oscar knew why he wanted to forget it all.

"On the very first day of battle 58,000 troops died. It was supposed to be a fierce attack with bombardments of mines and explosions to destroy the German frontlines but the attack wasn't a surprise to the Germans at all. Many stayed safe in their bunkers and used their machine-gunners to do some terrible damage."

Santu was trying not to break. The visions were harrowing in the extreme. How could anyone go through all that and not go crazy? Everyone was still and silent, listening to Oscar's story. Eyes were filling with tears and hearts were going out to him.

"I think," Oscar went on, "that the French lost 200,000 men and the British lost at least 400,000. There were just dead people everywhere. So was Private Tom. I remember looking at a blanket of bloodied people, all of them so still, it was awful. Then I must have passed out. I guess someone took me to a soldier's hospital. I must have been there a long time. I have a very big scar . . ." Oscar pulled up his shirt. The glowing zigzag was obvious to everyone.

Santu could tell Oscar was having trouble now but he had to remember. "Keep going Oscar. You are doing really well."

"Well, then I had to leave the hospital and I had nowhere to go. So I went with some other soldiers back to the frontlines. They took me to Passchendaele. That's when they made me an honorary soldier." A fleeting look of pride crossed his face. "Our main aim was to sweep through Flanders and breakthrough to the coast of Belgium so that German submarine pens could be destroyed. On July 18th, 1917," Oscar smiled sadly to himself—suddenly he could remember all these dates—"a heavy artillery barrage was launched at the German lines. This lasted for ten days. Again, just like Somme, the Germans were not surprised by us. Then after just a few days, very heavy rain poured down on us. Flanders became like a swamp, everyone got stuck. The artillery bombardment had destroyed the drainage systems and it was like a world of mud. The shell-craters filled with water so the advancing men could not hide in them and the fields became impossible to move through."

Outside, a crash of thunder broke through the dark as if it were ripping the sky in two. Oscar clapped his hands over his ears. All that time being so brave on the frontlines and now the truth: A frightened little boy who had lost everything and had only the fear of memory to consume him. With his hands clasped firmly over his ears he went on.

"It was so cold. So cold. We were moved on to Passchendaele Ridge. That's where the Germans used their mustard gas. They added it to high explosive shells you know. One of the soldiers wrapped his jacket around me covering my face and my upper body but this left him in danger. It's very bad. The skin blisters, the eyes become very sore, sometimes blind, and then you vomit. It burns your insides as well. It is very painful. It can take a person four or five weeks to die of mustard gas poisoning. Many men died slowly, horribly. Some of us kept going but it wasn't long after that they we faced a massive attack.

"By then it was late October, 1917. The Germans attacked with heavy artillery and the whole squadron was killed. I guess I was too. I remember a huge explosion. It was very sudden. It didn't hurt. I was 14 years old by then. I remember being annoyed that I would miss out on the chocolate we had saved for supper. I realized I would never eat it again, but I was glad to be away from there.

"But still, I couldn't shake the feeling of being lost. When I ghosted I was all alone. I couldn't see *any* of the other ghosted soldiers. I didn't like being alone. And that's when I realized all I wanted to do was go home: go back to my family; back where it was safe. But then I remembered it wasn't safe there either." Oscar looked distraught. "Home is where we all want to be.

"I think that is why, when I ghosted I spent all my time looking for other ghosted ones to help." Oscar was shaking his head looking desperate. "But I didn't even recognize my own sisters."

"Oscar, of course you were recognizing them. They were the ones you were looking for." Santu rubbed his mouth. Every word was important here. If he lost Oscar's hope he could be in real trouble. "I saw all your visions Oscar. You were looking for them after you ghosted. You were having a chance to go into the light but you would not because you had to find your sisters." Santu nodded hoping to encourage him. "Are you remembering now?"

Oscar did but it wasn't enough. "But after I found them I forgot. And then everyone forgot."

"You are needing to tell everyone who your sisters are Oscar."

Oscar hesitated. That was why he went to fight the Shadow. Once he remembered who they were he was even more devastated: Vengeance had seemed like his only option. He shook his head.

"Oscar," said Santu gently. "I am not going to be telling but I want you to. You do still want to save them don't you?"

Oscar nodded. "Buttons . . ." he stopped. It was impossible to tell them without breaking down.

"And . . ." encouraged Santu.

Oscar sighed. The coldness had finally found him. It was overwhelming and awful. "Bruises."

A swirl of shock ran with the cold, moist air through the upper storey of the church. Duel and Duette had felt something building; still, they were not prepared for this revelation. Daffodil had stopped herself gasping and Blaze had just sat dumbfounded. Annabelle found that she wasn't surprised by anything much anymore.

"Is this why you went to the Shadow?" asked Santu already knowing the answer.

Oscar nodded. "When I remembered, I was so angry. Everything was coming back to me so quickly: Fury and hate and anger . . . and pain," Oscar said correcting himself. "They were all screaming at me. I thought I could get Bruises if I gave the Shadow what it wanted."

"Oscar, what happened to the Shadow—why was it exploding like that?"

"I filled it with as much hate and pain as I could, and then, when I'd stored all the electricity from the lightning I blasted it with the positive charge." Oscar almost smiled. "Maybe if I'd just given it all the lightning charge instead I might have destroyed it . . . but my sister . . ."

"You are doing well Oscar. That was taking an amazing amount of strength. Did you sense Bruises in there?"

Oscar shook his head, dismayed. "It is just a mass of hatred."

Santu only wanted to make Oscar remember. There was no reason to make him regret. "Please Oscar, tell us who you are. We are caring very much."

Oscar eyed Santu suspiciously. "You care because you're stuck here like the last ones. I remember them."

Santu was suddenly confused. "Who are the 'last ones'?"

"The last ones who came here." Oscar was looking annoyed now. "They ran away scared. After that boy got taken they wouldn't help us." He threw a glance out toward the graveyards. "And that's where they all ended up anyway."

Shock resounded around the group and even Jake in his hazy state jolted.

"I am not understanding. Oscar what are you saying?"

"They all ended up over there." Again Oscar gestured in the direction of the graveyard.

"Did they get taken by the Shadow?"

"Only one boy did. The rest got taken by that other thing."

"What other thing?" asked Santu as a sudden rise of panic hit him.

Oscar shrugged. "It's not interested in ghosted ones, just live ones. Like you."

Santu's mind was reeling. He should have been listening to his suspicions. Doubt had been plaguing him more and more but he had ignored it.

"What can you be telling us about it?"

"Well," said Oscar, "It hates the Shadow. I've seen them fight. When that happens it's like watching the daylight fight the night."

Immediately Santu saw the vision. "This is very helpful Oscar. Maybe we can figure out more about it after you've gone." The fear in Santu's eyes gave him away.

Blaze was the first to notice. "Santu? What did you see?"

"I'm not sure," lied Santu. "You have helped everyone Oscar. Can you see that now?"

Santu's words were sinking in. But Oscar couldn't hear the truth without it being distorted by his pain.

"Oscar you are not this monster you say you are. You were never intending to hurt anyone. You helped save lives on the frontlines." Santu was feeling desperate. "Please Oscar, I am knowing that *you* know the truth. Don't let guilt bury it."

Santu's words were piercing Oscar's armor of blame. But it didn't matter.

"I told you," said Oscar indignantly, "I can't go without Buttons."

"Then," said Santu in a very risky move, "you had better go and get her."

Daffodil jumped up shaking her head. "I don't think Oscar should leave yet. He hasn't even told us his name."

"Oscar?" said Santu. "Are you wanting to tell us your name?"

Oscar shrugged.

"It doesn't matter what my name *was* anymore."

"Don't you think Buttons would like to know her brother's name?" asked Santu. "I am thinking she would love to know she has a brother. Can you imagine how excited she is going to be?"

Deep rumbles of thunder were instantly followed by a flood of sheet-lightning. Black trees suddenly grew closer before disappearing into the dark again. Oscar looked out into the pouring rain remembering what it felt like to be alone in the world. An image of Buttons' smiling face lit up in Oscar's mind. Maybe she would be so happy to find out that she had a brother that she wouldn't be so mad at him?

"My name," said Oscar finally, "*was* Ford Whitman.

"And," said Santu smiling, "what *were* the names of your sisters?"

Oscar surprised himself by smiling back. "Pearl and Jet. Buttons was called Pearl and Bruises was called Jet." Oscar looked wistful for a moment. "My mother and grandmother collected buttons. That's what buttons are made out of, Pearl and Jet. My parents obviously like to name us after things."

Santu understood. "Yes, you are named after Henry Ford's cars. So you also took a name that was from before you ghosted. And, in a way, so did your sisters."

"Suddenly Oscar looked dismayed. "If I'd just remembered our names I could have worked it out."

"Oscar, you have just saved Buttons. If you're sisters were born 3 years after you, and you were 14 in 1917 that means that you were born in 1903 and you ghosted in 1917 and you're sisters were born in 1906 and ghosted in 1916. They were only 10 years old."

Suddenly yellow light expanded all around Oscar. He looked horrified.

"No!" he cried. "I won't go! I can't go!"

Just as Oscar protested, the familiar burst of the white light holding Madame Glizsnort returned. But this time she did not look so calm.

"What's wrong?" asked Daffodil when she saw the look on Madame Glizsnort's face.

"We are losing time too rapidly. Something is not right." If it was the Calling she would not be able to hold on. "Only one?" Madame Glizsnort opined, her face looking worn and sickly.

This wasn't what the group had expected. A new game had begun and the rules had changed. Santu didn't like this at all.

"What has happened? What has changed?" asked Santu.

"I thought I had more time," Madame Glizsnort said checking over her shoulder. "Time is running out."

"Where are the others?" asked Daffodil.

"They are here! Can't you see them?" Now Madame Glizsnort seemed really distressed. "They cannot go without me." She patted a couple of invisible heads. "Here. It's Adam, Benjamin and Henri."

Daffodil was biting her lip trying to see what was apparently in front of her. Slowly Henri's image emerged. "I can see Scraps!" cried Daffodil. "I can see him." She looked excitedly around the room.

Scraps was waving happily unaware of whatever everyone seemed so fussed about.

"I can see Scraps now too," said Santu suspicion lifting his words. "What do you mean they cannot be going without you?"

"Please, we must hurry." It was too late for the truth now.

"Can't you do something about it?" asked Daffodil.

"I have done too much already." Madame Glizsnort looked like she had made some terrible mistake. "I cannot wait here any longer. I must take the next one. Now, please, hurry."

"Oscar," said Santu not knowing what else to do, "you are having to go. We can be sending Buttons without delay now that we are knowing about her. Please Oscar. Go." Santu wasn't sure if he was doing the right thing. For all he knew he could be sending Oscar somewhere worse. But he had seen the faces of the returned children and they had been full of joy. Of course, he could only see one of them this time.

"But the others!"

"Oscar, you said Dog would bring them back if you didn't show up. He will do as you asked because he is trusting you. Are you understanding Oscar? They are all trusting you. When they had no one else to trust in their lives, they are trusting you. You took their pain away and now we can cross them over. Everything is based on truth and trust. Now it's your turn to be trusting us."

Scraps was waving frantically. "Oscar! It is your turn! Oscar! We have all been waiting for you Oscar. Come on."

The warmth of the yellow glow around him was soothing away all the anxiety, anger, hurt and shame. Without all those crushing emotions, Oscar felt lighter, freer, and able to access all those other wonderful feelings like love and hope. Oscar looked at the people who had helped him. One by one he gave them a grateful smile.

"You can't leave anyone behind!" Oscar said. "You have to promise you won't leave anyone behind. The pets too. You have to make sure all the pets are crossed over. There's a Duck and Kat and Yellow the canary, and Buttons has a fluffy cat called Fidget and . . ."

"We promise Oscar," Santu cut him off. "You must be going now!"

Just as Oscar was about to go toward the light two other figures appeared beside the radiola. Oscar couldn't believe his eyes.

It was Buttons, holding Fidget, and Dog. Dog had kept his promise: He finally trusted Oscar.

"Buttons!" Oscar screamed as he flashed to her side and hugged her and the cat with all his might. Realizing how brief their time was, he rushed words at her like a storm. "You're my sister! I forgot, I'm so sorry! But I came looking for you. I looked for so long that by the time I found you I had forgotten who you were. But I knew to keep you safe. That's why I kept bringing more and more ghosted ones here. I didn't remember that I was just looking for you."

Dog could see that Oscar was bright with the light. He knew it was Oscar's turn and he tried to stop himself from feeling angry. It didn't matter anyway. Dog knew he wouldn't find the light so the others may as well.

The shock was too much for Buttons and she broke down in tears. She reached out for Dog's hand. Oscar was horrified: Buttons had turned to Dog instead of him. Oscar looked at Dog, his face full of hurt.

"Oscar," said Dog. "That place is very bad for everyone. Buttons doesn't remember anything anymore except me. She is constantly terrified. I'm going back and bringing the others now. We can't wait there anymore. It's destroying us. We don't care if it becomes unbalanced. We are lost anyway. It's a risk we have to take."

Madame Glizsnort didn't have time for this. "Please, I must take you!"

Oscar couldn't leave without Buttons—not now, she was here right beside him.

"Buttons, you're name was Pearl Whitman. My name was Ford. Bruises was called Jet. You were named because mommy and grandma loved buttons. So you remembered about the buttons. That's what you're called here. Remember? You were born in 1906 and ghosted in 1916 with mommy and daddy in a mortar attack. I couldn't save any of you. Please Buttons you have to remember."

Buttons was shaking her head and concentrating on holding her squirming cat. Some of what he was saying sounded familiar but other things weren't right. Fragments of memories flashed in her mind but none of them made sense.

"I'm sorry Ford my time has run out. We must go now! Come."

"Hurry, Oscar, hurry!" cried Scraps.

"Oscar," said Santu gently. "You have to go. I will be making sure Buttons is going next. I promise. I absolutely promise."

Oscar realized he was still fighting old emotions. But regret, sorrow, pain and loss had been of no use to him. He looked at Santu and let the warm yellow light take hold.

"Thank you," said Oscar as the bright glow around him expanded. The pull felt like liquid warmth filling his veins, a gentle caress, a hug. Oscar had never felt anything like it in his existence. He knew it would be alright now. He knew it was safe. All the ugly hateful distrust had washed away and he was left with the magic of the light. Bruises was gone but Santu would send Buttons next. He would wait for her just as he had all these years.

As Oscar entered the light, Buttons whispered something urgently to Dog.

"Wait!" screamed Dog.

Everyone turned to face Dog. Beside him, Buttons was lit up with yellow light.

"Go!" Dog screamed at Buttons. He pushed her gently toward the glowing white light. A surprised and excited Oscar reached out for her.

Dog flashed in and out before explaining to the crowd what was happening.

"When Oscar touched the light, Buttons remembered everything." Dog was staring at the glow, mesmerized by its radiance. "It must be the light. Buttons remembered the truth," said Dog without taking his eyes of his brightly lit companions.

Daffodil turned to face him. "What truth is that Dog?"

"Buttons told me that she and Bruises didn't die during the mortar attack."

"But Oscar saw them," said Daffodil.

Dog shook his head. "Yes, but they weren't ghosted yet. They both died later. Bruises died in the hospital—her legs had been badly crushed—but she stayed with her sister as a ghosted one. A nice man took Buttons out of the hospital to take care of her but he died shortly after and his wife forced Buttons out. Bruises found the ghosted cat to keep them company. But Buttons couldn't survive: There was no food. Eventually she became too weak. Bruises tried to help, but Buttons gave up. She ghosted in that same year, 1916, only six months after her sister."

Daffodil was worried that more grief and guilt would prevent Oscar from crossing over. He had thought his sisters had both died with his mother and father. Essentially he had left them under the rubble to be found by strangers. But when she saw what was happening she was filled with such awe that she would struggle to recall its grandeur.

Oscar was reaching out for his sister. The ecstatic look on his face said everything. It did not matter about their earthly lives anymore: Oscar and Buttons were going home.

The last image the observers saw was of Oscar hugging his little sister and Fidget clawing Buttons' chest in excitement. Madame Glizsnort's relief was obvious: Finally she could let go.

While everyone was in high spirits for Oscar and Buttons they were also feeling strange suspicions. Why wouldn't Madame Glizsnort answer their questions and why did it feel like she was running from something? Was there something else out there that was watching and waiting?

Things weren't adding up and they needed to figure out why and quickly.

With the heavy rain falling, nobody noticed that this time no angels sang.

Follow The True and Strange Story Of DAUZAT'S Report Where German Soldiers Tried To Enter A Church Which Housed a Miraculous Statue. When The Doors Wouldn't Open, The Officer Commanded They Be Blasted Open By A Cannon. Before The Command Could Be Enacted, The Doors Opened By Themsleves As If By Magic. But As The German Troops Began To Enter The Church, They All Fell Dead On The Spot ~ PAGE 8.

The Legend of the HOUND OF MONS has returned! The giant skulking hound reported to have dragged British soldiers to their deaths, now has another reason - It is the result of a hideous experiment by Dr. Ho-chmuller said to have taken the brain of a man gone mad by his hatred of the British and transplanted it into a giant Siberian wolfhound. After careful training, the wolf was released in No Man's Land to terrorize and destroy the hated troops of the enemy by tearing their bodies to pieces. It is said several English soldiers have been tormented and are suffering from terrible and un███ ███osis that ca███ ███ ███ tak█

Missing

This is the last picture of a boy missing after his parents have been reported dead. His name is Benjamin O. Walsh and he is the child of Ciaran Walsh & Darragh Walsh. He has a sister named Grace. His whereabouts is unknown and he is perhaps in hiding. If anyone knows of his situation, it needs to be reported to local police staff.

~Present day~

~A Clue in a Nightmare in the Abyss of What's Missed~

As the white light dissolved, Santu turned back to thank Dog but he had already disappeared.

"He's gone," said Blaze. "At least we will have all of them here together soon."

"If," said Daffodil, "they make it out of that awful place." The alternative didn't bear thinking about. "What do you think Oscar meant when he talked about the other creature, the one that will kill us anyway?"

Santu shook his head. "I can not know."

"I wonder why it hasn't attacked us yet?" asked Blaze.

"Maybe," said Daffodil, "it wants the ghosts crossed over first?"

"Why?" asked Santu. "Why would it be caring if the ghosts are crossing over or not? Oscar said it took the others before they could do anything to help. If it is just wanting 'live ones' why not kill us now?"

"Because," said Jake, "it can't." Jake's eyes were squinting into the fire.

Daffodil knew that tone. "What do you mean?"

"I mean it can't get to us. It can't move like the Shadow." Jake's mind was tumbling furiously. "Maybe it doesn't have to."

Daffodil shrugged. "Well how would it get us if it can't move? We can just run away from it."

349

"Not if it's barricading our way out," said Jake. Jake pulled his eyes away from the fire and stared darkly at Daffodil. "Like that mist out there."

Everyone was remembering the impenetrably thick blanket of fog that surrounded them.

"But I thought that was Madame Glizsnort's way of keeping us in?" said Blaze feeling confused.

Jake shook his head. "Oh it's keeping us in alright but the two aren't mutually exclusive. It's also keeping us out."

Tiredness suddenly struck Blaze and it was making it hard to understand what anyone was saying. "Out?" she asked.

"Out," repeated Jake. He looked around skeptically. "You really think this place is on the map?"

Blaze wished she hadn't asked. "So it can't kill us unless we try to leave?"

Jake raised his shoulders. "I think *it* thinks it's protecting this place; protecting the ghosts and anyone who tries to get out . . . or in." Jake raised his eyebrows.

Annabelle had been standing on the outskirts taking it all in. Looking out into the rain and lightning, she remembered feeling the same way: No way out; no way for anyone to get in. Trying to forget what this day represented, she let the rain fall across her face; let it soak into her skin. Perhaps if she made the outside of her body as cold as the inside . . .

"You mean," replied Blaze, "it thinks it's protecting the ghosts, this place, and the outside world, by *killing* us?"

Jake ignored her question and turned back to the radiola. He had already answered that.

"Then," said Daffodil determinedly, "we'll just have to destroy that too."

Santu was feeling ill. It was a mixture of nausea, exhaustion and hunger. "Let us focus on the ghosts first, yes?" This was unusual for Santu: Problem solving was his specialty.

Duel and Duette could read his confusion and fatigue. Duel threw a look at Daffodil and passed the thoughts on.

"Or," said Daffodil giving Duel a quick nod of thanks, "maybe we should rest."

No one was going to argue with that.

Beds were fashioned out of cardboard boxes and blankets were wrapped tightly around bodies. The only person who hadn't moved from the window was Annabelle. She had other things on her mind and the rest took a distant, second place.

Duel's back injury—from being flung backward and forward at the window—was starting to really hurt. He gratefully lowered himself to the floor next to the fire and let the heat warm his torn muscles before drifting into a dreamless sleep. Duette was having trouble removing Duel's pain from her mind. She had managed to subdue its intensity but she was yet to shed the throbbing. He had not said anything to anyone about his pain. Since their experience in the Shadow, her brother's strength continued to amaze her. Now she knew his courage crossed all barriers: emotional and physical.

"Oh," Daffodil said as she lay down beside Blaze, "try not to light anymore infernos please."

Blaze winced. "I won't. I think I know what sets it off now. I'm sure I know what to do."

"Great," said Daffodil with a yawn. "Let's all try and not die then."

The nightmares were cold, dark and vicious and Santu was well aware who was responsible. Even though he knew he was dreaming, he couldn't force himself to wake. Something in his visual cortex had been triggered and visions were coming to him without words. It was something he had never had to deal with before. And now, even in the middle of these torturous nightmares, Santu knew Annabelle was becoming more and more dangerous to herself. If she didn't turn back now, she wouldn't be able to. Right before Santu fell into a black abyss of viscous slime, he realized that Annabelle had left the building.

As the gray light of day rose, Annabelle trudged toward the graveyard. She didn't notice the cold rain or the freezing air. It felt like nothing to her. Annabelle had given up. The icy creation inside her had taken over and it took too much energy to fight. So she had stopped. A lifetime of struggling had taken its toll. Battling something inevitable was overrated.

By the time she had reached her destination the rain had eased enough for her to make out the gravestones. And the mist. She wondered what would happen to her when she went in there. Would it hurt? Would it take the ice from her? Would it make her feel regret before it consumed her?

First she would have to find the clue. Wonderboy, Madame Glizsnort and Blaze had all said it was there. The thought of Blaze made her sneer. Soon the handsome boy, Santu would mourn Annabelle's passing. And, in his mourning, Blaze would never have a chance with him. Funny thing was, Annabelle didn't think *he* wanted Blaze. In fact she was sure of it. Mind you, he didn't want Annabelle either. That made her sneer again. All boys wanted her—the unattainable angel—what was wrong with him?

The rain fell in her eyes and mouth. She was soaked to the bone. Annabelle had always thought that being waterproof was like having a superpower. No one had ever seemed to appreciate how cool it was. Now it just seemed annoying. Why couldn't the water just soak her up? Shaking the stupid thoughts from her head she moved around the gravestones wondering what it was she was supposed to find.

Finally, she saw it. One of the gravestones had been engraved with strange symbols. Why hadn't they seen them last time? Had something changed? It was the same gravestone that the strange man wearing the top hat had been digging; the one with the gaping abyss in front of it. The hole was so deep it looked as if it could lead all the way to hell. At least that must mean that Bruises soul hadn't been buried yet. The Shadow was probably playing with his last prize, torturing it, enjoying its agony.

Annabelle tried to get closer to the symbols to study them but the cavernous hole was in the way. And the icy ground surrounding it had turned to slush and mud which made it impossible to even lean over without risking falling in. Now that would be a horrible way to die.

Moving to the side of the grave and using the edge of the stone to grip onto, she managed to push her feet into the mud and bend her head round its side. She was dangerously twisted, her feet teetering on the slippery ledge of the bottomless pit.

Just as she was memorizing the symbols she felt her feet slide. In the horrible split second that followed Annabelle realized she was about to face a hideous death.

As she felt herself slipping, one last loud crash of thunder resounded around her and a fork of lightning struck the ground beside her like the last wave of a conductor's wrist.

✳   ✳   ✳

Jake was having trouble sleeping. The concussion was making his head throb and strange thoughts kept pushing themselves into his mind. His life had been such a waste: All those years studying antique objects, objects that people stored behind glass to study; just things, unused.

He had cut himself off from everyone. It was a protective device, he knew that, but it was also a way of pretending not to be alive. Sometimes he could dismiss all the awful abuse his mother had put him through, the acts of violence and hatred that had guided his early years—but the courts, and the foster people, loved reminding him. He wished he could just forget like the ghosts. But forgetting wasn't going to happen; not without a lobotomy or shock treatment—and there had been a few psychoanalysts who had recommended some equally hideous treatments.

Jake realized he had spent his whole life trying not to exist. Until now, until this place. Here, he had learned to sense humor; he had learned to laugh, to touch, to be touched, to feel. But it all came with a price: The recognition that everything he had done before added to nothing. Without human interaction, without experiencing the myriad of human emotions there is no life—you are just a thing. The irony was not beyond him.

Jake decided if he ever did get out of here he was going to run away. Run far away where none of the people from his past could find him. He would find a job; a job with lots of other people where he could make friends. The concept was bizarre. What did friends do together?

Just as Jake wondered if, after this was all over, he would see any of these people again, he heard a noise. As Jake lifted his head he saw Santu disappear down the stairs. Sitting up and looking around the room, he realized that Annabelle was gone too. Were they having some sort of tryst? Jake thought about it for only a second. That seemed highly unlikely.

Jake got up and looked out the window. Santu was running through the rain toward the graveyard. Jake didn't waste time. Dashing toward the stairs, he ran after him.

WORLD TIMES

Volume 752 - London, November 11, 1918   One Cer

ARMISTICE SIGNED, END OF THE WAR! REVOLUTIONISTS SEIZE BERLIN; NEW CHANCELLOR BEGS FOR ORDER; OUSTED KAISER FLEES TO HOLLAND

ARMISTICE FOR PEACE

An amistice has been signed by Germany, the terms of which are now in the process of being executed. The news of the abdication of the Kaiser came on Saturday. The leader of the most efficient fighting organization in the history of the world is believed to have boarded a train to Holland - which could also be where Hindenburg has fled. The Crown Prince has either been assasinated or on a voyage to Holland. More on Page 2.

GERMANY CRIES FOR FOOD

Addressing a joint session of congress, President Wilson stated that steps were being taken to supply the Central Powers with food on the same systematic plan which prevented the starvation of Belgium during the German occupation. Full Story Page 6.

— — —

ARMISTICE DAY

At 11:00 am today, on the Western Front, the truth of the final surrender has come to fruition. All allies and Germany sign the armistice. Report Page 3.

— — —

Tribute to KC

Turn to Page 7 for our full page tribute to cartoonist Kenneth Connelly, who sadly died in June from influenza. God Speed KC.

Utah - July 22nd. Wasatch National Park - 504 Sheep killed as lightning strikes.

— — —

Boston - Boston Children's Hospital is the first to trial the use of The Iron Lung. Polio sufferers may be save by the new breathing dev

— — —

U.S. - Spanish Flu virus has killed over 2o,000 in its first week. PAGE 3.

— — —

Western Samoa - Influenz epidemic has spread to Samoa, killing 20% of the population so far. This s

~Present day~

~And Down Will Come Baby, Cradle and All~

As Annabelle's feet slipped, her weight pulled her hands from the headstone. As she tried desperately to make another grab at the grave, she felt her fingertips press across the symbols. In the slow motion that adrenaline brings to its victims she suddenly understood what she had done to herself: Unable to change the past, she had changed her body; her insides; her being. What she had done to protect herself was in fact, slowly killing her. But she didn't want to die like this. Annabelle wanted to know the wonder of innocence, the kindness in a caress, the smile of love.

But time does not stop for remorse.

Annabelle felt herself slide downward. The awful truth of what was about to happen to her struck her so deeply that even the icy soul that was taking over her body cracked. Something drastic had changed her.

Just as the empty, arctic air caressed her falling body, a vice like grip ripped at her ankle. It didn't make sense. There were no vines, no roots. There was nothing that could save her.

"Annabelle!" Santu's voice rang out over the rain. "Pushing yourself up from the sides!"

Annabelle realized her face was deep in the mud at the side of the hole. She was upside down, dangling toward the infinity of the pit. Quickly, she scrambled at the slippery mud on the wall in front of her. Her efforts made Santu lose his balance.

"Stop!" he screamed. "Wait!"

But for the first time in an eternity Annabelle wanted to live. She couldn't stop her instincts: They were fighting for their life as well.

Santu was slipping. He hadn't had time to lasso himself to anything and now it was his weight against Annabelle's desperate attempt at survival. Santu wondered why he had bothered. Annabelle was dead weight anyway. She wasn't going to make it, so why had he risked his life for her?

Just as Santu felt himself slide toward the abyss, two hands wrapped around his waist and pulled with an unearthly strength. Santu didn't have time to think what it could be. Anything was better than that godforsaken hole.

As they all fell backward onto the frozen sludge they heaved sighs of relief. Santu turned to see Jake flat on his back behind him.

"Wow, you are a sight for painful eyes!" Santu was smiling but the tension in his face made him look hostile.

Momentarily Jake was confused. Why would Santu be angry when Jake had just saved his life? Jake shook the thought away: Old paranoia getting in the way of the truth. Jake wasn't going there ever again.

"Couldn't sleep. Thought I'd go for a walk," said Jake.

Santu erupted with laughter. "You are a life-preserver! You are candy with a hole in the middle!" he roared as if it was the funniest thing anybody had ever said. "But there's no hole!" Santu joyfully thumped Jake in the stomach.

Jake had no idea what Santu was talking about but his laughter was infectious. Jake lay back in the slushy mud with rain pelting down on his face and began to laugh like he had never laughed before.

Santu punched Jake's arm and then the air. "Never leave home without Jake!" he screamed to the sky. He felt crazy and stupid and wild.

Annabelle's heart was hammering in her chest as if it wanted to get out. She didn't blame it. Her body was not a good home for anything. Shame catapulted through her mind. She had nearly killed two people. She had nearly killed herself. Before, dying didn't seem to matter. In fact, she had welcomed the possibility. But when faced with it, the coldness inside her broke somehow, shattering into pieces: She could feel again, see again. What had she done to herself to have become so heartless?

Jake motioned toward Annabelle, and Santu grabbed her around the waist and pulled her a bit further from the hole.

"What the hell were you thinking?!" Santu was starring at her, all humor dissipated.

"I was looking for the clue." Annabelle's soft English accent had resurfaced; the exaggerated American twang, all but disappeared. "I think I found it."

Two things happened to Santu simultaneously: A vision of the symbols Annabelle had seen rolled inside his mind, and, suddenly he realized how really beautiful Annabelle was. Her soft features were shining with falling rain, her blonde hair clung wet to the sides of her heart-shaped face and her small rosebud lips sat in perfect dimension to her wide blue eyes—her wide *dark* blue eyes. She looked like a downtrodden angel. Something inside her had changed: The ice inside her had melted. How long had she forced her pain deep down? How terrible had her pain been to turn her into an ice queen? How awful had it been for her?

Jake could see something was different. Annabelle looked special somehow and even her voice was different. Santu was looking at her in an odd way too as if he were seeing her for the first time.

"That mist is getting thicker," Jake said, suddenly noticing how close the white fog had edged toward the gravestones. "I'm sure it was a lot further back last time we were here."

"Let's get out of here," said Santu. Jake was right. The mist had moved inward. He reached for Annabelle's hand. Surprised, Annabelle raised her blue eyes towards Santu. His face was true. She reached out and held on.

"Thank you," Annabelle said, her words gently spiraling in the air. The kindness in her eyes startled Santu. Was this who Annabelle should have been all along? If her mother hadn't abandoned her in an alley; if she hadn't been mistreated by all those awful men; could this be what she would have been like? Sadness welled inside him as if it were *his* great loss. As Annabelle's hand clasped his, he felt his skin flush hot.

"You should," Santu began, trying to disguise his thoughts, "be thanking our friend, Jake."

Jake felt his chest swell. No one had ever called him a friend. He nodded shyly.

"Then," said Annabelle, "thank you, my friend, Jake." Her soft voice rang out to Jake and, momentarily, he wondered: *If the grieving angel at the church entrance could speak, would she too have such gentleness in her voice?*

As they walked back through the rain and sludge they each felt a kind of previously unknown peace. Whatever happened now, they had found something in themselves that they were proud of.

And Annabelle realized, ironically, that for the first time that she could remember, she was celebrating 'life' on her birthday.

Blackwater Herald Moon Tribune Wednesday, April 30th, 1975— One Shilling

WORLD NEWS HEADLINES
NORTH VIETNAM WINS WAR

The battle between North and South Vietnam, which continued to rage even after America withdrew, has at last come to an end. The North Vietnamese have surrounded Saigon forcing the south to surrender today. Full story Page 4.

LOCAL NEWS HEADLINES
GLIZSNORT DONATION

Many decades ago, the Herald Moon Tribune began a series of stories regarding incidents occurring in Blackwater that began around 1918— coinciding with the cessation of World War 1. It was a story that would run for the remaining history of the paper.

Mr. Macalister Glizsnort and the late Madame Grace Glizsnort collected a wealth of articles and historical papers that ran for over 100 years from 1879.

The now retired Chief Superintendent Glizsnort has assisted the community for over 40 years and is proud to donate all these papers to the old unused church on the Cross Roads site. He says there is no other place to put the mounds of information.

"It is really fascinating," says Mr. Glizsnort, "but it overtook our lives for so long. I feel I need to remove it from our house. I wish I could finish Grace's

358

work but I have to accept that it cannot be solved. Even dedicated policemen have to accept this every now and then and so, now I will concede to failure."

Our reporter states that there are hundreds of boxes filled with articles and photographs of all the possible leads Madame Glizsnort discovered on her decades-long search for the truth.

The Herald Moon Tribune has rummaged through some of these boxes, finding intriguing contents. There are even mysterious photos of strange looking children that must have been taken perhaps 80 years ago.

The entire body of research is to be sent to the old Saint Catherine's Church of Redeemus where Madame Glizsnort felt the strongest pull toward these children. Although this church hasn't been used for decades, Bishop William Paracticus of the Church of St. Barnaby, in the close by Bainsbury, has gratefully accepted the many boxes of documents and even some old and rare items which will join the other antiques—like the old Radiola VIII that Mr. Glizsnort gave to his wife in 1938, and donated to the church a few years later. "We will store them in the old church attic as there is plenty of room there. I know no one uses the church anymore but it was important to Madame Glizsnort that the papers be sent there in the event of her and her husband's death. Although her husband is still with us, he feels it is a significant step to move them to this building which has meant so much to her."

Mr. Glizsnort reminds us of the terrible altercations that took place after this church burnt down. Memories of this awful time still disturb him. He is proud to have stayed in the town of Blackwater after it was abandoned but now that his wife has passed on he will move closer to his children, returning to his wife's birthplace of Dublin in Ireland. His daughter is pregnant with her second child and he hopes he will see Grace's lovely red hair continue through the generations.

"It will be nice to be near our children again," stated Mr. Glizsnort. "They had a difficult time of it when their mother became ill. But, I have always said I would wait until I was the last man on the sinking ship and now it has turned out to be so. Blackwater is a ghost-town now and I am afraid I must find some new energy if I am to live out my remaining years with fortitude. My life here with Grace and our growing children was a wonderful time but as it is with life, all things must come to an end."

Bishop Paracticus said: "If Bishop John Biggs were still here he would be proud to hold these documents at his church. Bishop Biggs spent many hours trying to help solve this strange mystery. Before he died, he told us that, perhaps in the afterlife he may find some truth about this matter to console him."

If anyone is interested in these donated articles please contact Bishop Paracticus and he will organize a visit to the once much loved Saint Catherine's Church of Redeemus to show you the mounds of unsolved research being held in its attic.

LATEST NEWS HEADLINES

London—*The new restaurant, 'McDonald's, or as some like to call it, 'The Golden Arches', has proved to be very successful after opening in October last year. "It is the first McDonald's for the country but definitely not the last," said a spokesman for the popular fast food eatery.*

Australia—*Color television has made its first transmission in Australia much to the joy of the general public. "I saw 'The Flintstones' in color!" cried one small child on the Sydney nightly news.*

Cambodia—*The Communist Khmer Rouge Forces have taken Cambodia. Page 4.*

COMING SOON TO LILLYPILLY THEATRE—'Jaws'—starring Richard Dreyfuss and Roy Scheider.

~Present day~

~My Love is like a Violin that's Sweetly Played in Tune~

At the church, Duette, Duel, Blaze and Daffodil were all having strange dreams. Symbols were flying at them in the darkness, bombarding them, demanding to be noticed. Daffodil forced herself awake. Even though it was freezing, her skin was slick with sweat. Yawning, she moved over to the fire. The gray skies outside were still falling with rain. At least Blaze hadn't burned them all to death in their sleep. Daffodil stared at her resting friend. Bandages were wrapped around all her limbs—both her legs, both her hands. How long would they all survive? Everyone had been badly injured at some point. Everyone except Annabelle.

Footsteps distracted Daffodil's thoughts. Suddenly she realized that people were missing. Swinging her head round to look for Jake she realized that he was one of them. She ran toward the staircase only to bump straight into a very wet Santu as he strode the top steps.

"What's going on? Where have you been?" The three of them were saturated. Daffodil was about to accost Jake next but saw Annabelle first. Annabelle looked completely different. Too stunned to go on Daffodil took a step backwards and let the three of them pass. Annabelle smiled kindly at Daffodil as she moved beside her. Daffodil's mouth dropped open in shock. Her eyes questioned the two rather proud looking boys.

The noise woke the others and Blaze stretched before remembering her injuries. Pain shot through her legs like razors.

"Annabelle went to look for the clue in the graveyard," said Santu struggling to take off his beloved leather jacket which was now covered in mud.

Daffodil shook her head. That didn't explain anything.

Annabelle blinked her large dark blue eyes. "Santu followed me." The words were gentle and pronounced, a perfect English accent.

Daffodil's eyes narrowed.

"And Jake," said Santu, "he was following me. Thank the Lord for that!"

"Jake saved my life, our lives," said Annabelle, her eyes downcast.

"Yes, he is a crazy, wonderful, nutcracker!" cried Santu as he threw an arm around Jake.

Daffodil was shaking her head. A million questions were screaming to get out. Why was Annabelle suddenly putting on a snobby accent? Why did she look so different? How did *Jake* save everyone's life? Why was Jake looking perfectly comfortable with Santu's arm slung around him?

Jake could see Daffodil was getting madder by the minute. "Annabelle found some new symbols on that grave that was dug up," said Jake. "And the mist is getting thicker or moving in or something."

Blaze's eyes were transfixed on Annabelle's face. She looked . . . beautiful—even dripping wet with her hair clinging to her face. The cold expression in her eyes had gone, melted into a dark blue gentleness. Had Annabelle and Santu done something together? Had he kissed her and made her hatred melt? That didn't explain the color of her eyes. Jealousy flared inside her and the fire behind her burst with flares.

Duel and Duette exchanged knowing glances.

"Blaze," said Duel as he shook his head and motioned toward the fire. Blaze hadn't noticed until then.

"Oh, sorry," she whispered as she forced the fire back down.

Santu went on to tell them exactly what happened and explained how Annabelle had touched the symbols before her near fatal plunge. When Daffodil confessed to having just dreamt about similar images Duel and Duette declared that they had also seen such images in their sleep.

"But," said Daffodil, "that doesn't make sense."

"Really?" said Santu with revived sarcasm. "You are suddenly surprised that things are not making sense?" He shook his head in annoyance. "Tell her Jake."

Jake shrugged. "She's nice now."

Duel and Duette suddenly and simultaneously became aware that they could read Annabelle's mind. They had never been able to penetrate her thoughts before. Something really radical had happened in that graveyard. The strange thing was that usually a person was thinking several different things at the same time—especially girls. Duel and Duette had learned to concentrate on the main thought-stream and let the peripherals scatter. But Annabelle had no peripheral thoughts; just one quiet preoccupation. All Annabelle was thinking about was the symbols and what she felt like as her fingertips stroked their forms. This thought replayed over and over without distraction.

"Well," said Daffodil, "what do these symbols mean?" Before anyone had a chance to answer her, the radiola burst into sound. The shock made everyone jump. Jake ran over to listen. Through the static he heard voices. Turning the dials very carefully, he refined their vibration. But Jake was confused. This wasn't a recording. It was as if he were somehow eavesdropping on a conversation.

Daffodil was spraying everyone with solution so that they could all hear what Jake was hearing. They crowded around the radiola waiting for a voice.

Jake was shaking his head. "This isn't a recording. I don't know what it is." He twisted the left dial just slightly and several voices burst out at them.

"It sounds like a telephone call except we are hearing both sides," said Daffodil as she listened to the tinny, distant voices.

"Shh," said Jake. "Listen."

"Operator . . . operator?"

"Yes Doctor Schmidt, please speak up we have a terrible line."

"Operator, I need to put a call through to Deacon Muller."

"Hold the line please Doctor."

"Hello, Deacon Muller speaking."

"Deacon, it is Doctor Schmidt here. I have a difficult matter to discuss."

"And what is that good Doctor?"

"I have a child's body in the morgue, a Melodie Wagner."

"Melodie Wagner?"

"Yes. I am sure you know her. She is the daughter of Elisabeth and Fritz Wagner."

"Oh, yes, of course, Melodie. Such an unusual name. Such a terrible circumstance. Very sweet face. She was sent to a children's home wasn't she?"

"Yes, she was sent to the German Soldiers' League Fund for Orphaned Children's Home. They have taken in so many of the little orphaned ones. It has been an appalling time."

"Yes. There are very bad stories everywhere. So then, Doctor, how can I be of assistance?"

"Deacon, I am afraid little Melodie has been found deceased. Cause of death was Polio. She had been suffering from it for a while but I'm afraid it accelerated alarmingly on her entry into the Home. Her respiratory system became paralyzed. I am sorry to say this but as her family is all dead there is no one to pick up the body and of course there is no one to pay for a burial."

"Oh, such bad news. So many children dying. What can I do to help Doctor?"

"The little girl is in our morgue and we can no longer keep her here . . . there are others . . ."

"Of course, Doctor. I understand. It must only be 6 months since her mother and the baby died. Just terrible."

"Yes Deacon. The mother died in childbirth. I couldn't do anything to save her or the baby."

"Very sad. And her father was killed only six months before the mother died."

"That is right Deacon. So many sad stories these days."

"Too many I'm afraid Doctor. The church shall organize to pick up the body and we shall bury her with her mother and brother. We will find a way."

"That is very helpful. Thank you Deacon."

"Doctor, do you have the details there: her full name; birthdates etc? Perhaps I can get a volunteer to add them to the grave stone."

"Yes, of course. Just a moment. Here they are. Her full name is Melodie—spelt: M.E.L.O.D.I.E—Sofie Wagner. She was born right here in St. Josef's Hospital in Bochum-Linden on March 19th, 1907. Date of death is November 12th, 1916."

"Right. Thank you Doctor. She played piano beautifully you know? Amazing for someone so young."

"Yes, not surprising considering her lineage though. I have heard her play on several occasions when making my house calls. Just lovely. Real emotion for such a young thing."

"Yes. Just awful. Well I will attend to the matter immediately. Should I go straight to the morgue?"

"Yes, that will be best."

"Alright then. Thank you Doctor."

"Thank you Deacon."

"Operator . . . operator?"

"Yes Doctor Schmidt, please speak up we have a terrible line."

"Operator, I need to put a call through to Deacon Muller."

"Hold the line please Doctor."

As Jake began to twist the volume dials down, a hideous twisting blast like a high-pitched scream, forced them all to cover their ears. Then, just as quickly, static charged through the channel once again. Outside, the rain was still drumming the ground, but no one noticed. The conversation they had just heard was occupying their thoughts.

"I know who that's about," said Daffodil. "You know that little girl that carries the baby ghost around and takes care of it; the one the calipers on? That's about her. She doesn't even realize that it's her baby brother." No one responded. Daffodil was faced with a sea of sad faces—of which one in particular took her by surprise. Silent tears were streaming down Annabelle's perfect face. Why was Annabelle's transformation the only thing she couldn't comprehend?

Daffodil walked over to the window. Darkness was about to blanket their world again. Loneliness suddenly gripped her: The freezing cold air; these horrible stories; no parents; Annabelle crying; it was all too much. Daffodil broke down. Small huffs of pain escaped her lips and tears flowed. They were the tears she had never allowed herself to cry—they came from a place inside her that was deep and dark and lost.

Jake didn't know what to do. Everyone was exhausted and hungry and confused. Some of them were badly injured and they were all emotionally wounded. He walked over to the window and wrapped his arm around Daffodil. He had no idea if it was the right thing to do but he had to do something. Daffodil turned toward him, all tears and hot skin, and rested her head on his chest. He wrapped both his arms around her quivering body realizing that he had never hugged anyone. Ever. A sad smile crossed his lips. Hugs felt good.

Suddenly Daffodil's head shot up. Her eyes were wide with fright.

Santu caught her look. "What is it?" he asked as worry crept up his spine.

"I just realized something."

"What?"

Daffodil was shaking her head as if it would make her thoughts fall into place. "How was it possible that we heard that conversation?" Jake gestured to the radiola. It seemed fairly obvious.

"No," said Daffodil. "You don't understand what I'm saying. That telephone conversation would have transpired *before* that radiola even existed."

Blaze was confused. "So were the looped recordings weren't they?"

"No," repeated Daffodil. "The ghosts started recording after the radiola was put up here—which could have been around the forties." She paused. "*That* recording, or whatever it is, is from 1916."

"Um, excusing me." Duette had noticed something very peculiar as well.

"What?" Stress rang in Santu's voice.

"Isn't anyone notice it?"

"Noticing what Duette?" Santu sounded like he was warning her not to tell him something he didn't want to hear.

"That not Anglais."

"What's unglazed?" asked Jake confused.

"No, Jake," said Daffodil suddenly realizing what Duette meant. "Duette is saying it wasn't English. But we all heard it; we all *understood* it."

"Also me. But not Anglais." Duette and Daffodil exchanged knowing glances. "I think," Duette went on, "that doctor said, girl born 'here' in St. Josef's Hospital, Bochum-Linden. That Germany."

"German?!" yelled Santu unexpectedly. "But the Germans were the enemies in both world wars."

"We are all enemies at some time in history," said Daffodil unimpressed. "We should all be allies at some point too."

Duette was getting frustrated with her inability to explain herself. "It not important what language is in!"

"Duette is right," said Daffodil. "We need to understand how this happened."

"Is like," tried Duette, "listening to reflection."

Daffodil suddenly understood. "Oh my god."

"What?" asked Blaze and Santu simultaneously.

"Oh no." Daffodil looked at her arms and legs like they were about to disappear.

"What!?" yelled Santu again.

Daffodil shook her head. "That message is not from . . ." her voice trailed away again. She shut her eyes and tried to figure out how to explain it. "Someone is trying to help us. I think that message is from . . . the periphery."

"The periphery?" asked Blaze in confusion.

"The spirit world." Daffodil shrugged apologetically.

"The spirit world!?" cried Blaze a little too loudly.

Daffodil nodded slowly. There was something else that she needed to say but she didn't know how.

"Is it Madame Glizsnort?" asked Blaze, head tilted, her mane of red hair dangling to one side.

Daffodil shook her head. "I don't think so." She gave Santu a look that terrified him.

Santu frowned. "You are not telling everything."

Daffodil sighed. "You see, it is really rare, but it has been documented . . . In the spirit world, language is not definable. I mean, language is universal; all language is understood." Daffodil waited for the information to sink in.

"You meaning," said Duette feeling rather annoyed, "I could be speaking French whole time!?"

Daffodil shook her head again. "No. We are not ghosted . . . yet." She shrugged. "It's those that are trying to communicate with us. In the spirit world."

"But who is doing this?" asked Santu feeling way out of his depth, all sarcasm gone.

"Haven't you noticed," added Daffodil, "that we aren't suffering from this cold the way we were before? Yes, we are all freezing but this weather should have frozen us to death by now. You said it before Santu. You said we would get colder until we understood." She was biting her lip now. "We are between two worlds. We can still feel what an earthly body would, but it is growing more distant, less real somehow."

In his heart, Santu knew Daffodil was right. Even though he knew it all along, he couldn't deal with it. And now he realized that he had been doing *that* with everything for much too long. Was that where all the frustration and anger came from?

Santu looked down at himself. With his muddy leather jacket removed he was only wearing his layers of tee shirts to keep warm. He looked out the broken windows at the plummeting, icy rain. He should be shivering uncontrollably. Would this be how it all ended: Being slowly removed from the world?

"And there's something else." Daffodil looked around the room. A sea of fear faced her. "I think we have been thinking about the Shadow all wrong."

"The Shadow? What's *that* got to do with *this*?"

"I think we have been fighting so that we don't die." Daffodil's brown eyes were wide, her fuzzy blonde hair framing her face like a corona. "I think we should be fighting to *be* alive."

"We dead?" Duette was trying to understand.

"Dead!?" Santu's face was filled with horror.

Daffodil held up her palms to stop the inevitable need to blame the messenger. "No, I don't think we are dead. And no we are not ghosts."

"But . . ."

"I think we are in-between worlds," Daffodil said simply.

"What the hell is being the difference!?" Santu's voice was unintentionally accusing.

Duette was annoyed with Santu. His outbursts were not helping anyone. "Santu. Being more calm please."

"Sorry." Santu huffed out his tension. "But you are just telling me I am dead."

"No," said Daffodil, "I didn't. I said, I think we're not anything." Biting her lip she went on. "Does anyone remember getting on the bus? I don't' mean *riding* on the bus I mean *getting* on the bus."

Everyone was thinking hard. Memories were sifting like dust in a storm, escaping like dreams.

Santu was nodding. "I am remembering, I think." His eyes were downcast and it was taking an awful amount of energy to make the recollection. Then he shook his head. "No, I am not remembering. I am not."

Jake couldn't remember anything after he got off the plane and they had taken all his electrical devices away from him. He remembered the awful, freezing-cold bus-ride—wailing animals, black trees and icy roads—but not what had happened before.

"What did they do to us?" Jake's face was sad. He had just started to enjoy being alive.

"I guess it was the only way," Daffodil said grimly.

Santu started hitting his legs. "Are we being in our bodies? What is this meaning?"

"I'm not sure," said Daffodil. "These are definitely our bodies. We are not lying comatose somewhere I'm sure of it. But somehow we are walking between two realms. And we will be staying here until we finish our job."

Blaze knew she was in her own body. No spirit body could hurt this much. "And after that?" she asked, wanting, yet not wanting, to know. "Is that what the mist is for? To finish us off?" Daffodil didn't know. What could she say that would keep everyone positive? If they all just waited to die then that's exactly what would happen.

"Maybe the mist didn't take that other group of children," Daffodil said adding a slightly judgmental tone to her voice. "Maybe they just gave up."

"So," replied Santu evidently still angry, "the mist is just eating them up."

Daffodil fired an angry glance at Santu: He wasn't helping anyone with that attitude.

Santu sighed. "Sorry. You are being right Daffodil. We have to fight this thing until the end."

"Yes," returned Daffodil wishing Santu hadn't added the 'until the end' bit. "We have to fight."

Everyone was nodding and encouraging each other. There wasn't much choice. It was either that, or sit down and wait to die—and Daffodil was *never* going to do that. At least the mood in the room had changed. There was also an added thing that they had gained from this: Now, they knew *how* to fight: Offensive not defensive. Daffodil knew that would make all the difference.

It all made sense to Annabelle. That icy formation inside her had accelerated after she had arrived here. It had grown quickly and remorselessly as if all her past cruelties were solidifying. As soon as she had fainted on that first day, she had known she wouldn't survive any of this. What would have been the point? But then she had faced that gaping abyss at the graveyard and, as her hand had brushed across those symbols, she had scrambled to save her own life. In the pouring rain it had felt like she was being washed clean of her past. Shame had come, yes, but it had dissipated and been replaced with peace. Why, she had no idea. Perhaps it was all a test: To live you must first prove you will fight for your own life. Now, she thought, perhaps her soul had been turned over to find its own value without her: And it had proved itself—maybe too late, but still, it had triumphed over all the evil and foul deeds that had plagued her past. The irony that rebirth had preceded her very likely death, albeit only just, was somehow comforting. At least heaven would greet her now instead of more hell.

Perhaps a stranger would look into this room from the darkness outside and wonder what these people were doing here? Would they think interference was a choice or a necessity? Of course they may think it strange, but would they hear the sadness, the loss? Would they worry about these strangers so obviously displaced? Or would they turn, twist their heads back toward the darkness, and seek their own way home? Possibly. But, in their travels, if they found what they sought, which is rare anyway, they would think about this group of strangers, so hungry for life and with so little right to crave it; and they would forever be unsure of their choice to walk away. Decisions are obviously the hardest when life and death are involved. I should know.

BOSTON BUGLE

Volume 752 - Boston, January 16th, 1919   One Cent

INFLUENZA NOW A GLOBAL DISASTER

THE INFLUENZA PANDEMIC HAS KILLED MORE PEOPLE THAN THE GREAT WAR. IT IS STILL IMPOSSIBLE TO GAUGE NUMBERS- BUT THE DEATHS ARE BETWEEN 20 MILLION AND 40 MILLION. KNOWN AS THE 'SPANISH FLU', IT HAS INFECTED NEARLY ONE FIFTH OF THE WORLD'S POPLUATION. AND THE DEATHS ARE RAPID IN NATURE: SOME HAVE CONTRACTED THE INFECTION AND DIED WITHIN HOURS - A VICIOUS TYPE OF PNEUMONIA DEVELOPING THAT SIMPLY SUFFOCATES AND KILLS ITS VIC- TIMS, MANY CHOKING ON A BLOODY FOAM THAT HAS GUSHED FROM THEIR MOUTHS AND NOSES. PHYSICIANS ARE POWER- LESS. MANY ATTRIBUTE THE DISEASE TO TRENCH WARFARE; MUSTARD GAS OR BIOLOGICAL WARFARE. MORE PAGE 5.

MYSTERIOUS STORY HAS COME TO LIGHT

Several years after the infamous campaign of Gallipoli in 1915, a group of soldiers have come foward with a story so bizarre, that it can only be true. Three members of a New Zealand field company have claimed that they watched from a clear vantage point as the Royal Norfolk Regiment marched up a misty hillside in Suvla Bay in Turkey, where they simply disappeared. The mist rose and the men were gone completely, Believing that the entire battalion must have been cap- tured, the British Government finally demand. The Turkish insist that these soldiers never made contact with the Turks and urgently claim that they did not capture them. It seems that no one has heard or seen of the British battalion again - the entire group of soldiers simply disappearing never to return.

Handley Page Aeroplanes

ENGLAND to INDIA
LONDON to CONSTANTINOPLE
ENGLAND to CENTRAL AFRICA
and have carried
PLOT and 40 PASSENGERS
over 6 500 feet high.

Talking Machine

GREAT BOSTON MOLASSES TRAGEDY

2 Million Gallon Tidal Wave Of Molasses Kills Dozens

Yesterday the Northend of Boston faced a disaster of immense proportions. Near Keany Square, a molasses storage tank - 50ft tall and 90ft in diameter - collapsed. The ground shook as the 15 ft wave r ushed through the streets breaking the girders of the Boston Railway and lifting a train off the tracks. Nearby buildings were swept off their foundations and crushed. A truck was picked up and hurled into the harbour. The wounded include people, horses and dogs. The many dead are so glazed in molasses that they are difficult to recognize. Over 150 have been injured and coughing fits h...
...ne one of the...

~Present day~

~RETURNS~

They had spent time resting, trying to sleep away fear and hunger. Some managed to drift into a light slumber and others did not have so much luck. Each had taken turns as a lookout which was a lonely vocation and led to too much thinking—every one of them glad to turn over their post to the next.

Duette was the last to keep watch. All she could see outside was heavy leaden clouds full of more rain. It had seemed interminable. She ached to wake someone for company. It was strange to feel like this. Her life had folded on and over itself in reserved isolation. She understood why now. It wasn't just people's thoughts that penetrated her mind; it was also people's feelings. How could she not have realized that all those misplaced emotions weren't hers? With Daffodil's potion she was learning to control her empath skills and strangely, company had become important. All those years spent rejecting people—what a waste.

Duette could stand it no longer. Darkness had just begun to fill the sky and gratefully, she turned around to face the sleeping bodies. Who would she disturb first? As she moved toward Duel something distracted her. Immediately she changed tack and ran to Jake instead.

"Look," said Duette. "Quickly to look."

Jake dragged his eyes open. His whole body felt like a dead weight. But, as soon as he saw what Duette was pointing to, he swiftly told her to wake the others. As each of them hauled themselves from the depths of sleep, they were faced with a surprising sight. Dog had returned with some companions. But Dog looked bad. His face was drawn and his radiance, faded.

Jake moved straight over to the radiola to alter the dials.

"Dog," said Jake into the radiola. "Are you alright?"

Dog disappeared and reappeared at the machine. "I can't remember anything. I can only remember that we are supposed to come here." He looked exhausted.

"It's okay Dog," said Jake. "You'll start remembering again now that you're here." He hoped it was true.

That seemed to soothe Dog's anxiety. He nodded tiredly. "I hope so. Why are we here?"

Jake wasn't sure if they should have that conversation until Dog started to remember. "Perhaps you could tell us who your friends are?"

Dog looked confused. He had forgotten that he had brought others with him. Turning to face his ghosted companions he tried to remember their names. "That's Duck," Dog pointed to a duck that was running around in circles. That was good he remembered that name. Who else? "That's Kat," Dog went on, "that's Yellow." Dog pointed to a canary that was sitting on a little girl's head—a little girl that wore shining white calipers and held a small bundle in her arms. "That's . . ." Dog couldn't remember.

All Dog's personality had gone: His suspicion; his anger; his doubt. He was like an empty vessel. Jake found it disturbing. Without memory, he realized, we are nothing. Good, bad, it didn't matter. Memory made us human. Jake swallowed.

"I think," said Jake not wanting to make Dog feel any more lost, "that this little girl," he pointed to the one in the flouncy white dress holding a doll, "is called Bitsy. Isn't she?" Bitsy was looking very scared. Jake gave her an encouraging smile. "You're the one who showed me how to use the radiola."

Dog looked at Bitsy to see if it was true but Bitsy shook her head. Dog looked back at Jake shaking his head too.

"And this," Jake said, pointing to the other little girl with calipers who was squeezing a tightly wrapped bundle, "is Melody and Baby." Melody nodded and held up the infant. Jake felt a huge sense of relief.

"Melody do you remember your name then?" asked Jake gently.

Melody nodded. Dog was surprised. He nodded too.

"Scruffy!" Dog unexpectedly yelled into the radio. "My dog, that's my dog! Scruffy. I remember."

"See," said Jake, "I told you you would remember."

Dog looked confused again. "Who's Oscar?"

"Oscar," said Jake "is the one who protected all of you. He has already gone into the light. He's waiting for you."

Dog tried to remember. "Into the light?"

"Yes," replied Jake hoping he wouldn't have to explain.

"Is that why we're here?"

"Yes."

"Well where is it?" asked Dog looking around.

"It's not here just yet. We have to make it."

"When are you going to do that?" asked Dog.

"When you remember a little bit more."

Dog looked disappointed. It had been a very dangerous journey here. The horrible place they had left, had collapsed behind them threatening to suck them back in. He had used all his strength to try to get them out of there. He hoped he had gotten everyone but he couldn't remember who was left. At least Scruffy was here.

"How long will that take?" asked Dog.

Jake was all out of answers. He looked over at Daffodil for help.

Daffodil shrugged her shoulders. "I think now that Oscar is gone, these ghosts will remember everything by themselves. It was Oscar making them forget. So tell him when it's fully dark. Dog probably just wants an answer."

Jake repeated the information.

"Oh," said Dog. He was feeling strange. Emotions were bubbling inside him and making him uneasy. "How do I know you're telling the truth?" Everyone in the room smiled. Dog's suspicion was coming back and that meant so was Dog.

"Because," said Jake, "you trusted us before. That's why you came back here. You saw Oscar go into the light and you went back to get everyone so you could all follow Oscar."

Suddenly Bitsy was in front of the radiola and was staring right into Jake's eyes.

"I'm Bitsy and this is Poppy," she said pushing her luminescent, ragged doll into Jake's face. "And I helped you with that." She pointed to the radiola.

"Yes, Bitsy, said Jake. "That's exactly right." Jake tried not to pull away but the bitter cold of the shining white doll was burning his face.

"I made it turn on."

"You certainly did Bitsy. You're very clever."

"I'm very clever," Bitsy repeated. "And I'm very old." Her strange comment confused Jake.

"Do you know how old you are Bitsy?"

"I'm only 8 years old in life years but I'm much older than that." Bitsy's expression was strange. Jake went to reply but before he could, Bitsy showed everyone how old she really was. The appearance of the little girl turned into the death mask of a very old woman—just inches away from Jake's face. All his instincts were screaming at him to run but he managed to hold his ground. He had, after all, had quite a bit of practice.

"Well," Jake tried to keep the effort out of his voice. "You certainly are old."

Dog said something in Bitsy's ear and Bitsy's face crumbled like dust. Her headless body floated there for a few moments before she returned to her 8 year old self. She flashed over to pat the Duck, laughing.

"I'm sorry," said Dog into the radiola. "That place has made us see such awful things. Bitsy has had a terrible time of it. Make sure she goes first."

"Well you're here now," said Jake not wanting to address the issue of who would be going into the light first.

Dog nodded. "I'm remembering things I don't want to remember."

"I'm sorry Dog. It must be awful. But you have to remember as much as you can."

Dog looked distressed.

"Maybe," said Jake, trying to stall for time, "you should rest? Would you like to do that?"

Dog nodded. "We are all very tired."

Daffodil was motioning for Jake to come over to the group.

"How do we do this?" asked Daffodil. "We know that the phone conversation we overheard was for Melody and Baby."

"Can we be replaying it for them to hear?" Santu asked Jake.

"Hopefully," said Jake. "I'll try to adjust the dials back. Maybe it's still there."

"Do you think they are ready to hear it?" asked Daffodil.

"Are we having a choice?" replied Santu. "Plus, everything is telling me to worry. I am thinking time is short now and we must be hurrying."

Jake nodded and headed over to the radiola. "Melody," Jake said before he began to shift the dials. "Do you think you would be able to come over here? I am going to try to find a recording that is about you and your family."

Melody looked hesitantly at Dog. Dog didn't see how it could do her any more harm than what she had already experienced. He nodded.

Instantly Melody flashed over to the radiola—her calipers glowing tightly around her legs. Jake tried not to flinch. He couldn't get used to the way they moved. He carefully tried to readjust the dials to where he remembered the phone conversation was held. A horrible high-pitched buzz shot through the air terrifying Melody. She disappeared and rematerialized back at Dog's side. Jake realized that he had found the right frequency for the exchange. As the voices of the Doctor and the Deacon sounded out from the radiola the little girl in calipers moved hesitantly forward.

The grim story unfolded again.

As Melody slowly understood the conversation was about her, she moved closer and closer to Jake. Once the conversation was over, Jake quickly moved the dials so that they could talk to her again but Melody had already started talking into the radiola before he could manage to fine-tune the signal.

". . . aby is my brother!" cried Melody in her clipped accent. "Baby is my brother! And my name really is Melody just spelled wrong." She was looking back at Dog with excitement. Then suddenly she looked confused. "But I found him in a field. He was naked and freezing cold." She was shaking her head. "Why was he in a field? How did I find him there?"

Melody hadn't taken on the special glow that usually preceded their entry into the white light and Daffodil was concerned. She motioned to Jake that she would take a turn.

"Melody, are you sure you found your baby brother in a field?"

Melody was nodding slowly as if she wasn't quite sure. "It was a big pasture with small blocks everywhere."

Daffodil knew instantly what Melody had mistaken for a field. "Melody, what were the blocks for? Did you look at any of them?"

Melody nodded again as she tried to remember. "Some had words on them. People's names. And there were dates as well." She thought harder. "Oh, I remember now. That was the first place I went after I ghosted. I was looking for my mama but I couldn't find her. But Baby was there." Melody looked sad.

"Melody, do you remember what a graveyard looks like?"

Melody's luminous eyes went dull. Clutching her brother tightly she nodded. "It was a graveyard?"

Daffodil nodded. "Yes Melody, it was."

"Baby was just floating there like he didn't know."

"Didn't know what, Melody?"

"That he was ghosted. He looked like he was waiting for someone."

"He was Melody. He was waiting for his big sister."

Suddenly Melody's calipers disappeared. "I saw the gravestone. Everyone's name was on it except mine."

Jake moved over next to Santu. "They mustn't have been able to get anyone to engrave the stone," whispered Jake.

"Maybe she was not even getting buried there," murmured Santu.

"But the Deacon said . . ."

"Something is maybe preventing this from happening." Then Santu had another thought. He called over to Daffodil. "The names on the grave stone . . . maybe it is saying what Baby's name is."

Daffodil had another thought. "What language was the gravestone in?"

"My language," said Melody looking down at her baby brother.

"And what language is that?" asked Daffodil trying to draw Melody's attention back.

"Same language as everyone is speaking."

"Well," said Daffodil, "I'm speaking English."

Melody started laughing. "But I don't speak English."

Jake laughed at the round conversation. "I guess it doesn't matter here?"

Daffodil smiled. "I guess not." Daffodil had to ask the next question. "What did the gravestone have written on it Melody?"

Melody thought hard. "It said: 'Here lies Fritz Wagner, 1890-1915, killed in action. Elisabeth Wagner, 1892-1916. In eternal rest with Baby, 1916-1916. God be with us." She looked cheerless. "That's why I called him Baby. I remember now. I guess no one ever named him."

Baby was gurgling away into the radiola as if he knew what was going on and wanted to add something to the conversation.

"Perhaps," said Daffodil thinking that it couldn't change anything, "you should give him a name, now?"

Melody suddenly looked delighted. "Otto!" she cried out making the name sound very foreign with a sudden brusque accent.

Daffodil was surprised by the swiftness of Melody's decision. "That's a great name. Otto Wagner. Daffodil looked around the room. Inexplicably, everyone was smiling, even Bitsy and Dog.

As Daffodil turned back to face Melody she saw that bright yellow light was encircling the little girl who had finally lost her calipers.

"You," started Melody as she looked down at Baby, "are my little baby brother named Otto." As the final word was spoken Baby puffed out a ball of glowing yellow light too. Melody smiled at him serenely. "We are going home to mama now Otto. You will never be cold again."

Everyone waited for the burst of white light that accompanied Madame Glizsnort. But after a few moments Santu knew his earlier concerns weren't unfounded.

"Where is she?" he asked in agitation.

"It's okay, Santu," said Daffodil trying to calm the mood of the room. "Let's just wait a bit."

They waited and waited. Santu was getting more and more fidgety and Jake was following suit. Everything seemed to be moving in slow motion. Daffodil was getting really worried. What would they do if there was no more white light? She didn't want to know.

"All of us," said Daffodil finally, "need to try to bring Madame Glizsnort here. Maybe try to, I don't know, imagine her here or something. You too Dog and Bitsy." Bitsy nodded not understanding what she was supposed to do.

Shutting their eyes, they tried to visualize Madame Glizsnort in her burst of white light. Moments ticked by until finally they all felt the change. Even with their eyes closed they could sense its brilliance.

"But," said Blaze, "Madame Glizsnort isn't in there."

Peering into the dazzling luminescence they could see nothing except the intense glare of white light.

"What do we do?" asked Daffodil.

Melody was already moving toward it as if pulled by invisible strings.

"Oscar," Melody called out, "Oscar, Baby is my brother. And my name really is Melody but spelled wrong!"

"Melody," said Daffodil quickly, "you can see Oscar?"

She nodded rapidly. "Yes, Oscar has come to take us home." Melody was delighted. "You kept your promise Oscar. You kept your promise."

"Melody," said Daffodil again, "is there an older lady in there too?" Daffodil was trying desperately to see what Melody could see.

"Just Oscar," said Melody before she and Baby were enfolded by white light.

"Wait, Melody . . ."

But it was too late. With a burst of illumination they were gone.

Before anyone had even had time to contemplate why Madame Glizsnort or the other ghosted ones weren't there, or why only Oscar had come, or even why they couldn't see Oscar, Bitsy had taken over the radiola. She was singing a song into it as if she were doing a recording.

Daffodil smiled at her. "That's a very pretty song Bitsy."

"Yes it is my favorite. I was singing it when I met her." Bitsy pointed at Annabelle.

Annabelle looked as surprised as the rest of the group. She shook her head as if Bitsy had made a mistake.

"Yes," said Bitsy confidently. "It's her. That is why she's here."

THE SOLAR BATH

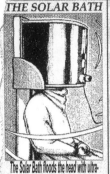

The Solar Bath floods the head with ultra-violet rays, clearing inflammation of the mucous membranes in the ears, nose, and throat.

STRANGE SIGHTINGS: BLACKWATER

Reverend Paul Augustus O'Connor of the Blackwater Church of Mortimus, has spoken out about the strange sightings that have intrigued the community. He has told the Herald Tribune that, "The children came and went before our eyes. They are ghostly in image and appear to be lost, perhaps trying, fruitlessly, to get into the church. I was unafraid and felt driven to offer them succor. As I approached them they vanished completely - as surely as an apparition from God himself."

The community are at a loss as to how to resolve the mystery. However, the population as a whole are trying to work together to help in any way they can. MORE P3.

FRANCE'S WAR DEBT

France's war debt to Britain is now 623,000,000 pounds. They also owe 798,000,000 pounds to the United States of America. Britain has approached France about repaying the debt but are sceptical about the funds being returned. **FULL STORY Page 5.**

CURSE SURROUNDS KING TUT'S TOMB

Since the discovery of Tutankhamun's tomb in 1922, constant rumors have resulted in announcement by Arthur Conan Doyle, that a "Pharaoh's Curse" is attached to the ancient site. With the death of Lord Carnavon and his brother only five months later, we are waiting for news on Howard Carter after he lifted the granite lid of King Tut's sarcophagus earlier this year. Presently the tomb has been closed again while Carter and the Egyptian Government battle of ownership. Story P7.

10 MILLIONTH MODEL T

The Ford Motor Company has manufactured over 10 million Model T automobiles this year. Henry Ford, a self made man has become an icon. His mechanized assembly line and his $5 a day rate for workers has made him a hero to the common man.

ADOLF HITLER FREED EARLY

After only 8 months of his 5 year sentence for his failed attempt after the unsuccessful coup at a Bavarian beerhall, Adolf Hitler has been freed from jail early. FULL STORY Page 9.

HUBBLE: "OTHER GALAXIES"

Edwin Hubble has announced the existence of other galactic systems. The possibilty of there being more galaxies in our universe has been professional historically ordinary...

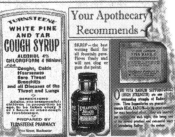

~Present day~

~BITS AND PIECES~

"What do you mean, 'why she's here'?" Daffodil was looking at Annabelle with renewed suspicion.

"She knows," said Bitsy. "She's seen me." Bitsy's face was hard.

Annabelle shook her head in confusion. "I swear I don't know what she's talking about." Again, the soft English accent drifted like bobbing notes around her and her eyes seemed at once innocent and unsure.

"The station," said Bitsy seeing Annabelle shake her head. "You cannot have forgotten the station."

Annabelle's heart sank. It had been real. "But that was so long ago," Annabelle said with her perfectly rounded words. The memory was a lifetime ago: a memory from the place she was born; a memory before music; of life before being dragged to America; a memory that had always been too hard to forget.

"Annabelle," said Daffodil, "come over to the radiola so Bitsy can hear you."

Annabelle's feet felt like lead. "I'm sorry Bitsy. I thought I'd imagined that."

Bitsy shook her head proudly. "I remembered and you didn't."

"That's true Bitsy. But why do I need to be here?"

"How much do you remember?" asked Bitsy.

381

"About meeting you? Not much I'm afraid. I was only four." There were too many other memories that had crowded her attention on that fateful night.

"It was the same train station where I lost my mommy and daddy. Don't tell Oscar but sometimes I used to slip out of the church and go back there. That's when I found you."

"That's right," said Annabelle feeling sick. She didn't want to remember the rest. That day had shaped her entire life; it had begun her descent into hatred and bitterness, feelings she had finally been freed from.

"You're mommy left you there all by yourself didn't she?"

"Yes," said Annabelle unable to stop a tear from rolling down her cheek.

Santu could see the vision. It was the same as the one he had seen the day he met Annabelle. It was a terrible image. A tiny, little girl left in the dark on a train station all alone. He closed his eyes and tried to push the visions away.

"Your mommy left you like my mommy left me."

"How did your mommy leave you?" asked Annabelle, only too glad to take the attention off herself.

"There was a mass-evacumation and everyone was running."

"A mass evacuation?" clarified Annabelle.

"Yes a mass-evacumation. There were so many people. We went to the train station to try to get away. My mommy was holding my hand but I think the people pushed me away. Dolly was with me." Bitsy held up her dolly as if it were show and tell.

"What happened after that?" asked Annabelle softly, her big blue eyes reflecting her sorrow. Daffodil was still having trouble getting over the gentleness of Annabelle's English accent.

"I was trying to see mommy as the crowd took me away from her. She was screaming." Suddenly Bitsy let out a mind numbing scream. It was hideous and painful and heartbreaking.

"That," said Jake, "is the same scream I heard on our first night. That's why I went out into the snow." Daffodil remembered the face at the window and nodded.

When Bitsy's scream had finally died down Annabelle uncovered her ears.

"We heard you scream like that when we first got here. It gave us quite a fright."

Bitsy laughed, turned herself blue, and flopped her tongue out of her head like she had been hung.

Annabelle pretended not to notice. "What happened next Bitsy?"

"There was a big sunburst."

Annabelle eyed Santu. Was *he* seeing what *she* was thinking? Santu shook his head. "I am not seeing an explosion. Not sure."

"Not explosion." Duette's voice was trembling. "Not bomb."

Annabelle glanced back at Duette. "Just a minute Bitsy. I think Duette might be able to help us."

Bitsy looked glum. "I can't hear her over there."

"Then, how about I pass on the information?"

Bitsy nodded reluctantly.

Duette's face was pale. Daffodil moved over to her side and assured her that she could deal with her empath skills now: "Just feel the flow of the potion." Duette nodded, not wanting to feel anything. Her breath had become rapid now but she tried to calm herself.

"She not explode . . . she go under train." Duette shook her head. She could feel the moment that Bitsy realized her fate. "I think she say sunburst to . . ." Duette rolled he wrist trying to find the words she needed.

"To forget," said Duel reading her thoughts. "To forget what had happened." Duette nodded at her brother.

"You've done really well Duette," said Daffodil nodding encouragingly. "It's okay, *you're* okay. You did it."

Duette looked exhausted but pleased. "Okay, I can do bit better now." Some color returned to her cheeks. But then everyone's attention turned to Bitsy.

"Why does that lady look sick?" asked Bitsy. "She didn't get left alone by *her* mommy too did she?"

Annabelle was still trying to comprehend that she and Bitsy shared a part of their lives. Liverpool Street Station. Annabelle had thought about that place every day for 13 years. And now she remembered it all.

"Well," said Annabelle gently, "your mommy didn't really abandon you. It wasn't her fault."

Bitsy screamed into the radiola again. She didn't understand that it wasn't anyone's fault.

"Bitsy," said Annabelle when the scream had worn itself out, "do you blame your mommy?"

"She let me go just like your mommy let you go."

"But your mommy didn't want to let you go did she? I mean she screamed because she was upset that you were dragged away. Your mommy didn't want to lose you."

"Then why didn't she hold onto my hand better?"

"I'm really sorry that happened to you Bitsy but I really think your mommy loved you and wanted you to stay with her."

"Not like your mommy?"

"No," said Annabelle realizing that the grief she had held onto for so long, was no longer there. "Not like my mommy. But you know what Bitsy?"

"What?" Bitsy asked warily.

"I don't know why my mommy did that to me but I don't blame her anymore."

"You don't?" Bitsy didn't understand. "But when I found you, you were so sad. I tried to take you with me. But you just kept crying. It was horrible. I didn't want you to cry. I wanted to bring you back to the church with me. But then that man came and took you."

Annabelle swallowed. She hung on to her newfound peace and pushed the memory out and away from her. That memory didn't matter either. She couldn't allow the awful experiences of her past to destroy her anymore. She had been given a second chance, a future, and that was what she had to hang onto.

"Yes," Annabelle said biting her lip.

"I followed you. I know what happened."

Santu was feeling sick. Trying to drive the images from his head, the sinister evil hatred of everything in the world pushed him to the ground. Annabelle saw him crumple and knew immediately what he was seeing, but she wasn't going to let the shame and hatred form inside her again.

"Well, you see Bitsy, we have both had some very bad experiences." Annabelle decided it didn't matter that Bitsy didn't remember how she died. It was more important for her to be free of the sense of abandonment. "Now it is time to let them go."

"Let them go where?"

Annabelle smiled at the simplicity of the question. "That Bitsy, is an excellent question."

Bitsy smiled proudly.

"I think," said Annabelle, "that they should go on a very long holiday."

"Oooh, where should they holiday?"

"Hmm, what about The Devil's Triangle?"

"I would like to send them there. Is that a real place?"

"Absolutely," said Annabelle feeling freer than she had her whole life. "What do you say then?"

"I say," said Bitsy looking cheeky, "that I think The Devil's Triangle is a good place for them. How do we send them there?"

"Well, we close our eyes and imagine all those awful things leaving our bodies and our minds. They can travel like light out of our heads and across the planet to The Devil's Triangle where they will be buried deep below the water and earth never to escape again."

"I can feel it!" cried Bitsy. And to everyone's amazement they could actually see a cool white stream ribboning from Bitsy's head. It stretched long and narrow, toward the ceiling.

"I can see it," said Annabelle. "Keep going Bitsy, keep going."

As the white wisp of long ago memories curled away from her, Bitsy's face relaxed.

"I'm sorry I couldn't save you," Bitsy said to Annabelle, still with her eyes closed.

"That's alright Bitsy. It was nice of you to try."

"It's gone," said Bitsy with a simple expression of calm. "I'm glad it's gone."

"Me too Bitsy," said Annabelle. "Me too."

"But so is the sunburst." An icy, white tear curved down Bitsy's cheek. "I remember now. It was the train . . ."

"Yes, Bitsy, but that just proves it wasn't your mommy's fault."

"She saw me going under the train. There were so many people. Everyone was pushing. The train was very full. All those frightened faces pushed up against the windows. It was moving, the train, it was moving. It was trying to get the out of the station . . . That's why she screamed."

"Yes, Bitsy, that's why she screamed."

"Yes, I just wanted to be with her."

I know Bitsy. But imagine being able to see her again."

"How?" asked Bitsy tiredly.

"Well, we need to find out some more about you."

"Like what?"

"We need to know things like: When your birthday is; or, what year you were born."

Bitsy shook her head. But then her eyes lit up. "It's in spring." She looked very proud of herself. "I remember because mommy used to say I was born with the sunburst of spring. That's why she liked that word so much. Sunburst."

"That's very helpful Bitsy. Do you think it was March?"

Bitsy shook her head.

"Do you think it was April?"

Again Bitsy's eyes lit up. She nodded enthusiastically. "I remember now." She looked both sad and proud. "My birthday is April the 4th. And I remember when I was born too."

"And when was that?"

"Aren't you going to ask me how I remembered?" Bitsy looked disappointed.

"Of course, Bitsy. I'm sorry. How do you remember?"

"Because our house had the same number. My mommy made me remember it in case I got lost. She liked the joke."

"The joke?"

"That our house was my home because it celebrated my being born."

"Well that is amazing Bitsy. You're very clever to remember all that."

"It was my life you know. I should remember my life." Bitsy's voice was becoming breathy. Tiredness was overtaking.

"Yes, that's true Bitsy. It is very good that you remember." Annabelle needed to hurry this along. "And what was the number on your house?"

"I was born in 1908 and I was eight when I ghosted."

Annabelle released a sigh. "So that means you ghosted in 1916."

Bitsy shrugged. She didn't remember how to do math.

"Well, Bitsy, all we need to know now, is your real name."

Bitsy was thinking hard. Most of the crowd had their fingers crossed. Daffodil noticed that Santu even looked like he was praying. She thought it wasn't a bad idea.

"Maybe," said Daffodil, "we could all join Santu in a prayer? It couldn't hurt right? Maybe, whatever is helping us needs a bit of help too?"

"I agree," said Annabelle remembering the feeling from the symbols.

Bitsy nodded at Annabelle's explanation. "I will pray for mommy."

"Yes," added Annabelle, "just concentrate on your mommy."

Bitsy nodded and closed her eyes.

Annabelle took a deep breath and nodded. Everyone closed their eyes and implored all and any beings that could help. Together they believed it was possible and that belief made it so.

A tiny voice emanated around them. It was Bitsy. "Florence. Florence Myrtle Fiddick." At once they all opened their eyes.

"Florence!" said Annabelle, her voice full of surprise. "Just like Florence Nightingale!"

"No," said Bitsy confused. "Florence Fiddick."

"Yes," smiled Annabelle still reeling in astonishment. "Yes Bitsy! You are Florence Myrtle Fiddick!"

All of a sudden Bitsy burst with yellow light.

"Oooh, look at me, look at my dolly!" said Bitsy as she turned to face Dog. She was thrusting Poppy at Dog as if he may have missed the fact that she and her doll now glowed with light. "It feels warm! It feels like a warm bath!"

Dog looked on. His happiness for Bitsy was real and true, yet he felt somehow removed from it all. Perhaps it was a form of self protection—he was never going to be touched by that golden light. But the right thing had been done; he had kept his promise and everyone had had the chance to go home. Bitsy was the last one. A sad smile lifted his face. He hadn't remembered anything since his return here. Not like Bitsy had. All he knew was that his name was Dog, and his dog was Scruffy. His friends Oscar, Melody and Baby had gone into the light. And now Bitsy was going too. There was nothing else: No memories of Before; no family; no names; no birthdays. Dog knew he was doomed. He waved at Bitsy. Bitsy darted to his side and he felt the warm glow of yellow light that surrounded her. It was like being teased with something you knew you could never have. Dog reached for her face but as his hand reached toward her, he jolted. It was not his light.

"Go home Bitsy, go all the way home. I will miss you most."

"Dog, you have to come too." Suddenly Bitsy looked terribly upset. "Please, Dog, you're like my brother now, you have to come too."

Dog nodded knowing he was going to lie to her. "I promise Bitsy, but it is your turn first." Bitsy would forget all about him after she entered the light.

Daffodil was panicking again. So was Santu. Again, the white light orb hadn't appeared to take Bitsy away and Bitsy was glowing like a yellow flaming star ready to go.

"What's going on?" Daffodil was finding it hard to keep still. "Bitsy is ready to go home."

"It took a while last time too," said Santu trying to keep the edge out of his voice.

"I know, but it feels different this time." Daffodil looked out the window. "And the daylight is coming."

Santu turned quickly to check outside. The rain had reduced to a drizzle and Daffodil was right: The sun was trying hard to penetrate the grizzly skies.

"You want to try that prayer thing again?" asked Santu desperately.

Daffodil shrugged the question to the group.

As they all closed their eyes to concentrate they didn't see the fog outside move.

~Present day~

~To sleep is to prepare~

B y the time they had opened their eyes again, a huge ball of glowing white light had grown in front of them.

All the animals were gravitating toward the light. The duck was biting at the cat's tail, the canary, with wings outstretched but not flapping, was following, and even Scruffy, Dog's pet was riding the yellow glowing ribbons toward the white light. Peering into the great shining brightness, Dog felt its pulsating grandeur. Still, he couldn't hide his distress. Wanting Scruffy to go into the light didn't stop him from feeling like he was being ripped in two. Scruffy had been his pet through all these ghosted years. Now Dog would really be alone.

Annabelle was worried and her questioning glances around the room proved her suspicions were founded. "Can you see anyone in there Bitsy?" Annabelle asked as Bitsy drifted toward the white light with the duck, dog, canary and cat in tow.

Bitsy nodded. "I see god," she said before turning to wave to Dog. Dog had never seen Bitsy smile like that. It was wonderful and sad and amazing. Dog waved back. How lonely he would be now. Scruffy had bounded away from him and toward the radiance without even looking back. Why hadn't he told the silly mutt he loved it? Just once. More than once. Dog's throat squeezed tight and he battled the looming tears that were burning his eyes. He wanted to say goodbye but his voice was lost, as he guessed, so was his soul.

Bitsy and her animal companions dissolved into the brilliant orb. They all heard her giggles well after the light had disappeared.

"The daylight is here Dog," said Annabelle. How could she console him about Scruffy? Dog looked devastated.

Dog nodded. The immobilization was flooding through his body. He wondered what would happen now. He was going to have to tell them he couldn't remember. Even the animals had found the light. There was no going home for him. Would they accept it? Would this mean they would all have to face defeat? Dog's eyes closed as the light rose. He would be still for a time now and in that time he could be nothing: Not Dog; not anyone. When the night came he would face the fury but until then he would just be nothing.

Blaze curled up on a blanket of newspapers trying to put out of her mind the furious ache that coursed her ankles and cut hands. It felt like fire had infiltrated her blood and her soul, creeping into her limbs; curling flames up through her injuries. She smiled at the irony.

Jake couldn't think of anything else now except sleep. It was like a long lost friend come to take him away from all of this. His fitful efforts without static had proved worthless in a world where concentration was everything. Until coming here he had never prayed before. There hadn't been much point. If there was a God, and he let such awful things happen to one of His children, then He wasn't much of a god at all. But Jake wondered if he hadn't been looking at it all wrong. Maybe praying was just a positive way of sending messages out into the universe: Messages that just might bring something good back to him. He turned the radiola dials until he heard that low hum of comforting static, sank down beside the purring machine, closed his eyes and thought big.

Santu had thrown everyone snack bars which had been mostly ignored. Sleep will trump hunger when it's so overdue. Slumping against a wall, Santu tried to chew on the block of sweet sticky nuts, but he couldn't taste anything. Perhaps it was because he was stuck in this nothingness, halfway between life and death, halfway between desire and truth, halfway to nowhere, no-when, and no taste buds.

Annabelle caught Santu's fatigued expression. Looking around the room, she faced a group of exhausted teens that looked as if they had fought a war and weren't sure if they'd survived or not. War seemed to be everywhere here. And it was far from over. Somehow Annabelle knew that she was about to face the biggest battle yet. She would be ready. She would make sure that whatever happened, this time *she* would be making the choices. There was no way anything was ever going to make her go back to being angry, bitter and self destructive.

Duel was rubbing his back trying to ease the pain of torn ligaments. Duette and Duel had rallied as only twins can. Sadness for Dog had passed between them, and a brief acknowledgement of their sure demise also traveled from one to the next. But they were more resolute than ever. Fighting was all they had ever done and fighting would be how they would go out.

Sleep cried for them, begged them to drift toward it, offered them reward for it. Sleep had no enemies, no opposition: It was all part of the scheme and it knew its own power. Before long, they all felt its will and succumbed to its force. Sleep felt better to have these children in its wake. It could offer them much needed succor; it could help guide them, for, there was an unforeseen tragedy coming their way and they would need rest to comprehend its divinity.

What they couldn't know, was that the coming daylight had saved them. When Bitsy had gone into the light, the Shadow was thrown into fury. Almost finished with consuming Bruises, it would soon bury her deep, deep down in the bowels of the earth. Time was the key to success. If it did not find another to feast on soon, weakness would drive it into the earth to look for lost souls—distasteful spirits of scum—weak and unsatisfying. Those souls had abandoned everything and were virtually useless to a ravenous void in desperate need of satiation. The unending hunger had become intolerable but it would not be long before the Shadow would have its fill. As soon as darkness allowed some much needed power, the dark mass would seize them all. There was enough feed inside that damn building to sustain its voracious appetite for a long, long time—or until the next ones came. And there were always more.

Choosing patience out of necessity, the Shadow consoled itself that all would be put right very soon.

Nearly everyone had anchored their sheets to something substantial and had curled up on the floor desperate to fall into a deadening slumber.

Daffodil, however, still stood at the window observing the sky. The rain had stopped and there was a fresh earthy smell to the air. Wisps of blue had managed to penetrate the gray icy clouds that had sealed them inside this no-when for so long. It was strange and almost disconcerting. Daffodil had grown used to their island-like isolation and her first instinct was doubt. She was surprised at herself. Had this place forced her back into a state of distrust or was she just learning to recognize it?

Either way, something was changing and Daffodil couldn't tell if it was good or bad. She swiped a look at the ground below as she moved over to join the others. The sweeping vision of green had told her that a thin sprinkling of grass was beginning to sprout. Too tired to wonder how that was possible, Daffodil sidled up to Annabelle. "The ice is melting."

"Yes," murmured Annabelle. "I guess life is here after all."

Cuddling up to a pile of newspapers, Daffodil smiled half-heartedly. Miracles *had* occurred here. Perhaps there was still a chance. If this place could sustain life; if grass could grow again; maybe there was hope after all.

As they drifted into the mysterious world of sleep each of them touched their own destiny.

Static Recording No.13—On Loop

D⊕G. 1906-1918. GH⊕STED AGED 12.

*U*m, hi, I guess. Oh yeah, Oscar says to tell you my name. That's pretty funny Oscar since I don't remember *my name. Fine. In this place, whatever this damn hell is, I have been called Dog. That's pretty much what I am, a crappy dog. What! Fine, Oscar says to tell you I'm called Dog because this stupid dog has been following me around since I ghosted. He doesn't remember* his *name either.*

Yeah, alright Oscar, don't have a coronary. The dog is called Scruffy. Glad we got that outta the way. What else do you want me to tell them? I don't want to tell them that. No. Why?

Fine. Oscar says I have to tell you what I remember so that everyone can go home. Personally I don't give a damn about going home. You have to have one first. I mean it's just a load of hogwash. We died and now we're here. The end.

Crumbs, Oscar, your face is as long as a gasman's coat! Yeah, yeah, alright, alright. Geeze. Who died and made you god?

Right, so I was born in the same year as those earthquakes in San Francisco . . . what year was that? Oh yeah, that's right, the almighty year of 1906. I remember that was all anybody ever said when they found out it was the year I was born. 'Oh, all those thousands of casualties' . . . Gadzooks. I wish had been in San Francisco! Then the earth could of just swallowed me right there and then.

I had a big family. I think my baby sister died first. Chicken Pox. She was about three. Then my brother got German Measles. He was seven. Not long after that my other two sisters and my father where going to the market in our horse and cart and there was a bad snow storm which trapped them in the middle of nowhere. They were six and eleven and my father was, I don't know, old. My mother and I were the only ones left. But then my mother caught Typhus. I think she was twenty-something.

Do you like that story? No? Oh so sorry. Oscar they didn't like the story.

Do you want me to tell them the lovely story about little red riding hood? That's much better isn't it—she gets eaten whole by a great big damn wolf.

Hey! Oscar stop it! Hell Oscar, no need to make my legs disappear.

That's better. Geeze.

I don't remember much else. I know I was alone. I don't know why I didn't get sick but I didn't, so don't think that's how I ghosted because you'd be wrong. I reckon I did it myself. I mean, I was alone, I was just a kid, I think twelve, everyone left me. What would you do? Anyway, no one gave a damn.

Yeah, righty-o Oscar, you gave a damn—you gave me a damn headache, that's what you gave me!

Anyway that's the last thing I remember. The vision of falling. The panic. You know, that's just human to panic a bit even if it's something you want to do. Hey Oscar. Oscar knows about panic, I've heard his recordings. Yeah. Something bad is coming. Something worse than hell.

~Present day~

~A IS FOR ATONEMENT~

"I can't remember, I can't remember, I can't remember!" Dog had been yelling into the radiola trying to get someone's attention. All the human people were lying on the floor looking dead. Darkness was starting to fall and none of them had woken yet. "I can't remember!"

But no one could hear Dog because Jake had reset the dials.

Dog was feeling frantic. The Shadow was going to come, and no one was doing anything. Somehow he had always known it would be his fate. Him and Bruises: soul mates in a lost world of chaos and blackness. "I can't remember!" Dog was exhausted. The other place had really wrenched the last bit of fight left in him. He drifted over to a window. The dark skies outside felt different: Perhaps it was the first time in a long time that he could remember seeing stars?

Dog looked at the dead people lying on the floor. Why weren't they ghosting? Where had their souls gone? Had they just spirited themselves away without taking him? He drifted over to the boy by the machine. There was a faint static noise humming from it. He sat in the middle of the boy's body.

Jake woke with a fright, his heart frozen. As he jolted upright, Dog leapt up in the air. To Jake, Dog looked both shocked and angry. Blinking himself awake, Jake saw how dark it had gotten and how still everyone was. He knew what Dog was thinking. After the life Dog had led, death would be the first thing he concluded. Quickly, Jake jumped up and adjusted the dials.

Somewhere from the impermanent world of sleep, Jake sensed a memory. In the static he had heard Dog's words and now he understood. Yes, Oscar had made them all forget, but Dog had even more reason to push the memories away; Dog had taken his own life. If it wasn't for Oscar, this last remaining ghost would have been lost in the ether forever. What Dog's fate might have been if Oscar's pure heart had not found him, Jake did not want to know.

The darkness in the recording made Jake shiver, the weight of it almost real. Perhaps his ability to hear inside the static was changing? It was disconcerting but it helped him retrieve the information. The main question was: How to tell Dog?

"Dog," said Jake when he had reset the dials, "it's okay, we're just very tired, we're not dead." Jake beckoned to Dog who had flashed over to a corner. "Please Dog, come over here so I can talk to you."

Dog wasn't moving. He eyed Jake suspiciously.

Jake heaved a sigh. He didn't want to disturb everyone but until each person was moving, Dog wasn't having any of it. Jake untied the sheet wrapped around his waist and nudged each of them gently. There were annoyed groans and yawns but as consciousness unwrapped the covenant of sleep they each pulled themselves back to the in-between world that was holding them captive.

Jake moved back to the radiola. "You see, Dog, you didn't hurt anyone. They were just asleep. Now, please come over here and talk to me."

Dog eyed each of them. So they weren't dead. He didn't make them all die and he wasn't all alone. Something inside Dog felt weird, a shift of some kind that he couldn't quite understand.

Santu was the first to speak. "What is going on?"

Jake moved over to Santu so that Dog couldn't hear him. "I heard a recording in the static when I was sleeping." Jake had everyone's attention now.

"What were you hearing?" asked Santu rubbing his eyes with his palms.

"It was Dog. It was awful."

"I can't remember! I can't remember! I can't remember!" Dog was screaming into the radiola. Could they hear him now?

Jake went to talk to Dog but Santu grabbed his arm. "Jake, wait, first be telling us what you know."

As Jake explained, Dog continued to yell into the radiola.

"Now, I have to go talk to Dog before he thinks we're scheming against him. He's very upset."

"No kidding," said Santu waving at Dog.

"Dog," said Jake, "we know you can't remember. Please don't be upset about it. We're trying to think of a way to help you. Okay?"

Dog looked disgruntled. He kind of liked yelling into the machine. It took his mind off what was about to happen.

Daffodil was trying to stop an endless yawn. "Jake," she said, her eyes barely open, "put your sheet back on."

"Oh yeah, just a minute," said Jake as he leaned toward the light of the radiola again. "Dog, I just want you to stay calm. It's really important." Unfortunately, that wasn't what Dog wanted to hear.

"I can't remember! I can't remember! I can't remember!!" Now Dog was screaming at the top of his voice but his lips weren't moving: His mouth was arched open baring his teeth and his face was ashen, but noise was pouring out of him like vomit.

Jake panicked. This was really bad. "Dog," Jake yelled back trying unsuccessfully to outdo him, "you've got to stop!"

"I don't deserve to go! I don't deserve to go! I don't deserve to go!" Dog couldn't stop now. It was an outpouring of all the anger and hatred that he had kept jailed inside suspicious and distrustful bonds for too long.

And, it was just what the Shadow had been waiting for.

Gathering all the strength it had left, the black vortex of hatred raced toward the wrath it could feel in the air. Delight seized its centre. It would get its fill at last. So many tastes: Pity, fear, resentment, rage; all wonderful in their own right. And this time it would take them all.

Winds whipped up from the earth; the disgusting taste of fresh grass blades pulled from the mud, were spat far away: New growth must be destroyed. How had this happened? How much control had the mist taken from it? No matter all would be righted now.

Before anyone had a chance to prepare, the fury of the tempest was upon them.

The Shadow had come and it was full of madness. There was no time to be lost. It soared high up in the air stirring and whisking its conflicting currents into faster and faster rotations. Under its pressure, several huge and ancient tree carcasses bent, before snapping like twigs. All the hatred and fury and blame thrashed and surged through the windstorm; whispers coiling in the undertow.

With maximum power achieved, the Shadow then blasted its way downward aiming for the building full of bitter flesh. Smashing at the side of the heavy wall, it cracked the exterior before heaving itself at the upper level widows.

The smell was delectable, the plan made all the more real.

With the top of its whirlpool spinning in one direction and its base in another, the Shadow had cultivated enough potency to push past the irritating, protective crystals and their ridiculous glow of love and compassion.

As it forced itself inside, the whispers of its intent surged through the air like dust, swirling and swathing its grated charcoal filth over everyone—ensnaring them in its trap. When the dark mess finally hit the powerful crystals, its outer layer cringed. But any attempt to recoil was thwarted by the might of its core. Throwing another burst of energy outward, the winds reached further inside, so close now to the plump meal of disgust and shame, so very close.

The currents aimed for the boy hanging onto the wooden structure, the thing that hissed that awful static. No matter, the interference was no match for this dark windstorm. And the boy had more hateful things done to him in his short life than the Shadow could have imagined. What delight. There were plenty of others too, but consuming the boy would take a very long time—just like that lovely girl with the bruises.

Tearing harder, it forced itself beyond the borders of the room and, eating hundreds of flying newspapers for appetizers, pitched toward the boy. All those ancient articles of horror and fear swirled into the funnel, yellowing birds curling and flapping toward their doom.

The room was being torn apart. The east wall of the church was collapsing threatening to take the second floor with it. The severity of the vortex's power was greater than ever before. Everyone was hanging on for dear life. Being buffeted around by their tethered sheets was agonizing, especially with the injuries Blaze and Duel already carried. This was no ordinary attack: It was a deluge of loathing and censure, with enough vehemence to destroy them all. Each of them knew it and each of them vowed silently to fight with everything they had left.

Voices circled the victims, filling their heads with doubt and self-hatred. Daffodil cried out for the others to take no notice, but no one could hear her against the battering of the whirlwind and those awful whispers.

Jake should have listened to Daffodil earlier. He could feel the Shadow's intent immediately. The loose sheet—the same one he was supposed to have re-tied to the radiola—had coiled away with the currents, flapping and twisting into the vortex, dissolving within seconds. Jake's only chance had been to hang onto the old wooden device, hold on for his life. But his fingers were slipping. And the old radio was being pulled in toward the windstorm anyway. In the inevitability of the moment, Jake understood an overwhelming truth. In those brief seconds, he promised himself, no matter what happened inside that dark thing, he would not let its hatred break him.

Optimism is admired in most circumstances but here, in this cruel and thankless place, it is a foolhardy enterprise. Still, there are those that have found such strength. And Jake will always be remembered as one.

The echoing whispers began to laugh. 'Ahh, there are many delights here! A suicide too. That shall be next. But life and its pity are much too delectable—they must be taken first! Come boy, you hanging on to that block of wood. You have faced the most abuse, and by your own maker too! You have seen the death of love taken out on you and your soul is forever contaminated!' The reverberating voices clattered around Jake's ears. 'Come to us. We shall feast upon all that you are.'

Laughter ricocheted around them all.

"Don't listen Jake," screamed Daffodil.

But the voices didn't stop. 'Never discount the strength of hatred and anger. It is the most delicious thing in the world. And the most powerful.'

Jake's felt like his flesh was being torn from his bones. The winds were too strong, the cruelty too real. He was losing his grip; the sweat on his skin was betraying his strength. As he tried to reposition his fingers, he felt them slip.

Annabelle felt her sheet give way. The old fabric that was tying her to life was ripping. A torn sheet was no match for these wild currents. She tried desperately to grab hold of the tearing pieces but it was nearly impossible to do anything whilst being pummeled by whipping winds.

Jake's grip gave way. He felt himself being pounded up and down as he flew backwards, feet first, toward the mouth of the Shadow. Desperately, he tried to grab anything, anything at all, but everything was moving in the same direction: En route to destruction.

Santu had reached out desperately to try to grab onto Jake's clothing but the fabric slid through his fingers too easily. For a split second Santu and Jake locked eyes. Fear joined them, an often visitor, this time to escort life from a boy that had never had a chance to know of the beauty of existence.

Annabelle had made the same reckoning and she was finally ready. Her second chance had been given to her for a reason: Suddenly, she knew why those symbols had given her fleeting freedom and why she had to do what she had to do. *Come on*, Annabelle screamed to herself just as her delicate fingers finally found the split in the cloth. Gritting her teeth, she knew what would come next.

Just as the swirling winds raised themselves to maximum potency, Jake knew there was no way out and Annabelle was ready to make her last offering.

Finally, the only thing that was anchoring her to life, was giving way. The hiss of splitting material gave Annabelle a speedy count-down to her doom. Just as if she were to detonate a bomb or perhaps blow out candles on a birthday cake, the numbers fell through her mind just as the pull took hold.

"No!" Daffodil screamed as she saw what was happening. "No, Annabelle, no!"

Annabelle gave Daffodil a fleeting look of inescapability before being hauled toward the rotating mass. By milliseconds, Annabelle managed to intercept Jake's ultimate oblivion. As Jake slammed into her, Annabelle was ready. With all her strength, she pushed the boy away. It had little effect but gave her just enough time to be drawn into the Shadow first.

Annabelle's frightened expression was the last they saw of her as she disappeared into the dark obscurity.

With the winds still frantically thrashing, Jake knew he was next. Annabelle had only given him a second more of life. Still it was an extraordinary act. Knowing his demise, Jake lifted his head and smiled at Daffodil. She would never know how he felt about her; she was the kindest person he had ever met. He wanted so much to hold her again.

Just as the hideous tempest reached for the boy—the very boy that held so much delicious abuse—it suddenly lost velocity. Jake thumped heavily down on the floor smashing his chin against the boards.

The Shadow was choking, gagging at its very core. Its wind draughts were now reversing as if they were trying to expel something putrid. The retraction of the currents sent Jake flying in the opposite direction, toward the radiola again, the force crushing him against the once sturdy machine.

The spinning force of detestation now appeared to be hesitating. Outer winds were still whipping with vigor but its center had stopped still as if it were confused, perhaps even afraid. Feeling like a snake that swallowed a dinosaur, the Shadow drew back its multitudinous voices; its own violent roars still heaving through the air, swelling and exploding in bursts.

But within its heart, an implosion struck at its very core. The violent, twisting, black cloud suddenly shrank back as if struck by its own hateful snakes. Its arms drew back as if for support, its mouth closed in shock.

They watched it teeter: Backwards, backwards, forwards, backwards. Like a drunken warlord it staggered, its intention reversed, as it headed toward the graveyard, its threat retreating with every second.

Exhausted and breathless Daffodil screamed. "Where's Annabelle!?"

"Is she on ground?" asked Duette as she tried to untie her sheet. Her hands were shaking so much she couldn't even make her fingers bend to her will. Duel managed to untie himself and went to help his sister.

"I can't see!" screamed Daffodil.

Blaze crawled over to the window and then using the window ledge she pulled herself up.

"Blaze," said Daffodil. "Be careful. That wall is about to crumble."

"Her sheet tore. I saw it. She ripped it through!" said Blaze ignoring Daffodil's warning.

"What?" said Daffodil as she kept searching the dark grounds.

"She did it on purpose." Blaze turned toward Jake. "To save him."

Daffodil couldn't concentrate on what Blaze was saying. She needed to get out there.

"I have to go." Daffodil moved to run toward the stairs.

"Wait." A small voice called out to her from the radiola. Daffodil turned to face Dog's familiar sound.

"Wait for what?" asked a dazed Jake as he rubbed his head.

"She's not on the ground," said Dog.

"What do you mean?" asked Jake amazed that the dials were still in place. "Where is she?"

"It took her like it took Bruises." Dog's remorse was obvious.

"You mean it really took her?" asked Jake. "The Shadow really has her inside it?" It all seemed so surreal. Annabelle was really gone?

Santu could see Daffodil's distress. He moved next to her and touched her shoulder.

Daffodil couldn't accept it. "Duette, Duel, can you read her mind? Can you sense anything?"

Duette glanced at Duel. Neither of them wanted to tell Daffodil what Annabelle was going through. They shook their heads simultaneously.

"No," said Daffodil knowingly. "Don't do that, tell me what you just said to each other."

"She not succumb," said Duette. "That all I know. Her last thought that she surprised by her strength and she not succumb."

"But what does that mean?!" cried Daffodil. "If she didn't succumb, what does that mean?!"

Duette shook her head. "I cannot know. I sorry Daffodil."

Daffodil was looking around the room at everyone as if they could explain it to her. How could this have happened?

"Didn't you see this Santu? Didn't you see this happening?" Daffodil cried accusingly.

Santu was shocked. "Laying blame is not going to be helping anyone Daffodil, and besides, Annabelle has barely spoken since we are getting back from the graveyard. I thought it was because she was adjusting."

"Adjusting? Adjusting to what?!" Daffodil felt like she was on a merry-go-round. "Why is everyone talking in riddles!?" Collapsing to the ground Daffodil burst into tears. "Annabelle had changed—she had a whole new life to live."

"This is what I mean Daff," said Santu. "She was adjusting." He motioned to Jake to comfort Daffodil.

Santu had some other worries he needed to figure out. Why had the Shadow recoiled like that as soon as it had gotten hold of Annabelle? He moved over to the radiola to question Dog.

"Dog, this isn't your fault. It is very important you are understanding me."

Dog was curled up and floating in a ceiling corner. Finally he had learned how to make himself go really high and Oscar wasn't here to see it. When Santu spoke to him he just squeezed up tighter.

"Dog, you are needing to come down here to talk to me," said Santu calmly. "You are not thinking you owe us this much?" Dog looked down at Santu and then flew toward the radiola.

"I'm sorry," he whispered into it. "I'm really sorry."

"Dog, this is not your fault. None of these things that are happening to you Before, and none of these things here are your fault. You must understand this."

"But," said Dog very quietly, "I don't remember."

"You don't have to be whispering Dog. That thing didn't come here because you yelled. It wants all of us. It would have been coming anyway."

"But your friend is gone. She went like Bruises did."

"Yes," said Santu trying not to let his voice give him away. "I know. This is why we have to get you home. Then, *we* can all be going home too."

A pearly tear slipped down Dog's gaunt face. Shiny and white, it dripped to his chin before disappearing.

"I am not wanting you to cry Dog. I am wanting you to be happy."

"But I don't remember."

A hideous roaring sound cried out in the distance. The echo rocked the ground around them, rattling the crumbling walls of the church. Startled looks crossed from one to the other.

In the shock, Dog disappeared.

As Annabelle felt the pull of the Shadow, she hoped she had done the right thing. Hopefully she had stopped it from taking Jake. Her last look at everyone had been difficult: Their horrified faces, their outstretched arms, their relief.

They could have been true friends, yet she had been rude and bitter and distrustful. But then there had been the graveyard, and those strange symbols, newly etched across the headstone like a child's attempt at hieroglyphics. And then she had slipped and fought desperately to save a life that she had only ever wanted to have over. Annabelle had always known she would not have much time on this earth but she hadn't guessed it would all end in such a cruel way: Regaining innocence only to sacrifice it again so quickly. But it was the only way to save them. It was true: Innocence trumps hate.

The winds were hauling her in: Fierce and full of the loathing she had once known. Her skin felt like it was being ripped from her body: A thousand icy splinters stung her; a thousand barbs wounded her soul, scratching and slashing at it. Blustering currents tore at her hair, each strand ripped from its root. Blood would come now; no one could survive this monstrosity. Unseen voices screamed all around her, daring her to fight, laughing at her pain. Yet there were other voices too—but they were not of the Shadow. Where they came from Annabelle was unsure but she knew there was hope. And then she saw who she was looking for: The faded image of a little girl with bruises, and eyes so sad they would break a strong man's heart.

Just as she felt the hideous mass reach for her heart, she knew there was only one thing to do. As she felt herself explode into a million pieces, Annabelle said goodbye to the world.

~Present day~

~Ghosts of Mist and Shadow~

Everyone was crowded around the sturdiest part of the crumbling wall looking out the window. In the far distance they could see that the core of the Shadow had swelled. A white light distended at its middle while the dark base and swirling top battled each other like opposing teams.

"What's going on?" asked Blaze as she leant on the window sill.

"It looks," said Jake, "as if it's fighting with itself—trying to tear itself in two to get away from that glow."

Daffodil gasped. "Annabelle."

"What?" asked Blaze staring intently at the dark windstorm. "You think Annabelle's doing that?"

Suddenly the white light inside the Shadow shot upward through the top of the black swirling spiral and sped quickly toward the moon, a shooting star in the dark night.

They watched, speechless.

"Where do you think Dog has gone?" asked Jake finally. If they couldn't find Dog, they had just watched their own future.

Daffodil went over to the radiola. "Dog? Dog it's all right now. The Shadow has gone. You can show yourself again." But Dog was nowhere to be seen.

Santu wasn't getting any visuals. "Maybe he is just hiding. Keep calling him." As Daffodil leant into the radiola's light gently calling Dog's name, Santu instructed the others to look up any newspapers from 1918.

"Check the 'Deaths'. A suicide: Something to do with falling. A 12 year old boy. And I am knowing this sounds a bit yellow bananas, but look for a name that is like a dog; maybe a type of dog or a name that you would be calling a dog? I don't know. Just be keeping this in mind, yes?"

The others nodded and went to work.

✳ ✳ ✳

Time moved on. Articles were discussed and dismissed and Dog remained invisible to them. The strain of watching their fellow companion die a hideous death, and knowing that her pain would last for days while the Shadow slowly consumed her, was beyond unnerving.

They tried to eat the snack bars that Santu handed out but they were Annabelle's. It felt strange and insensitive, but they had to eat.

Daffodil would not give up. She continued to talk to Dog explaining that they missed him and that they needed him to come back. Everyone was counting down the time knowing that each passing minute was a minute closer to their untimely demise.

Finally it became obvious that Dog wasn't going to show himself just because they wanted him to. As Daffodil turned away from the radiola something amazing stopped her in her tracks. The brilliant celestial body that appeared in front of her was overwhelming. Its pulsating grandeur was hypnotizing but there was something else, something instantly familiar. At once Daffodil realized who she was looking at.

The ambient light that flooded the room grabbed everyone's attention. And, in that slow motion moment, each person knew what everyone else was thinking.

Annabelle.

"Annabelle. What happened to you?" Daffodil's voice was almost a whisper.

Annabelle smiled. Of course, they couldn't understand yet. "There is much I need to tell you." Her voice was soft and kind, her face radiating love. "I have been inside the Shadow. It is a cruel master of many and it is powerful beyond reckoning. But inside it I saw my truths as if they were written for me to value. Revelations have been many and wondrous." Annabelle sighed. So much to tell in so little time.

"The Shadow holds no power over innocence. This is most important. There are many voices inside that hideous vortex. Some are cruel and hateful. I believe they are its essence; what *made* it. But there are other voices too. They are the voices of light."

Duel remembered his brief experience in that horrible thing. "I heard them too. They gave me hope. I used them to help Duette and me."

"You are very strong Duel," said Annabelle sounding worldly. "Do not ever let anyone tell you otherwise. To sense those voices you have truth and goodness inside you."

Santu was confused. "Are the voices helping to save you also?"

"The only reason I was able to fight, was because I had been cleansed of all immorality and my cursed past. I was cleansed because of the graveyard." Annabelle looked directly at Santu. Her radiance streamed out toward him.

"The graveyard?" Santu asked mesmerized.

"Santu, you remember I told you about the symbols on the gravestones?"

"Yes."

"Please listen carefully. Those symbols are made from light. They are to protect innocents when they are finally buried by the Shadow—protect them from the eternal abyss. If you believe in destiny, then you will believe this is as it's meant to be." She sighed. "I found Bruises in that thing. She was almost gone. So strong. I found her heart. It glowed still for her sister. That is how she resisted being fully consumed: Love." Annabelle's voice had grown quiet, barely audible. "Love," she repeated in wonder.

"Annabelle," said Santu, "where is Bruises now?"

"She is safe now." Annabelle shook her head in amazement. "The soul fragments."

"Is that what happened to you? Is that why you changed after touching the symbols?" asked Daffodil.

"The symbols have been made by the force that is trying to help set all these souls free. It fights the Shadow."

Jake was confused. "What force?"

"I believe that is where the good voices come from also. I believe that it was made in the same way as the Shadow: By people's emotions. But I believe it was born from hope not distrust."

"But how did *you* get out of that thing?" Jake doubted it was 'love'.

Annabelle smiled at Jake's scrunched up face. "The purity of my soul," she said gently. "The innocence created by the rebirth after touching those symbols. I probably could have destroyed it but again, the purity of my soul would not allow it. The strangest truths are always filled with irony."

"So the Shadow still killed you?"

"Yes," said Annabelle looking down at her own bright form. For the first time, her face became sad for all the living she had wasted. "It has much evil inside but it was the powerful turbines of wind that will tear a body to pieces. As much as this may be so, it could not take my soul." She smiled now and the light source around her flamed even further. "I made sure of that."

Questions were bombarding Daffodil's brain. "Have you seen Madame Glizsnort or any of the ghosted ones that have passed over?"

"No. I was taken to see my mother, not in the skies but in the earth. In life, as in death, she is weak and fearful and gave herself no credit, but she also gave herself no blame." Annabelle looked momentarily disappointed. "She says she abandoned me because she truly believed that someone would find me and take me in, never intending for such awful things to happen to me. Nevertheless, her reasoning is small and selfish. Responsibility is what we are born to earth with and we must endeavor to take it into our hearts. I was lucky to get a second chance." Annabelle nodded towards Santu and then Jake.

"How do we know if they have all gone home?"

"Ahh," said Annabelle remembering what it was like to feel distrust. "Where do you think the white light would have taken them?"

Santu couldn't see any images coming from her words. How could they trust her? "Where are *you* saying it has taken them?"

The soft ringing laughter of Annabelle's sweet voice rang out around them. "Home," she said simply. "Which is where I must take Dog. Do you remember Madame Glizsnort telling us that after she died she tried to find her Lost Children? She said that when you first ghost you are free of all attachments and you are able to take others into the light." She waited for them to understand. "Madame Glizsnort was too late. When she finally found them, after she ghosted, they couldn't see her. Madame Glizsnort has fought the Calling. And that is wrong. There will be grave consequences."

Daffodil felt the hairs on the back of her neck stand on end. What had Madame Glizsnort done?

Annabelle knew she had said too much. "I have a little time before my Calling, I can take Dog with me." Daffodil and Jake exchanged horrified glances. They both ran to the radiola and started calling for Dog again.

Dog hadn't gone anywhere. They just couldn't see him. The radiance of the beautiful lady in the light had made him nearly invisible. He didn't want to be seen before; he wanted to be left alone. Now that he *wanted* them to see him, they couldn't.

Annabelle felt the sadness of the little boy. Her eyes turned toward him. There was a faint glow high up near the ceiling beams. Smiling kindly, she reached out her hand.

As Dog floated down Santu called to Daffodil and Jake and motioned for them to see what was happening. Annabelle took Dog's hand and beamed. Her light spread all around him. The delighted look on Dog's face was amazing. The soft sounds of angels singing hummed around them.

"I feel warm," said Dog as he stared into her lovely eyes. "I forgot how nice it is to feel warm."

"We are all part of this grand plan, Dog." Annabelle looked across to Santu. "Santu, you saved my life so that I could save another. And Jake saved yours so that you could also."

Santu had no words. Annabelle hadn't just saved Dog; she had probably saved them all.

"But," started Santu.

"Hush now," said Annabelle. "You must listen. Jake has heard enough information about Dog to engrave his gravestone. It is very important for these ones we have helped to have a life marked in stone. These engravings will also weaken the Shadow further."

"Do you know how we are destroying the Shadow?" asked Santu.

"You already know Santu. The means is with you and has been all along." Annabelle looked between Duette and Duel. "Together, you two have the power." Annabelle smiled at the memory of what their anger toward her had created. "With Daffodil's help, all will be righted and the balance of this place will be returned."

The group was looking at Duel and Duette as if they had been keeping this a secret. But the twins simply shook their heads in confusion. They had no idea what Annabelle was talking about. But Daffodil did. When she thought about it, it was obvious, especially after Oscar's performance with the lightning.

Still holding Dog's hand, Annabelle looked into his eyes with boundless love and compassion. "Destroy the Shadow," she said, "and the other force will be there to help you."

"What about you Annabelle?" Santu asked.

"I am at peace. It is all I really ever wanted. It is a shame my life was wasted with hate and self-pity but luckily I found virtue before I passed on. Be sad for the child who could not see love or kindness but do not be sad for me now."

A tear rolled down Daffodil's cheek. She had truly disliked Annabelle when she was cold and cruel. It would have seemed impossible to feel sorry for that person. But Daffodil knew better than to judge. After all, there is a certain amount of innocence required to love and Daffodil sensed that Annabelle had been tainted by cruelty from the moment she was born.

Annabelle smiled in Daffodil's direction. "Now I must take Dog home. I have been hearing them call me for a time and I must answer soon. They have told me Dog's real name is Cane Abelle." She smiled at Dog. "Did you know that Cane in Corsican is dog?"

Dog looked delighted. His surprised face circled the room.

"How did Oscar know?" asked Dog. "Everyone was named for their living days and not their ghosted ones."

Annabelle laughed. "That, my new friend, is because we all need names. Our names in life as in death, define a purpose. It is usually unintentional by the living but they often pick up the threads of past lives or loves to entwine them about us; to help in the design; to guide us forward without taking away our past. Oscar was very intuitive."

Jake had one last question. It was probably inappropriate but he had to ask. "So Dog can go into the light even though he . . ." The words jagged in his throat.

Annabelle finished his sentence. "Even though he took his own life?"

Jake nodded and eyed Dog apologetically. Dog had remembered as the last loud roars of the Shadow trundled through the sky. That was why he had disappeared. But now in the light, holding the angel's hand, Dog's thoughts had smoothed and his torment had all but disappeared.

Annabelle sensed Dog's calmness. "Love is love, Jake. I know you have not had much of it in your short life but you will and it will be so wonderful you will cherish it every day. There is no blame here. If you want to be loved you will be."

Annabelle finally looked at Blaze. Her kindhearted expression surprised Blaze. It was no secret that the two had disliked each other. Blaze softened under her stare. Streams of light reached out toward Blaze as she sat holding her bandaged feet. There was something about Annabelle's gaze that was extraordinary; it sparkled up through her ankles and through her body. Was Annabelle healing her?

Annabelle continued. "What Dog did was born of desperation. That is understood." Annabelle's finger ran across Dog's fringe. "As angry as Dog got, he never really gave up hope. Scruffy proves that. Scruffy *was* his hope."

In the excitement of it all, Dog had forgotten to ask about Scruffy. "Will he be there?! Will he be where I'm going?!"

"Yes of course. Scruffy can think of nothing else except you. He is waiting." Annabelle looked for more questions but there were none. "I will take Dog now and then you must destroy the Shadow." Annabelle looked at Daffodil. "You know what to do."

Daffodil nodded. "Thank you Annabelle." The words seemed too simple. Daffodil shook her head.

Annabelle smiled sweetly at her. Annabelle's face was angelic, her dark blue eyes warm and gentle. Daffodil felt her heart swell. Annabelle was conveying thanks in her own way. Daffodil smiled at the beautiful girl turned angel.

"Goodbye Dog," said Daffodil. "Goodbye Annabelle."

Annabelle waved and Dog copied her.

Before they disappeared, an angelic song expanded around them and the old crumbling church was filled with incredible harmonies— the musical chords of a thousand instruments, all deftly orchestrated by Annabelle. Daffodil smiled. Annabelle was still in control of certain things—even in the afterlife.

~Present day~

~SHADOW SHIFTS~

"What do we do now?" asked Blaze as she ignited the cabin fire by focusing her thoughts. Outside, the rain was drumming again, a manic countdown to an unknown future.

"I guess," said Daffodil, "we figure out how to destroy that bloody Shadow."

Everyone was still feeling the exuberance that Annabelle had left them with. There was a strange ambiance that now surrounded them and it was filled with hope and excitement and chance.

Blaze laughed. "Too bloody right." Blaze had managed to control the fire until it was creating perfect flames and then she released her focus. Controlling fire was becoming second nature. Santu was impressed that she had learned to manage her power so quickly.

Slowly, Blaze unwrapped the bandages on her ankles. The purple angry bruises that had stretched around her swollen skin had disappeared—so had the swollen skin. It was an Annabelle miracle. That's what Blaze would call strange occurrences from now on: Annabelle miracles. It was an odd feeling: Being thankful for events that had been caused by someone you thought you despised. Blaze shook the loathing away. If she had been taught one thing here, it was not to hate: Hatred and anger destroyed. Blaze walked on her mended legs. *'Thank you and sorry,'* she whispered as she walked backward and forward.

Duel saw Blaze walking as if she had never been injured. No one had told Blaze but he was sure that without Annabelle's help, Blaze would never have been able to walk properly again—especially without proper medical help. Then, suddenly, Duel realized that his back didn't hurt anymore. The searing pain charging up his spine had ceased and, without the pain, he could think again.

Duel threw Daffodil a meaningful look and together they nodded in confirmation.

"You tell them," Daffodil said to Duel.

"We annihilate the Shadow with positively charged lightning." Duel decided to keep it simple. No point in confusing everyone.

"Lightning?" asked Santu.

"Yes," said Daffodil as if it were obvious. "Do you remember when Annabelle annoyed the twins and they shot that bolt of electricity or whatever it was at her?" Santu had forgotten. Jake had not.

"Why didn't anyone say anything? I thought I imagined it."

"I think," said Daffodil, "that it was so surreal that everyone wanted to pretend it *wasn't* real. Remember, it was only our second day." It seemed so long ago now—almost another lifetime. And in some ways it was. They were all forever changed; they had all begun new lives.

"So what do we do now?" asked Blaze as she jumped up and down, checking her legs.

"That depends," said Daffodil.

Jake was watching Blaze with curiosity. Why couldn't she just accept that her legs were healed? "On what?" he asked.

Daffodil looked over to Duel and Duette. "On whether you two know how you did it the first time?" Duel and Duette returned looks that said they did not.

Santu thought out loud. "You directed it toward Annabelle. Were you being angry?"

Duette remembered what she had felt right before it happened. "Yes, much anger."

"Me also," said Duel. "I think I was feeling Duette's anger too."

Daffodil was worried. "You can't fuel it with anger though, that's really important. It has to come from a positive place."

Santu was feeling frustrated. Duel and Duette didn't seem to have a clue how to recreate the event.

"Perhaps," said Santu you are needing to understand how lightning works?"

The twins shrugged and nodded.

"Lightning is being a form of electricity and electricity is being formed by opposites: The negative and positive charges. The ice and water in the clouds is needing to be electrically charged. Inside the cloud, the cold air is having ice crystals and the warm air is having water droplets. The droplets and crystals are bumping together and moving apart in the air, yes? This rubbing makes static electrical charges in the clouds; the positive charges are moving up inside the cloud and the negative charges are moving down." Santu nodded toward the darkness outside. "Perfect conditions: The sky is full of these cumulonimbus clouds from the storm."

Instantly Duel understood how it had happened.

"We were the positive charge and Annabelle was the negative."

Santu shrugged. "Is possible."

Daffodil realized how obvious it was. "The Shadow is a mass of negativity." Why hadn't she seen it earlier?

Santu nodded. "Good point. We would have to be drawing it to the church somehow."

Daffodil realized where Santu was going. "Of course. Lightning always strikes the highest point in the area."

"Exactly," said Santu. "Positively charged particles will be rising up taller objects like trees and houses."

"And church steeples."

"Exactly. Then the positive charge, from the earth or the steeple, is reaching out to the negative charge with a streamer. When these channels are connecting . . ."

"You get lightning." Duel finished Santu's sentence.

Daffodil had an idea. "I can line the walls of the church with lodestone and lightning-strike crystals. I have some really rare ones—nice and clear, all the way from Diamantina. They will increase the power of the charge." Daffodil started rifling through her case. "Quartz is piezoelectric which means that it actually generates electricity when it's under pressure. That's why they use quartz in watches and other electronic items. When the pressure builds, the electricity has to discharge and . . ." Daffodil pulled out a stone and held it up for everyone to see. "It causes this zig-zag in the quartz."

"Great," said Santu finally feeling like they were getting somewhere. "We are needing updraughts and downdrafts to create charge separation."

"The Shadow," said Blaze.

"Some gold stars for you," said Santu now caught up in the buzz. "We are going to be needing a tremendous amount of charge to destroy it."

"Isn't that dangerous for Duette and Duel?" asked Blaze.

"We are having to somehow be using the positive charge of the earth and the insulating properties of the atmosphere without inhibiting the electric flow." Santu was thinking hard.

Duel and Duette were feeling anxious.

"But," started Duel, "there is only one thing you haven't figured on."

Santu looked surprised. "What is this?"

"Duette and I have no idea how to do this."

Jake had been taking it all in but there was one thing nobody had considered. "Has anyone realized that the lightning could destroy the church?"

Santu nodded. "I think we are needing to demolish this church."

Jake didn't understand. "But the radiola; all those newspapers; the love letters . . ."

"These are all just things, Jake," said Santu. "These are all the things that kept those ghosted ones in their loop. They are free now and their past should be too. I would have been thinking that you would be the first person to want to burn all that sadness to the ground."

Jake was shocked. He turned to Daffodil in confusion.

Daffodil hadn't thought that Jake would be so attached to all that stuff. But now it dawned on her: All those things signified Jake's new life; they represented his future.

"Jake," said Daffodil, "all that stuff helped guide you to find yourself, that's true. I understand why you don't want to destroy it but none of it is necessary now. You've found out who you want to be and now you have to to let it go. It's not yours and you don't need it."

Jake felt strange. Why did he care about old newspapers and an ancient machine? And then it all fell into place. That's why he had turned to antiques and old things; that's why he had spent endless hours researching the whereabouts of rare objects: He was looking for a different past; other people's pasts. Every one of the objects that he studied had a story and none of those stories were about him. They were like life rafts in an ocean hungry for his misery.

Jake's sad smile made Daffodil's heart go out to him. Somehow she understood what he was thinking.

"You're right," said Jake finally. "I don't need that stuff."

Daffodil returned his smile. Santu patted Jake on the back.

"So," said Santu triumphantly, "we burn it down!"

Everyone laughed, even Jake.

"Now," said Duel, "we just have to figure out how we create lightning."

Time had slipped by and the murky daylight had returned. Drizzle fell quietly, muffling thoughts and dazing minds. Slumber summoned them like the urgent call of a lost friend and they acquiesced without much of a fight. But with the dreams came the nightmares: Dark and strangely familiar, comforting in their own cruel way. Santu dreamed of the snakes that had coiled through his subconscious for years; Blaze dreamed of fires and burning children; Daffodil found herself lost in a void where no one could see or hear her; Duel's father's ears bled; Duette's mouth sealed; and Jake, without electrical interference to hush his mind, tossed under the weight of storms and their static. And in doing so each of them faced their fears.

Jake nudged Daffodil. "I know how Duette and Duel need to make lightning." Jake had woken with a start. The dream had been fierce and unrelenting but it gave him verification too.

Daffodil stirred. She stretched trying to hurry the tardiness of consciousness along after deep dreams. "Wake the others first Jake," Daffodil said. "Give them a minute to wake up though, okay?"

Jake woke the others and waited impatiently.

His dream and its static, the storms and the sacrifice had made Daffodil protest loudly. But as he spoke, Jake's confidence made her see that this was the only way. He smiled at her, grateful that she would feel this way, but this wasn't about him; this was about all of them and Jake could see no other way out.

Slowly everyone came to understand. And for that Jake was thankful.

Blaze was also going to have to test herself. She would have to use her power tactfully: not too soon, not too late. It would be difficult and she may be faced with the decision of taking another life but it was a job that had to be done.

Darkness had descended again, and with it, the rain had returned. Plans had been made and discussions had gone on long enough to convince everyone they had a chance to destroy the Shadow and escape. The problem was that neither Duel nor Duette could practice without a negative charge. That meant that their first performance would be their only performance. The danger was not beyond them. If they failed they would be swallowed whole and the others would follow. The responsibility was too enormous to contemplate.

Once again, with Daffodil's potions and Duel's ability to transcend minds, they were all put into a mind-bond. They must all stay positive; think affirmative thoughts, no matter how their fears taunted them.

First, they would head to the church. Daffodil would line the perimeter with lodestone and lightning-strike crystals and then they would each climb the tall, black, skeleton-like trees. Each of them would hold tight to the quartz crystals that would reflect the positive energy that the twins would create, and aim the streams of power toward the Shadow.

All of them except Jake. Jake was to remain inside the church. He was the sweet meat that the Shadow craved. Yes, Jake had chosen himself to be the sacrificial lamb. After all, it was he that the Shadow wanted more than anything. So, the dark mass of hatred would have him. Perhaps, he thought, he should have touched those symbols in the graveyard. Maybe then his soul would be saved. But, as Annabelle had said, if you believe in destiny, then you will believe this is as it is meant to be. At least he could save Daffodil.

In theory it all sounded like it could work.

Santu had told them as they prepared: "If I am right, the Shadow will be destroying itself."

"And if you're not?" asked Duel.

"Then my friend, I am wrong."

Taking deep breaths, they ventured out into the cold, rainy night.

The trees were slippery—slick with the falling rain—and climbing them was taking more energy than they had in reserve. Daffodil had lined her crystals around the church and had watched Jake go up to the second story where they had all spent so much time together. Tears rolled down her cheeks—there was no need to hide them in the rain. Jake had simply walked into the church as if he would do it a hundred more times; again and again. He had not said goodbye, he had not turned back. He had simply gone back to all those things he now realized he no longer needed. Perhaps he would listen to one last recording; perhaps he would read a love letter from a man of war to a teacher that had lived so many years before; perhaps he would allow himself a tear. Daffodil did not know and she would probably never find out.

Gritting her teeth she climbed one of the old trees. Her hope of having a vantage point into the church vanished. She would never see him again. After tying herself to its top, she closed her eyes and prayed. Perhaps her mother and grandmother would greet her when this was all over.

Duette and Duel swapped thoughts easily. However crazy this all sounded they were confident that they could at least give it all they had. No one was considering goodbyes. No one was considering the consequences of failure.

In their combined state of consciousness, they knew when Jake was ready. Duette and Duel readied themselves, trying to sense the conflict in the air. From the tops of the trees, the moonlight revealed a cloud-filled night sky, the darkness crouching around them in wait, the rain caressing their skin with sorrow.

From this height they could see the heavy mist that enclosed their camp, the same mist that threatened them with no way out. Still they remained staunch. Together they contemplated a future, a future with every one of them in it.

Jake was touched. He had never felt such comfort. This was what it was like to have friends. They felt his gratitude and returned it twofold. But then it was time for Jake to remember.

The recollections came to him in a rush of abhorrence which the others deflected. Their positivity was key. Still, they could not prevent some of the information from seeping into their weary minds. Poor Jake had had an insufferable childhood. To make him remember all that horror was cruel. But Jake didn't stop. He let the memories come at him with full force.

"Remember to breathe Jake," said Daffodil to the night. "Remember to breathe."

The arrival of their aggressor came more quickly than anticipated. The shape-shifting winds of the violent mass approached with such velocity and fury that they were all taken aback. Jake felt its presence and quickly tightened the several sheets which tied him to the radiola. Ultimately, the Shadow would take him—but not without a fight.

Santu spoke to the twins in his mind: '*Stay calm, just be thinking of this as a job. Anger can be constructive too. Stay positive!*'

The Shadow soared toward the church, its currents pitching it forward. Delectable miseries were waiting for it. Finally! And there was someone alone. And *so* lonely! All those wretched memories oozing from the boy— the boy it had wanted most.

Defeating the soul of such loss, the victim of such terrible hatred was irresistible. *Devine.* And so close. The taste of victory was beyond thrilling. The rotating winds swirled in rage, thrashing at the night air, its fingers reaching through the smashed windows of the church toward Jake.

Jake felt the fierce turbines pulling at him. His body was being tugged, feet first, toward the destructive force. As the vortex spun harder and faster, Jake felt the radiola shiver and jolt in the direction of the windstorm. In a bizarre moment Jake felt as if the radiola was fighting for its life too. With eyes shut tight and holding on firmly to his tethers, Jake began reciting a prayer. It was one he had heard long ago, from whom, he had no idea, but right now it was all he could do to stay calm.

Duette and Duel went to work. They summoned their fury toward the black swirling shape, enticing it, reminding it of all it could have; confusing it.

The Shadow faltered. The hatred had moved. Had the boy left the crumbling building? Another delicious call of loathing was coming from *outside* the church. Bewildered, it hesitated.

And that was the moment they had been waiting for.

Duette and Duel switched all their emotions to positive ones. They thought of their brave father, Duel's heroic fight for his sister, Annabelle's strength, every accomplishment they had ever made, and they threw it all at the skies. They forced their powers into the cumulonimbus clouds, aggravating the water and particles of ice, forcing them to create positive and negative charges.

Palms spread outward, Duette and Duel drove the streaming light upward: Negative and positive charges forced together.

Now the Shadow's fierce winds were storming toward *them*.

But something was happening that they had not expected. In its confusion, the Shadow was separating: Part of it moving toward the church and part of it moving toward Duette and Duel. And it had grown. How it had amassed such power was beyond all of them but it was twice the size and it had grown extraordinarily strong.

Daffodil saw what was happening. 'Jake!' she screamed. 'The other half will take Jake!'

But Duette and Duel were already trying to thwart the unexpected division. With his right hand Duel was firing a lightning stream into the hurling winds by the church, and with his left, he was discharging more energy into the surrounding clouds. Duette was doing the same, firing a charge into the hideous mass as it approached them.

Like lions in a cage, the sparking steps of jagged light zapped back and forth inside the clouds. The air was crackling with pent up energy, the atmosphere ready to implode with their combined power.

The sky was lit up like a festival.

Spiraling currents forced themselves at the already crumbling wall of the church. Spinning backward and forward like a washing machine teetering on the edge of a cliff, it managed to dodge the lightning streams.

Jake felt the winds now pushing and pulling at him as if he were a retractable toy. He was bashing his head into the radiola one minute, and then being heaved away from it, the next. If it went on too much longer he'd be knocked unconscious and he did not want to enter that thing without having a fighting chance.

"Now!" screamed Duel.

And with that, Daffodil, Santu and Blaze held their large quartz crystals up above their heads. Duel and Duette spread their hands and arms wide and with a striking movement the electrical storms inside the clouds shot out around them.

The noise was tremendous. Massive lightning rods coursed the sky finding striking points with the quartz crystals. The force nearly knocked them to the ground but their makeshift attachments held fast. The quartz ignited and the lightning grew in strength, doubling in width and crackling and booming like a sonic rip.

Duette and Duel forced the light strikes around the sky to gather even more power before throwing them at the two halves of the Shadow.

The sound was horrific even to a vengeful ear. A thousand voices screamed out in agony—the sounds of a war that should never have become so. Louder than the roaring of the lightning, the sky was filled with their cries.

But nobody stopped.

The two whirlpools sped toward each other as if, united, they would be stronger.

That was a mistake.

When the tossing currents met, the twins were able to force all their strength into the one mass. For Duette and Duel being united *did* escalate their power. As they pumped the massive lightning explosions into the tormented vortex they sent their final message to Jake.

Now it was Blaze's turn.

Duette fired an immense bolt of light toward the church steeple. The strike had the effect they were hoping for: The church roof immediately surged with fire.

Daffodil prayed for Jake. She hoped he had been quick enough.

Blaze had gone straight to work, encouraging and pushing the flames, forcing them down through the broken windows and across the wooden floors. As each flare of fire struck a box of articles, a burst of flames ignited another fire and so on until the inside of the church was engulfed.

When the fiery upper floor finally fell through to the ground level, Duette and Duel forced the Shadow backward. It was still struggling, putting up a fight that could have refloated the Titanic but they hadn't finished the attack yet.

As the voices from inside the Shadow screamed, the twins pushed it further and further, backward, toward the church. The lightning-strike crystals and lodestone burst into light creating an intense force-field that electrified the entire building. By the time the hideous mass had realized its fate, it was too late: The Shadow was being forced into the electrified inferno.

High pitched shrieks filled the air as its defeat became obvious: The tomb of hatred had lost the fight and it knew—no triumph would be had now.

The church fire had been fanned further by the insidious winds and was now curling amongst the dark currents like fingers suffocating a child. The lightning streams that were still being thrown at it were carving great slices from it that immediately shriveled to dust. As the Shadow was chopped and burned and slowly destroyed, wisps of black rose up and out, high into the sky; perhaps the souls of all those trapped inside being freed.

Just as Duette and Duel began to struggle with the immense effort of it all, the Shadow finally erupted in a massive explosion: The strength of which they hadn't predicted. The violent release of energy was so ferocious that all the trees, including the ones on which they were perched, were snapped in half.

As they fell backwards, toward the ground, they could each hear an unknown prayer being recited in their minds.

If there had been time, they would have seen the grieving angel's arms rise.

Blackwater Herald Moon Tribune
Tuesday, August 16ᵗʰ, 1977—
One Shilling

ELVIS 'THE KING' DEAD

*A*t 42 years old, Elvis Aaron Presley has been found dead on the bathroom floor of his Graceland home in Memphis, Tennessee. The autopsy report has been sealed from the general public until 2027—50 years from today.

'The King' shot to fame in the 50's with his suave moves and catchy songs combining gospel, rock-and-roll and rhythm and blues crossing all the racial divides of the time.

In 1958 Elvis was conscripted into the United States Army and, as the U.S. were not involved any wars, he was sent to West Germany where he received his Sergeant's stripes in February, 1960.

Elvis also acted in many Hollywood movies and became an idol to the majority of the U.S. population.

LOCAL NEWS HEADLINES
LAST RUN FOR PAPER

Although the The Herald Moon Tribune is run by volunteers, we are sadly announcing the ceasing of business one week from Friday. Blackwater now has too few residents to continue the production of the paper. We want to assure the few remaining locals that we have done everything we can to persist but we also have become victims of the situation which has caused extreme financial hardship for the last few community members.

Blackwater has now receded into a ghost town: Streets are empty, shops have closed their doors, even leaving stock still on the shelves. Homes have been vacated without even being sold. Unfortunately, at this stage, the town looks to be lost forever.

Before we go we must offer our gratitude to the very dedicated and hard working Herald Moon contributors: Mr. Walter Bailey and Mr. Thomas Bentley, Mrs. Agnes Underwood, Mr. George Winchester, Mr. Stephen Montgarcy, Miss Lynette Turnley, Mrs. Pieta Rosely, Mr. Douglas Hornby and all the other locals that helped us turn out a great anecdote.

We wish to thank our loyal readers and offer appreciation to those of the community that stood up and fought for this paper right until the very end.

Now, my friends, it is that end and we sign off in sadness and with a great sense of loss for all that has been. We must however, keep the hope, that one day, we will ink up the printing presses and reel off one more great story.

Until then, goodbye Blackwater.

~Brought to you by~

PSYCEDELIC SWIMMERS—*The Best Psychedelic Beachwear On The Market!*

BUZZ RECORDS—*New Vinyls:* Saturday Night Fever ~ The BeeGees; Rumors ~ Fleetwood Mac; Bat Out Of Hell ~ Meatloaf—**All The Latest Hits!**

~Present day~

~The Mist Will Rise~

S antu was the first to come around. The bright light hurt his eyes and he raised a palm to shield them. Blinking several times, he tried to understand what he was seeing. His head was throbbing and he felt like his blood had been drained from his body.

The six of them were lying in a circle, their feet meeting at the middle. Although completely surrounded by mist, Santu recognized the graveyard. White fog rose like a tower around them—it was so thick that all he could make out was the gravestones that had been left for the ghosted ones and a small circle of light high above him.

At least Jake had made it out of the church. Santu nudged him. Jake grunted before squinting his eyes open.

"Jake, your head is being covered in blood."

Jake sat up, wincing as he did. "So is yours."

"Oh," replied Santu as his fingers touched the sticky fluid on his forehead.

"Are we dead?" asked Jake looking at the white mist that encircled them.

"Maybe," said Santu feeling the back of his head for damage.

Jake nudged Daffodil.

"Time to wake up and be dead," Jake said drolly.

Santu laughed and then rubbed his ribs. "Do not be making me laugh. That was a hell of a gravity check."

Daffodil heard Jake's voice and was hit with a rush of relief but she couldn't open her eyes.

Jake motioned for Santu to wake Blaze, who was lying very still beside him. Santu prodded her. Blaze murmured her annoyance and Santu rolled his eyes and shrugged at Jake. Jake smiled.

"Try the other two," said Jake.

Santu forced himself to stretch his feet forward to bump Duette and Duel.

"Come on," said Santu exhaustedly, "wake up."

Daffodil had managed to sit up but her eyes wouldn't open.

"I can't see," she said.

"It is helping," said Santu, "if you are opening your eyes."

"Oh you're so funny Santu." Daffodil lifted her heavy arms up to her face and pulled her eyelids apart with her fingers. "Are we dead?"

"This," said Santu, "is a popular question."

Blaze had managed to force herself up. "What's the popular answer?"

"Well," replied Santu, "my favorite one is being 'no'."

"Yeah," said Blaze looking pale and ill. "I'm voting on that one too."

"Great," said Santu. "Then we are choosing not to be dead. What do we do now?"

Daffodil was still holding her eyelids open. "Everyone is covered in blood."

"Mmm," said Santu. "The explosion."

Daffodil suddenly remembered it all. "Oh yeah that's right. Did we kill it?"

Santu nodded. "I think that is why we are here."

Duette and Duel were too exhausted to speak. Both of them had bad burns on their palms and their bodies felt like they had been thrown under a stampede of elephants. But they had done the job. They had destroyed that horrifying Shadow. Whatever that meant for them now was unknown but they mentally congratulated each other, amazed at what they had been capable of.

Everything was suddenly dawning on Blaze. "Why are we in a circle?" She thought again. "And how did we get here?"

Santu raised his head up to the towering white fog around them.

Blaze was confused. "You think the mist brought us here?"

Santu shrugged. "I think it might have been healing us too."

Daffodil had let her eyes close again. "Yeah, I don't think falling out of a 40 foot tree does a lot for your health."

Jake felt unbelievably tired. "So what do we do now?" Slowly he lifted himself off the ground and went over to look at the unmarked gravestones. There was no longer a gaping hole in front of the gravestone meant for Bruises. Beneath the thin layer of mist covering the ground, Jake could see a fine cover of grass. He stared at the symbols on the gravestone—the same symbols that Annabelle had touched.

"I guess we mark the gravestones," said Daffodil skeptically.

"With what?" asked Santu. "I am forgetting to pack my gravestone engraver."

Daffodil used her fingers to open her eyes again. She stared directly at Santu. "Oh you're all kittens and cream today, aren't you?"

Santu laughed. "I am a fluffy kittens," he said with a girlish lisp, his shiny black curls bouncing up and down.

Daffodil ignored him and lifted herself off the ground to go talk to Jake. If she raised her eyebrows really high, her eyelids opened enough to see.

"Hey," she said to Jake. "I'm really glad you made it out. I couldn't consider not ever seeing you again."

Jake was deep in thought but he was glad to have Daffodil there. "Thanks Daffodil."

"I know it must have been awful for you."

Jake shook his head. It was over now, no need to go back there again. "Daffodil, do you think if I touched those symbols it would have the same effect on me as it did Annabelle? I mean, it would be good to be free of it all."

Daffodil sighed. "There are some things we cannot change, things that have happened to us, things we cannot control. But Jake, it is better to focus on today. If you worry about what might have been, if you had a good mother, or your father didn't die, then you are not considering how great you are now. The past doesn't have to define who you are but it definitely can show you the person you want to be. If you touch those symbols, you take all that you have learned here away. When Annabelle was here, she didn't discover anything that could change her—until she touched those symbols—so for her it was different."

Jake stared at the strange markings. To be free of all the humiliation and hurt would be incredible. But Daffodil was right: He had just learned how to be himself without any of those other considerations. When he first got here none of them knew about his past, none of them judged him. He was free from it all. He had learned to communicate, to touch, to feel, to laugh. And he had been useful. Memories may have formed him, but they would not define him. Jake shook his head. He did not need the symbols to change him—he had already done that himself.

"No," Jake said finally, "you're right Daffodil. I don't need them."

An idea unexpectedly dawned on Daffodil but it was asking a lot and she wasn't sure what to do.

"Um," she said quietly. "I think I know a way we can engrave these stones but it's a lot to ask."

"What Daff?" asked Santu. "Anything could be helping."

"Well, I think if Blaze, Duette and Duel have enough energy they could help."

Blaze was ready. Whatever she could do, she would. "I can do it. Tell me what to do."

"I think," said Daffodil, "that lightning and fire could scorch the stone."

Daffodil caught Duette looking at her burned palms. The wounds looked painful beyond comprehension. Daffodil felt awful. Shaking her head she turned away from them. She had nothing to help: no crystals; no balms.

Even though Duel was burned and bloody and exhausted he was excited that he had found this new power. "I can do it without Duette. Let her rest."

Duette closed her eyes in relief. She had always been the strong one, but perhaps not anymore. Duel had come into his own and she was proud and thankful that he now felt confident enough and powerful enough to take the lead. She nodded at him and her eyes conveyed what her thoughts could not. Duel was filled with pride. His sister understood him and it felt like a new bond had been made. It would be such a great story to tell their father. Would he ever believe it? Would they ever see him again?

"What do we need to do?" asked Blaze.

"I think Duel will find that he can create the charge by himself now," said Daffodil. "And Blaze, you can manipulate the force by adding fire."

Daffodil turned to Jake. "I'm sorry Jake but there is something else you should realize."

"What?"

"Jake, you hear inside static." Daffodil waited a moment for the information to sink in.

"Yeah," replied Jake nonplused, "and I hear very high-pitched sounds." He shrugged his shoulders.

"Static," said Daffodil, "is energy, electricity."

Jake nodded; that was obvious. "But I don't make the static, I can just hear inside it."

"I'm not sure that's true Jake."

"I don't understand."

"Jake, no one else touched that radiola except you. I didn't want you to lose your confidence so I didn't tell you about that power socket."

Jake was confused. "The socket made it work."

"The socket had no electricity running to it Jake," Daffodil said gently. "The church had no lights, no heat, no electricity."

Jake looked accusingly at Santu. "But Santu, you plugged it in. You saw it had electricity. Didn't you?"

Santu who had been stretching, was caught off guard. He grimaced. "Jake if that receptacle had worked it would have thrown me across the room. You saw the point. It was scorched and burnt out."

"But why didn't you say something?" Jake was looking from Daffodil to Santu. He didn't understand what they were trying to tell him.

"Jake," said Daffodil softly, "don't you think it's a bit unusual to *need* static to go to sleep?"

Jake didn't. He had never thought about it. Static helped him sleep so he listened to it. He shook his head defensively.

Santu didn't see the big deal. "Jake it is pretty cool you know."

Jake felt like his head was too heavy for his body. He sank to the ground trying to understand what they were saying. "It's just another reason for everyone to call me a freak."

Santu shook his head. "No one here is calling you anything but a hero."

Jake wasn't listening.

"Jake," said Santu. "You are volunteering yourself as bait to tempt that godforsaken monster of a thing. You are risking your life for all of us. You even escaped a burning building. You are are being a legend, a man of stomachs." Santu collapsed down next to Jake and pretended to punch him in the abdomen. "*And* you can be making electricity. What do you think would have happened if we could not have used that radiola?" Santu didn't wait for a response. "We would all be inside that Shadow having our souls devoured, this is what."

Daffodil nodded. "He's absolutely right Jake."

"Yep," Blaze added, "chew toys. That's what we'd be right now, chew toys for the Shadow."

Duette and Duel through positive thoughts at Jake.

Jake knew straight away what they were doing. He smiled at them. "I just never realized."

Daffodil smiled. "And now you do. So you want to find out if it's true?"

Jake shrugged. "Let's find out what I can do."

Santu slapped Jake on the back. "Give it all you have got."

"Okay," said Daffodil taking a deep breath. "It's like a triangle. If Jake can create the electricity then Duel can create the discharge and Blaze can control it with her firepower. Duel if I tell you what to write on the headstones I think your telepathy will help Blaze with the delicacy of the composition."

"Let me just get focused," said Duel. The others nodded and tried to do the same.

Daffodil shut her eyes tight and tried to remember everything they had been told about the ghosted ones. "Ready when you are," she said finally.

"Ready," said Duel as he placed his palm on Jake's shoulder.

Blaze was on the other side of Jake. "Me too," she said as she placed a hand on Jake's other shoulder.

Jake shut his eyes trying to imagine the wonderful relaxing sound of static. As he focused he felt his mind slip backward as if his thoughts were sliding on the downward loop of a rollercoaster. Trying to stay steady, he concentrated harder.

Duel felt the change in the air. Quickly he seized the energy and threw a thought to Blaze.

But Blaze was already on top of it. To her it felt like the oxygen her fire craved. It was exhilarating but she would have to work hard to keep it under control. Steadying herself she focused on the headstones. As the bright discharge flew from Duel's fingers, Blaze centered her attention and held up her free hand waiting for Daffodil's words to guide them.

As Daffodil spoke, Blaze curled her forefinger in the air, divining the cursive script that would finally be engraved upon these gravestones.

They all listened to Daffodil's words remembering each ghosted one as she spoke.

'BUGSY'
Adam Adams (Scottish)
Beloved son of Catherine and
Professor Hamish Adams (Entomologist)
b.May 8ᵗʰ 1910-d.June 14ᵗʰ 1917
Orphaned aged 2
Killed by air raid attack in London aged 7
Loved and loved by, his Bugs.

'WONDERBOY'
Benjamin Oisin Walsh (Irish)
Beloved son of Ciaran and Darragh Walsh (Volunteer Private)
b.November 19ᵗʰ 1910-d.December 27ᵗʰ 1918
Orphaned aged 7
Died from Influenza aged 8 years
Loved Comics and Games

'SCRAPS'
Henri Emile Thenault (French)
Beloved son of Antoinette (Nurse)
and Francois Marcel Thenault (Pilot)
b.September 1ˢᵗ 1909-d.September 1ˢᵗ 1919
Orphaned aged 8 years
Buried alive after illness aged 10 years
Likes Playing Spider-Jacks and Whispers
Dislikes green potatoes
Forever with Tooting the Mouse

'OSCAR'
Ford Whitman (American)
Beloved brother of Pearl and Jet ('Buttons' and 'Bruises')
b.1903-d.October 1917
Died in German attack on frontlines near Passchendaele

Orphaned Aged 13 Died Aged 14
Loves cars
Will always be remembered for protecting
the Lost Children and ghosted animals

'BUTTONS'
Pearl Whitman (American)
Beloved sister of Ford and twin sister Jet
b.1906-d.1916
Orphaned aged 10
Lived for 6 months after Jet died
Died of starvation aged 10
Loves Fidget and collecting buttons

'BRUISES'
Jet Whitman (American)
Beloved sister of Ford and twin sister Pearl
b.1906-d.1916
Orphaned aged 10
Died from injuries after mortar attack aged 10
Stayed with her sister until the very end
Sacrificed to the Shadow but loved forever

'MELODY'
Melodie Sofie Wagner (German)
Beloved daughter of Elisabeth and Fritz Wagner
b.March 19ᵗʰ 1907-d.November 12ᵗʰ 1916
Orphaned 8 years
Died from Polio aged 9 years
Loves the Piano and her Baby Brother Otto

'BABY'
Otto Wagner
Beloved son of Elisabeth and Fritz Wagner
b.1916-d.1916
Orphaned aged 0
Died at birth
Beloved brother of Melodie

'BITSY'
Florence Myrtle Fiddick (English)
b. April 4ᵗʰ 1908-d.1916
Died during mass evacuation aged 8 years
Loves Whispers and Collecting things
Loved and Loved by, Poppy

'DOG'
Cane Abelle
Last surviving member of his family
b.1906-d.1918
Orphaned aged 12
Took own life aged 12
Now with Scruffy

Jake couldn't believe what was happening. He was creating electrical energy. His whole body thrilled with the charge. Both Duel and Blaze were using it to reproduce their powers. Jake smiled to himself: He truly was a freak—everyone had been right about that—but if this is what freaks could do he wanted more of it.

As the last words were etched into the gray stones, memories of the ghosted children and their lives filled the air. Grief and sorrow were palpable but there was a light within the sadness that reminded them that these orphaned ghosts had finally found home.

As these thoughts swirled around them like living beings, the surrounding mist began to mirror the yellow glow of the ghosts' reflections. Mesmerized, they watched in wonder at the manifestations.

And then, as if in a dream, each gravestone began to glow like a sun. Speechless, they shared confused looks.

"Don't be frightened," came the familiar voice of Madame Glizsnort. Looking much older, she appeared tired, a woman who had struggled with what life, and death, had to offer. "We are all here to thank you." Madame Glizsnort's arms were extended out directing everyone's gaze to the ghosted ones around her. Floating in a circle was: Bugsy and his bugs; Scraps and Tooting; Wonderboy; Oscar; Buttons struggling with Fidget; Melody; Baby; Dog and Scruffy; a very active duck, a cat and a few other animals, all chasing each other, twisting in and around the luminescent children.

The only ones missing were Bruises and Annabelle.

Daffodil felt faint. "You haven't found Bruises?"

Madame Glizsnort smiled kindly at Daffodil. "Bruises is waiting for us. She is in there."

Everyone looked around. There was nothing except mist.

"In the mist?" asked Daffodil.

"She is waiting for the final moment. By destroying the Shadow you have saved Bruises soul. Well, you, and Annabelle, and the symbols."

Blaze was confused. "What do you mean?"

"It is of no concern to you now. You have done something more extraordinary than anybody else on this earth. Including me. And I have had more than a vested interest."

Santu's suspicions were rising again. "What are you meaning, 'a vested interest'?"

Madame Glizsnort smiled. "The name given to me by birth is Grace. Grace Walsh." She waited for some kind of recognition. Everyone's faces were blank except one.

Blaze looked at everyone wide eyed. How could they not realize? "Your Wonderboy's *sister*?"

"Benjamin's sister, yes."

Something twisted inside Blaze. "But Wonderboy is . . . he is my ancestor."

"Benjamin. Yes." Madame Glizsnort smiled.

"But if Wonderboy is *your* brother and he is *my* ancestor . . ." Blaze felt strange as if she were being turned inside out.

Understanding was dawning on the others.

"Oh my god," said Daffodil. "That would mean Madame Glizsnort is your great great grandmother!"

Blaze felt sick. All those stories of mental illness running in the family came back to her. Wonderboy's own mother took an overdose of barbiturates after the death of his sister Sarah. Her death left them orphaned, alone in the world.

"Why did you think you were chosen Blaze? Because of that ridiculous medal?"

Blaze's mind was reeling. "But the fire. I can start fire."

"That my dear, also runs in the family."

Was Madame Glizsnort reading minds too now? Terror stripped away any veneer of calm. Blaze wondered how much danger they were really in.

Daffodil was trying to understand what was happening. "Are you saying you can create fire too?"

Madame Glizsnort looked grave. "Unfortunately, I too have been taken to the brink of death. My mother did not just imbibe those opiates herself; she also administered them to me. Benjamin heard me screaming for him to leave and that's what he did—he ran away." A fleeting look of sorrow crossed her face. "There was a moment where I knew death had come for me—even at such a young age. But, as I'm sure Blaze is aware, sometimes we are offered a choice at these times. *I* chose to live, which of course, meant that ultimately, I chose to suffer." She suddenly looked hesitant. "I too . . . ," she hesitated, "accidentally burned down a very important building—one you are now quite familiar with."

"The church?" asked Jake trying to follow the weird conversation.

"The sky was full of lightening," went on Madame Glizsnort. "I panicked. I loved that church, and I was sure my ghosted brother, Benjamin, was hiding there. I could feel the electricity in the air, it was teasing my gift, arousing the anger I felt after I lost my brother. My fury ignited the fire. Then I ran. Remorse has been a cold friend that has stayed by my side all these years." Madame Glizsnort sighed. "That one act destroyed our town, turned people against each other, created the Shadow. All these ghosted children may have been treated differently if not for that. It is a secret I have kept until now; a secret I should have divulged long ago. Perhaps its disclosure will finally bring me peace."

Daffodil was amazed. "But what happened to you? You disappeared."

Madame Glizsnort smiled wanly: So much life; so much living; so much lost. How lucky she had been to have such a wonderful and supportive husband and such loving children. Still, she never forgot her brother. Grace's mother's childless best friend had found Grace under the kitchen table, desperately ill. She had also found Grace's mother—dead. Unable to find Grace's brother, the woman had grabbed the little redheaded girl and run home with her, hiding her behind the closed curtains of fear to coax her back to life. When the news of her brother's death filtered through, the woman knew she would have to take Grace away. Far away. England was as far as she could afford. It was far enough. No one came looking for the little girl with no mother. There were so many lost and missing children after the first great war—too many for law enforcement to consider. The adoption papers were not processed until years later when the system was so clogged with strays that one less was a godsend.

If her brother hadn't run away . . . Somehow, Grace had always known her brother was one of the ghosted ones and she had never let him go. Now she could finally send him home, with help of course, but still he would be going home. Would her resistance to the Calling prevent her from going with him?

"What happened to me is that I found all of you: The strongest, the bravest, and the most gifted people on this planet. You were each handpicked, and you are each responsible for the outcome. I wish I could offer you more than a 'thank you'."

Wonderboy was flashing in and out in excitement. It was a curious image: Madame Glizsnort, an old woman and her brother, a little boy; siblings.

Santu felt displaced, as if his body were looking back at his soul. There were no visions but there was something else that was much worse: Grief. He didn't understand why he would be feeling such deliberate melancholy but a deep pit of sadness was pulling him from life.

"What is going to be happening now?" Santu asked not really wanting to know the answer.

"This is the inevitable moment. Together you have achieved more than I was able to in my whole life." All the ghosted ones were floating above them and laughing. They rotated around the group as they played with their pets.

"Why didn't you come back?" asked Santu.

"Ahh," smiled Madame Glizsnort. "There are so many questions and so many answers. I remember what that was like. Allow me explain it to you in simple terms." She thought for a moment. "When I arrived here, I was allowed to bring newly ghosted children into peace. But I was supposed to leave all earthly obsessions behind. This was to balance out my providence. I was supposed to just observe but I could not release the pain. I ignored the Calling, I orchestrated your arrival here, and that is forbidden. There are rules everywhere."

Irony twisted in the golden air. The breath of change moved within each of them and somehow they felt destiny exhale upon their short lifelines.

Jake's heart was racing. "I don't understand what you are saying."

Madame Glizsnort looked disappointed. "I moved with caution and secrecy but I was discovered and was made to retreat. In truth, I should have accepted my failure. My husband was wiser than I could ever have been." Madame Glizsnort looked ashamed. "But you have succeeded where I could not. I had faith in you and I was not mistaken. It took all my resources to find you and bring you here."

Santu could contain himself no longer. "So you have been conspiring to bring us to this place with no regard for *our* safety?" Santu's mind was racing. "And what about Annabelle? What about her? What about the danger for all of us?"

"For that," said Madame Glizsnort, "I am sorry. But you have heard their stories. Did you not feel their desperation?"

Jake did. But Jake was feeling something else too. "If the ghosted ones have found home, why aren't they there?"

Madame Glizsnort looked suddenly annoyed.

Jake wasn't about to change his attitude. Not now. Not after all this. "You're not letting them go are you? You're keeping them with you. Why? Are you using them to protect you? Are you going to make them ignore the Calling too?" Jake was feeling furious. Had they almost sacrificed their lives so that Madame Glizsnort could hold the ghosted ones captive all over again?

"They still have time." Madame Glizsnort was unable to hold back her fury. She stopped herself from speaking any further.

Jake wasn't satisfied. "And Annabelle? Where is she? Is she 'Home'?"

"Do you want the truth about Annabelle or do you want me to tell you something that would make you feel some kind of earthly power that would give you the right to decide what was right or wrong for her?" Madame Glizsnort's tone was cold.

Jake was ready for a challenge. "I want the truth . . . if you can manage it this time." Daffodil and Santu exchanged glances. What had happed to the Jake they knew? No stuttering, no hesitancy, no fear.

Madame Glizsnort appreciated the boy's fiery attitude. She had felt those same emotions once too. "Alright. Annabelle understood only one thing: Rejection. Her mother had left her with a legacy; and not the one that you think. Having her mother abandon her was not the sole issue. Annabelle's mother was also gifted. But she rejected her gift, even to the point of rejecting her child. Until Annabelle saw those symbols on the graves she did not remember what happened to her mother the day she was abandoned."

They all stood, silently waiting for Madame Glizsnort to finish. She seemed irritated now, as if they should already know. "Annabelle's mother threw herself in front of the train."

Daffodil was horrified. "In front of her daughter?! Why?!"

"Because," said Madame Glizsnort, "she believed that her gift was evil. Because she believed that she was saving Annabelle."

"But," said Daffodil wrapping her arms around herself, "she left her little girl."

"Yes," said Madame Glizsnort, "she did. But what Annabelle's mother could not have realized was, that by committing such an act, especially in front of her daughter, she left her child with a gift that would turn against her. In its negative form it could only lead to Annabelle's ultimate demise."

Santu couldn't hold his tongue any longer. "Annabelle had given up."

"Yes Santu. But then she touched the symbols."

"What *are* they? Why were they doing that to her?"

"Santu, you need to accept that she was asking for help. In this place you are free to imagine your way out." Madame Glizsnort's voice was dutiful. "In *this* place you are free to be who you need to be."

This made Santu even angrier; *he* had not needed to change. "Are you saying that Annabelle needed to be dead?" Before the question had left Santu's lips he knew the answer.

"Even with your visions Santu, you completely misjudged your companion." Her piteous gaze lay heavily upon him. "Annabelle wanted to be free. And she wanted every tortured soul to be free. If all of you had actually looked past her discomfort you may have seen that."

At once they felt the pull.

All the playing ghosted-ones surrounding them stopped still, their glowing yellow lights pulsating.

Madame Glizsnort looked into the golden mist and saw what it was she was waiting for. There would be consequences for her but her ghosted ones would finally be free. She would find them again, somehow. "You have all done this before you know." Her smile was strange, all knowing. Santu wanted to fight her, be cruel to her, but his body was not doing what he wanted it to do: Lethargy was consuming him; his mind was dry; his voice immobile.

The mood had changed.

The Mist was enclosing upon them. The images of the ghosted ones were disappearing; their ecstatic waves were fading in the golden glow and each and every surviving member of The Secret Society for Gifted Teens was about to face the only thing that they couldn't change.

There were so many questions and so few answers but none of it was choice and all of it was inevitability. Who could say why they were really picked? And as the inescapable realization dawned upon each of them, they saw Annabelle's golden image floating high above in the approaching mist. She held a little girl's hand: It was Bruises.

Annabelle's voice rang out like a choir of angels. "Thank you all. To be free and at peace is all I have ever imagined. Now I have it. And now you must make *your* choices. Remember this is just another beginning."

The thick white mist came swirling upon the six remaining members of the group. They each felt it, slowly at first, then more rapidly, until each of them dropped to the ground unable to speak or move.

Blaze knew immediately that she was dying. It felt strange but not unpleasant. Her mind had almost stopped now. It would have been nice to hold someone's hand.

Jake felt the numbness course through his body. It was almost peaceful, like being immersed in a warm bath. The ever-present chill had left his bones, finally. Jake's last words weren't heard by anyone.

Santu was disappointed. He had truly believed he could get everyone out of here safely. He now understood his vision. It hadn't been a mistake at all.

Daffodil's eyes were closed. At least she would see her parents again. But, if she had one last wish it would have been about Jake.

Duette and Duel exchanged thoughts right up until the end: Their father would grieve for them but he would know that they would now be with their mother. They swapped goodbyes before losing consciousness.

Blackwater Tribune
Sunday, November 12ᵗʰ, 1989— One Pound

WORLD NEWS HEADLINES
BERLIN WALL COMES DOWN!

*F*or 28 years the East and West of Germany has been separated by a massive guarded wall, 27 miles long (43 km). Erected in 1961 by the Communist government, the wall was made to prevent the East Berliners from escaping to the West. Many, held captive, tried to escape and were shot to death by the guards. Now finally, after Czechoslovakia and Hungary have allowed 'crossovers' from their borders, the Communist government has announced that East Germans are free to travel to the West.

Some Easterners have climbed the wall amid cheers from the other side, and together, both East and West have begun pulling the mortar apart with their bare hands.

It is suggested that the current East German leader, Egon Krenz, who has actually welcomed democratic reforms may be charged with manslaughter for the deaths of all those who tried, unsuccessfully, to cross over.

LOCAL NEWS HEADLINES
BLACKWATER TRIBUNE RE-LAUNCH!

CONGRATULATIONS BLACKWATER! The Blackwater Tribune is very pleased to announce our re-launch. After being forced to close our doors nearly 13 years ago due to issues with the town's population, we can now rejoice in the fact that we are back in business again!

Our last hope was that we could fire up the printing presses and give the public a good story and that is exactly what we have been preparing for. So brew yourselves a coffee because you are about to be reading history in the making!

For the new comers and visitors to Blackwater we must start by briefly recapping the history of the town since we shut down. And what a history the town has had!

Although the new settlement of Blackwater was rebuilt nearly 2 miles away from the original township it still retains the comradery and companionship that made it 'Town of the Year' in 1937—before the angst and quandary led to its demise.

Our thriving Trade Centre, consists of a variety of businesses combining the most up to date technology, with stores reviving the history of the town. The modern and brand new 'Movie Worlde', is packed with VHS video tapes of all your favorite movies. And you'll find, 'Ye Olde Lolly Shoppe' stacked with jars of humbugs, licorice and butterscotch. Several trend shops are housing the latest fashions in taffeta dresses and bleached-wash jeans.

The Savior's Church built on Strawberry Lane in 1947 has become so full of parishioners that extensions are being drawn up by the local architect, Sam Haffey. They should be completed within a year.

And the tourists are flocking in! The tumultuous history of the Saint Catherine's Church of Redeemus, which was turned into a museum, before mysteriously exploding over a year ago, has become the starting site for the new 'Ghosts of Lost Children Tour'. Just after the strange explosion the gravestones, left unmarked for so long, suddenly revealed the markings of the Lost Children's identities. The graveyard and several other places of interest, including the school, are included in the bewitching excursion that has visitors attending from all over the world.

The Blackwater Heights School—the original residence of Madame Glizsnort, the well known teacher of 'The Large Orchard School House'—has become a very large school with over 300 pupils. The beautiful grounds of the old Glizsnort Residence have become a wonderful 'teaching garden' following in the footsteps of the innovative tutor who passed away 20 years ago. The fact that Madame Glizsnort died from a mental illness—barely even mentioned at the time and simply described as 'derangement'—only adds to the historical interest of the residence. Children often report sightings, claiming they have seen her wandering toward the old graveyard seemingly still searching for those Lost Children she could never find.

Join our new journalist Lochlan Maiddock as he delves into the history of the Herald Moon Tribune and speculates what could have been done to save the beautiful town of Blackwater during such harsh times.

ODE TO A GREAT JOURNALIST

Some may remember the stories of war Henry Frienly brought us in the days of World War Two. Henry was a fine journalist who held his cadetship at the Blackwater Herald Moon Tribune and made excellent contributions to the paper from the age of 17.

When the population in Blackwater became too sparse for him to continue his determined stories, he moved to London with his family and began working for the London Daily where he produced many awarded pieces.

With typical purpose and fortitude, Henry volunteered to record the stories of war and, in Vietnam, he found his skills and grit were ideal for this type of coverage.

Henry reported hundreds of stories as a war correspondent before falling victim to the very situation that had become his life. In July 1970, as Henry sat in a café in Saigon, waiting for his next assignment, a bomb-blast struck the area killing several hundred including our heroic journalist. Henry was just 49 years old. He was survived by his wife and 2 children. After his wife's passing last year, both his daughter and son have since moved back to Blackwater: The circle of life.

These are the kind of journalists that we can award with our hearts. We thank Henry Frienly; we thank all the journalists that have fought their own war to bring us the stories of the world. Unfortunately there will be more wars, and we can only hope that enlightening us with these stories will bring us faith and not misfortune.

A Special Welcome—To all our new residents over the past year! We look forward to providing you with up to the minute information and rejoicing in the fact that the Blackwater Tribune is once again the local read.

~Brought to you by~

~Present day~

~Blackwater Shire~

"Excuse me, are you alright?" A young dark haired girl was prodding one of the unconscious bodies lying on the ground. "Are they breathing?" she asked a tall thin man walking past.

The touch of the man's cold fingers on Santu's neck woke him immediately: Icicles burning his skin.

"Yeah, this one is alive." The man scowled. "Probably on drugs or something."

This didn't seem to appease the girl. "Please wake up. Please."

Santu tried to open his eyes but the bright light burned his vision. What was happening to him? Why was he being prodded and annoyed? He managed to shield his eyes with his arm before sitting up. Coughing, he noticed white smoke puffing from his mouth.

"Oh!" cried the girl. "Have you taken drugs? Do you need a doctor?"

Santu shook his head. He couldn't remember anything. He rubbed his eyes and tried to squint into the bright sunlight to make sense of what was going on. Three strangers stood around him, bent and peering into his face as if he were some fantastical curiosity.

"I do not think so," Santu said sounding unconvinced. Had he taken drugs? Why was he laying unconscious on a grassy reserve in the middle of a strange town? "Where am I?" he asked.

"You're in Blackwater Gardens," said the girl.

"Who are they?" asked Santu nodding toward the other unconscious teenagers lying near him.

"I don't know," said the girl. "Don't you know who they are?"

Santu couldn't think. His head felt as if it were floating away from his body. He clasped his skull in his forearms trying to stop the sensation. Again he squinted into the daylight to try to find something familiar. As he turned his head, he saw rows and rows of blocks marking undulating grassy hills.

"What are they?"

The girl turned to look at the stones. She seemed surprised by his question. "They're gravestones. You're *in Blackwater Gardens*," she said again as if he were stupid.

Suddenly, thoughts and memories and flashbacks all bombarded Santu's brain. "Oh my god!" he cried as he scrambled over to the other bodies. Madly, he shook the boy next to him and then the girl on the other side. "Wake up! Wake up!" Yelling hurt his brain but he couldn't stop until they were all conscious. "Come on! Wake up!"

As each of them struggled into consciousness, more and more memories flooded Santu's mind: The bus; Madame Glizsnort; the ghosts; Annabelle. Spools of images fell over themselves to try to get to his conscious mind before he forgot everything.

Santu screamed at their empty expressions. "Remember, remember everything!"

Then Santu saw the boy's heavy eyes blink open. Again he screamed at his friend to remember. Shaking the redheaded girl and the boy and girl who looked a bit like spies, he yelled out Annabelle's name, he yelled out everything he could remember.

The young girl that had tried to wake them, backed away, terrified of the strange boy and his companions. But, bizarrely fascinated, she watched from a distance. Others in the cemetery assumed the boy's motive was grief and left him to scream it out with his God. They shook their heads: they knew what it was to feel unquenchable sorrow. A few said a quiet prayer for the bereaved group but most walked on, not wanting to deal with the usurping of youth that comes with the death of a loved one.

Daffodil was in a sitting position but she was swaying like a drunk and her eyes were vacant. She felt herself being shaken but it was far off, not her own body. Ignoring the interruption to her lovely somnambulate state, she let her head fall heavily backwards, her mouth opening like a gargoyle.

Santu suddenly remembered the girl's name. "Daffodil! You be waking up right now or I'll take away your crystals." Santu knew there were no crystals but he couldn't think of anything else to jolt her back. If they allowed themselves to succumb to the pull they would be gone forever.

"My crystals?" murmured Daffodil.

"Yes!" screamed Santu. "If you are not waking up I'm taking them." Then he shouted to Blaze. "And you, Fire-starter!" Santu shook her hard. "Remember fire, good fire, fire that saves, not destroys." He saw Blaze start in shock, her daze exploding into memory. Then it was Jake's turn. "Jake you are being one of us now! Remember! You are creating electricity! It was not a dream Jake. We are still here for you but you have to be waking up!"

The screaming boy had woken Jake from his first wonderful sleep. Jake had never experienced deep slumber like that. It was warm and kind and inviting. He didn't want to leave it but the boy was making so much noise he wanted to yell back at him.

"Shut up!" screamed Jake as he sat up bleary-eyed.

Santu jumped up. "Jake! Come on Jake, you can be sleeping later!" Santu grabbed Jake by the shoulders and pulled him into a standing position. "Help me Jake! Help me wake Duel and Duette."

"Who?" asked Jake bewildered.

Blaze was standing up now and her eyes were focused on the bemused people in front of her. "Who are you?" she asked as she staggered toward Santu.

Santu had to think for a second. Who was he? Who was he? He had been given his name for a reason. Visions. Saints.

"Santu!" he said at last. "Santu."

"Blaze," said Blaze suspiciously.

"Yes," said Santu amazed, "the Fire-starter!"

"Amongst other things," said Blaze feeling the memories come flooding back. "Who is Daffodil? I remember someone called Daffodil."

Daffodil held up a shaky hand. "I think that's me."

Blaze wrapped herself around the girl with the messy blonde hair as if she were greeting a long lost relative. "All I know is that I like you."

"Same," said Daffodil. "Same."

Jake was standing and staring wide-eyed at the scene. He was captivated by the girl called Daffodil. He wanted to hug her like the redheaded girl was hugging her. But he didn't like being touched. Tiredness was biting his soul. All he wanted to do was sleep. Slowly Jake's eyelids blinked him back into the drifting kindness of oblivion and his body gently sank to the ground.

Blaze's hug calmed Daffodil's anxiety for a moment until she saw the boy with the sad eyes drop to the ground. And then, something inside her broke. Without understanding, she tore herself away from Blaze and ran toward the boy descending into unconsciousness.

Santu was now thrashing Duette and Duel to jerk them into awareness but they wouldn't wake. It was like they had made a mutual decision to fall away from life and their bond was so strong that it couldn't be broken.

"Help me," Santu was screaming. "Anyone that is remembering, help me before it's too late!"

Blaze came running. She pounced on Duette and for reasons beyond her understanding, started calling her a 'frog'.

In the split second that Santu took to contort his expression at Blaze's crude abuse, Duel managed to open his eyes. Words came out of Duel's mouth but they were from gluey lips that thought they would never speak again.

"Duel," yelled Santu, "speak up! I am not understanding you." And then, realizing that Blaze's rude comments were, for some reason, working on Duette who was lashing her arms defensively in front of her, Santu also started yelling the word 'frog' in Duel's warming face.

Finally, still with eyes closed, the twins simultaneously rose, their flailing arms fighting to the death.

Daffodil was cradling the sad boy's head. Without understanding why, she began to rock his body as if she were embracing a child not far from death. "Please," Daffodil whispered, "don't die."

The warmth of the girl, her familiar scent and the lovely tone of her voice, made Jake remember a time when he did want to be alive, when he did want to be hugged. Memories, recent and formidable, rose in his mind. There was another side to him; a new side . . .

Suddenly Jake remembered. "Daffodil?" His raspy voice belied his excitement.

"Yes Jake, it's me. You remember?"

"How could I forget you?" Jake said trying to open his eyes. "You brought me to life—twice."

Duel struck a punch at his unknown assailant. It missed.

"Woah," laughed Santu. "It is helping to hit someone if you are having your eyes open."

Duel struggled to do just that. He struck out again anyway. "Want a frog?" yelled Duel. "Well I can give you a green eye."

Santu laughed in relief. "This will do," he cried. "This will do."

Duette started slapping Santu. "Who attacking my brother!?"

Santu couldn't have been more amused. "Duette! You must fight! You are a fighter and you must fight me! FROGS!" Immediately Duette opened her eyes to face the aggressor.

After Duette smashed Santu in the face, he realized that he may have gone too far.

Blaze was glad to have dodged the punch. She stared at Santu as if she were trying to divine the truth from him. "I don't know who you are."

"I am Santu."

"Your name doesn't mean anything to me."

"You have known me and you have trusted me."

For some reason Blaze believed him. "I'm sure I will remember," she said sounding unconvinced. But there was something about that sing-song accent that reminded her . . .

Daffodil felt like her body had finally solidified. "So where the hell are we Mr. Know-it-all?"

Santu smiled. "Blackwater Gardens—obviously." Whatever had happened to them, it hadn't changed Daffodil.

Daffodil sniffed. "It's quite nice."

Santu laughed. "I think you'll find it even more 'nice' if you are looking over there."

Everyone's gaze followed.

A row of old gravestones punctuated the soft grassy down of the hilly ground. And upon each small stone lay the scorched marks of strangely familiar names. Below each of the epitaphs there was a row of peculiar symbols.

"Oh," said Jake, "I remember." His creased brow reflected the torment.

"So do I," said Blaze almost surprised. How had these memories crept into her mind?

"I think," said Daffodil, with her new found deliverance, "that we remember what we are not supposed to remember."

~Present day~

~It's Not Whether You Win Or Lose~

Thickly branched trees spread leafy boughs out across the manicured lawns and the gravestones shone bright in the warm sunlight. There was no snow, no rain, and no dark.

"Why aren't we dead?" asked Blaze staring at Bruises's headstone.

Daffodil shrugged. "I don't know. But I think we aren't meant to be alive."

"This place looks sort of familiar," said Jake.

"Perhaps this is the same town . . ." Santu didn't know how to finish that sentence. *Of where we were before . . . ? Of where we fought the Shadow in the dark icy hell of no-time . . . ?*

Daffodil knew where Santu was going. "Maybe this is now? Maybe this is what that place we were in looks like now?"

"Perhaps," said Jake quietly, "this is where Madame Gliszort came from."

Santu looked down the hill. "I am not seeing a church."

"That," said Blaze, "is probably because we blew it up."

"True," said Santu. He looked around. A few people strolled through the graveyard and others knelt in front of the stones with their heads bent.

"Excuse me," said the young girl that had been watching the strange antics of the group from a distance. "If you're looking for the church, you can't see it from here."

Blaze was confused. "The church didn't burn down then?"

The girl shook her head and then nodded. "Oh there was a church here decades ago." She rolled her eyes. "That church got burned down and rebuilt and blown up and rebuilt." She hedged closer to the group. "There's a whole tour you can do."

Santu was horrified. "A tour?"

"Oh yes. There's this entire ghost story thing about the church being possessed by spirits and then around the time of World War Two everyone in Blackwater freaked out about it and there were all these fights and stuff." She shrugged. "Well, the people became divided and then something sinister took over the town. They reckon that the hatred caused it. Pretty much everyone left."

Daffodil sighed. "You mean it became a ghost town?"

"Yeah, how come you guys don't know any of this stuff?"

"The church," said Santu, "what happened to the church?"

The girl looked annoyed. "The original church?"

"Yes!" It was Santu's turn to be irritated.

The girl screwed her nose up at him. "Find out for yourself." She began to walk away. "And stop taking drugs, they kill you."

"Wait, please." Daffodil ran to the girl's side. "I'm sorry. We are travelers and we are very tired. We haven't been taking drugs, I promise. We just would really like to know about the church. I mean, you've made it all so interesting, we're just dying to know."

The girl hesitated. Daffodil smiled sweetly at her. "Well," she said looking around the group again. Faces stared expectantly at her. "Well, the original church turned into a museum," the girl pointed in the same direction as 'their' church would have been, "but that burnt down too. So weird. They reckon it was like the building just exploded or something. They say that when it blew up like that, all the people started coming back to Blackwater. Like the evil had lifted or something. Eerie. Anyway, it didn't matter; another church had been built on Strawberry Lane decades ago." The girl pointed behind them. "About 2 miles that way. That's where everyone goes now."

"Thank you," said Daffodil. "Your help has been fantastic."

"So, do you need help or not?" the girl asked looking perplexed.

"No, no," said Daffodil, "we are going to go home now."

Shrugging her shoulders, the girl turned and walked away. It was a shame they didn't want to talk about the graves they were sitting in front of. She had a ton of stories about those.

"What do we do now?" asked Blaze.

Daffodil rubbed her eyes. "I guess we figure out how we get home." Duette gets her wish now. We go home."

Duette smiled at Daffodil. And then punched her brother's arm. Duel's shock gave her enough time to do it again before running to Daffodil's side. Duel shook his head and smiled at his sister. He threw her a thought warning her of surprise retaliation. She told him she would tell their father. And there it was: The bond that had made them who they were; the bond that had changed everything. And home was waiting for them.

After all the horror of the past days, the word 'home' should have been welcoming but Santu was deeply disappointed. "Are we having to?" The others laughed. Except for the twins, home didn't have any true meaning for any of them.

"Actually, I think we do." Daffodil threw an encouraging smile toward Jake who looked very troubled.

In fact, Jake was distraught. "But I live in another country. I'll be thousands of miles away from you . . . and everybody else, of course." His eyes studied the grass at his feet.

Daffodil smiled self-consciously. "Santu, don't you want to go back to Guernica?"

Santu thought about it. His life had been wasteful in Guernica. He had spent his days chasing pretty girls and paying little attention to the realities of the world, denying his abilities and hiding the truth—simply trying to pretended that all that his mother had left him did not exist.

"Not really." Santu sighed. "No one would be missing me." Then he had a thought. "Perhaps I can be coming to Australia with you?"

Jealousy charged through Jake's veins. Instinctively he grabbed Daffodil's hand. "Then I will go to Australia too."

Daffodil's face turned scarlet. Embarrassment and excitement burned her skin. She felt her grip tighten on Jake's hand which made Jake's heart pump even faster.

"Wait," said Daffodil. "You all know you can't just go and live in another country. You have to apply for visas and stuff." She paused not really wanting to say it. "From your own country. And you need money. The Society organized it all for us."

"Yeah," said Santu quietly. "It was just a bit of fun, yes?"

Jake's shoulders dropped and then he had a thought. "Why don't we all just stay here?"

Before anyone could answer, an old bus pulled up in front of them, the brakes squeaking like a dying bird. The flaking paintwork and cracked windows gave them an unsettling memory.

"Oh, that's weird," said Blaze as an old man approached them. The man's face reminded her of someone, someone from a long time ago. "He looks like the guy that drove us here—or there—or wherever we were—or are."

"Yeah," said Santu, "but he is really old."

Bert stood in front of them with a gentle smile on his worn face.

"I have been waiting a long time for this day," he said. "I've been writing the date on every calendar for a very long time just so I wouldn't forget." He was looking at each of them as if he was testing his recognition. "I promised Grace."

"But Madame Glizsnort is . . ."

"Yes," said Bert interrupting Blaze. "I knew her as a young woman—so long ago now." Bert suddenly looked very proud. "I was told you would only show up if you had completed your task." He smiled. "So I'm guessing that congratulations are in order." Turning back toward the bus, Bert saw the newly marked gravestones and smiled to himself. Grace had chosen this group wisely. "Now," said Bert sounding authoritative, "it's time to go. Come on, everyone, on the bus." Bert marched toward the ancient bus, each unyielding step a demand for them to follow.

Blaze was confused. Madame Glizsnort had lived until she was fairly old. Why did Bert say he knew her as a young woman? "Should we really follow him?"

Santu turned toward Blaze and gave her the kind of look you only get once or twice in a lifetime. It was a look of gravity, a look that told her she needed to learn to have faith, that sometimes, suspicions were nettles amongst baby's breath and that just sometimes, none of it had to do with bravery and all of it had to do with trust.

Everyone moved forward except Jake. Daffodil felt the pull on her hand and turned to look back at at the boy who had taken her lost heart.

"We'll keep in contact Jake, I promise. I don't want to be miles away from you either."

"Can you promise that you won't forget me?"

"That," said Daffodil with an elated smile, "is something I can definitely promise."

"I'm going to find a way. I'm going to visit you."

Tears welled in Daffodil's eyes. She nodded. "We will work something out."

"Okay," said Jake suddenly sounding very Australian.

This was all very strange: They had been thrown together as complete strangers; forced to befriend each other; forced to push themselves to extremes; forced to face their secrets. One of them hadn't made it out alive. And now they were expected to just go back to their old lives; abandon the friendships that had saved them.

Bert's voice rang out toward them. "Come on you two, I don't have much time."

Jake didn't care about Bert or the time. Jake knew he might never see Daffodil again. Drawing all the confidence he had gained since meeting her, Jake took a deep breath and squeezing Daffodil's hand, he pulled her in close to him. Instead of fearing the closeness of another human being, Jake felt exhilarated. Looking into Daffodil's brown eyes he tried to capture the moment—a moment he wanted to remember always. He leant in and gently kissed her. And she kissed him back. A lightening thrill ran through his body. Electricity. Daffodil smiled and kissed him harder. It was like they were surrounded by white-energy.

Santu led a roar filled with whistles and cheers before Blaze, Duette and Duel joined in.

"Alright!" yelled Bert. "You can do that on the bus! For goodness sake, kids these days! Move it along right now!"

Jake and Daffodil smiled at each other before relenting and traipsing toward the bus. Neither of them released their grip.

Bert, finally happy to have everyone on board, started the engine. It rattled and coughed before lurching slowly forward. There was just enough time to get everyone to the airport and to their individual terminals before nightfall. The bus picked up speed and chugged toward the aerodrome.

Each parting was met with a mixture of sadness and appreciation. Contact details were swapped and promises made. It was agreed that none of them would ever be the same after what they had experienced together. As a group they remembered and farewelled Annabelle. As each of them left the bus in turn, Bert returned all their devices and issued them with their plane tickets. There were a few tears but mostly a steadfastness that they would carry with them all the way home.

As Jake tightened his seatbelt, he saw a piece of old newspaper sticking out of his pocket. Unfastening the belt again, he pulled out the yellowing paper. It was folded several times in perfect creases. One side had nothing significant on it aside from a few old-fashioned apothecary ads, so he turned it over.

The shock made him struggle to comprehend what he was seeing. An old black and white image showed Jake and each of his new friends grouped together and posing, all be it unsmiling, for this very photograph. Blaze stood on the end next to Santu, and then there was Duel, Duette, Jake and Daffodil. They wore strange clothes and curious expressions and appeared to be standing in front of an imposing but ugly building. On closer inspection, Jake thought he could make out a wispy white shadow behind Blaze but it was difficult to be sure. Frustratingly, the wording below the article had been torn off and there was only a few letters that were readable—nothing that made sense.

It sent a shiver up Jake's spine. Quickly, he folded the yellowing paper into its perfect creases and shoved it back in his pocket before twisting his earpieces into his ears and turning the static up really loud.

THE SUN EDITORIAL
Saturday, March 19th, 2016—
Two Pounds

NEW NAME, SAME HONOR

Welcome to your newly named daily newspaper. As readers are aware, due to the surge in the population over the last few decades, the Blackwater Tribune has been sold to the Broadford News Corps. We now welcome Blackwater residents with this first edition of THE SUN EDITORIAL.

We thank you for your loyalty to the paper and we hope The Sun Editorial has as much fascinating news to capture over the next 100 years.

We hope you don't mind if we indulge in a retrospective journey before we begin our expedition into the unknown.

Journalist Peter Silverman has penned a few words to introduce us to our new place in the world of Blackwater. So sit back with an espresso or latte at one of our thriving local cafés and take a glimpse into the past and its people.

EDITORIAL by PETER SILVERMAN

My, how the world has changed in these last 100 years: Everything mobile, moveable, as if the speed of change has forced us to take all our possessions with us as we move through life.

The telephone exchange has become the mobile phone.

The phonograph has become the iPod.

The radio has become the wide screen 3D digital television.

The typewriter has become the laptop.

The novel has become the eBook.

Letters have become email, text, twitter and the like.

Our friends have decided we must always be in contact via image, words, noise and emotion. Freedom is everywhere and nowhere.

Information has become the grass; opinion the weeds; and now the sky is that which blazes with the images of them all.

And yet, with all this change, we are still humans of human form, of human emotion, of human grief. Stories have been told amongst these pages that have saddened, confused and amazed us but we have found value in them; found someone or something we can relate to; felt compassion, anger, conviction.

One of these great stories was that of the Lost Children.

First spotted at the end of World War Two, they have, ultimately been accused of being accountable for the demise of the town. In the 70's the city was classified as a ghost town.

Today The Sun Editorial declares this day, Saturday the 19ᵗʰ, of March, a day of remembrance—a day to acknowledge the grieving of war; a day to acknowledge Blackwater; and a day to remember to be sympathetic and open minded. Judgment is not for us to declare.

Today we can acknowledge the graves at the Cross Roads site and pray for a clearer future where intolerance is invisible and compassion and truth are our allies. We hope that these children have found their peace and that they have been united with the love they so needed. Our new dictum shall be: "Praise be to goodwill and kindness and hope shall reign upon us all."

This paper may have a different name but we shall not forget.

As in the words of the time: Godspeed you all.

~Brought to you by~

BERT'S WIND-UP WATCHES—*Join the trend and return to our old-style watches. All watches include double screen for internet and music adaptation.*

~Epilogue for Annabelle~

The information of Annabelle's death was passed on to the authorities anonymously. The implicit understanding was that she had taken her own life. The information was accepted without question even though there was no body. What did that mean for Annabelle? In a way that *is* what Annabelle did. Still, if she had cared to look back at earth, she would have been disappointed. It was easier for them to lay the blame with her rather than seek out her murderer.

But really, who caused her death? Was it her mother? Life's cruelty? Her gift? A swirling mass of hatred?

Must we accept that there are always more questions than answers? Perhaps. But now, Annabelle no longer looks for answers. Life used her up, and not even reclaimed innocence, could change her fate. For that we are sorry. But not so sorry that we will prevent it happening again and again. Life is complicated and who are we to change that?

I have waited patiently, waited for them to grow toward me, waited for them to breathe assurance, waited and watched. It is time for me now. It is my turn to call for help.

M ardi Orlando is an author & illustrator who lives on the coast in
Australia with her husband of fifteen years.

She has written several novels including a book of poetry, *The Life Expectancy of Wind*—illustrated with fascinating fantasy artworks. There are also several young adult novels including: *The Light Voyager*—a thrilling fantasy, *The Amazing Life of George Fred Fiddlington*—a full colour scifi story; and *Adventures of The Wishall*—a beautiful and magical full colour book for children.

After studying psychology she worked with many associations whilst continuing to indulge in her two passions: Science and New Age Philosophies. She has also travelled extensively and has found an open mind essential in all walks of life.

Other Titles by MARDI ORLANDO
www.mardiorlando.com